The Breeder Cycle
Book 3

Clone

K. B. Hoyle

This book is a work of fiction. Names, characters, places, and incidents are either a product of the author's imagination or are used fictitiously. Any resemblance to actual people living or dead, events, or locales is entirely coincidental.

ISBN: 1-6730-3351-2

ISBN-13: 9781673033519

BOOKS BY K. B. HOYLE

The Gateway Chronicles

Book 1: *The Six*

Book 2: *The Oracle*

Book 3: *The White Thread*

Book 4: *The Enchanted*

Book 5: *The Scroll*

Book 6: *The Bone Whistle*

The Breeder Cycle

Book 1: *Breeder*

Book 2: *Criminal*

Book 3: *Clone*

A Story of the Devastations: *Hunter*

DEDICATION

To Grandpa Bob and Grandma Sally, for your enthusiasm for this series

CONTENTS

Clone

Clone

1

Clone.

My feet slap against hard rock.

Clone.

Jolts of pain through my heels, through the balls of my feet.

Clone.

Arms pumping. Sucking air in and pushing out. It's not enough.

Clone. *Pax is a clone.*

Careen around a corner and scrape against the wall.

He's a clone. A clone. A clone. A—

I smash into someone. Apologize. I think I apologize.

Keep running.

I don't know where to go. I have no place to go. I dash through Asylum, looking for someplace to be alone, someplace I won't be found.

My feet carry me to the familiarity of the hangar and I cross the expansive space to Celine's X-1. The hatch yawns wide open, and I leap inside and collapse against the far wall, the metal digging into my skin, the darkness engulfing me.

With my hands over my head, I rock myself back and forth as the pounding of my blood in my ears envelopes my senses. But the sound can't push out the horror.

This is impossible. It's *impossible.*

My heart feels like it's bleeding through my chest. Blood. My hands are sticky with it. It runs through my fingers from the gaping hole over my heart. I hold them up, but they are dry. It's a hallucination. It's—

"Celine?"

A familiar voice cuts through my delirium. I look up, but I can't see. I can't stop crying.

"Celine, *êtes-vous ici*?"

An animal snuffles up beside me and licks my face, my hands—licks the blood from my hands. *No. There's no blood. That's not real.* The metallic bang of heavy feet climbing into the X-1 precedes the scent of sweat and dirt and the presence of a man.

"*Bon dieu*, Pria! Are you okay? Arrow—quit." He kneels beside me and shoves Arrow away.

"Henri!" I sniffle and throw myself into his arms.

He wraps me up. "Hey, it's okay. What's going on?"

"I . . . I . . ." I can't say it. Even though it's true, I can't say it. I gulp back a sob and bury my face in Henri's shoulder. I don't mind the smell of sweat and dirt. He's familiar and reassuring. "I can't tell you."

He holds me tighter and whispers French words I don't understand until my breathing slows.

"What are you doing back already?" I ask, my voice wavering.

"I had to see my sister." He sets me onto my heels and cups my face. "I think—" He lets out a heavy breath. "I think I found our dad. And I think he's still alive."

I stare at Henri, trying to process his words and feel happy for him. Something deep down tells me this is happy news that normal people would be overjoyed to hear. But I am not a normal person.

Tears stream down my face, and I hate that I can't tell Henri, my friend, why I am so upset. But I can't betray Pax. "That's . . . wonderful," I say in a strangled voice. Then I close my eyes and try to regain control over my shuddering sobs.

"Pria?"

I open my eyes. Henri's face is smudgy and blurry. A watery brown mask through which I see two darker dots for eyes, a gash of a mouth, an appendage reaching toward me . . . I flinch away as Henri's fingers brush my cheeks. He's wiping my tears.

"Are you going to tell me what's wrong?"

How can I tell him? *How can I not tell him?* If Pax is a clone, then he is connected to the Unified World Order uplink, and if that's the case, then he could be a traitor . . . "No," I say through gritted teeth. I grab my head and squeeze, lowering it between my knees.

Because I can't. I just can't. I love Pax too much to betray him without at least giving him a chance to explain himself.

"You're scaring me a little," Henri says. He rubs his hand in a slow circle on my back. "Why don't we get out of here and go see Doc?"

"Not Doc," I say. "I'm not sick."

"Well, then what—"

Whistling. Getting louder. Henri looks over his shoulder, and I wipe my nose on my arm as Celine clambers into the hold of the X-1 holding a metal wrench and a rag. The clang of the tool hitting the floor punctuates the end of her whistling.

"Henri! What are you doing here?" She flings herself at her brother, who rises and catches her in an embrace just in time to swing her around.

"I don't believe it!" Celine says. "I thought I wouldn't see you back for a year, at least. I just . . ." She catches my eye as she trails off, and she furrows her brow. "What's going on?"

I stand and try to force a smile, but there's no way to hide the fact I've been crying. "I, uh . . . got all the way back to our apartment and realized I didn't have my key," I say.

Celine pulls away from Henri and puts her hands on her hips. She looks me up and down. "Uh-huh. The rest of the story, please."

I give Henri a pleading look. "You need to talk with Henri," I say, hedging. "He has something important to tell you."

"I don't doubt that," Celine says. "Otherwise he wouldn't have come back. But I think we're both wondering why you look like somebody has died. *Has* somebody died?"

I shake my head as new tears slip out the corners of my eyes.

"Unless *you* know what this is all about," Celine says to Henri.

"She won't tell me," he says. "She's right, though. I do need to talk to you. It's important."

Celine lets out a heavy sigh. She takes my shoulders and gives me a little shake. "All right. If I give you my key, do you promise to go straight back to our apartment and wait there for me?"

I nod. She didn't ask me to promise to tell her what's going on, and judging by what Henri has to tell her, I'm guessing it will be some time before she comes home. Hopefully I will have figured out how to compose myself by then.

Celine pulls her key from a chain around her neck and presses it into my hand. "I'll see you in a bit. Whatever's going on, we'll figure it out together."

I give her a paper-thin smile. What would she say if she knew what I know now?

Henri pulls me to his side and presses a kiss to my forehead. "See you soon, yeah?"

"Okay."

As I walk down the ramp of the X-1, I touch my fingertips to where he kissed me, the chain of Celine's key swinging from my other hand. The spot on my forehead seems to tingle. I'm glad Henri's back, and safe. I was afraid for him, out in the wilderness with those monsters—with the Golems.

When I'm halfway across the hangar, I hear Celine shriek, and I smile. I hope Henri's intelligence is good and their father really is alive. They deserve to gain a family member—rather than lose one—for once.

But my smile fades. Because I have to confront Pax before I do anything else, before I even keep my promise to Celine about going back to our apartment. I have to confront him, because whatever he says will determine whether or not I turn him in to Luther.

I ball my fists. Right now, for the safety of everyone in this compound, I have to find out if Pax is hiding anything other than *what* he is.

I have to confront the clone.

2

I take a deep breath to brace myself before opening Pax's door. I don't knock.

Still dressed only in linen pants, he sits at his table with his head in his hands. The chair across from him is pushed out and angled toward me, as though he set it up that way in expectation I would arrive. Maybe he did.

I close the door, and he looks up, his face twisted in anguish and covered in red lines like he's clawed himself. His hair sticks up on end. He drops his arms to the table with a dull thud and tenses as though to rise.

"Stay there," I say, surprised at the strength in my voice and the wave of revulsion that washes through me at the sight of him. "Don't move."

Pax freezes, and I hold his eyes with a fierce gaze—his eyes that only a short while ago had seemed so beautiful to me. Now they seem cold, dead, manufactured. He might as well be a Golem.

I turn my head, trying to rid myself of that thought. I'm overreacting. Aren't I?

When I turn back, he still hasn't moved, honoring my wishes. I look him up and down—evaluating every contour of his arms and chest, the shadows resting between his collarbones and shoulders and the dip where his neck meets his breastbone, his pulse beating beneath his jaw, the blue veins underlying the pale skin of his wrists. He looks so *human.*

"You're not," I say. "Not human. You're a clone. You're a UWO clone."

Pax swallows hard. Then he says, "Yes." The admission seems to cause him even more pain than he already appears to be in. He grimaces and veins pop out in his temples. His face and neck turn almost purple, and for a moment he looks as if he might pass out.

My face crumples. Even though I already knew it, it's hard to hear him admit it so readily after all these months of hiding it. "Why?" I ask, my voice squeaking.

"I'm . . . not sure how to answer that," Pax says. He takes a deep breath and massages his forehead.

"*Why*?" I march to the table and slam my fists on the hard wood. "Why did you make me care for you if you're not even human?"

His golden lashes flicker. "That was never my intent," he says. "I tried to keep from getting too close to you—"

"*Ha*."

"I'm sorry I failed!" he says over my guffaw, silencing me. He groans and digs his fingers into his hair, hiding his face in the shadow of his arms. "I'm sorry," he says again, quieter.

My legs can't support me any longer, and I fall into the chair across from him. "How?" I ask. "You said—you said the UWO wasn't close to perfecting human cloning. So *how* can you be . . . sitting here . . . being what you are?"

Pax's shoulders are shaking, and when he looks up, there are tears in his eyes. They unnerve me now. A clone shouldn't be able to cry—to feel. That's an indication of humanity, and he's a manufactured *thing*, a monster.

"I lied," he says. A tear escapes from each eye to streak down his cheeks and cling to his jaw, quivering. "I was afraid of what Luther and the others would do to me if they found out what I am."

"Afraid." I snort, choking on my pent-up tears. "Can you even feel real fear?"

Pax makes a strangled sound in his throat, and another set of tears falls to join the first on his jaw. He sniffs and looks down, and the beaded tears finally drop to the table, making dark starbursts on the wood.

I feel a warm trickle down my own cheeks, and I swipe the tears away, impatient with my weakness, with my sorrow, and with my sympathy for Pax's brokenness. He *lied* to me. I must hold on to my anger so I can maintain the resolve I need to get to the bottom of his lies.

"You also said you didn't know anything about the cloning process."

"I don't," he says. "Just because I *am* one doesn't mean I know how they made me." He raises his head and looks at me. His eyes are red, but tearless now. He seems to be getting a hold of himself.

I, on the other hand, am losing my grip. Love and revulsion war within me. I need to know more, and I don't want to know more. I want to pretend I never felt that implant on the back of his neck. If I could go back and change what happened, I would.

But then I would never know the truth.

More tears slide down my face. "Is anything you told me about yourself true?"

He stares at my chin, his jaw working and his face contorted, and then he looks me in the eyes with a pleading sort of expression. "Yes," he finally says. "I only lied when I had to."

I let out a heavy breath and twist my fingers together, squeezing so tightly I lose feeling in them. "Tell me the truth now," I say. "All of it. Tell me who you are."

Pax's eyelids flutter and he looks side to side, like he's thinking fast about what he should say. "I was . . . incubated . . . by Sanctuary Mother," he says in a rasping voice. "She did give birth to me, just like I told you. That much I know, but—"

"How do you know that?"

Pax's shoulders sag. "Because I was kept in a special lab after birth—not one of the labs you saw, but a lab in the cloning facilities down beneath Sanctuary. I came out genetically flawed—as you know—so they kept me to determine what went wrong. I told you Mother ordered my termination after she found out I was still alive, but that part's not true. She was in charge of the tests they ran on me and had no intention of letting me die until they had determined all they could."

The way he talks about it—about being tested on like a lab animal when he was only a baby, and by his own mother—makes me ill. I know my incredulity must show in my twisted lips and furrowed brow, but I can't school my features. Nobody should have to go through what he went through, not even a clone. "Why?" I say, because I don't know what else to say.

"Because I'm one of a kind." Pax says this in such a strangled voice I almost reach out and take his hand out of habit. He abruptly shoves away from the table and goes to the far wall.

Bracing himself against it with both hands, he hangs his head and breathes like he's running out of air.

"Pax . . ."

He holds up a hand but doesn't turn to face me, and then he clutches his middle and doubles over. After grabbing a bucket from his shelf, he becomes violently ill. I look away.

"I'm sorry," he says when he returns to the table several minutes later.

I sneak a look at him. His eyes are even more sunken now.

"It's difficult for me to talk about," he says.

I nod. I want to say it's okay, but I can't. "Are you trying to tell me," I say, "there aren't any other human clones like you out there?"

"That's exactly what I'm telling you."

I shake my head. "Why wouldn't they create more? Even though you didn't turn out exactly as they wanted, I mean . . . look at you! You're perfect!" I bite my lip and look him up and down. "Nobody would guess you're . . . manufactured."

"I was an anomaly," Pax says. He breathes deep. "That's another reason why I infiltrated Sanctuary—it wasn't just to acquire a Breeder so I could hook up with another Nest. It was so I could go back to where I came from. So I could keep an eye on the cloning procedures and see if they'd come close to creating another *me* yet. They haven't."

"It doesn't make sense."

"I know."

I fold my arms, thinking. "How long has it been since you were b—created?" I almost said born.

Pax's eye twitches, but he quickly conceals the look of hurt that flashes across his face. "Almost twenty-five years."

"And in all that time, they haven't replicated the process they used to make you."

"Not at Sanctuary, at least, and that's the main cloning facility in North America."

"It just doesn't make sense."

"I know. I can't explain it any more than you can," he says.

"So how *did* you get out of Sanctuary?"

"It happened more or less the way I told you. A medical technician took pity on me. I must have been three years old when she set me free. She removed my microchip and smuggled me out—gave me to a Nest, and everything happened from there just as I described it to you when we first met."

I study his eyes, holding a steady gaze with him, remembering his story of growing up in a rebel Nest, of running away with his friend Jacob when that Nest was firebombed, of finding himself alone as a child years later when Jacob was killed by an Enforcer. Pax isn't blinking or twitching or looking nervous at all—now. Is it possible this is really all there is to the truth?

No. There has to be more. "What about your implant?" I ask.

"It's not connected." He touches the back of his neck. "It hasn't been since I was two."

"That's not possible. Everybody knows clones die without the uplink to the UWO net. Even Wallace hasn't figured out how to extend the animal clones' lives beyond a few months after disconnection."

"Like I said, I'm an anomaly." Pax shrugs. "When I was two, they took me off the uplink to see how rapidly I would deteriorate—if it would match the rate of the animals or differ because I was made from human biological material. I didn't deteriorate at all, so they left me disconnected and kept observing."

"And you know this because . . ."

"The medical technician who saved my life relayed the information to the person she left me with at the Nest."

"You mean to tell me the rebels who took you in knew you were a clone and they didn't *care*?"

"At least one of them knew, and no, I guess they didn't care. But they all died when the UWO firebombed that Nest, so my secret died with them." Pax rubs his forehead, giving me a sidelong glance. "Until now."

Until now. I wipe at my eyes and study him intently, as Luther would do. He seems sincere; I see no signs of deception, but he's also managed to hide his being a clone for this long without detection.

"How do you *know* you're no longer connected to the UWO uplink?"

"In all my many years away from them, do you really think they wouldn't have picked me up by now if I were still connected?"

"Unless . . ." I almost can't get the words past my trembling lips. I swallow and try again. "Unless you're a plant. A traitor. Unless you're the one who's been betraying us for weeks." The words tumble out of me, an accusation I can hardly bear to vocalize because it seems Pax has proven he's *not* a traitor in so many ways already. But I have to speak it. I have to see his reaction.

He drops both arms flat on the table between us with a *thunk*, giving me an agonized look and baring his wrists, as though offering me his life's blood. The hurt my accusation causes is manifest in his eyes; he doesn't even have to say a word. But he does, and his voice is low and strained. "I won't pretend to be surprised you no longer trust me," he says, "but I am telling you the absolute truth. I know I-I repel you—"

I flinch.

"—but I'm asking you to put your hands on my wrists, to feel my pulse so you know I'm not lying."

I stare at his pale skin, longing to reach for him, and longing to kick away from the table and never touch him again. But he's vulnerable, and I love him against all better judgment.

I love him. And I have to know.

I touch my fingers to the veins of each wrist, keeping as little skin-on-skin contact as possible. Even so, it's impossible not to note how warm his skin is—how human he feels—how steady his heartbeat throbs.

Pax waits a moment and then says, "When I took you from Sanctuary, I admit I had my own agenda. But from the moment I started to care about you, my priorities changed." He pauses and licks his lips, and I find I can't break his gaze. When I first met him, I wondered if his peculiar blue eyes with their specks of floating gold would drive me mad. Now, in this darkened cave, they look like pools of deep water in which I could easily drown. I think I *would* drown, if I didn't know what he was.

"I always wanted to save the world," he continues, "and coming here, with you, seemed the right course of action all along. But at some point, I can't tell you exactly when, it became about more. More than me, and what I thought I had to do." His voice drops even lower. "I could no sooner betray you—betray *any* of these people here—than I could cut off my own arm. So, no. I am not a traitor. Since I came to care about you, I have never knowingly acted in my own interest over yours. Everything I've ever done, and everything I will do if I am permitted to go on living"—his earnest look deepens—"will be for the good of you and everyone here. I promise you that, and I ask you—I beg you—to remember it."

If I am permitted to go on living. He's really, actually, afraid Luther might kill him for being a clone.

Then again, even *I* feel, deep down, that he is an abomination.

But he's also telling me the truth.

Pax may have lied about a few details of how he got out of Sanctuary as a young child, and about being a clone, but he's not a traitor. He's never betrayed me.

Relief courses through me. I'm so happy, I could cry. But I've already *been* crying, so my relief just has a calming effect instead. "How did you manage to lie to Luther about your infancy?" I ask in a quiet voice. As far as I can tell, that's the only part of his story he would have had to pass off to Luther as the truth. Luther never would have thought to ask Pax if he was human or not.

"A lot of practice," Pax says. "A *lot* of practice. I've told myself that story so many times *I* almost believe it."

His arms twitch beneath mine, and I remember I'm still touching him. I look down, reluctant suddenly to let go without asking at least one more question. "Why bother with all this? Why run the risk of being discovered? Why not escape to the wilderness and live alone somewhere? And don't say it's because of *me*."

He twists his lips to the side and blinks hard. "I'm nothing but a science experiment—I know that. I can't help what I was born, but I can choose what I do with the time I have. I can choose what I make of myself." He leans toward me, the skin of his wrists contracting beneath my fingers. His eyes look as clear as I've ever seen them. "When I realized I had a choice, everything changed."

3

I'm in danger of letting myself lean forward to meet him. He's a magnetic force drawing me in, but I can't let him. I *can't* feel what I feel for him. He betrayed my trust and, more importantly, he's not human. So I remove my fingers from his wrists and lean back instead.

"You have one of those undetectable chips in the back of your head along with your implant, don't you?" I say.

Pax sighs and sits back as well. He rubs his fingers over the familiar spot on the back of his neck—the spot he always rubs when he's anxious or unsure, the spot that sets him apart from everybody else on the planet—and nods. "It's *part* of the implant."

"But Wallace said that was new technology, and you're twenty-four years old."

"Not as new as he thought. I received state-of-the-art equipment when I was made, and again later. As long as I was with the Program, they ran tests on me—I think they tested equipment on me, too."

I shiver. "So they didn't *remove* the implant, but it's not connected to the UWO net."

"Exactly," he says. "They wanted to be able to easily reconnect me to the system if I showed signs of needing it. Leaving the physical implant in place was the best way to accomplish that."

I prop my elbow on the table and rest my head on my hand, feeling overwhelmed. "How are you not dead already?" I ask in a whisper. "*How?*"

"I don't know," he says. "But I bet they'd be interested in finding out."

"So the headaches . . ." I raise an eyebrow, leading him, but he doesn't take the bait. "How do they fit in? Are they related to your implant being disconnected?"

He blinks. It's like the blink he does when he's lying, but he hasn't responded yet, so I can't place it. Maybe it was just a blink. "I don't know," he says after a long pause.

Is that a lie? Is he lying to me? "But your headaches are getting worse—more frequent."

"Yes."

"Are they related to *me*? You seem to—that is . . . Whenever we get too *close*, it seems as though they get worse."

"I can't . . . say for sure." He grimaces and studies his hands.

But, why? Anxiety is tearing apart my insides. Fear for Pax. Confusion. Desire to comfort him. And I hate that it is, but I can't help it. "Are you dying?" I ask in a strangled whisper.

"It's possible," he says. "I guess it's possible, yes. I suppose that would make sense."

I have to bite my knuckles so I don't scream. I sit with my head bowed, trying to regain my composure, trying to mull through any way this doesn't end in tragedy for Pax—and all the while hating that he's made me love him. "But there's no way for you to know for sure, because you're one of a kind, and it's not like you have someone studying you anymore." *Like Wallace—Wallace could study him.* A flicker of hope flares within me. Maybe Wallace could help him. What would Wallace say to all this? I lower my hands and bite the inside of my lip instead.

He nods and rubs the back of his neck again.

"Do you have a headache now?" I ask.

He hesitates. "No."

Why the hesitation?

We stare at each other in silence. I don't know what else to say. I want to scream and strike out at him and fall into his arms and hold him and never let go and curse his name. But while all of that would be justified, none of it would be rational, so instead I just stare.

A strange panting and snuffling sounds at the base of Pax's door, breaking the tense silence. Pax furrows his brow and looks around me. "What—"

I glance over my shoulder as a whine and then a scratch joins the snuffling. "Arrow," I say on an outburst of breath. Celine and

Henri are coming back. They can't find me over here, not like this.

I stand, scooting the chair back so hard it almost tips over. "I have to go."

Pax rises in a fluid motion, and I flinch away from him, but he holds up his hands, palms out in a placating gesture. "Wait," he says. "Just wait."

Tense, I balance on the balls of my feet.

"Please—I'm begging you," he says. "Please."

He doesn't have to vocalize what he's begging me to do or, rather, *not* do. It's obvious. His secret, possibly his life, is in my hands. I give a short nod. "I won't tell anyone," I say.

He lets out a heavy breath, his shoulders sagging, and says, "Thank you." He takes a step toward me, hands outstretched.

I back away. "But whatever there was between us"—I keep my voice steady even as the tears threaten and my throat tightens—"is over. I can't—I just can't—with a . . ." I look him up and down, and then drop my eyes.

"With a clone," he says, his voice dull.

I nod. "Do you understand?"

"Yes. I understand."

Arrow's scratching and whining becomes insistent.

"Good," I say and go to the door.

"I never intended anything between us," he says, so quietly I wonder if he's talking to himself. "Not ever. I didn't even know it was possible."

"It's not," I whisper. Not anymore.

4

Arrow tries to push into Pax's apartment when I open the door, but I knee him out and snap the door shut. A quick look down the hall tells me Arrow is far ahead of Henri and Celine—I don't see them yet. With a sigh of relief, I use Celine's key to open our apartment and slide inside. Arrow bounds past me and settles onto our couch while I stand like a statue in the center of the space, unsure what to do with myself.

Pax's lies sting, but what hurts the most is that I can't be with him. I wish I'd never developed feelings for him only to have to give up those feelings. I feel like someone has hit me in the gut, and all I want to do is cry, for hours and hours. It's an insane pain—a pain I don't understand. I allowed myself to hope for . . . something. Especially after he kissed me, twice! He has feelings for me, too—the same feelings, probably, as I have for him. But humanity cannot be manufactured—it must be bred, *bred*, the way I've always been taught! What makes us human can't be replicated in test tubes and grown in petri dishes. Pax cannot be human, and we *cannot* be together.

Right?

I scrunch up my face and my fists until my nails bite flesh.

Besides all that—which seems insurmountable on its own—he said he never intended anything between us. He doesn't want me. *He doesn't want me.*

Did I reject him? Or did he reject me?

Does it matter?

With a groan, I drop next to Arrow on the couch and curl into a ball. Arrow licks my face. The licking hurts, pulling against resistance, reminding me of the fresh line of stitches on my forehead from where I hit it during our mad escape from Denver Commune.

A sharp whistle blows, and Arrow whines and hops down. A moment later, the door opens, and Celine enters, followed by Henri.

"—what the possibilities are, though," Celine is saying. She paces to the far end of our apartment, spins on her heels, and faces her brother. "I can't—I can't even . . ."

"I know." Henri sounds like he's said those two words multiple times already. He looks at me for a long moment before slinging a large bag to the floor.

I sit up and try to school my features, scrunching up my face against the rage of emotions threatening to come howling out. I want to flee—to run and hide from everyone, even these two friends. But I have no choice but to stay.

Henri sits beside me, his actions slow and measured like I'm an animal he doesn't want to spook. For a moment, I fear he's going to put an arm around me, but instead he stretches them up over his head, lacing his fingers together. He looks at me out of the corner of his eyes, but when I catch his gaze, he returns to following his sister's movements around the apartment.

Celine hasn't stopped moving, as if by her pacing she can work out what her brother has told her about their father. "Did he tell you what he told me?" she says, jabbing a hand my direction.

"Just that he thinks your father may be alive," I say. "But no details."

Celine barks a laugh and shakes her head, running a hand over her ridge of hair. "He heard a *rumor* about a secret factory up north of Reform where UWO prisoners are kept as slaves, essentially. He thinks that's where Dad is—has been for all these years."

"You just heard a rumor?" I ask. "Did you find any evidence?"

"I saw a factory, yes."

"You saw a building that could have been anything." Celine swings her arms wide.

Henri exhales heavily. "I saw a building in the mountains that could have been anything, true, but my source who brought me there swore on his life it was a UWO factory—that he'd once been a slave there, and that he'd known a French African man who went by Rousseau."

It's Celine and Henri's family name. This man Henri's source spoke about—he could really be their father.

"Did your source say how he escaped?" I ask. "How long ago did he know your father?"

"Four years or so, by his reckoning. He's been with Reform ever since. Didn't mention how he got away," Henri says. He yawns with a groan and covers his mouth. "It's getting late."

"What sort of factory is it?" I ask. "What is the UWO making there?"

Celine shoots me a pointed look, as if to encourage me to keep pressing.

"Industrial equipment and the like." Henri shrugs. "The guy said he didn't really know what it all was—just looked like parts of ships and stuff."

"Well, that doesn't make sense." I frown at Celine. "Right?"

"Right."

"What do you mean?" Henri looks back and forth between the two of us. "What are you two getting at?"

"Why on Gaia Earth would they use human slaves for that sort of work? Surely the UWO has all that automated by now. Human workers for that stuff would just be . . ."

"Inefficient," Celine says, finishing my thought.

Henri leans forward and rubs his eyes. "So you think my source was lying? Why would he lie?"

"Maybe he needed a cover story to get into Reform," Celine says. "Charlie can't be any more trusting than Luther."

Henri yawns again, covering his face. When he emerges, he scowls at his sister. "I think you're just afraid."

Celine scoffs. "Afraid? Of what?"

"Of getting your hopes up that Dad might actually be alive." Henri hefts his tall frame from the couch with a groan, displacing Arrow, who goes to sniff under Celine's bed. "I'm exhausted. And I need a shower. We can talk about this in the morning."

Celine bites her lip and turns a circle. Then she says, "Stay tonight . . . please. Sleep here. Pria won't mind—will you?" She throws me an earnest look, her eyebrows raised.

"Oh," I say. "No, that's fine."

"Sure, sis." Henri looks around. "Do you have a towel I can use? Clean, preferably." He eyes one of Celine's usual piles of clothes.

"That pile's clean." She gestures toward the foot of her bed.

Henri rolls his eyes and goes to rifle through it.

I stand and stretch, feeling my forehead stitches. My whole face hurts from the stress and strain of crying and fighting with Pax. Talking with Celine and Henri has been a welcome distraction, although the weariness of the day is dragging me down. I can't even begin to guess at what time it is. Quite late, I'm sure. Was it really only this morning that we left Helene's house in Denver Commune? It feels like a life-age ago.

Celine comes to me, holding her head in her hands. With a heavy sniff, she throws her arms around my shoulders. I stiffen, and then try to squeeze her in return.

"You're a terrible hugger," she says against my neck. "But that's okay. I understand it doesn't come naturally to you."

"You . . . took me by surprise," I say. "I didn't know this was a time for hugging."

She guffaws and pulls away. To my surprise, she's smiling.

"Alright, I'm off to shower," Henri says. "Hey, Pria, walk me out?"

"Uh . . . okay."

We walk to the door together, Arrow following at our heels. "Stay," Henri says to him as he picks up the bag he dropped.

Once outside, Henri shoots a look over his shoulder at Pax's door and then leads me by the elbow several paces down the hallway. "What with everything I've got going on with my sister, I don't want you to think I've forgotten how upset you were when I found you in the X-1 earlier. I know you're not okay."

My face falls, and Henri grimaces.

"I get that it's a forbidden topic." Henri's brown eyes are warm and welcoming and full of concern. "But at least let me know if you're going to be okay."

"I . . . I think so." I square my shoulders—sniff hard. "Yes, I will be." Pax doesn't get to destroy me; I refuse to give him that power.

"If you need to talk about it—"

"I don't think I'll *ever* want to talk about it."

Henri pulls back and purses his lips into a frown.

"I'm sorry." I look at the ground. "But that's the truth."

"Okay. I can respect that."

"Really?"

"Really."

I look back up at him, and he cracks a half-smile at me. "Will you tell me how you got this, though?" He brushes his fingers over my stitches.

"That's a long story."

"I plan on being back for a long time."

"You're not leaving again?"

"Not until we go rescue my dad."

"You really think you found him?"

Henri sighs and smiles. "I really do." He folds his arms. "And as long as I'm here"—he throws another look back down the hall toward Pax's door—"I wanted to know if anything has changed between us."

"I'm not sure I understand."

Henri rubs the top of his head. "All right. I'll just say it. Are you and Pax together now? Like a couple?"

"*Oh.*" Blood rises to my face and I feel a rush of threatening tears. If only Henri knew how ill timed his question is. "No," I say, keeping my voice—and expression—as tight as possible. "No, we aren't. I don't think we ever will be."

"Oh. Good." Henri gives me a quick grin before turning toward the bathroom.

He whistles on his way down the hall, but I put my back to the cold, stone wall and swallow my tears before rejoining Celine in our apartment.

5

The rumbling timbre of Henri's snores wakes me long before I'm ready to get up, and I can't find my way back to sleep no matter how hard I try.

I roll onto my back and stare at the shadowy ceiling, caught in a deep lethargy that tells me I haven't gotten nearly the amount of sleep I need, wishing Celine had let Henri go to his own apartment and that I was sleeping in peace right now. My head hurts where my stitches are, and a bit of cold metal is burning a hole in my breastbone. I grope at my chest until I find it—the square of saved information that constitutes my entire life with the UWO. Helene gave it to me. Pax told me to throw it away.

Why was that, again?

It doesn't matter. He lied to me about who he is, so why should I listen to his opinion about how to deal with who *I* am?

I sit up and swing my legs out from under my blankets, dangling my feet over the edge of the low bed and onto the cold stone floor. What time is it? Wallace rises early, but is it *too* early to go and see him? He's the only one I know of who could read this drive for me.

I tuck the metal square back inside my undergarment and reach for my boots. I'm not getting back to sleep now that I'm thinking about this, especially not with Henri's ongoing snores issuing from the couch. I might as well see who is up and about. I shove my feet into my boots and lace them before tugging on my thickest sweater and buckling my holster with my ringer around my waist.

All the lights in our apartment are off, but as I tiptoe by I can see Henri's long form sprawled on the couch—one leg stretched far out on the floor, the other bent up at the knee. Arrow, lying beside him, whines and lifts his head.

"Shhhh," I say, putting out a hand for him to sniff.

Celine, as usual, doesn't budge or make a sound in her sleep.

"Where are you going?"

Henri's low whisper takes me by surprise as his hand shoots out to touch my ankle.

"For a walk."

"For a *walk*?" With a deep inhalation, he sits up, draws his legs in, and rests his forearms on his knees. "It's the middle of the night. What's going on?"

"Nothing's going on. I just can't sleep."

Henri holds out a hand, and after a moment of hesitation, I touch it and he folds his fingers around mine. His hands are much larger than Pax's, making me feel dwarfed, like a child. He tugs until I come closer—displacing Arrow, who gets up, turns three circles at the foot of the couch and lies down again. I perch on the edge of the couch.

"Tell me what's going on," he says, his voice rising to a rumble instead of a whisper.

I chew the inside of my lip and meet his eyes. How do I explain this? Does Henri even know about the mission I just returned from? Not unless Celine told him last night, but I somehow doubt she did. They were too distracted discussing the possibility that their father might still be alive.

"Have you had a chance to talk to Luther since you got back?" I ask.

"No," he says. "I haven't talked to anyone but you and Celine. Saw a few people in passing, obviously—the guards who let me in, and whatnot. I'm sure Luther knows I'm back, but"—he shrugs—"there will be time to talk tomorrow."

I nod. "Well, Luther and Charlie—"

"Charlie?" Henri frowns and sits forward, releasing my hand. "Charlotte Grebel? She's here?"

"Yes. They, uh . . . sent Holly and me and some others on a mission—"

"They *what*?" Henri's voice rises to full volume, and Celine snorts and rolls over.

I touch his shoulder and lower my voice. "It's okay. Obviously I'm fine. We're all fine." Except for Nyck Ridley, who is dead, but I don't have to tell Henri everything right now. "On this mission, I was given a memory drive with information about my life. It's . . . my file. My UWO file. Do you understand?"

Henri narrows his eyes. "How on Gaia Earth did you get that?"

"I'll tell you more about it later—when it's not the middle of the night. But you wanted to know what's going on, and that's it. I can't sleep. I want to see if Wallace is awake yet."

Understanding dawns on Henri's face. He sits back, blinks, and nods. "You want him to read the drive for you."

"Yes."

"Of course you do."

"You . . . don't think it's a bad idea?"

He shrugs. "Why would I think it's a bad idea?"

Because Pax did. I duck my head and twist my lips to the side.

Henri taps my chin until I return my gaze to him. "Of course you want to know about your childhood."

"Even if it's from the perspective of the UWO?"

"Even then. I think you should know what sort of information they collected on you."

I nod, my chest swelling. He understands.

Henri stretches and yawns. "I should come with you."

"No. Stay, please. I think this is something I need to do on my own. And you really need to sleep."

He furrows his brow. "I don't like you wandering around alone in the middle of the night."

"I'll be fine."

Henri yawns again, his head already drooping between his shoulders. "All right, then. Be safe, yeah?"

"Okay." I stand, and he lies back down on the couch.

"You have a weapon?" he says.

"Yes."

"Good."

As I turn toward the door, I hear his breathing lengthen. I put my hand on the doorknob, and he says in a sleepy voice, "Maybe Lovey Dovey and Moon are up and about already. They're always good for company."

I catch my bottom lip between my teeth as the shock of tears stings my eyes. Turning back to him, I whisper, "Oh, Henri . . ."

But there's no response.

He's already fallen back asleep.

With fumbling hands, I open the door and slip out. After closing it behind me as quietly as I can, I stand in the flickering dimness of the auxiliary lights with my hands pressed to my mouth. I can't be the one to tell him. I can't.

6

I must have really misjudged the time, because virtually nobody is awake. I pass a handful of guards on my way down the hall. They nod at me and when I look back over my shoulder, I find them watching me as if wondering what I'm doing. The main hall is dark and empty—the cooks haven't even started breakfast preparations.

I stand looking around the cavernous space, indecisive. I tap my fingers on the cold metal of a tabletop that looks as if it came out of the Commune, annoyed anew that I'm awake and not sleeping. I should be sleeping. I had a terribly long day yesterday. What am I doing wandering around in the middle of the night?

But I can't go back to sleep now. I don't want to wake Wallace, so maybe I'll just take advantage of the time before dawn to explore the cave system here at Asylum. There are still many passageways down which I've never been.

I smile at a female guard who crosses in front of me as I choose a narrow tunnel that winds in the direction of the infirmary. The guard hesitates as though wanting to speak to me, but then hurries on without saying anything. The tunnel I've chosen branches almost immediately, and light spills out of the right-side passageway—the one toward the infirmary. They always keep the lights on in the infirmary.

I choose the left-side way and find myself in what looks like a residential wing. It twists a bit, not a straight hall like where Celine and I live, and the doorways are narrow and low. One of the doors hangs slightly ajar and a familiar female voice drifts out of it, muttering words I can't quite make out. It's Charlie.

So I'm not the only civilian in Asylum awake right now.

I pause outside the door and lean close, trying to make out what Charlie is saying, but her lilting accent is so strong and it sounds like she's been crying. Her words are garbled beyond distinction. A foul smell wafts out of the room as though she hasn't washed since returning from our journey yesterday, but it's mixed with something else that reminds me of a night not so long ago with Celine and Pax.

I wrinkle my nose and twist my fingers together. Should I help her? I don't know how to comfort her in her grief. I don't know what it feels like to lose someone you love.

Charlie gives a little gasp and then sighs. I tap on her door and it swings open further. "Charlie?" I whisper. "Are you okay?"

Silence falls.

"Charlie?"

The door opens the rest of the way and Charlie looks up at me with bloodshot, bewildered eyes. "What the bloody hell are you doing here?" she says. She's wearing the same clothes she was wearing yesterday except that she's discarded her jacket and outer shirt and wears only a thin-strapped undershirt. Her pale, freckled shoulders are bare and raised with tiny cold-bumps, but I'm distracted by the drips of blood running down her palm and fingers and the smears of blood on her cheeks.

"What's happened? Where are you hurt?"

She snorts and stumbles back.

I dart a look around the tiny living space. There are only four pieces of furniture: a bed, a small table, and two chairs. On the table is an open bottle and a bloody knife.

Charlie wipes her hand across her cheeks, leaving a new smear. "You wouldn't understand." She turns her back on me and plods to the table with heavy steps, then sits and stares at the bottle and the knife in turn, as though trying to decide which to take up next.

I follow her, my eyes glued to the three open and bleeding lines across her inner forearm.

Charlie picks up the knife and studies the blade. "You wouldn't understand," she says again. "I'm taking the pain away. I can't . . . bear it, otherwise." She hiccups and rubs her cheeks again with her empty hand. "I have to be strong."

She doesn't look strong. She looks weak and defeated, sitting hunched and bloody over her bottle and her knife.

She fixes me with a glare as though I've censured her aloud. "Sit down, Pria. Let's see how strong *you* are."

My stomach twists in dread. Is she going to ask me to cut myself? I won't do it, but I feel caught, having stumbled into something private I shouldn't be seeing. Squaring my shoulders, I move to the chair opposite her and sit.

Charlie takes a swig from her bottle and then slams it down on the table. "Have you ever lost someone you really loved?" she asks me.

I don't know what to say. I lost my baby just before I met Pax. And it hurt to lose Lovey Dovey, but I'm only recently learning the very great depths of what love is. Somehow, I don't think either of those answers—however valid they may be—will satisfy Charlie. I shake my head.

"I didn't think so." Charlie positions the tip of the knife above the topmost cut on her arm—each of them as evenly spaced as if she'd measured out the distance. Faint white scars mark her other forearm in telling hash marks. She's done this before. "It feels," she says, pressing until a blossom of blood springs to the surface, red and violent, "like you've lost," she presses harder, drawing the knife in a slow, straight line, "part of your very own life."

How can she bear it? The pain must be excruciating, but her hand doesn't waver.

"Like you've shed your own blood." She finishes the cut and lifts the knife, watching the blood pool and drip in rapid droplets to the wooden tabletop. She lets out a deep sigh and closes her eyes. "Worse, even."

"You need medical attention," I whisper. I can't help it—the words slip out.

"You need to mind your own damn business." She raises the knife again.

"*Stop.*" I lurch forward.

"If you haven't the stomach for it, then leave."

"Ridley wouldn't want you to do this to yourself," I say.

She points the knife at me. "You didn't know him at all."

"No . . . not really, but . . ."

She makes a coarse sound somewhere between a sob and a laugh and says, "But you're not wrong."

"So you'll stop?"

She blinks at her arm. The first cut is scabbing. She touches it. "Just leave, Pria."

I push back from the table and stand, wondering if I should tell somebody about this.

"What are you doing wandering around in the middle of the night, anyhow?" Charlie asks.

"I couldn't sleep," I say, my restlessness seeming inconsequential now. "I was going to see Wallace, but it's too early yet." Then, because it seems I have an opportunity to keep her distracted, I pull the metal drive out of my shirt and show it to her.

"What's that?"

"My UWO file. Helene downloaded a copy before erasing me from the system. I'm hoping Wallace can—"

"No." Charlie's eyes fly wide and her nostrils flare.

"What?"

"I said, no." She holds out her hand, palm up. "Give it to me."

I cradle my file protectively to my chest. "What do you mean? I need to—"

She springs to her feet, knocking her chair over behind her and flipping the knife so she's gripping it like a weapon. "You give it to me now, or *I'll kill you*!"

7

"W-what?" I palm the drive and back away with quick steps as Charlie comes around the table.

"Give it to me," she says, brandishing the knife. "*Give it to me*!"

"No!"

"Do you have any idea what will happen if that falls into the wrong hands? If that gets back to the UWO? How can you be so stupid—so selfish as to bring that back here? *Give it to me now*!"

She looks crazed with rage. I lunge for the door, heart racing, but Charlie catches me by the elbow. I lash out reflexively, twisting and kicking her in the knee the way Sing trained me to. Charlie goes down with a cry, and I run for it, down the twisting tunnel and toward the main cavern, certain she's going to follow me. If I can find some guards—

Charlie tackles me from behind, and I go down hard, scraping my chin on the rock floor. I'm amazed at her speed and strength, especially given her current state. Knees in my back, she grapples after my clenched fist.

"Give . . . it . . ."

"*No*."

She digs her knee into my spine and I cry out.

"What is going on out here? People are trying to sleep." A man says behind us.

I can't see him, but Charlie must turn to look, because her weight shifts and I'm able to shove her off.

"Break it up!" the man says, coming closer.

"Sorry! I'm sorry," I gasp as I get my feet under me, but then I flee once again, not even bothering to look back.

Charlie gives a guttural cry and is after me a moment later, followed by the shouting voice of the man. I shoot out into the main cavern. Relief courses through me as I see a group of three guards running toward us.

"Help me, please!" I dash straight into their midst and don't stop until they've circled around me. One of them, a man large enough to lift Charlie bodily from the floor, stops her from throwing herself on top of me.

"What is the meaning of this?" Another guard swings around to face me as Charlie bucks and kicks and screams in the arms of the other.

"She has to—give it to me! She's . . . selfish . . . thoughtless . . . she's—she's . . ." Charlie's losing steam as her words trail off, and she suddenly collapses against the guard and weeps.

"She's injured," says the only female guard of the three. "Are you, too?"

"No." I lean heavily over my knees, trying to catch my breath. "It's all her blood."

"What is she talking about?" says the guard in front of me.

"It's . . . kind of difficult to explain."

"Ridley," Charlie says with a whimper. "Nyck! The whole mission will have been for nothing. Nyck will have died for *nothing*."

Oh.

I clench my hand tighter around the metal square, the realization striking me with such suddenness I feel stupid for not seeing it before. Ridley—Charlie's Ridley—died on the mission to wipe out my UWO identity, an identity I hold in my hand because I couldn't let it go—not completely.

She's right. And while I can't empathize with her grief, I understand now.

But it's my life, and I can't throw it away without at least looking at it, just once. "I swear to you I will destroy it as soon as Wallace has finished helping me read it," I say.

"No. *Now*," Charlie says through gritted teeth.

"Charlie, I—"

"*Now*!" she screams.

"Charlie," says another voice.

Luther is here.

He looks as though he's come straight from bed, as his hair is mussed and he's wearing loose clothing. "You're disturbing the entire compound."

"Do you know what she has?" Charlie points an accusing, bloody finger at me.

"Not here—not now," Luther says. He grabs her outstretched wrist and turns it over, looking at the cuts. "You need the infirmary."

"But she has—"

"Not now," he says, firmer. "Later. In private. When you're sober and bandaged. Infirmary, now." He nods at the big guard who is still holding Charlie, and the man half-drags, half-supports Charlie toward the tunnel leading to the infirmary.

Luther rounds on me, his eyes heavy.

"I'm so sorry," I whisper, but he holds up a hand.

"Whatever it is you have"—he shoots a quick look at the two remaining guards—"now is not the time or place to discuss it. Take it back to your apartment and hide it somewhere safe until we can sort this all out."

"You're not going to confiscate it?"

He raises an eyebrow. "I'm not in the habit of confiscating people's personal property over private disputes. Even if those private disputes spill out into public . . . displays."

"Thank you, Luther."

"Don't tell anyone what you've done with it, and tomorrow we will talk about it. But for now, go back to bed. In fact—I'll escort you."

He thanks and dismisses the guards, and we walk back to my apartment in silence. At my door, he puts a hand on my shoulder and says, "I trust whatever it is, it's worth preserving if you fought so hard for it."

"To me it is."

"I also understand you've had precious little to call your own in your life. I will do my best not to take that away from you."

I suddenly can't talk, but I purse my lips and nod.

"Hide it well," he says again. He shoots a look over his shoulder at Pax's door, and then lifts a hand in farewell before walking away.

8

Arrow growls when I enter the apartment.

"Shhh," I say. "It's just me."

He quiets and settles back down with a snuffle.

I don't know what else to do with the memory drive, so I slide it between my mattress and bedframe. I remove my boots and gun holster before I lie down on top of my blankets and stare at the inky ceiling, trying not to dwell on my encounter with Charlie as the minutes and hours drag on. It's impossible not to think about her, though, so I stop fighting it after a while. How would I feel, if our roles were reversed? What if it had been Pax who had died and Charlie who had brought back something that could make his sacrifice worthless?

I twitch and throw an arm over my face. I can't think about Pax like that anymore. For one thing, he and I have never been together in the way free people can be together—in coupled, romantic relationships. For another, I've already determined I *can't* love him, not now that I know what he is. And for a third thing, he's never even said he loves me, nor have I said it to him—aloud.

But . . . *but* . . .

If I'm honest with myself, and if our roles were reversed, I think I might be just as upset with Charlie as she is with me.

I sigh and roll onto my side. It is exhausting being a free person with free emotions. Tonight I almost envy the people on the inside—those on the UWO's emotion-numbing decipio drug.

To my surprise, a yawn pushes out of me. Ironic, now that it's certainly almost morning and I will have to be up and alert for what will likely be a long meeting with Luther—a long meeting, and a difficult one. Of course, most meetings with Luther are. If Ridley had survived the Golems at the end of the mission, we could report complete success.

I yawn again, so wide my jaw clicks. As I drift into oblivion, I wonder vaguely if that could be considered a genetic flaw—a superficial one, to be sure, but a flaw nonetheless. I'm flawed. I'm not perfect. I'm . . .

9

"Pria. Pria." Henri's voice, and his hand, warm on my cheek. "Wake up." He taps me—three light taps.

I blink and come slowly awake, with the feeling Henri has been trying to wake me for some time.

"I didn't hear you come back in last night," he says.

"Mmph."

He offers me a hand, and I take it, letting him pull me into a sitting position. But then his grip tightens. "Is this *blood* on you?" He turns over my arm and looks me up and down.

Oh. Great. "Yes, but it's not mine. Don't worry." I try to pull away, but Henri doesn't let me.

He raises his eyebrows. "Don't worry?"

"It's dried, see?" I tug at my clothes. "And I'm not injured. It doesn't belong to me."

He finally releases my hand. "Then whose is it and why is it all over you?"

I sigh and rub my face, wincing as I hit my stitches and my chin—newly bruised in the scuffle with Charlie. "It's a long story, and I don't know if Luther would want me spreading it about."

"Luther? I thought you were going to meet with Wallace?"

"Wallace?" Celine says from the table. "Why did you want to meet with Wallace in the middle of the night?"

I look her direction. She has a loaf of bread and some preserves spread out. "It's a long story," I say again. I clear my throat and run a hand through my hair, long enough now that it's sticking up on one side. "And I didn't get to meet with him. As you said, it was the middle of the night. I don't know what I was thinking."

"So you just came on back here, covered in blood?"

I clear my throat again and avoid Henri's eyes. "More or less."

Celine walks over and hands me a slice of bread. "Plain, as you like it." She puts her hands on her hips and gives Henri's leg a kick. "If she doesn't want to talk about it, she doesn't want to talk about it. She's not hurt, so lay off."

I finger the toast and meet Celine's gaze. She raises an eyebrow as if to tell me she knows I need some space. I swing my legs over the side of the bed. "Luther wants us right away, yeah?"

"Pretty soon. We can eat breakfast first."

"I should probably change out of this shirt and wash up before we go, too."

"Yeah. Wouldn't want people asking questions, would you," Henri says.

"Don't be like that," Celine says. "Go to the bathroom, Pria." She tosses a clean shirt at me. "I'll teach Henri some manners while you're gone."

Shoving the bread in my mouth and the shirt under my arm, I leave the apartment. Hurrying down the hall so I won't be stopped by anyone else who might be off-put by the dried blood on me, I duck into the bathroom and into a stall. I shimmy out of the ruined shirt and into the new one Celine gave me. I throw out the bread with the ruined shirt, not really hungry after everything that has transpired, and go to the washbasin. It takes a long time to scrub off the dried blood, which clings to my skin like it has become a part of me. Charlie's blood—that she spilled of her own accord. I shake my head.

Someone enters the bathroom behind me. I turn to find Pax there, staring at me. I freeze, dripping tepid water onto my toes. His face is drawn and haggard, like he hasn't slept all night. He opens his mouth to speak, but a group of girls comes in and passes between us, giggling. They are all about my age, and when they see Pax, they giggle louder and put their heads together, as if they are connected by a single mind.

I take the chance provided by the distraction and flee.

Celine and Henri spin toward me when I slam the door. Even Celine seems worried now, her expression drawing down into a puzzled frown. "Hey—you okay?"

"Yes. Yes, I'm fine. You ready to go? Are you coming for the meeting?" I ask Henri.

"I'm going to come by, yeah, but I don't know if Luther will want me to stay or not. He probably wants to debrief the rest of you first." Henri goes to the table and helps himself to some bread, spreading it with liberal amounts of preserves. "I still can't believe he sent you to the Commune," he mutters. "What a terrible idea."

"It was the only way."

"The only way to do what?"

"Erase my identity."

"Why did Luther and Charlie want to erase your identity? What are they planning?"

"It has to do with something called Gentri—"

Celine gives a loud cough and shakes her head at me behind Henri's back.

I frown at her, uncertain.

Henri turns to his sister. "What? What's your problem?"

"I just think Pria shouldn't be the one to tell you about this plan."

"Why not?"

"I think you might . . . overreact, that's all."

Henri rounds on me. "What were you going to say? Gentri—what?"

"Uhhh . . ." I've already given him the first half of the word. Can he not figure out what I was going to say?

Henri raises an eyebrow. "I can wait. You know I'm going to find out anyhow." He lifts his bread toward his mouth.

Celine rolls her eyes and sighs. "Fine. Gentrification, all right?"

Henri freezes with his piece of bread poised at his lips. He looks from me to his sister, and he then throws the bread down onto the table, preserves splatting to the wood. "Like hell," he says.

10

"Henri." Celine follows him around the apartment as he storms to the door and gives a sharp whistle at Arrow. "Henri—wait."

"Over my dead body." Henri yanks open the door.

Celine throws me a desperate look and follows him out. "*Henri.*"

I push my feet, still damp from my trip to the bathroom, into my boots, tripping over myself in my haste to catch them.

"Henri." Celine is taking two steps to every one of Henri's long strides, but he's ignoring her. "It's already been decided. What are you going to do about it?"

"Try to knock some sense into Luther. Whose terrible idea was this, anyhow?"

"Charlie's," I say, jogging to catch up. "It was Charlie's idea."

Henri stops so fast Celine runs into him. "It was *Charlie's* idea?" He spins to face me. "You can't mean—"

"She said she thought of using me for it after you told her about me."

Henri flares his nostrils and grits his teeth. "*Cette salope manipulatrice et sans scrupules. Comment ose-t-elle utiliser ce que je lui ai dit pour mettre Pria en danger? Si j'avais su, je n'aurais jamais rien dit. Quand je mettrai la main sur elle . . .*" He smacks his fist into the palm of his other hand and turns to continue striding down the tunnel.

"What did he say?" I whisper to Celine.

Celine rolls her eyes my direction. "Really? You're a genius, and you can't figure it out?"

"I don't speak French."

"Oh come on, Pria." Celine starts after her brother again.

I sigh, but she's right. I can't say I don't know what he means, not really.

It's unsettling. I don't like this version of Henri—this angry version. He looks too much like Etienne when he's angry.

When we arrive at Luther's office, Henri bursts in without knocking. "What are you playing at, Luther?"

Celine and I follow him inside, but huddle together by the door. Celine puts a hand on my arm as though to hold me back.

Luther rises from his table, his brow furrowing and his eyes flashing. "The meeting hasn't started yet."

"You can't—you can't *possibly* be thinking of sending Pria to Washington! Luther"—Henri slams his hands on the table—"they will find her out and *they will kill her.*"

"Keep your voice down," Luther says, leaning in to meet Henri's aggressive stance.

"Why should I?"

"Because James is still here."

Henri lets out a huff and hangs his head. "You are not going to keep me from saying my piece," he says in a heated whisper.

"I don't doubt that."

Luther's son peeks out from under the table and stares with wide eyes up at Henri. His lip quivers, and Luther comes around and picks him up. "I'm going to take James to the nursery," he says. "We can talk when I get back. In the meantime, sit down and cool off."

Luther sweeps past us with a cursory glance, and the door slams behind him.

The silence after Luther leaves the room is full and deafening. Henri doesn't sit as Luther told him to but balls his fists and taps a foot. Arrow comes over and nudges his leg with his nose.

"Nice job, bro," Celine says after several long seconds have passed.

"I'm not interested in your opinion," he says.

"Obviously. But did you bother to think about asking Pria for hers?"

Henri looks over his shoulder at me. "Pria doesn't have any idea. *Pria* doesn't realize she's just a pawn in this game."

Annoyance flares within me, and I narrow my eyes. Who is Henri to tell me my own thoughts? "A pawn." I look at Celine. "That's a piece from that game you like to play with Elan—the one you always lose on purpose, right? Chess." Celine snorts and nods.

I look back at Henri. "I'm naïve, but I'm not stupid."

Henri's face falls and his shoulders slump, "I didn't mean—"

"And I don't appreciate you talking about me like I'm not here."

"That's not what I—"

I hold up a hand, and he falls silent with a grimace. "This is not a game, and I am not a pawn," I say. "I consented to the Gentrification plan because there is no one else who can fill the role of female Breeder. I'm finally free to make my own decisions, and this is a decision I have made."

"A decision she made while *you* were gone, by the way," Celine adds, poking her brother on the upper arm. "And a lot happened while you were gone to make everything more . . . urgent."

"And you were the one who told me I shouldn't let other people tell me what to do," I say.

"Yes but . . ." Henri shakes his head. "This is not what I meant. This plan is suicide. And *Gentrification*? Do you even know what that could mean?"

The door opens and Luther re-enters the room. "I thought I told you to sit down." His eyes flash.

With a deep sigh, Henri pulls out a chair and slumps into it. Celine and I sit, too.

Luther massages his brow as he sits across from us. "None of us knows what Gentrification means—not really. All we know is that it's an *elevation*. An opportunity to get *in* where none ever really exists. We have to take it."

Henri rubs the top of his head. "I just want to know why. Why choose something so risky for her to do?"

"We don't have a choice."

"Bull."

"Call it bull if you want. It's the truth. After . . ." Luther shoots a sharp look at Celine. "Have you told him?"

"Told me what?"

Celine shakes her head and hunches over her knees. Her face crumples.

"All right." Luther leans forward. "While you were gone, we had some casualties. A hunting trip went south, and a lot of people were killed."

Henri raises his chin and swallows. "Who died?"

"Most of the usual hunting crew."

"Moon?"

"No."

"Lovey?"

"Yes."

Henri's eyelids flutter, and he puts his hand on Celine's shoulder. "Did she suffer?"

"No."

"Was it a Golem that did it?"

"Yes."

Henri closes his eyes and pinches the bridge of his nose. "Where is Moon? Is she okay?"

"She's gone."

"What do you mean, she's gone? I thought you said she survived!" Henri's voice rises to a shout.

Luther clears his throat and raises a placating hand. "Moon brought us Lovey's body, but after the funeral, she left. She hasn't returned. We don't know when—if—she will."

"Great Gaia," Henri mutters.

Luther continues. "When she came back with Lovey's body, she also brought us a head from one of the Golems involved in the attack. Wallace took it apart and discovered that the UWO has been upgrading their uplink and microchip technology."

"Meaning?" Henri's voice is rough with emotion.

"Meaning they now have technology for implanting and tracking people that no sensors of ours can detect."

"So have Wallace develop new sensors."

"It's not that simple, and you know it."

"No. I don't know it. What are you saying? That we can't liberate any more people from the UWO because they could be implanted?"

"With undetectable, untraceable trackers, *yes*. And yes, for the safety of everyone here at Asylum, everyone for whom I am responsible, that is exactly what I am saying."

"That's not acceptable!"

"That's why we must get the evidence we need to move on the UWO *now*. We can't wait. We can't . . . look for another option. This *is* our chance. We will send Pria and Wallace to Washington as Gentrification candidates so they can infiltrate and steal the files. This is our best shot, and possibly our last. We simply cannot compete with the rate of progress of the UWO. We have one Wallace. They have hundreds, thousands maybe, just like him."

Henri pounds his fist on the table. "Luther—"

A knock sounds on the door.

"Come in," Luther calls, without taking his eyes from Henri.

Pax enters. He nods and sits at the table on the other side of Henri—as far from me as he can place himself.

I swallow and sit up straighter in my chair, knitting my fingers together. Celine sniffs and looks from me to Pax and back to me again. She raises an eyebrow and tilts her head in a way that tells me she will surely be asking me questions about my behavior later.

I will have to be strong, because I can't reveal his secret. I can't.

More knocks. More people enter. Holly, and Bishop, and Elan, and Mari, and Wallace. They fill the empty spaces at Luther's table, but I don't look at them; I stare only at Pax.

Now that I know about it, I can't help but look at his neck where his implant chip is embedded. Is the chip *visible* as a bump beneath the skin? If I stare too long at the spot, will other people notice? Will I give away his secret without intending to?

"Pria." Celine punches me on the shoulder. "Hey."

The fact that they're trying to get my attention finally registers. Pax meets my gaze. His eyes are sunken in, his skin pale, and his cheeks hollow. I can guess what is going through his mind.

"She's too tired. Are you sure she doesn't have a concussion?" Henri says. "We should do this tomorrow."

Annoyance flashes through me. Why is Henri talking about me *again* like I'm not here?

"Are you able to talk about the mission, Pria?" Luther asks.

I tear my eyes from Pax—Pax's devastated expression—and look at Luther. "Yes. Yes, I'm fine."

"What's up with you?" Celine shakes my shoulder. She sounds concerned now. "Are you okay—really?" Her eyes flick up to my forehead, and I touch the line of stitches.

"You want a report, Luther," I say, ignoring her questions. "Let's report."

11

"Where's Charlie? Shouldn't we wait for her?" Elan says.

"She won't be able to make it," Luther says. "She's overwrought."

I meet his eyes and silent understanding passes between us. We won't ever tell anyone what happened. Charlie's behavior, her cutting, will remain our secret and hers.

"I suppose that's to be expected," Celine says. "I don't think I'd want to be here, either, if it was Elan who . . ." She clamps her mouth shut and shakes her head.

"All right," Luther says when the silence stretches on. "Who wants to start?"

"You could start by telling us why you thought it was a good idea to send Pria back into danger," Henri says, his voice a low growl. "And why, apparently, you think you need to do it *again.*"

"You weren't here for the deliberations, and the mission is done," Celine says. "Get over it."

"I want to talk to Charlie," Henri says. "It was her idea, wasn't it? I don't give a damn if she's overwrought. I want to talk to her. She should be here. She took the information I gave her about Pria and *used* it!"

Luther leans forward. "I would have done the same thing."

"*What?*"

"Any of us Nest leaders would have. What do you think, Henri? That we're just trying to survive here? We can't be content merely to survive while the Unified World Order stands."

Henri's eyes flash. "Sarah does it. She's been doing it for years."

"I am not Sarah, as you well know. And if your opinion has so changed, then perhaps you should leave here and go join her."

Sarah? I frown at Celine, but she shakes her head in a "not now" gesture.

"We're in a war for our lives, man," Luther says. "For the survival of the human race, and all people everywhere. Charlie had a plan—has a plan—and Pria and Wallace are the keys to executing that plan. Of course she *used* the information you gave her. And so far, with the exception of one casualty, the plan has gone off without a hitch."

Henri leans forward to match Luther's stance. "Without a hitch? Pria was injured! And now you want to send her to Washington. She has *no idea* what she'll face there!"

"I have more of an idea than you do," I say.

Henri turns to me, already shaking his head, but I slam my palm on the table.

"No! Stop it, Henri. I've lived most of my life under their control, and that's more than you can say."

"Under their control—not as their target. Now that you're a criminal, they will kill you."

"They already think I'm dead. That's why we went to the Commune—to declare me dead. And it worked!" I look around. "Right? We accomplished what we set out to do."

"Yes, you did," Mari says.

"And Pax . . ." Luther lets out a long sigh and lifts his hand in a feeble gesture. "Pax once again demonstrated not only his fidelity to our cause, but the inadequacy of my security detail."

"What did Pax do?" Henri asks, his voice low.

"Charlie wanted to test him," Elan says. "So she had him 'arrested' by some of our own men—sent him on a wild goose chase after some supplies we already have. Pax beat them all and rendezvoused with us in the Commune instead. Saved all our lives, truth be told." He looks down the table at Pax. "We wouldn't have gotten out of there without you."

Pax nods without smiling.

"How did you get out?" Luther asks.

"The old sewage system," Pax says, his voice quiet and strained. He clears it and starts again. "I used the system as a boy hiding in the Commune, so I knew how to navigate it."

"Is that so?" Luther's question sounds benign, but his gaze is piercing.

Pax meets Luther's eyes and folds his hands. "It's so."

"And once you were well outside the Commune limits?"

Elan speaks. "We split up. Pria was injured and couldn't run, so Pax took her on his motorcycle back to the X-1. But then the storm rolled in and the Golems attacked, and it all went sideways."

I flinch and close my eyes, flashes of memory assailing me. Golems roaring and chasing us through the thunder and lightning and rain. Nyck Ridley falling from the open hatch of the X-1. Charlie screaming.

"Pria."

"Yes?"

"Anything you want to add?"

I trail my fingers along my stitches and blink my eyes open to find Pax looking at me. "No," I whisper.

There's a beat of silence before Elan says, "They'll be on to Helene now. There were Enforcers at her place when we were there. And after what happened when we escaped, I don't see how she'll be able to talk her way out of suspicion this time. There must be some way of helping her. Of getting her out."

"There's not," Luther says.

"But—"

"Helene knew the risks when she joined our cause, and the sacrifice she might have to someday make. It's another reason why we have to act now. It's *another* reason why Gentrification is our last hope."

"It's a bad idea," Henri says.

"Yes, you've made your opinion perfectly clear." Luther sighs. "What I don't understand is why you're back. I was under the impression you were going to stay with your brother in his ostracism."

"I was going to, but I discovered something up north—north of Reform."

"There's nothing north of Reform," Mari says. "Just wilderness."

"That's what I thought, too. But a man from Reform told me about a UWO factory in the woods, tucked far away like they didn't want anyone to know about it, the perimeters crawling with Golems. Rumor has it they keep slaves inside, and there is one there who goes by Rousseau."

Luther raises his eyebrows. "You think it's your father?"

"How many Rousseaus can there be left in this world? Our

mother is dead. Guy is dead."

"I see." Luther taps his middle finger on the table. "And Etienne?"

"I told him if he broke the conditions of the ostracism and showed his face back here, I would kill him myself."

"What do you hope to do with this information?"

"Isn't it obvious? I'm hoping to launch a rescue mission."

Celine gives a desperate-sounding laugh and shakes her head.

"You disagree, Celine?" Luther says.

"I just think . . . I mean, come on, Luther! Our father's been gone for thirteen years. I think this whole thing is a little far-fetched. Doesn't this factory in the woods sound sketchy to you? Why would this man from Reform know anything about it? He claims he used to be a slave there, and yet he couldn't even say for sure what it is they build. What use would the UWO have for such a factory, filled with human slaves? Henri wants to launch a rescue mission when we have—what—five weeks to get Pria and Wallace ready to go to Washington? Shouldn't that take priority?"

Henri rounds on Celine. "Don't you want to get our father back?"

"Of course I want to, I just—" Celine shoves away from the table and stands. "I mean, am I crazy? Don't we have more important things going on right now?"

Luther says, "It's okay, Celine. There's no need to get angry."

"I'm not angry!"

"She's afraid," Pax says.

"I'm not afraid of anything, and don't you tell me what I'm feeling!" Celine jabs a finger at Pax, and then storms from the room.

"I'll go after her," Elan says, his voice quiet in the aftershock of her explosion. He lets himself out.

"Well?" Henri says.

"Well?" Luther opens his hands.

"Will you consider a rescue mission?"

Luther squares his jaw, a distant look coming into his eyes. He must be weary—what with Gentrification plans, his brother's exodus from Asylum with a sizable portion of the community, the death of Ridley and Charlie's subsequent breakdown, and now this—but he doesn't seem to be letting it weigh him down. Is it worth going after Antoine Rousseau now, in the midst of all this?

"I'll consider it," Luther says. "But Celine is right—we do have other pressing matters at hand."

"Like Gentrification." Henri leans back and rubs his head, a ready scowl on his face.

"There is a lot to do to prepare," Mari says. "A *lot.* Five weeks is hardly enough time."

"Pria and Wallace will have to look as though they've just come from Breeding compounds," Holly says in a brisk voice. "They'll have to be at peak health or the UWO techs will know immediately there's something amiss."

"I'm always at peak health," Wallace says. He sounds almost irritated.

"I don't doubt." Holly shoots him a wry grin. "But you are also pushing the upper age limit for male Breeders. There could be some question of why you were even chosen for Gentrification at all."

Wallace huffs quietly through his nose.

"Lucky for you, since the advent of the microchips, all we have to do is implant in your arms the microchips of the Breeders we're swapping you in for, and their readers will tell them you are whoever those Breeders are. Simple. Elegant, even."

"You mean once I override the chips with our images," Wallace says. "Pria and I may be dead according to the UWO system, but we wouldn't want any facial recognition scans to contradict the imagery on the new microchips." He says it as though it will be as easy as taking a walk.

Holly blushes. "Yes. Of course. Once you do that, then you should be set."

I grasp my wrist and massage it. I can't help it. Of course, the point of dying was to be able to do this—to be able to take on a new persona to fool the system.

"There's another thing," Holly says. "I'm sure you've thought of it—I *hope* you've thought of it, but they'll expect the Breeders to be on—"

"The decipio. Yes. We know." Luther nods.

"The microchips will be able to detect it in their systems. Some data—like blood type and identity—is stored on the chips. Other data is read by the chips. If they're not on it, the microchips will alert the techs when they're scanned in."

"We have some decipio-laced water here—pilfered from the

supply going to the Commune."

I dart a glance at Luther. I hadn't thought of that. "I should start taking it right away," I say with a thrill of fear. I shake off the feeling and sit straighter in my seat. "Wallace is resistant, so it won't effect him when he takes it, but I'm not. Is there any way for me to build up a resistance to it?"

"Possibly," Henri says. "Awareness is half the battle."

"Henri's right," Luther says. "People have become resistant before, for other missions." He laces his fingers together. "I'll have some delivered to your apartment this afternoon. Start small. Don't drink it exclusively. Resistance isn't necessary for you to succeed as a topsider, but it will help you if you can achieve it. And, Holly?"

"Yes?" Her expression is drawn and pale. I think she's nervous about my taking the decipio.

"You can help us know exactly how high a concentration they will expect both her and Wallace to have in their bloodstreams. As well as anything else the microchips will read on them."

Holly nods curtly and folds her arms.

"There's much to do in the next five weeks," Luther says. "Pria, if you'd stay and have an extra word with me, please, the rest of you can go. The engineering debriefing will be in twenty minutes in the hangar."

Everyone shuffles out, but Pax lingers. His hand flinches several times toward the back of his neck, and he keeps clenching his fist and pulling it back, as though afraid of drawing attention to his implant. He seems lost. Is he waiting on Luther? Is he debating coming clean about what he is?

I meet his eyes once, and then he turns and leaves the cave.

12

Luther waits until his office is empty, then he looks at me keenly. I know what he's going to ask before the words leave his mouth.

"What were you and Charlie fighting over this morning?"

"A memory drive containing my personal UWO file."

Luther leans heavily on his table. "What?" he breathes.

I take a step back. "A—"

"Never mind. I heard you." He hangs his head and lets out a long breath. "Pria . . ."

"I know."

"That's precisely what we sent you to the Commune to erase."

"I know."

"If that information were to somehow make it back onto the UWO net before we can bring down the UWO, all of this will have been for nothing. Many lives will have been risked—Ridley's life will have been sacrificed—for *nothing*."

Guilt gnaws at me. Luther's quiet censure is somehow much worse than Charlie's screaming indictment, worse than Pax's urgent disapproval.

"But, Luther, it's my life."

He opens and closes his mouth, staring at me. "They don't—they never have—defined who you are."

I bite my lip, trying to find a way to articulate why it is so important to me. "But they watched me grow up, and they observed me . . . they *shaped* me, at least to a certain degree. Who I am is partially a construct of their design. None of us belongs *only* to ourselves, do we?"

His gaze remains intense.

"The UWO didn't get everything wrong. I was raised a part of something much bigger than myself. Everyone who's born here is, too. The difference is, you let your people have agency of their own, have . . . identity. You value the individual. My individuality was denied to me, my agency defined for me. I want—I need—to see what the UWO saw in me. To see why they chose me to be a Breeder. To understand myself. I still don't feel like I know who I am, not fully. Let me look at the file, and then I'll destroy it. I promise."

"You'll need someone to help you read it," Luther says.

My heart leaps. "You'll let me look at it?"

"It belongs to you. I wasn't going to take it from you. I just . . ." He sighs. "I just wish you hadn't risked bringing it out of the Commune."

"Thank you. And I'm sorry. Charlie is right to be so angry with me."

"Charlie." Luther grimaces. "She is . . . well, she's not what I expected. Sharper, and more vulnerable, and more dangerous all at once. But if it wasn't for Charlie, where would we be right now in our fight against the UWO?"

If it wasn't for Charlie, I wouldn't even have my file. I quirk my mouth to the side and say nothing.

"Anyhow," Luther says, straightening and rubbing his hand through his hair. "Take the memory drive to Wallace. He can help you, and he won't judge your decision to keep it."

"That was my plan."

"Do it today, Pria. Right now."

I nod and turn to go.

"And, Pria."

I look back.

"I do understand," Luther says.

I blink and nod. Wrenching the door open, I hurry out.

13

I ease past a group of girls outside the bathroom. They laugh in a breathy, giggly way and press back against the wall. One of them is the girl with bright red hair who reminds me of Pax. I don't want to think about Pax. I just want to get my memory drive and take it to Wallace. I just want to know what the UWO knew about me all those years of my life.

I pull out my key and grab the door handle, but the door swings easily in, loose and unlatched.

"Celine?" I poke my head inside, thinking she must have come back here with Elan. She never did return to the meeting.

But the apartment is empty. And ransacked.

Celine's piles of clothes are overturned and thrown about the room. Our drawers pulled out, their contents dumped on the floor. Cupboards opened and rifled through. My bed . . .

I catch my breath. My mattress hangs askew off the frame. Grasping the corner of it with cold hands, I lift it up.

Gone. My memory drive is gone.

No. Not *gone*—destroyed. Silver pieces of smashed metal and circuitry lie scattered beneath my bed, just enough of them to make up the small drive.

I drop the mattress with a *fwump* and then sink to my heels. With trembling fingers, I pull the pieces to me—try to reform them into some semblance of what they used to be.

But it's no use. It's utterly destroyed.

Charlie did this.

I clench the pieces in my fist until they bite into my skin. She did it, and she wanted me to see—wanted me to know and to feel the loss, as she felt the loss of Nyck Ridley. *Now I'll never know who I am.*

"Who the hell broke our door?" Celine's voice carries in from the hall.

I look over at her with heavy eyes. She's fingering our doorframe, which is splintered, fragmented into tiny shards around the knob and latch. I didn't notice the bits of shattered wood when I came in, too distracted by the mess inside.

"And—what the?" Celine takes several slow steps into our apartment. "What happened here?"

"I don't know," I whisper. I hide the pieces of the drive, too ashamed to tell her.

Celine sighs. "Guess there's nothing to do but start cleaning up. Are you okay? You weren't here when it happened, were you?" Then her eyes flash in sudden alarm. "Were you attacked again?"

"No, I . . . I wasn't. I'm fine."

"Did you ask Pax if he heard anything?"

I shake my head. "I think it happened during the meeting." Charlie wasn't at the meeting; she had plenty of time.

"*Still*." Celine hurries into the hall. A moment later, she's pounding on his door.

I shove the pieces of the drive into my pocket, but I can't make myself rise from the floor—not just yet.

When Celine returns, Pax is trailing her.

"Said he didn't hear anything," Celine says.

He takes a quick look around before his gaze alights on me. "Are you okay?"

There's a strange resignation to his question, as if he expects me to say no. And when I meet his eyes, he looks away.

I don't answer.

"So what's missing?" Celine says into the void of awkward silence.

"What do you mean, 'what's missing?'" I get slowly to my feet.

"Oh come on, Pria." Celine balls up some of her clothes and tosses them into a new pile by her bed. "We've had a break-in. Surely something was stolen." She casts an exasperated look at Pax.

"You mean this sort of thing happens a lot? You—you know what to expect?"

"I wouldn't say *a lot*, but it happens sometimes, sure. Unfortunately." She scowls and kicks at the shards of a broken bowl. "People don't trash other people's houses for fun. They must have been after something."

I bite the inside of my lip and hold my breath. Would Celine react the same as Charlie if I told her about the memory drive? I don't want to bring it up in front of Pax, though.

"What? What is it?" She's eyeing me with hands on hips. "Spit it out, princess."

"It's . . . nothing."

"Fine." Celine snaps the word, and a look I can't quite place chases across her face. Hurt? Anger? "Keep your secrets. Covered in blood this morning. Moon-faced and won't even look at Pax. Now this. Whatever. Look—I need to go report this to Sing. You just . . . just stay here and keep cleaning up. I'll be back in a few." She stomps out, brushing past Pax, who opens and closes his mouth as she does.

Pax steps closer to me, approaching like I'm a wounded animal. He says, "Covered in blood?"

I clench my teeth, wanting him to go—wanting him to stay. "It's fine. Nothing to worry about. It wasn't my blood." I right a chair and sit down in it, hard.

I don't understand what I've done to Celine, but I sense I must have hurt her, somehow. And I can't think straight with Pax standing there, staring at me in the wreckage of my apartment.

He picks up my pillow and sets it on my bed—straightens my blankets so they are no longer hanging askew. His movements are careful and deliberate, as if I could explode at any moment, or he could. Maybe both are true.

We haven't been alone like this since we talked about him being a clone—since we agreed we couldn't be together. Then, he was in pain. Now he just seems . . . on edge. Taut, like a bowstring ready to snap.

I'm about to tell him just to *go* when Henri's voice sounds. "Holy Gaia, what happened here?"

"Celine called it a break-in," I say, thankful for the reprieve from the tension.

"What was taken?"

"Nothing," I whisper. It's true. Nothing was *taken.*

Except for my past.

"Hey. Hey!" Henri is there, sliding his arm around my shoulder. "It's going to be okay. You look like someone has died."

I feel like my one chance at knowing myself has died, but I don't say that. Instead I take a bracing breath as Henri tightens his arm around my shoulders and I look again at Pax, standing now by the splintered door.

"I'm going to go," he says. No reason . . . other than to get away from me.

Because he is a clone and I am a human, and not only can we not be together, but for some reason I cannot fathom, I cause him pain.

It wasn't like this, in the beginning with us.

I nod and Pax leaves, and Henri says, "He didn't want to help clean up, huh?"

"He hasn't been well," I whisper, still staring at the door.

Henri huffs. Moving around the space, he starts picking up furniture and pushing broken dishes into a pile. "Anyhow, I ran into Charlie on the way here. She could have come to the meeting, but she skipped out." He snorts. "We had *words*."

"What does that mean?"

"That means I told her exactly what I think about her using you for Gentrification."

"And?"

"And it doesn't change anything. But at least I said my piece." He sighs and sets the rest of our chairs upright. "Pria. I really wish you would reconsider."

"You know I won't. You know I *can't*."

"Sure you can. You always have a choice."

"Not really. Not this time."

"I hope you're not just saying that because of how you've been programmed to think by the UWO."

I flinch. *Programmed to think*. I cast another quick glance toward Pax's apartment. "I won't deny that I'm more . . . prone to suggestibility than maybe some of you. But I recognize that this way is probably the only way. Can't *you* see that?"

Henri grumbles something in French, and then says, "Yes. I suppose so."

"Then why don't you want me to go?"

"You know the answer to that."

"Because it's dangerous."

"Beyond dangerous. You'll be going directly into the mouth of the beast."

"What beast?"

"It's a metaphor." His mouth twitches into a smile. "I guess you didn't grow up with a lot of stories."

"No."

"I just don't want you to get hurt. I think you've been through enough." He spreads his arms. "And now this. You can't seem to catch a break, Pria."

I can't. And something niggles at the back of my mind that it shouldn't be this way—that something about my life isn't normal. Then again, who am I to say what *normal* even is?

14

Later, after Sing and Henri both leave, I straighten the covers on my bed again, even though Pax already did that. The pieces of the destroyed drive rattle in my pocket. Luther wanted me to destroy it after I looked at it; Pax wanted me to throw it away without ever looking at it. I guess now that Charlie took matters into her own hands, everyone has gotten their way but me.

"Was I imagining things, or was it colder than an icebox between you and Pax earlier?" Celine says, breaking into my thoughts.

I catch my breath, and then turn to her, squaring my shoulders. "Pax and I will never be together. I can't tell you why, because he asked me not to. I'm sorry."

Celine blinks. "That's it?"

"I'm . . . not sure what you mean."

"I mean, that's all you can tell me? *Me*. Your best friend."

"It's important. I promise."

"But you do love him, don't you?"

Can I love someone—some*thing*—who is not even human? "I thought I did, but now I'm not sure."

To my surprise, Celine breaks into a grin. "Don't worry. It's actually pretty normal to feel confused about love." Her grin slides off her face. "Although I am sorry something has come between you two. I like Pax." She rights a shelf and says, "Okay, so what about this mess? What is this really all about? Can you tell me that, at least?"

I hesitate.

"Oh, come on." Celine puts a hand on her hip. "This doesn't have anything to do with Pax, does it? Spill."

"I . . . brought something back from Denver Commune."

Celine's eyebrows shoot up. "Oh?"

"My UWO file," I whisper, not wanting to look at her. "On a memory drive. I intended to read the drive and destroy it. I know it was a terrible risk to bring it out of the Commune, but I just wanted to know about my past—to know who I am."

"Sure," Celine says in a quiet voice, and her lack of censure encourages me to look up.

"But Charlie found out I had it, and she—she threatened me. She must have broken in here while we were meeting and—"

"She *stole* it? That conniving little . . . Let's go get it back!"

"Celine, no. She didn't steal it. She destroyed it." I reach into my pocket and pull out the pieces. "See?"

Celine lets out a hard breath. "Gaia Earth, Pria. I'm so sorry."

I shrug, my lips twitching with the urge to cry again. "I would have told you earlier, but I was ashamed."

"And that's why you were covered with blood this morning. Charlie attacked you—you guys fought."

I nod.

She mutters a curse and covers her face. "I'm sorry I was so short with you. I just don't like feeling like my friends are keeping things from me. And you're the best friend I've ever had."

"You too," I say.

"Yeah, well, you weren't allowed to have proper friends in the breeding compound, were you," she says, dismissing my remark with a smirk.

It's true. They kept us so drugged up on the decipio, we weren't capable of forming real bonds of friendship.

I go to Celine and look down at her, arms outstretched.

"What are you doing?" she says.

"Offering you a hug. It's what friends do, right?"

Celine laughs. "Yeah, princess. Sometimes, yeah." She pulls me in and squeezes tight.

When she releases me, we get to work cleaning up. It takes us hours, but we get everything back in its place. And when we're nearly through, a knock sounds on the door—it's Holly, dropping off my first dose of decipio.

"Here we go," Celine says. She comes and sits across from me, clutching the vial. Holly didn't stay, but said she would be back the next day with my second dose.

"It's just a small amount. Holly said she'd bring you up to the right dose gradually. You most likely won't even feel this." Celine hesitates.

I hold out my hand.

Celine licks her lips, sighs, and then gives it to me. "Fine. Okay."

"What's wrong?"

"Nothing. I mean, I'm . . . I don't want you to not be you anymore."

"I'll still be me."

"I know." Celine wrinkles her small nose. "I know this is probably the silliest thing to be worried about in this whole plan, because your *life* will be in danger, but I don't want you to forget us—our friendship. The decipio is designed to numb your feelings. I need you to hold on. To me. To Henri. To Pax, despite"—she gestures vaguely toward our door—"*whatever* is going on between the two of you. I need you to fight it—not just for the mission but, selfishly, for me."

"Oh." I blink rapidly against an unexpected swell of tears.

"That's good," Celine says, half laughing as she sniffs back her own tears. "It's good that I can wring some emotion out of you. That will help!"

"You were trying to make me cry?" I wipe my eyes.

She shrugs and grins. "You have so many years' practice either repressing your emotions or being on that stuff." She scowls at the bottle. "You need some help to resist it while it's in your system so you don't lose yourself entirely. I meant what I said. You're the best friend I've ever had. Hang on to who you are."

"I'll do my best." I finger the vial for a moment more, and then upend it into my mouth.

It tastes like water. That's because it is, I suppose—water laced with a drug I took for years without realizing it. I wait to feel different, but Celine is right. It was a small dosage—probably too small to make any sort of immediate difference.

I set the empty vial on the table. "So that's that."

"Yep." Celine clears her throat and stands. "You wanna go find Charlie and confront her about the memory drive?"

I stand, too, thinking of Charlie's wild, sad eyes, of her bloodstained wrists, of her desperate behavior, and I shake my head. "What's the point? She destroyed it."

"Yeah, but you can at least tell her off. That was your property."

"Celine . . . she was"—I bite my lip—"she was not in her right mind. I think I just have to accept that it's gone." And I'm not too keen on confronting Charlie again, after the last time.

Celine gapes, blinking like she can't comprehend my words. "But, it was your entire life."

"It was my entire life up to the point Pax came into it," I say with a tilt of my head.

Her mouth curls into a knowing smile. "It always comes back to Pax somehow, doesn't it?" She sighs and stares at our door. The lock is still broken and will be for at least another day, until Henri can install a new one for us. So we've decided to move a dresser in front of the door for security.

"What are you thinking?" I ask when she continues to stare, her gaze intense and distant.

"Something feels off, but I can't put my finger on what. Maybe I'm just exhausted." She casts me a serious look, her head canted, her brow straight, and her eyes piercing. "Does Pax know?"

My pulse leaps. "What? Does Pax know what? *You* brought him over after the break-in."

"What you told me before—that there will never be anything between you."

"Oh . . . Yes." I drop my eyes to my clasped hands. "He knows."

"Huh," Celine says. "How long has he known?"

I raise my eyes slowly. Technically he's known for a long time. *Technically*, he's known from the beginning, since he's always known he was a clone. He knew, and still he kissed me. He knew, but I was not alone in drawing close to him—he drew close to me, as well. Until something *changed*. Headaches. *When did the headaches begin?* But he stayed closed, kissed me even, despite the headaches. Was that it, or was there something else?

"Pria?"

"Why?" I say. "Why do you want to know?"

Celine shrugs a slender shoulder. "Curiosity. *You're* an open book, but that one"—she jabs her thumb in the direction of Pax's apartment—"has always been a puzzle that needs figuring out."

I give Celine a wan smile and avoid her eyes.

She's not wrong, because that's exactly what I'm trying to do, isn't it? Figure out the puzzle. Except a puzzle is a game, and this is no game.

15

The sounds of sawing and hammering seem primed to grate on my last nerve. A headache has formed up the back of my head, radiating into my sinuses and eyes, and no matter how I massage the bridge of my nose, it just gets worse with every passing second.

"I need to get out of here." I heave myself off my bed and look toward the door where Henri is working. He determined that he had to rip out the entire frame and put in a new one to replace the splintered lock. Celine left early this morning to go to work in her shop, so it's been just me and him. Not even Arrow can stand the noise. Bishop isn't expecting me for a couple of hours yet, but I have to find someplace else to be.

"Can I get by?" I ask Henri. "Sorry to leave you alone, but—"

"It's fine, it's fine." He lowers himself off a stepstool and moves aside so I can pass. "I'm sorry about all the noise. I'm surprised Pax hasn't come out, too."

I give a feeble shrug and try not to look toward Pax's apartment. Truthfully, I have no idea if Pax is home right now or if he left early this morning. Maybe he's just sitting in there, alone.

"Are you dying?"

"It's possible."

I flinch, and a squeak, almost a whimper, escapes my throat.

Henri frowns and puts his hand on my shoulder. "Hey, you okay?"

"Headache," I gasp. "I have a bad headache."

"Oh—I'm sorry!" He looks at his hammer with a grimace. "You should have said something sooner. I can always come back."

"No, it's fine. This needs to be fixed. I'm going to go to . . ."

Where? Where am I going to go?

"The infirmary," Henri says. "Holly will give you something." He shoots a conspiratorial grin down the corridor. "We're not supposed to use the medical supplies for things as trivial as headaches—we're supposed to ration them for the bad stuff, you know? But Holly's a softy and she's new enough not to know better." He trails his hand down my arm and squeezes my elbow. "Feel better. I'll have this done by the time you get back from work today. Promise."

I wander down the corridor, but I don't go to the infirmary. I'm aimless in the worst sort of way—the way that leaves me caught in my own turmoil of dark thoughts. *Pax—is dying. Pax—is a clone. Pax—doesn't love me. Pax—can't be with me. Pax—is a liar. Pax—is inhuman. Pax—*

I bump into someone, jamming my nose hard enough to make my eyes smart in my already throbbing head. Reeling back, I slap my hand to my face and mutter an apology.

"Pria," Luther says. He steadies me with a hand to my shoulder. "Please excuse me."

"No, it was me—I wasn't watching where I was going." I rub my nose vigorously, but tears spring to my eyes nonetheless.

"Actually, I was hoping to speak with you today anyhow. Come to my office?" He gestures.

I nod and follow him, glad for a destination, and a distraction.

We don't speak again until we're alone, seated at his table. Luther folds his hands and says, "I wanted to talk to you about Pax."

I go still and look up, moving only my eyes. "Oh?"

To his credit, Luther reddens. "I know this is probably none of my business, but I take very seriously the well-being of the people under my charge. And with Gentrification coming up, your relationships in particular matter to more than just you."

I grit my teeth and resist pinching the bridge of my nose, although my fingers twitch with the effort. "You mean if I want to build resistance to the decipio, the best way for me to do that is through *cultivating my emotions*."

"Ah. So Celine told you."

I nod.

"Well, it will go better for you if you are at least somewhat resistant. And I thought this aspect of preparing for Gentrification would be easy for you, given your relationship with Pax."

I raise my eyebrows and drop my mouth open in protest, but Luther holds up his hand.

"People who are in love should be able to most easily resist the dulling effects of the decipio, once it is reintroduced into their sys—"

"I'm *not* in love with him, and I never have been." I stand, sending my chair toppling backward.

"You do yourself a disservice if you pretend there isn't anything more than friendship between you and Pax," Luther says. "He knows it. You know it. Everyone around you knows it. That is why I have been discouraged to see something seems to have changed between the two of you since you returned from Denver Commune. Something drastic, and I don't know what, or why."

I sit again, slowly. Have I been so obvious? Have *we*? My heart thuds in my ears and my vision fogs, and with a start of horror I realize I can't keep the tears from streaming down my cheeks.

Luther leans forward, and his voice is hard. "Has he done something to you? Has he hurt you, Pria? Is there something you need to tell me?"

Has he *done something* to me? Only ripped me apart down to my very soul. Yes, he has hurt me—hurt me far worse than I ever thought possible. But I know this isn't what Luther means, and I cannot betray Pax, even now.

"No." I wipe my eyes. "He hasn't hurt me. It is a . . . quarrel, nothing more."

Luther sits back and fingers his lips. After several silent moments spent studying me, he says, "It will go easiest for you, with the decipio, if you can keep the strongest emotions you feel always before you. They will grow dimmer the more of the drug you take, like you're feeling them through a fog, but they will help you to hold on to yourself. This quarrel notwithstanding, your love for Pax will help you survive."

I try to bury my pained laugh under a cough.

"I'm sorry if that's not what you want to hear, but it is the truth. And . . . whatever has happened to estrange you, remember it is easier to share a burden than to use it as a shield."

But this is not a burden I can share.

16

I wake up, sit up, and frown, shaking my head as if that will clear the decipio, even as I know it won't now I'm a couple of weeks into taking it. The fog rests on me even when I sleep, and for the first time I realize it was when I began to dream in Sanctuary that I must have started to break free.

In the Commune, the decipio is in the water supply, but not at the Breeding facilities. That's what Holly told me. At a place like Sanctuary, they regulate it in pill form so they can increase or decrease the supply for each individual Breeder at need. Holly also told me there had been an oversight in the administration of my decipio—that Mother had been *livid.*

I remember the first day one of the pills disappeared from my daily meds—the pink pill. I was told Mother had removed it from my prescription regiment.

The pink pill was the decipio. It suddenly seems so clear, even as the rest of my world threatens to fade into a grey oblivion. Why—how—in a place as regulated as Sanctuary, could a drug as important as decipio be taken out of a Breeder's drug rotation? Was it an accident, as Holly said, or an intentional move by Mother?

Did she want to push me over the edge?

And when Pax got me out of Sanctuary, I didn't feel any more emotional on the outside than I had on the inside. "Because I was already off the decipio," I say under my breath.

"What's that?" Celine plops down beside me, tilting my worn mattress. She shoves a piece of toast toward my hands. "How are you feeling?" Her voice is light, but worry hovers in her eyes.

"Nothing, I'm just . . . thinking." I give her a thin smile and take the toast.

"Well, get dressed. We need to head to Wallace's."

"Oh?" I put the toast in my mouth so I can grab my boots. I sleep fully clothed these days.

"Yeah. He sent a message that we should come to his shop. Something important for the mission."

I finish lacing my boots and stand, taking the toast out of my mouth. Something important for the mission. I should *feel* something about that, I guess. But I don't.

It almost makes me want to pinch myself.

The walk to Wallace's shop is quiet—the passageways subdued. Ever since Brant left with about fifty residents of Asylum, it's felt this way—far too empty. How can so few people rise up against the might of the UWO?

But that's why they need us to succeed. Because it must be more than just these few. It must be the combined might of the rebels in North America. Somehow, we must convince them to fight. This is why we need the files from the capital. This is why everything is relying on what Wallace and I will do in Washington.

We stop outside Wallace's cave and buzz to be let in. I brush the toast crumbs off on my pants, wondering what it is Wallace has for us today. I've been working hard on so many things: combat training with Sing, literacy lessons with Bishop, strategy and tactics with Luther. Even basic field first aid with Holly, just in case.

Wallace lets us in and we enter his cave together, our footsteps growing louder as the space opens up around us. Cold. It's always cold in Wallace's workshop, where the ceiling rises to cavernous heights that swallow even his bright lights.

Voices greet us, and I'm aware of his presence before I see him. Pax. He stands with Wallace at a worktable, his arms crossed over his chest and his head tilted down, watching something. He stiffens when I walk in with Celine, and I know he's as aware of me as I am of him.

Two weeks. Two weeks without speaking to each other. Two weeks of pretending he doesn't exist, of passing him in the corridor with eyes averted. Two weeks of pushing to the back of my very self the feelings Luther urged me to keep at the fore.

Two weeks. And if it wasn't for the decipio, I think I would feel like I was dying.

Pax seems to be doing much better without me around. He no longer looks tormented all the time—no longer twisted with barely repressed pain. The headaches, I think, must have gone away, confirming my suspicion that I have something to do with them. In my mind, I know I'm glad for him, even as the decipio strips me of the sensations associated with the knowledge.

Maybe the decipio is good for both of us, as we enforce our separation. I know Luther told me Gentrification would go easier for me if I tried to resist it, but why would I resist *this* when it helps me weather what would otherwise be eating away at my very soul? Luther doesn't know what Pax is—that we can't be together. He doesn't know I *must not* encourage any feelings for him.

I embrace the numbness. I embrace how it helps keep me from running back to him, and Pax—

Another person buzzes to be let in. It's Holly. Wallace looks up and says, "Good. We could wait for Luther and Elan, but this will do for now. I'm sure they'll be on their way, and I've already informed them."

"Informed them about what?" I ask, carefully avoiding looking at Pax.

Wallace steps aside so I can see his worktable, on which is spread bits and pieces of the severed Golem head Moon brought back from the attack on the mountainside weeks ago. I frown slightly and look to Pax—I can't help myself.

"I reverse engineered the casing," Wallace says, drawing me back. "The casing they're using for the upgraded Golems." He lifts a clear plastic tray holding two tiny granules, like metallic grains of rice. "Pax?"

Pax picks up a detection rod and waves it slowly over the tray.

"Nothing," Wallace says. "Now two can play at having untraceable trackers."

"So you're going to implant those in me?"

"Holly is. In *us*." Wallace hands her the tray, and she surveys the contents with raised eyebrows.

"We've never been able to track our topsider operatives before," Luther says, joining us. "It was always too risky, in case our signals were intercepted or our people were captured and our technology hacked. Now, thanks to their own technology, we can. If anything goes wrong—if you have to flee, if you can't make the rendezvous—we'll be able to track you and meet you."

"Helpful, since we'll be on the other end of the country," Wallace says. "But more than that, this gives us a way to download files that's much more effective than that hack we used in Sanctuary." Wallace taps the edge of the tray. "These things can hack, download, store, and transmit across long distances—information as well as location. We can't go traipsing into Washington without a means of fulfilling our mission, now can we?"

"No . . . of course not." I haven't given much thought to that part of the mission—downloading the files and sending them back to Luther and the rest here at Asylum—so preoccupied was I with surviving it. I shiver and hug my chest. "So, are you implanting those today? Now?"

"Yes," Luther says. "We thought it would be wise to get them in place as soon as Wallace had them ready and make sure nothing malfunctions before you go."

"Okay. Where . . ." I look down at my arms.

"Your hip, I think." Holly walks a circle around me and then looks Wallace up and down as well.

"I fixed this up for the implantation," Wallace says, hefting a wicked-looking syringe. "Should be easier than a surgical placement." He gestures to a bare table over which is situated a bright light. "You first, Pria?"

Celine walks with me to the table, eyeing the syringe with a disgusted frown. As she helps me up, she says, "Why aren't we in the infirmary for this? Is it even safe to do this here? Did you sanitize that thing, Wallace?"

"Relax—I have what I need," Holly says in a low voice. She hands the tray with the implants to Celine and then takes from her pocket a small bottle of what I recognize as alcohol. "Lower your pants a few inches, please, and turn on your side." I do as she says.

"We want to keep this as secretive as possible," Luther says, his voice far too close.

Celine rounds on the men. "Privacy, please."

"Of course!" Luther says.

Luther and Wallace remove themselves to stand by Pax at the worktable, and Holly swabs my side with the cool liquid. I close my eyes, not wanting to think about the long needle puncturing my skin—about the foreign technology entering my—

I gasp at a sting of pain, chased by a wash of numbness.

"Just the local anesthetic," Holly says. "You'll feel pressure when the big needle goes in."

Pressure. And then it's over, and Holly is wiping blood off my hip and pressing on a bandage that sticks, and I roll off the table and stand.

"When the anesthesia wears off, you are going to feel that," she says.

I give her a grim smile and massage my side, wandering away from the table as Wallace steps up for his turn.

I don't want to be near Pax, so I take a turn around the space, scowling up at Beatrice, the Golem. I stop at the animal enclosure on the far side and stare. It's abandoned, clean, empty of any animals or even any sign of them. "Where are they?" I say.

"Dead, obviously," Wallace says.

I spin around. He's done already, standing and adjusting his pants.

"What do you mean, dead?" My voice is shrill, too loud. I can't control it.

Celine gives me a startled frown. Even Luther seems taken aback.

"They were clones—you know that. Hell, you were here when one of them died." Wallace walks to my side and puts his hands on his hips. "I got this batch to live longer than any of the others, but they always die in the end. I need some more to study. If Lovey and Moon were still here, I'd have some already." He tightens his mouth as though their absence is a personal affront—as if his friends have simply gone off cavorting somewhere. "After all this Gentrification madness, I'll find myself another clone, somehow, and keep at it."

My heart races like there is no decipio in my system. *They always die in the end.* If Wallace only knew—if he *knew*—he had the perfect clone specimen working with him every day. One who has been disconnected from the UWO net since he was a toddler and has survived.

Survived *so far.*

I swallow hard and drag my gaze to Pax, who stares at me as though we haven't been avoiding each other. In whose eyes I find trust in me, but also fear—a plea for his very life.

Luther was right. What I feel for him—these are feelings strong enough to keep the decipio at bay.

But they are feelings I cannot have; they are feelings I do not want.

I cannot love a man who is not a man.

I shove them down deep and let the fog roll over me again.

Pax looks away, and the spell is broken.

17

Celine nudges my shoulder. "Hey. You okay?"

"Nothing. It's nothing." I lace my fingers behind my neck and turn a circle, avoiding her.

"After Washington," Luther says to Wallace, "hopefully you won't *need* to keep studying the clones. If we can bring down the UWO—"

Wallace guffaws. "Yes, yes. But do you really think their unholy practices are going to die with them, even if we do succeed?"

Pax coughs and my eyes shoot back to him. "Luther, I've been up all night," he says. "May I leave now?"

"In a bit." Luther holds up his hand. "There's another thing we need to go over today."

Wallace's buzzer sounds, and he goes to let in Elan and Henri, who walk in holding each other's shoulders and grinning.

"—and I tipped my cup to let some out, because you know how Coop can get when we play those games, but he wasn't buying it." Elan looks around at our solemn faces and swallows his mirth. "Sorry." He removes his arm from Henri's shoulder, and he and Celine migrate toward each other like magnets.

"Now that everyone's here," Luther says, "it's time to discuss the issue of Antoine Rousseau and how to progress with our plans in light of the information Henri brought back."

The last sign of humor slides from Henri's face as he stiffens and raises his chin.

"I've given it much thought, and here is my conclusion. Now, of all times, just as we're organizing this mission—this most important of missions—someone has mentioned your father's name in connection with a *factory* of some sort, north of Reform. It must be for a reason."

"What do you mean? What reason?" Henri says.

"The man who told you about the factory was from Reform, was he not?"

"Yes."

"And this whole plan for Gentrification, it came from Charlie and Ridley—"

"Also from Reform," Wallace says.

Luther tilts his head. "My brother's . . . *discontent* with my leadership should be enough to tell you not everyone is of one mind when it comes to how we should deal with the UWO. It's possible you were given information that would lead you back here to divide our interests. To weaken and confuse us. *Now*, when we need to be unified."

"Especially now that Brant has already split our numbers," Elan says in a quiet voice. He reaches for Celine's shoulder, but she flinches away.

"Or," Henri says, "there is no subterfuge, and the man spoke the truth." He balls his fists. "Luther, if our father is alive, I cannot leave him as a slave of the UWO."

"I know."

"You . . ." Celine looks between Luther and Henri. "I'm confused."

"That's why we have to investigate your claim. But I can't spare many people right now, not with Gentrification approaching. And we can't launch a rescue operation until we are certain."

"What are you suggesting?" Henri asks. "A reconnaissance mission?"

Luther nods. "Exactly."

Henri scans the room at the few of us gathered. "Who?"

"You and Celine. He is your father—your blood. Go investigate the factory, and report back. Leave in the morning."

Celine gapes. "In the morning? So soon?"

"The sooner you leave, the sooner you can return. You're the best pilot we have, Celine, and you will be sorely missed, but . . . it is right for you to go after your own family."

"It's better than nothing, I suppose," Henri says.

Luther lifts his hands. "What else would you have me do? Now?"

"*Not* send Pria into danger again. Send a large force up to this factory instead. Rescue my father and other innocent *slaves*. Find your brother and convince him to come back. Figure out another way to defeat the UWO."

I shuffle over next to Celine, who is covering her mouth with both hands, her eyes vacant. She turns to me as I approach and lowers her hands. "Tomorrow?" she mouths.

I shrug. Henri's petitions will come to nothing. Luther's mind is set; *my* mind is set. We will move forward with Gentrification, and it is the *right* move.

I hope.

Celine makes a strangled noise and dodges around me to throw herself into Elan's arms. If anything goes wrong, on either of our missions, this could be the last day they have together.

18

"Wake up! Pria—wake up!" Celine's insistent voice shakes me from another dreamless sleep. I groan and roll onto my back, off a hip that screams in pain.

What on Gaia Earth?

Pressing my hand to the painful spot, I sit up and squint at Celine in the dim light. She looks feverish—sick? Or excited?

"Ow. What is it?"

"Come on. I have a surprise!"

Excited. Strange.

I stand to find my whole leg is sore, pain radiating from the nexus beneath my hand. What did I do to myself?

"When the anesthesia wears off, you are going to feel that."

Oh. My new implant—shoved unceremoniously into the fat and muscle of my hip. Luther can now track my movements. I'm part of a system once again. I pull down the band of my pants. A dark bruise has formed around a small scab. With a sniff of disgust, I right my clothes and eye Celine as she bustles around our apartment. She's gathered a pile of clothes next to her travel bag, spread out on her bed.

"You . . . woke me up to watch you pack?"

"No, dummy." She runs her hands over her hair and looks around. "All right. I think I'm about ready! Put your shoes on—I'm going to get Pax."

I freeze halfway to my boots. "*Why?*"

"You'll see."

And then she's gone, the door swinging shut in her wake. Sounds of her pounding on Pax's door—demanding that he wake up—

make their way to me. I lace my boots and stand, and then I go to her bed and peek through her haphazard pile, but nothing gives me a hint of what has her in a tizzy. It's just clothes, supplies for her trip. Nothing special.

Celine bustles back into the room. "Pax is coming."

"Is he as confused as I am?"

Celine quirks her mouth. She shoves the pile of clothes and supplies into her bag and zips it up. Then she slings her arm through mine and tugs me toward the door. "Come *on*."

"When are you going to explain to me what's happening?"

"But that would ruin the surprise!"

In the corridor, Pax stands, bleary eyed and tousled with his hands shoved in his pockets. Like a jolt of adrenaline, his proximity parts the fog of my decipio, and I take a deep breath. Celine nods at him, but practically drags me past, leading the way into the yellow haze of the auxiliary lights.

"What time is it?" I say, glancing over my shoulder once to see if Pax is following. He is.

"A little after midnight."

"Where are we going? You're not leaving already, are you?"

"Of course not."

"That's not really an answer."

Celine giggles. She actually *giggles*.

I give up trying to get information out of her. I would guess she's drunk, but she doesn't smell like alcohol, and she seems steady enough on her feet. We pass a few guards, who nod and smile, and then we turn down a corridor I recognize.

"Isn't this where Elan lives?"

Celine beams.

We find Henri lounging against the wall outside Elan's door, yawning and scratching his chin. Gold light pours out of the space within. He straightens when he sees us and gives Celine an exasperated scowl. "We're leaving on a mission in the morning, and you drag me out of bed for this?"

She punches his arm, and for some reason, tears glimmer in her eyes. "Shut it," she says. Then, "Pria, would you go on in with Pax?"

"O-okay."

Pax extends an arm, indicating I should go first, so I do. Inside, Luther and Wallace are seated in chairs, and—for some reason—

Bishop stands on the far side of Elan's table holding a piece of paper. Elan stands on the fore side of the table. Bishop smiles at me and says, "Ah, you've arrived. Sit, please."

Pax and I sit on opposite ends of the couch, as far from each other as we can get. I feel him watching me, but when I look, he glances away.

The door opens again, and Celine and Henri enter. She's holding Henri's arm and grinning from ear to ear, happier than I've ever seen her. Luther and Wallace stand, and I frown. *But we just sat down?*

Pax gives a quick look around and then stands as well, so I follow suit. But then Henri has led Celine to the front of the room, and she's facing Elan, and Henri releases her hand and steps back.

"Thank you, everyone, for coming at such short notice," Bishop says. "When Celine and Elan told me today that they wished to be married, I had no idea they meant *tonight*." He shrugs and smiles. "But how could I say no?"

"*I* could have said no," Henri says, but the corners of his mouth twitch and his eyes shine in a way that shows he's actually quite pleased.

Bishop raises his chin. "You may be seated."

Everyone sits but me, and Henri, who hovers by his sister's side. "You—you're getting married?" I say.

Celine rounds on me, and for the first time since she woke me, there is uncertainty in her eyes. "If we don't do it now, we might never get a chance. Do you understand?"

Coldness rushes through my veins. "Because you might die."

Silence hangs heavy in the space for a long moment—too long—and Bishop clears his throat and removes his spectacles to clean them on his shirt. I guess I said something I shouldn't have, something inappropriate for a marriage ceremony. But that is what Celine means; I'm certain of it.

Elan is the one to break the silence. "One or both of us may die, yes, before we can be reunited."

"So . . . you want to be married." I'm struggling to understand why this is important and groggy with tiredness and the decipio flowing through my system. "But it doesn't change anything about how you feel about each other. It's just . . . a construct of the old world." I rub my forehead.

Celine releases Elan and comes to me. "I know this is strange for you—that you were probably taught that marriage helped destroy humanity, or some nonsense. But, Pria, this is one of the most important *choices* Elan and I can make. If we don't do this now, tonight, and we go and die on these missions, I know I will feel like the UWO has denied me of this as surely as if I were one of those poor saps down there in the Commune. Marriage will bind us together, until we're parted by death, like our souls are joined. I can't explain to you how and why, I just know it to be true."

I widen my eyes, but I have no more words. So I resume my seat, and Henri comes to sit between Pax and me. And together we witness Celine and Elan exchange vows I don't understand beneath a mountain of stone that hides them from a world in which their troth would bring them a sure and quick death.

19

After the ceremony—after Celine and Elan embrace and exchange a long kiss that makes me look away in embarrassment—I yawn and touch her shoulder and say, "Are you ready to go back home?"

Celine tilts her head and gives me a smile that seems almost pitying. "No, Pria. I'm staying here. I live *here* now."

I part my lips and furrow my brow. "But you're leaving in the morning."

"And I will stay here for the night and—if my mission is successful—I'll come back here after I return. The apartment is yours now."

Mine . . . To live in all alone?

My uncertainty must show on my face, for Celine squeezes my arm. "Pax is right across the hall—he won't let anything happen to you. I think most everyone in this place is afraid of him, to be honest, after what happened with Etienne. I'm sure he'll walk you back." She raises her voice. "Pax, come here, will you?" She gestures over my shoulder.

"No, that's—" I start to say, but then he's beside me, and I swallow my protest.

Celine pulls me in and hugs me tight. "I know I dragged you out of bed for this, but I'm so glad you were here. There's no one I would rather have shared this with than you. I'll understand if you don't see us off in a few hours."

"I wouldn't miss it," I say against her shoulder.

Wallace, Luther, and Bishop leave, but Henri lingers, talking and laughing with Elan. Henri flicks his gaze my way, but Pax steps between us and says, "Are you ready?"

"Yes."

We exit Elan's apartment together, but separate. Separate, as we've been for weeks. Pax lets me walk a couple of paces ahead of him and maintains that distance as we head down the corridor. My shoulders stiffen and I glance back once, twice, three times, but he won't meet my eyes.

It's better this way. Better for us not to pretend.

Celine didn't know, when she sent us off alone together. She doesn't know the depth of our separation. How can she?

I look back at him again, at his bowed head and shoulders. At the way his freckles disappear into his pale skin in the dim light and his hair looks dull and redder. How could anyone guess that someone so far from the UWO ideal was created by them as an exemplary facsimile of humanity? No wonder they wanted to study him—to study what went wro—

Pax looks up suddenly, as if he can no longer bear my scrutiny, and I spin back around, my heart racing as fast as my thoughts.

The rest of the walk is long and quiet under the auxiliary lights, and when we get to our corridor, I go to let myself into my apartment without a word. My key fumbles and scrapes in the new lock and, as I wrestle with it, I hear Pax's quiet voice behind me.

"Thank you," he says.

I press my forehead to the door and close my eyes, not wanting to turn around. If I turn around, he'll read everything I still feel for him in my face. "For what?"

"You know what."

I should go back to bed. I should open my door and close it in his face and stop talking to him, but weeks without contact have left me aching for any sort of connection we might share. For . . . his company.

"I will protect you," I say. "You don't deserve to die for what you are," I whisper the words against my door. Then I do turn, because such words deserve to be spoken to his face. "Whatever you are, you have a right to live."

Pax's face is oddly shadowed—half in the yellow light of the auxiliary bulb, half in the dark—but when I speak those words, his expression crumples and tears slip down his cheeks. He turns fully into the light and wipes his face.

"Whether or not I deserve to die is not the issue," he says after a long pause. He straightens and faces me, eyes red. "But I do ask for time."

A chill runs down my back. It starts at the top of my head and travels clear to the base of my spine, and I'm not even sure why. Perhaps it's the look in Pax's eyes—a look that holds both calculation and a certain recklessness.

"Time to do what?" I say.

He quirks one side of his mouth as he draws his lips tight.

"Pax?"

He backs to his door and opens it with a sharp jerk.

"*Pax.*"

But he leaves me alone in the hall, and all I can think of is the look in his eyes and the empty stall in Wallace's workshop that used to hold cloned animals.

20

I sleep only fitfully for the rest of the night, and when I drag myself from my bed, my hip screams in pain. I rub it and grumble under my breath as I limp to the door and let myself out.

I stand, blinking stupidly at Pax's door for a long moment, expecting him to appear. But there's no reason he should. He didn't say he was going to get up to see Celine and Henri off, and I don't need an escort to the hangar. He's probably fast asleep after our late night.

Trying not to feel self-conscious, I start down the corridor alone. The muscles in my hip feel as though they've tightened around the tracker Holly inserted last night. Maybe they have and that's part of the healing process. As I enter the more populated areas of Asylum, I try to make my limp less pronounced, but still I feel as though people must be watching me.

Not many people, though. It's only dawn, and Asylum is just waking up. The smell of coffee in the dining cavern, familiar to me now, churns my stomach as I pass through. I clench my teeth and increase my pace.

The hangar is empty except for Celine, Henri, Luther, Elan, Holly, and the usual posted guards. Arrow sits by Henri's legs, panting, and Celine raises her chin to me when I enter. A relieved smile parts her lips.

"You made it."

"I told you I would."

"You're limping." Celine squints.

I shake my head and run my hand through my hair, bedraggled from tossing and turning all night. "It's nothing—just the tracker."

"I said it would be sore," Holly says from her squat on the floor. She zips Celine's pack and stands. "There, you're all set with an emergency medical kit. All the basics."

"Why didn't Wallace make trackers for me and Henri?" Celine says, hefting her pack off the floor with a scowl. "What if we get lost, Luther? Don't you care what happens to us?"

"No time, and not enough material," Luther says. "Wallace assures me he can replicate the casing in the future, but for now—"

"It's fine, it's fine. I get it." Celine adjusts the straps on her pack and rolls her shoulders. "This is still heavier than I would like."

"Aren't you just going to stow it in whatever aircraft you're taking?" I say, looking around the hangar.

"No flying," Henri says. "This is a stealth mission."

"You can't mean you're *walking* all the way!"

"My thoughts exactly." Celine looks longingly at the X-1. "I'm wasted on the ground."

"I understand, but I don't like it," Elan says.

"We can't risk your being spotted—especially with how little we know of this factory," Luther says. "Going by foot is slow, but it is always the most secure."

"Then why aren't we going by foot to Washington?" I ask.

Henri chuckles and Holly gapes.

Celine furrows her brow at me like she's trying to figure something out. "You're joking, right? You must be . . . except you hardly ever . . ."

Henri's chuckles turn to a deep-throated laugh.

"Do you have any idea how far away Washington is?" Luther says. His voice sounds carefully calm.

"I guess . . ." I glance around at my friends and suddenly feel as though the decipio has muddled my thoughts as well as my emotions. "I guess it's a great distance away, based on how everyone is reacting."

"You could say that." Celine smirks.

I embrace her as tight as I can and feel, through the decipio, a nudge of fear that it might be the last time. The feeling is numb and farther away than it should be, but it's there. When we pull apart, Celine's eyes shine with tears, and she smiles through them. "It's okay," she says, cupping my cheek. "I know you're still in there." She steps back and goes to Elan, but I can't watch their farewell because Henri joins me, his face serious.

"Another goodbye," he says. "It seems we're always saying goodbye to each other."

"Henri . . ." I want to tell him what I feel, or . . . don't feel. But is now the right time? Does he know already? I peer at him, trying to gauge his feelings.

"I think I know what you want to say," he says.

"You do?"

"Well, sure." He rubs his head and grins crookedly at me. "You're on the decipio. It's hard for you to feel anything, for anyone, right now. I can't imagine what that must be like. *Literally* I can't imagine. I've never taken the stuff myself." He shudders. "I haven't wanted to put you under more stress—to make you feel like you had one more thing to worry about as you're trying to prepare for this ridiculous mission." He huffs in displeasure and rolls his eyes to the cavern ceiling. "Anyhow, I just want you to know that if I've seemed distant, it's not because I don't care about you, it's because I *do*. I'll always care." He looks at me long and hard.

I suck my bottom lip between my teeth. I should love this man—this good man who loves me—or at least believes he does. And somewhere deep inside, where I've come to learn what love is and all the different facets it can take, I *do*. But it's not the same sort of love I feel for Pax, and I hate myself for that.

I still love Pax more than every breath, even the bated ones I hold for Henri.

"I care about you, too, Henri. But I'm sorry I can't—"

Henri holds up a hand. "Please, let's not. Not right now. If I make it back, and if you make it back, and after you flush that decipio out of your system, *then* we can talk about you and me, yeah?"

"Henri, are you coming or not?" Celine's voice is sharp. "I didn't even take that long to say goodbye to my husband."

"Husband?" Holly says. "When did *that* happen?"

Henri takes a deep breath and nods slowly. Then he whistles for Arrow, who bounds to his side and, together with Celine, they leave the cave.

21

"Husband? Really?" Holly folds her arms and watches the fluttering net as it settles in their wake.

"Last night," I say. "They did it late last night."

Holly and I stand side-by-side, silent, and I wonder what she's thinking—if she's as baffled as I am by the compulsion Elan and Celine felt to marry so quickly. Then again, Holly adopted a child as soon as she joined Asylum. Maybe she understands such things as *family* better than I do.

"Join me for coffee?" Luther says to us.

Elan and Holly readily agree, but I wrinkle my nose.

Luther chuckles. "That's right—you don't like it. Pria, why don't you wake Pax and let's meet in my office? Elan, will you get Wallace? Holly and I can get the coffee."

I agree, and with a backward glance at the cave entrance, I make my way out on the heels of Luther and Holly. They talk amiably in low voices. Luther's hands are in his pockets, and I remember when Brant accused him of giving special favors to Holly because she reminded him of Katarina—Luther's wife. His *dead* wife. I tilt my head and watch them more closely, watching for signs of favor between the two of them. Maybe Luther will marry again. Maybe he'll marry Holly. Is that a thing people do outside of UWO control—marry a new spouse after they've lost one? Does *falling in love* happen to someone more than once in their life?

"Pria?"

I look up with a start. Without meaning to, I've followed Luther and Holly to the counter in the dining cavern. Luther's accepting a pitcher of coffee, and Holly is taking up a tray of mismatched cups and mugs.

"Sorry. Pax . . . I'll get Pax."

But I don't have to go far, because he's striding into the hall, dressed in black pants and a gray shirt that makes him look even paler than usual. He has an Air-5 strapped around his waist and looks ready for a day of work. As he heads toward the exit that will take him to Wallace's, I hurry to intercept him.

"Pax."

He swings toward me—expectation lighting on his face before he can school his expression.

"Not that way. Luther's—we're all meeting in Luther's."

He nods and changes direction, and I stop and press my hand to my chest where my heart races. The rush, the exhilaration, of being near him. There are moments—unexpected moments when the decipio doesn't stand a chance.

I feel eyes on me and turn. Seated at a table not five feet away is Charlie. She hunches over a bowl of porridge, her blue eyes dull, but her gaze hostile. With a sneer, she shifts from watching me to Pax's retreating form, and then she gestures with her spoon as if to say, "Run along, now."

I do. There's no sense in provoking her, or being provoked by her. I never did confront her for destroying my memory drive. She did it out of grief for the man she loved. In a way, I can hardly blame her.

With quick steps, I catch up to Pax at Luther's door just in time to find Luther fiddling with the lock, his movements awkward around the full pitcher of coffee in his other hand. Pax offers to take the coffee, and I stop beside him and let myself relax into his presence—as well as I am able. He doesn't shift away from me, even though he practically fled from me in the dining hall. I give him a tight smile and wonder . . . wonder if we've come to a sort of truce, now that some time has passed. Time Pax says he needs.

"Are we meeting in the corridor, or going inside?" Wallace says from behind us.

"Come on in," Luther calls. And then he returns to the now open door and takes the coffee from Pax. "Thank you."

I square my shoulders and follow after Luther, trying to act as normal as possible. When we're all seated, the others pass around the coffee to everyone but me and Pax, who doesn't like it either, and Luther settles back and says, "Now, let's talk Refuge."

I wrinkle my forehead. "Refuge?"

"On this mission in Washington, if you and Wallace get separated or can't get back to our rendezvous, you won't be able to return here on your own—not without aid. That's where Refuge comes in. You have a signal to Refuge programmed into that implant in your hip."

"Is it another Nest?" asks Holly.

"Yes," says Luther with some hesitation.

"And no." Elan leans forward and grips his coffee cup in tight fingers. Steam rises from it and coats his face like sweat, but he doesn't wipe it off.

"A Nest that's . . . not a Nest." I look sideways at Pax to find him sitting so still he hardly seems to be breathing. His pulse beats a steady rhythm in his neck, and for a single moment, he tightens his teeth. Then he gets up suddenly. "Bathroom," he says. "I'm sorry, I . . . I'm not feeling well today."

"Of course." Luther gestures for him to leave.

"Refuge stays out of official rebel matters, mostly," Elan says as I watch Pax walk on stiff legs out of the room. "They are completely off the grid."

"They are their own grid," Wallace says in a low voice.

"They could be the base of all our operations," Luther says. "They could easily lead us. *She* could easily lead us, but she won't do it." He takes a long drink of coffee and winces as though it burns him. A cloud seems to hang over him.

"Who's *she*?" I say.

Elan hesitates and, instead of answering me, looks at Luther. But Luther doesn't seem inclined to answer either, so Elan says, "Their leader, Sarah."

"So this Sarah is like Brant? She wants to stay out of the conflict—just . . . survive."

"Oh, hardly that. No." Luther sets his cup down a little too hard. "Sarah—her people—they're very involved, in their own way."

I frown. "I thought you said—"

"They don't work with us. At least not directly." Luther raises his cup again. "But they're always there if we really need them."

"So what do they *do*, if they don't directly help the rebel cause?" I'm so confused, but I try not to show it. I don't know how the various rebel Nests operate in North America, so I can't tell whether what Luther is describing is out of the ordinary. And

Luther is behaving so strangely.

"They were the first, so we think. And so they claim," Elan says. "The first organized place of refuge for people who were *other*—who were outside the UWO's control. Now of course, this was some two hundred years ago that they formed, and they have somehow remained all this time. It's remarkable that they have."

"Because they're close to Washington," Holly says. "How close?"

"About a hundred miles," Luther says.

"That's not that close," I say.

Luther looks at me, and in his eyes there is intimate knowledge, and deep memory. "It's very close. For an operation of people living outside UWO control for two hundred years, that is very close."

Holly shivers. "I wouldn't want to be that close to Washington—not now that I'm free. I never even wanted to go there when I was in the system. It just seemed"—she raises her coffee cup and lets the steam fan over her face—"oppressive."

"Well, we'll need you to go with Pria and Wallace," Luther says. "Pax too." Luther glances toward his hallway where Pax disappeared. "I have jobs for you."

Holly sighs resignedly.

"What else do we need to know about Refuge?" I say.

"Refuge is our contingency," Elan says. "I know where it is—I've been there before. I have their code, which I gave to Wallace."

"And I programed the code into the trackers Holly implanted in us," Wallace says. "So if everything goes sideways and we somehow survive and have to flee for our lives—"

"Refuge is where we're supposed to go," I say. "How does this code help us?"

Luther says, "You head southwest from Washington into the wilderness. The chips are programmed to send a distress code to Refuge once you're within fifty miles of them. They will find you." He glances again toward his hallway, but Pax has not returned. "Pax's job is basic security—to protect everyone on the mission at all costs, but especially Pria and Wallace. He's posed as an Enforcer for so long, I figured one more time—"

"He'll be in terrible danger," Holly says, shaking her head. "Washington isn't like other places in the UWO."

"I'm well aware of that," Luther says. "And I'm sure Pax is, as well."

"I am what?" Pax says, coming back into the room. He's pale, but otherwise seems fine.

"Aware of the danger in Washington. Luther wants you to pose as an Enforcer for the Gentrification mission to protect Pria and Wallace," Holly says.

Pax nods. "Of course, I can do it. I would have insisted even if you hadn't asked."

"I figured as much." Luther turns to Wallace and me. "When we swap you with the Breeders who have been chosen for Gentrification, Holly will remove their wrist microchips and implant them in you so your medical information reads as theirs." I can't help tightening my mouth as my hand goes, almost on its own, to the sore spot on my hip. More implants. "She'll also attend to any other medical needs on the mission."

Luther rubs a hand over his bristly chin and considers us with tired eyes. "I'm sorry to say we know very little about Gentrification itself, aside from what we've already told you. You will be elevated to Gentri status. Beyond that—what that means, how you will be treated—we just don't know. *I* don't know. I cannot prepare you for what you will face. It's been so long since the last time it was implemented, and the whole process is done with the utmost secrecy. We have tried to consider all possible outcomes of this mission—everything that could go wrong—but there is no way to anticipate it all. The success or failure rides heavily on your ability to play roles you were once told you were born for. What pains me the most about this is we freed you from this life, and now we're sending you back into it. Or . . . some version of it, at least." He raises his arms in a feeble gesture.

I should feel more fear than I do, but the decipio has me at an almost pleasant medium. I give Luther what I hope is a consoling smile, and then I glance at Wallace. He's immune to the decipio. No matter how much is coursing through his veins, it can't effect his emotions. Is Wallace afraid?

Wallace sits in uncharacteristic solemnity. Then he drains the rest of his coffee in a long swig and slams the cup down. "I would leave tomorrow if we could," he says.

"How are we getting the files?" I dart my eyes from Wallace to Pax, and back to Luther. "Do these implants work like the hack we used last time—downloading automatically if we get close enough to the right computers?"

"No," Wallace says. "In Washington there will be too much information—too many computers and systems to set something like that to auto-download. And it would take me more than a lifetime to sort through and decode it all, assuming I even survive. So I equipped each of our implants to download, store, and transmit information from a specific computer only when activated."

"How?"

"Through a vid-screen. There are two passcodes you need to memorize before we go. The first unlocks all files on the computer or system the vid is linked to. The second begins a transfer of files to our implants, and from our implants here to Asylum."

I nod. "How long will the transfer take?"

"Fast—nearly instantaneous. And that's really it. Find the right computer and vid-screen, download the information we need, get the hell out of there." Wallace shrugs and says in a wry tone, "Easy."

22

The decipio takes me so deep that before it's time to leave, not even Pax's presence can shake me out of my emotional lethargy. It's funny how now that I'm aware of it, I think of it all the time. For eighteen years of my life, this drug pumped through my veins, and I never knew it. This level of benignity was normal—until it wasn't. At least now I am aware, even if I can't feel.

All the plans have been set. Everything is in motion. Mission preparations beyond my control and outside my awareness have been completed and all that's left to do is depart. Bishop has kept me in the know as much as possible in our daily sessions, but even his knowledge only extends so far. He doesn't know how Luther and Charlie and Wallace and Elan determined which Breeders have been chosen by the UWO. Or how they figured out when to intercept. We can speculate, Bishop says, but it would be a waste of valuable time. He wants to make sure I can read and write well before I go.

"They won't expect that of you. It could give you an advantage, once you're there," he says.

So I learn. I know enough already that when I apply myself, the pieces finally come together. And finally Luther calls Wallace and Pax and me to his office late one night and tells us it's almost time.

He spreads a roll of paper onto his desk and weighs down each corner with disparate items: two books, a cup, and his recording cube. "I am sorry to say we know nothing, really, about the layout of the Autocrat's mansion," he says. "Once you are inside, you will be on your own." He taps the paper. "What we do know is that the mansion and the grounds where the Gentri live are enclosed by a massive wall and a moat of water. The wall enjoins with the capitol building, which is the city-facing side of the mansion. We do not know if there is any way in or out aside from through that building." He rubs his face. "The moat diverts from the Potomac River and nearly encircles the entire compound, except at the capitol steps in the square before the building, where it is diverted underground."

Wallace, Pax, and I lean over the paper together. The diagram looks hand drawn from a bird's eye view. There is nothing sketched within the outline of the wall.

"If all goes well, Elan will pick you up . . . whenever you can escape," Luther says. "Your trackers will indicate when you are outside the walls. Pax will aid as he is able."

Looking at the crude map, it seems unlikely Elan will be able to do anything for me or Wallace. Unlikely we'll get out of that fortress at all. Unlikely Pax will be able to offer any sort of aid against such a bastion.

"It could take some time, of course, for you to complete your mission. Days. Weeks, even." Luther tightens his lips and looks between us. "It's impossible to make any sort of real plan for you once you're inside. Nobody really knows what goes on in that place, let alone during Gentrification. It might not even work."

Wallace lifts his chin. "It will work. There's two of us—one of us is bound to figure out a way."

I cut a glance at him. Wallace and I will most likely be separated once we've been Gentrified. And if I get the files first, I'm expected to leave without him—and vice versa. Anything could happen to either of us, or to our friends, hiding and waiting for us to emerge.

But it doesn't really matter if we make it out, does it? If we get the files, our trackers will transmit the information here, to Asylum, and the rebels will have the information they've sought for so long. What more will they need us for?

"Are you having second thoughts?" Luther says.

"No," I say, even though my chest feels oddly hollow. "No."

Luther clears his throat. "My hope," he says, "is that you will get in and out with what we need before anything terrible happens to either of you."

Pax stands swiftly and says, "Bathroom." He's so pale he's white around his lips. Walking with long, quick strides, he leaves the room.

I try to muster the concern I know I should feel for him, but instead I manage only interest. Does he have another terrible headache? Another illness? Being sick could hamper him on the mission.

I return my attention to Luther to find him watching me with worry creasing his brow, clenching his hands into fists now. He swears and wipes his forehead. "I wish there were another way," he says. "Any other way. But I just don't see how—not if we're ever going to bring them down."

"I know the risks. I'm ready," Wallace says. He looks at me.

"Me too." But I can't feel the readiness I assert. And somewhere deep inside, I wonder if this will be the end of me.

GENTRIFICATION

23

In the morning, Holly erases all my scars. I stand naked before her in a private room of the infirmary as she scans my body for any marks I have accrued in my time as a rebel—anything that could mark me as "imperfect." The serum is cool as she brushes it here and there, and my skin tightens and relaxes in response to it, knitting back together. I rub my fingers over the smooth skin of my forehead and marvel at my complacency with being immodest.

"There," she says at last. "You're all finished. Try not to injure yourself in the next hour before we leave." She hands my clothes back to me.

"Have you taken care of Wallace already?"

"Just did—before you."

So we're ready. There is nothing left for us to prepare.

We exit the infirmary together, but Holly peels off toward her apartment, mumbling something about "time with Trent." I suppose she would want time with her son before the mission. None of us have any idea how long it will take.

Elan stands beneath the X-1 in the hangar, running his hands over its smooth surface as if checking for imperfections—not unlike Holly just ran her hands over me, looking for the same. His mouth is drawn and he looks as though he hasn't slept well in a week. I feel certain he's thinking about Celine, out in the wilderness virtually alone.

Pax is half-dressed in an Enforcer uniform. The green jumpsuit hangs from his waist over a plain white shirt. I wonder how he feels wearing it. Like an imposter—a faker? Another skin of deception on top of the one he always wears.

As I watch, he shrugs it on the rest of the way and zips it up to his chin, concealing the mass of freckles there that betrays his otherness. He hasn't, however, darkened his hair or eyes for this mission. Perhaps it's because we might be gone far too long for it to make any difference. Or because Washington is that dangerous a place for rebels. If Pax is caught, no amount of trickery will fool the UWO. There is no doubt he will be killed.

I shiver, and I welcome the rush of feeling.

Bishop approaches. "Well, Pria." He settles into an easy stance beside me, and together we watch supplies being loaded onto the X-1.

"Well?" I say.

"I would offer some advice, but I'm afraid I have none. *Don't die* seems a bit trite, and it is entirely outside your control."

"You could admonish me to remember how to be a Breeder."

"Ah, but you remember that all too well."

He's right—I do.

Pax, Enforcer helmet in hand, sits on a crate nearby. He faces away, but somehow I know he's listening.

"It's a mercy," I say, biting my lip.

"What's that?"

"The decipio. Making me go back on the decipio."

"Oh?"

I look at Bishop. "I do remember how to be a Breeder—how to act like they expect me to. But the taste of freedom has spoiled me for good. I could never really go back, and if it wasn't for the decipio, I think I would be quaking with fear. People are always telling me I can't hide my emotions, but on the decipio, I don't even feel them."

"Is that why you haven't tried to fight it?" Luther asks. I didn't even notice him, but now I look up to see him standing over me. Behind him, Pax has turned his head my direction.

"One reason," I say.

Pax looks down.

"Well, I hope for your sake that the drug hasn't taken you too far under." Luther sighs and rubs his face. "We need you back, Pria. We need you to fight and survive this. Just because we're putting you back in their system and back on their drugs doesn't mean we are sending you to the slaughter. You are important, do you hear me?"

"I'll get her out," Pax says in a low voice. "Even if I die trying."

Like emerging from a pool of water, a shock of emotional clarity rushes over me, and it's all I can do to keep from crumpling into sobbing bits. But then I go under again, the emotions muffled beneath waves of numbness.

Luther looks between us and says, "Admirable, Pax. But I would prefer to have you both back. All of you." He looks at Wallace, as well.

Two women come forward. I don't recognize them, but they gesture for Wallace and me to sit on the edge of crates. They roll a cart with hair-cutting tools between them.

Of course. We're going in as Breeders.

It doesn't take long, the shaving of our heads. But as my dark waves fall around my shoulders and into my lap, I can't help fingering the locks and casting a look at Pax.

He's staring at me, his face pale and his eyes shuttered—as if he's not really seeing me, but remembering . . . The first time we met? When he rescued me from Sanctuary after I went back? Every time my head has been shaved, it's been a symbol that I belong to them.

But there's no way to know what Pax is thinking. There never is.

"Are we ready?" Elan says, joining us, and both Pax and I look up at him. "The supplies are just about loaded, and Cooper is prepped."

"Holly isn't here yet." Luther takes a few steps away to talk with him and, beyond them, Charlie hovers in the shadows, watching the preparations. Ever since Denver Commune—ever since Ridley died—she's been withdrawn and removed from all planning. But it makes sense she would be here, now, to see us take off. Without her coming to Asylum with Ridley and Dougal in the first place, we wouldn't have even hatched this plan.

Dougal, who tried to assassinate Luther. Dougal, who Pax killed.

There was something odd about that whole scenario, wasn't there? The memory claws behind my thoughts like the emotions that won't come out, sudden and insistent. I furrow my brow. Now's not the time.

"We're on a tight schedule," Elan says. He holds a vid-screen and checks something on it. "Tighter than we thought. I think the Breeders may have upped their departure."

"Bishop, go get Holly." Luther says. "The rest of you, get on board."

Bishop hurries off, and Wallace and I stand and brush the hair off our laps. Wallace, with his head shaved, looks both foreign and familiar. Younger, vulnerable. We face the X-1.

"Luther, they've left Sanctuary and will be in the Commune soon," Elan says. "We need to go."

"Breeder!" Charlie shouts, and I glance back over my shoulder to see she's talking to me.

"You'll be our best chance at beating them, not him." She jerks her chin at Wallace.

"Why?"

"Because to get the files, you will have to get close to the Autocrat himself," she says. "Wallace will not have that opportunity, but you might, and you must be prepared to do whatever you need to do."

I clench my jaw and nod.

"I hope you learned what you needed to from that memory drive, but if you place your own interests over everyone else's this time around, it could mean the destruction of the world. Remember that." With a fierce glare, Charlie balls her fists and walks away.

I remain frozen for only a moment, and then I join Pax and Wallace in the X-1, thinking. She hopes I learned what I needed to? She can't think I had time to read the drive before she destroyed it, can she?

Holly clambers into the hold clutching a large pack, which she slings to the floor. She huffs down beside it and wipes her cheeks. Her eyes are red from crying.

Cooper follows after her, giving me a polite nod even though we don't really know each other, and then he joins Elan in the cockpit without a word. I hadn't realized Elan needed a copilot, but I'm glad for it.

Luther climbs inside and looks around. He opens and closes his mouth and then says, "I don't need to tell you we have only one shot at this. I trust you—all of you. Whatever happens, we can end our lives knowing we resisted. We didn't give up."

He turns abruptly and leaves.

The door whines as it shuts, sealing us away from Asylum and a life I've grown accustomed to. I don't know if I'll return.

Wallace straps in to a seat along the wall, and Pax does the same. Holly and I remain on the floor facing each other, wordlessly staring.

With a lurch, the aircraft lifts off. We glide toward the cave entrance—invisible to us in the hold—and out into the forest of Colorado Province.

24

Every now and then, the X-1 shudders. I can't remember if it's always done that, or if I'm just noticing it now. I lift my head and scratch the base of my skull before resting it back against the wall of the hold. Pax catches my movement with a darting look that tells me he's nervous. Sweat glistens on his upper lip and his fingers drum on the helmet he holds in his lap.

Pax is rarely nervous.

Wallace huffs an impatient sigh and bounces his knee. We've been flying for a couple of hours. Apparently we're circling, waiting for something.

I have to go to the bathroom, but there's no place to do so on this aircraft. I tilt my hips up to alleviate pressure on my bladder and try not to wriggle.

The X-1 banks again.

Holly grips a hanging net to steady herself. She's standing, stretching out her legs.

"I see them." Elan's voice breaks the long silence of the hold, and Wallace bounds up like his seat is on fire.

"It's about damn time," he says. In a few long strides, he joins Elan and Cooper in the cockpit.

With a whirr of the engines, Elan accelerates, and Holly stumbles sideways.

"A little warning would have been nice," she calls.

"Sorry—strap in."

Holly picks her way to my side and plops down, clicking the harness over her. "What do you think we're doing? How are we getting a hold of these Breeders?"

"I have no idea."

We accelerate even more for a short stretch, and then Elan drops us out of the sky like he shut off the engines. I wince and grit my teeth at the pressure on my bladder, and then with a *whoosh* and a reversal of engines, we come to a swift stop. I hear the landing gear go down, and the X-1 settles on the ground.

"Quickly, Pax," Elan says, appearing in the hold with a small, handled case. Cooper is close on his heels.

I look around. Pax has put on his Enforcer helmet, and he's fingering his Air-5. I'm missing out on some plan Pax is privy to.

"They'll be overhead in minutes. We only have one shot at this."

Pax nods and Cooper stretches as if readying for battle.

Elan slams the ramp release button. "Holly, Pria, stay here with Wallace. Hopefully this doesn't take long. If we don't succeed . . ."

Wallace stretches his lanky form to full height and catches the overhead netting. "Come after you?"

Elan's grip tightens on the case. "If we don't succeed, abort the mission and fly back to Asylum. And tell Celine . . ."

"What?" I say.

But he just gives a tight shake of his head and hurries outside.

Pax follows him without a backward glance, at me or anyone else. After he leaves, I round on Wallace, but he is already heading back to the cockpit.

I follow. "What is that thing in Elan's case? What are they doing?"

"Short-range EMP," he says, and I raise my eyebrows. "Electromagnetic Pulse. Strong enough to cause a malfunction of an X-1's systems, but not strong enough to make it crash outright. Considering the, uh, *precious cargo* they're transporting, they'll land to check systems. Probably send an SOS to the Commune, too—an SOS I'm about to intercept." He taps the instrument panel.

"Just like that?" Holly says from over my shoulder.

"Just like that," Wallace says. "This's the easy part. Pax, Cooper, and Elan will board their X-1 and take out the pilot and any accompanying Enforcers. Then I'll clone their systems so the UWO net believes our X-1 is their X-1, our pilot is their pilot, and so forth. You get the idea."

The lights and panel flicker and go out, plunging us into temporary darkness.

"That's the EMP," Wallace says in a hushed voice. He runs his hands over the instruments as, with a whirr and a chugging sound, everything flickers back on again, returning to normal in a matter of seconds.

Wallace fiddles with the panel, resetting systems, I imagine. "The clock is ticking now. Too long a delay on the delivery of the Breeders from Denver Commune will raise suspicion, and we really don't want the UWO to look too closely at our little corner of the world, do we?" There's a flurry of lights on the panel, and Wallace snatches up a headset as a tinny voice comes through.

"—experiencing technical malfunction. Landing forty-six miles east of Denver Commune, south by—"

And then Wallace has the headset firmly in place, so I can hear no more of the transmission.

"Copy location down, Transport Gemini," Wallace says after several moments. "We will stand by."

Wallace grins at me and Holly, releases the com button, and says, "Easy."

25

My bladder discomfort has gotten so bad I can't take it anymore. "I'll be outside," I say.

"Wait. Hey—where are you going?" Wallace swivels to face me.

"I need to relieve myself. I'll be right back."

"I have to go, too. I'll come with you," Holly says.

We descend the ramp together, but then we look around in dismay. I expected mountains and rising red rocks and trees and shrubs, but here it's just . . . barren.

"Well, I guess we can go behind the X-1 and turn our backs on each other." Holly pokes my shoulder when I don't respond. "Come on. Quick before the men return."

A spot on the barren horizon must be the other X-1. Forms are moving against the flat landscape—people. But I can't make out who.

Holly and I are quick about our business, and then we stand together at the foot of the ramp and watch for any hint of how things are playing out. Finally, Wallace shouts out to us, "Are you done, or what? They're ready for us!"

"We're not walking to them?"

"Not when we have an airship, we're not. Get in."

Holly and I clamber back on board, and Wallace lifts off without bothering to close the ramp. We cling to our seats as the sandy ground passes beneath us, and then Wallace lands again.

"Let's go," he says.

I lead the way, waving the dust cloud from our landing out of my face. The other X-1 has its ramp open, and Elan waits outside with a grim smile. "Only one Enforcer, just as you thought," he says.

"I already started the cloning program," Wallace says. "All you have to do is keep an eye on it."

Elan nods and ducks back inside our X-1, passing Holly on her way out.

"Why don't we just take their X-1?" I say.

"It's easy to clone programs and unwise to fly an unfamiliar bird into battle," Wallace says. "Besides, I have all the hardware I need to reprogram the microchips already built into our X-1. Come on, let's have a look at them—we don't have much time."

I flex my fingers and follow him into the interior of the UWO X-1. After the bright light outside, it takes my eyes several moments to adjust.

Quick, sharp breaths draw my eyes to the two Breeders huddled against the wall under Pax's guard. The male—tall and broad-shouldered with dark hair buzzed to his scalp and symmetrical features carved into olive skin as if with machine precision. Anyone would call him handsome, but I feel no tug of attraction. My perception has changed now. Unless that's just the decipio in my system, numbing me to all *sexual desire*, as Celine would call it.

My eyes flit to Pax, and then back to the Breeders against the wall.

The female—I don't recognize her from Sanctuary. I don't think I've ever seen her before. But looking at her is still like looking into a mirror of my past. We could be sisters, practically twins, for how similar we look. If she straightened, we would stand within an inch of each other in height. And when she catches my eye, a flicker of recognition lights there. She knows I was a Breeder.

I shift my attention to Holly, who has brought her medical kit. "They should change first. If they put up a fight, they will get blood on the tunics, and we don't have spares."

The female Breeder clutches the front of her tunic—a garment I remember well. "Change? W-what is—?"

"Don't worry," I say, holding up my hands. "No one here is going to hurt you. We just need to swap clothes with you." I indicate Wallace and myself.

The Breeder's knuckles whiten. "I can't change clothes! Not here. I need to go to Washington."

The male Breeder seems stunned into silence, but cool calculation runs through his eyes—the intelligence that made him fit for the Program.

He gives Pax only a cursory glance, but he eyes Wallace from head to toe. "You won't hurt us," he says.

"No," Wallace says.

The male Breeder jerks his chin in quick compliance and pulls his tunic up and over his head.

"What are you doing?" The female Breeder covers her eyes and hunches her shoulders. "I don't understand what is happening."

I try not to flinch or cover my own eyes as the male Breeder shimmies out of his trousers and hands them in a bunch to Wallace.

"Undergarment and shoes, as well," Wallace says.

I do turn around then, and the female Breeder wails—*wails*. Her reaction, although not impossible on the decipio, seems too strong. Something is amiss, perhaps? I can't tell. Maybe I am the one who is too emotionless, since I never did anything to resist the emotion-numbing drug. Maybe I really did go too far under. I study the toes of my boots until the sounds behind me say Wallace has handed over his own clothes and the swap is complete.

"Pria," Pax says. "Holly has you covered. We'll wait outside."

Wallace, now dressed in the beige tunic and trousers of the Breeder, touches my arm and says, "Hurry."

The men shuffle out, and I look at the female Breeder, who no longer cowers but stands with fists raised to her waist and her teeth bared. Holly stands behind me with a Ringer trained on the girl.

"Your turn," I say.

"No."

I take a deep breath. "I know this is difficult for you to understand—"

"You're like me. But you're not in a Breeding house."

"No, I'm not." I square my shoulders and look her in the eyes. "I'm free."

She recoils like I slapped her. "That's disgusting. *You're* disgusting. Traitor. Criminal!"

Someone pounds on the outside of the craft—Wallace probably.

I shake myself. Grab the hem of my shirt. "We are swapping clothes."

"No."

"Either you swap clothes with me willingly, or she stuns you and we undress you and leave you naked on the floor." The lie falls too easily from my tongue, but I can't meet her eyes when I say it. I would never—could never—do that to anyone.

Holly could, though. And the Breeder must see the threat as a reality in Holly's eyes, for she gives a furious, gasping sob—probably feeling stronger emotions than she ever has—and rips her tunic from her shoulders.

This Breeder still seems far too emotional, given the decipio. This shock must be just enough to break through her fog. I almost envy her rage.

In moments, we stand facing each other in each other's clothes, and the sterile stench of her Breeding tunic is so suffocating I want to rip it right off again.

The men return, and Pax makes the two Breeders sit against the back wall.

"Right arm," Holly says to the male Breeder, holding out her hand.

"What are you going to do to us?" the female Breeder says, even as the male Breeder complies.

Holly ignores the girl's plaintive question. "If you don't want to die, you will sit very still." She preps the male Breeder's arm for the shallow surgery, and when she makes the cut and his skin springs apart and his blood trickles out, the female Breeder gives a thin scream and then slumps over.

"Good," Holly says through tight lips. "Almost got it . . . there." She removes the male Breeder's microchip and places it into a hard plastic container beside her, which she snaps closed, and hands to Wallace. "Don't lose that."

"What is that?" The male Breeder lifts his chin. He accepts a bandage from Holly and presses it to his wrist.

Wallace hesitates, and then he says. "It's a microchip. It's how the UWO keeps track of their citizens. Everyone is microchipped."

"I never knew."

"It's privileged information."

"Why do you need mine?"

"That's also privileged information."

The Breeder looks down—studies his unfamiliar clothes. "What are you going to do with me now? I was about to Gentrify. My life was about to mean something even greater to the UWO."

"Well, now it can mean something greater than even the UWO can imagine," Elan says from behind us. "Wallace, the cloning program is complete. Ready whenever the rest of you are."

"I'll check it." Wallace ducks out.

The female Breeder groans, but Holly is wiping her hands on a cloth and sitting back on her heels. "Finished," she says. "We have what we need."

Pax nods and gestures me out of the X-1, but I hesitate, watching the two Breeders on the floor. "What will you do with them—and with their pilot and Enforcer?"

"We'll put these two to sleep like the others, and Cooper is set to fly this craft back to"—Elan glances at the male Breeder, who is watching us with alert eyes—"*back*," he finishes. "From there, you know the drill."

I nod. Luther will decide.

"Have Cooper tell Luther *that one*"—Holly looks meaningfully at the female Breeder—"is nearly immune to the decipio already. She's likely to be less of a threat than the other."

"Noted. I'll let him know," Elan says.

Nearly immune already. I wasn't imagining things. I twist my lips and cast one final look at the poor girl, keeled over on the floor in my rebel clothes. I've stolen her life, her future, from her. But if she's already been waking up, she'd soon have longed for freedom anyhow. By stealing her life, I've saved her life. I hope.

26

We take off before Holly implants the chips, and after she does, I sit and stare at the numb spot on my arm—numbness the only indication anything at all has been done to me. The scar-erasing serum has removed all trace of the cut and the glue. After the anesthesia wears off, though, I know my arm will ache.

Wallace takes my elbow and drags me to my feet.

"Hey, what?"

"Over here. This flight will take a while. Sit." He pushes me into a seat nearer to the front. "Be still."

"Okay." I glance at Pax, but he just shrugs.

Wallace taps a vid-screen on the wall, and a transparent curving screen arcs over my right wrist. Numbers and letters light up on the screen while my wrist warms.

"There," Wallace says. He slumps into a seat beside me, and a second screen curves over his wrist. "I designed this to reprogram microchips to new hosts. They will merge all our biological data with the UWO data on the chips. Just in case," he says.

"Just in case, what?"

"Just in case they do any physical tests or checks. If they check your actual blood or saliva or hair against what your microchip has on record, after this, it will match." He casts a side-eye at my screen. "You are becoming B-Twenty-one of Sanctuary House."

I press my free hand to my forehead. I'm becoming a number again.

Pax says, "And when we land in Washington and they scan the microchips, the new data will sync with the UWO net?"

"That's right," Wallace says.

"How long will this data merge take?" I look at my arm.

"Couple of hours. We'll be nearly there by the time it's finished." Wallace settles back and closes his eyes.

With the decipio in my system, I'm too numb to feel afraid that this whole thing might not work. So when we begin our descent and Pax puts on his helmet and Holly's face goes pale, I just tilt my head and look with interest at the door, waiting.

"Holly," Elan calls from the front. "Come up here with me and strap in. You're posing as my copilot."

Fumbling a little with her steps, Holly hurries to do as he says.

A lurch grabs the X-1 and we shudder sideways with a groan.

"They have us now," Wallace says under his breath. "No going back."

Pax straightens and flexes his hands inside his light-green gloves.

We wait.

The pull on the X-1 alleviates as Elan makes some adjustments, and then we glide in a swift swoop down, down to the ground in a smooth landing.

The ramp whirrs open, and I blink into artificial lights. It's early evening, and we must be facing east, for the sun is far behind us, casting the landing platform into the shadow of our X-1. Beyond that, the world is lit by bright lights on high poles. I squint against them, holding up a hand to shield my eyes.

Elan walks up between Wallace and me, and he stiffens into a sort of military posture. At the base of the ramp stand a man and a woman dressed all in white, little more than silhouettes in the bright lights. The man holds a vid-screen and the woman a scanning wand.

"Breeder delivery from Sanctuary, Denver Commune. Gemini Transport," Elan says in a voice that sounds almost bored.

"You're late," the man says. "We expected you thirty-nine minutes ago."

"We experienced a system malfunction forty-six miles east of Denver Commune and had to put down to run a full diagnostic. I have already submitted the log to my superiors, but I can transfer it to you, if that is required."

"No, Citizen. It would be more efficient to carry on." The man nods at the woman, who gestures Wallace and me down from the X-1.

And so I go, putting one foot in front of the other, leaving Pax and familiarity and safety behind. As I step into the lights of Washington, I don't dare look back.

The woman waves her wand over each of us, and the man watches his screen. He nods, satisfied, and the woman says, "You will follow me."

We do. Behind me, I hear the man say to Elan, "Report back to Denver Commune. You will be seventh in line for takeoff. Control will signal you."

Then they're too far behind for me to hear anything else, and we're passing under the first row of bright lights and a cityscape comes into view.

Buildings overlap each other one after another to the edge of my vision like the mountains on the horizon in Colorado Province. But here the effect is horrifying rather than idyllic. Smoke belches from funnel stacks to our right, turning the coming sunset hazy, and to our left lie rows and rows of the low octagonal buildings Denver Commune is composed of.

Grey. Everything is grey. Aircraft buzz and hum, slow and fast, all over the city in crisscrossing lines, but farther off there appears to be a break in the press of sameness—a break with a smudge of green and perhaps a change in the type of building.

"Come, now. Hurry." The man in white passes us with clipped steps. He turns and gestures. His dark hair is smoothed back from his face with some oily substance, plastered to his skull.

The woman takes my elbow to steer me. Wallace follows the man to a white vehicle that waits, hovering, not ten feet away.

I climb into the same vehicle ahead of the accompanying woman, and she shuts the door after us. It is just big enough on the inside for four adults, but even so, our knees practically touch. It must be automated, as there is no pilot.

"We have to hurry," the man says, studying his vid-screen as the vehicle lifts into the air. "You are the last to arrive. He does not approve of tardiness."

"Who doesn't?" I ask. I hope it's okay to ask a question. Wallace doesn't shoot me any look of warning. He has shut off his usual manic energy like water at a tap—replaced it with a calm boredom as he watches the buildings zoom by out the windows.

"The Autocrat." The woman taps her wand on her knee and peers at me through her dark brown eyes. "He will see you all tonight at the Gallery Party. But he seemed most especially interested in meeting you, B-Twenty-one." She sweeps me with her eyes, and there is something calculating there. "Most interested indeed."

27

I'm glad that shock is more a state of mind than an emotion, because I can't hide mine. I blink and my mouth drops open as I take in a sharp breath. Even Wallace's brow goes furrowed.

"Yes," says the woman with a pleased, slow smile. "He has asked after you particularly. This will be the first Gentrification our illustrious leader has had the pleasure of partaking in. He has read all the files on all the Breeders and seemed most intrigued by yours."

"*Read* all the files?" I ask, trying to keep my voice steady.

"It is considered cheating to view images or videos of the participants—even for the Autocrat," the man says without looking up from whatever it is he is doing on his screen. "It ruins the fun."

"Oh yes. Really spoils it." The woman taps her chin and looks back and forth between Wallace and me. "But I think he will be most pleased with the two of you. I think they all will be. Don't you agree, Richmond?"

"Mmm," the man, Richmond, says.

I lick my lips and cast a glance at Wallace, weighing my words carefully. "I didn't realize Gentrification was supposed to be fun. The UWO called me to a duty, and I was happy to comply."

"Fun for the Gentri. It's a grand tradition. Fun for you, too—if you let it be." The woman reaches forward and strokes a hand down my cheek, her eyes straying to Wallace's face.

"Elsa," Richmond says, and Elsa jerks her hand away. "You know the rules."

I sit back from Elsa, cheeks flushing and heart thumping, confused and disoriented. I retreat into my thoughts, wondering why B-Twenty-one might have been singled out by the Autocrat. What captivated him about her file, about her history? Will he be able to tell I am not her? Why am I—*is she*—being singled out at all in this elevation to Gentri status?

We bank over the city, and I look out the window—down onto a stretch of grey rooftops that give way moments later to a stretch of what looks like brownish water. And then . . . a wall. Tall and thick and militaristic with towers and battlements—but we're beyond it before I have time to study it, and all the colors change.

A green lawn stretches for as far as the eye can see. And statues—great twisted statues covered in gold and silver, I think, standing at odd intervals lining the lawn. It's difficult to tell in the failing light. Our vehicle flits low and fast over the lawn between them, heading toward a central building of white stone that rises at the end of it all.

"These statues were built after the Great Incursion, to mark the peace," Elsa says, as if we asked. "Each one formed from the rubble of an ancient monument."

"Ancient monument?" I say.

"Along this way, there used to stand monuments to the old way of life. A failed way of life. The Incursion of the Unfamiliars was violent—it destroyed almost the entire city. The only building left standing was the old capitol. Everything else was ruined."

"The first Autocrat took the capitol building as his seat of power," Richmond said. "But people only ever viewed it as a symbol of failure. He could not rule from there."

"That's why it became the palace, and why the wall was built." Elsa's eyes gleam oddly in the lights of the vehicle.

"Palace? I thought he lived in a mansion," I say.

Elsa giggles. "No. The *Gentri* live in mansions. The Autocrat would never lower himself to such a dwelling."

"Doesn't the palace connect to the capitol building?" Wallace says. "Where he actually rules from?"

"We have a couple of curious ones," Richmond mutters.

I blush and cast a sharp look at Wallace.

But Elsa just says, "Indeed." She touches my knee. "No wonder he is captivated by you."

I twitch my knee away.

The vehicle settles softly onto a green lawn, and with a hiss of air the door opens to an indigo sky shot with purple and red.

Elsa and Richmond exit first, and then they extend hands to us. "Welcome to your new home," they say together.

But when I step out and behold the rising white sides of the Autocrat's palace, the green flag of the UWO flying from every corner of the building, the wall stretching around us all . . . I know it is not a home. It is a prison.

28

"Come along now. We must get you inside before you're seen." Elsa prods me between the shoulder blades. "The Gallery Party is in three hours, and you're nowhere near ready."

Wallace and I are ushered up toward the building, along a concrete walk and through doors that are impossibly huge. I can't help but crane my neck to look up as we pass through them. I have never seen architecture like this before, not even in Bishop's books. The doors seem too heavy for human hands, yet they open at a touch, letting us into a corridor lined with rich, dark wood and walls of paintings. Real artwork, not the scorched fragments Bishop cherishes in his archives. The floor is tiled with marble that gleams with sparkling veins, like the building itself is alive.

"Look at her stare," Elsa says. "It's almost precious."

"What about you, B-Four? You don't seem too shocked by all this," Richmond says.

"I am not shocked," Wallace says in a cool voice. "I deduced what Gentrification must mean when I was selected for it. And if there is an elite class in the UWO, that class must live an elite lifestyle. It further makes sense the Autocrat is part of that."

"And it doesn't bother you that this decadence exists?" Richmond asks. "Such opulence surely must *offend* your upbringing, no?"

"Why should it? Does the Autocrat not deserve to live in a way that suits his status?"

"Well I can see why he was selected," Elsa says.

Our footsteps echo along tiled floors until we come to a set of metal doors—an elevator.

The elevator carries us down, and when the doors open, the space beyond looks more like what I expect from the UWO: Clean lines and white walls, glass-paneled rooms, and technicians walking around wearing tunics and carrying vid-screens.

"This way, B-Twenty-one," says Elsa, and Richmond draws Wallace after him in the opposite direction.

Elsa and I pass several rooms inside which sit young, beautiful women on medical beds. Each one has long hair and is dressed in a garment I've never seen before. Something like a tunic, but luxurious and shimmering. Their faces seem oddly sharper—more distinct—but I haven't time to study them before Elsa pushes me sideways into an empty room.

A technician follows us in with a wheeled machine. "We barely have enough time," she says.

"I realize that. I will work on her while the stimulation is in process."

"Strip down. Everything off," the tech says.

I obey, thankful I swapped even my undergarments with the Breeder on the X-1. Any article of rebel clothing from Asylum would have raised an instant alarm.

"This won't hurt, but you will feel an uncomfortable tingle." The tech fits a halo down over my scalp and then sets some controls on her machine. It hums to life, and my head warms, then prickles as if with electricity.

"What is it doing?" I say.

"Follicle stimulation." Elsa answers for the tech. "We can't have you going before the Gentri bald, now can we?"

"You're giving me hair?"

"We're growing your hair. Be still."

Elsa regards my face and body with a critical frown. Every spot Holly used the scar-erasing serum on seems to burn under her gaze, and it takes all my willpower not to grab my wrist—the spot of my last surgery. But after a long perusal, Elsa gives a nod of approval and turns to a counter to roll out a tray of items.

"Now, let's see how we can improve you."

The "improvement" consists of poking and prodding and zapping with tiny lasers at spots like my eyebrows and nose and upper lip and other places that would have sent me into waves of tearful humiliation if it wasn't for the decipio. Then I am told to lie down while more machines are brought in to scan my body with prickling, sometimes searing, laser points, and I bite my lips and bear up under the pain, even as confusion rambles through my mind. They seem determined to remove all hair from my body, except for my head, which grows heavier every moment. Then Elsa plasters and paints my face until I feel sticky and immobile, and sweet perfumes are dusted over me, and I ache, ache all over.

Another tech enters, wheeling a rack of shimmering clothes. I glance over with only my eyes, my head still stuck inside the halo machine.

"Red, I think," says Elsa, running her hands over them. "It is his favorite color."

A chime sounds once, twice, three times.

Elsa raises her chin at the tech in charge of the follicle machine, and the woman adjusts the settings.

I breathe a sigh of relief as the warmth subsides into coolness and the tingling finally ceases. The tech removes the device, and Elsa leans forward to run sharp-nailed fingers through my hair from my forehead to—

I gasp and look down. To my waist.

My hair falls in soft, heavy waves all the way to my waist where it bunches into spirals.

"Yes, B-Twenty-one," Elsa says. "You are exquisite." She moves to stand behind me, trailing cold hands along my shoulders. "A true work of art. A testament to the Controlled Repopulation Program." She combs my hair back some more, tucking it behind my ears, adjusting it to fall to one side. "A symbol of the might of the Unified World Order."

The tech who brought the clothes now brings a mirror.

I don't recognize myself. It is the face of a stranger, painted with dark lines and shadows around the eyes and red lips like blood. My hair rises in a swooping arc above my forehead and then falls back, so long it is pulled nearly straight until my shoulders, where the waves appear. I do not know who I am.

A chime again. And a second. Only two this time.

Elsa tsks. "Yes, yes," she says, as if in answer.

The tech takes the mirror away and returns with what looks like soft, shiny red cloth draped over one arm.

"Stand," Elsa says. "Raise your arms."

She gives me no underclothing to wear, and the fabric feels like cool water sliding over my head and along every curve of my naked body. It falls to the floor, where it pools around my bare toes.

"Silk," Elsa says. "This is a dress—a *gown*, to be precise."

I touch my left shoulder, where the gown is held up by a clasp and a red stone the size of my thumb. My right shoulder is bare.

"A ruby—worth more than anything you've ever touched in your life. How do you feel, knowing such things exist? Knowing they were *kept* from you?"

"I feel . . ." My mind races. How would, should, a Breeder respond? How would I have responded before Pax set me free?

But the question itself is a trap. As a Breeder, I should feel no individualism—no feelings to set me apart from the whole.

I blink and say, "I feel honored to be chosen to hold such secrets. I trust that, with the Gentri, I may serve the UWO better than ever before."

Her mouth turns up in a coy smile, and she beckons me after her. "Follow me."

The tech hands me no shoes. I guess I am expected to go barefoot, so I do, and the silk gown glides behind me like a trail of blood.

29

One chime sounds as we join with the other women. All those women I saw on the medical beds, I now realize, are Breeders. Long dark hair, trains of gowns in varying jeweled colors, bare feet that make hardly a whisper across the floor. At the elevator, we meet the male Breeders, and I find Wallace easily. He has hair again, but now it is oiled into ringlets and styled to make him look even taller. His face gleams, too, as if with a fresh shave and lotion, and the shape of his eyebrows looks sharper. He wears a shiny black jacket open to his bare chest, which gleams like his face. His black trousers match his jacket, skimming bare feet.

The other men wear the same outfit as Wallace, but in varying colors. All gleaming, all shining.

The elevator opens and Elsa chivies four Breeders inside with her: two males, two females. After it closes, I move to stand beside Wallace as discreetly as I can.

But we do not speak to each other, or reach out for comfort—not that Wallace is big on comfort, anyhow. Here, we are certainly being watched.

I try to count how many Breeders there are, but as they keep disappearing into the elevator in batches, it quickly becomes a futile task. Soon, it is just Wallace and me and another male and a female in a yellow dress like the sun. Richmond stays with us until the end, and when Elsa returns with the elevator, she is red in the face and a bit out of breath.

"Last, but not least. No, *certainly* not least," she says, gesturing us into the elevator.

Once inside, she says, "You may eat and drink anything you like.

Answer any questions posed to you, and for the love of Gaia Earth, don't make a fuss if anyone touches you. If the Autocrat addresses you, you are to avert your eyes and refer to him only as 'Your Illustriousness.' The next time you hear a chime sound, you will go to the crystal daises at the edges of the rotunda. Richmond and I will give further instructions at that point."

The elevator doors open, and I blink. Music, light and airy, wafts from an opening. Music, the sort of which I used to dance to for exercise in Sanctuary, but more beautiful—freer in form and melody. Elsa walks us toward it, past walls painted with murals cast in shadow.

We step into the rotunda, as she called it, and I gape upward in awe. The ceiling rises to dizzying heights, and the paintings here are lit by powerful lights. Images that tell a story of the UWO's past, portraying a world torn apart by famine and plague, and spaceships and Golems—*Unfamiliars*—raining fire from the skies. Men and women in dark green uniforms and goggles march in unified patterns against them until . . . another panel, a peace between the "races." Bountiful harvests erupt around the construction of new cities with octagonal buildings—ranks of people pour out of UWO structures, people who all look the same. The UWO banner is raised against a bright sunrise.

I lower my eyes and exchange a long look with Wallace.

What if we're wrong? What if everything happened exactly as the UWO said it did? What if they are the saviors of humanity, and not the destroyers?

"Do you like it?"

The voice is rich and deep, tempered with the confidence of a man who never stumbles over his words.

When I turn to him, I know he is not just some member of the Gentri. I know his face well—a face that seems not to have aged since I learned it in the Agoge as a child, despite the years he has been in power.

"Do you like it?" he says again. "The artwork."

I avert my eyes, as I was instructed, and say, "Yes, Your Illustriousness. I do like it."

"You are the first to tell me so," he says. "The first to admit to personal opinion."

My heart stops and blood rushes to my cheeks. I am certain they are as red as the gown I wear when I say, "I seek only to serve,

Your Illustriousness."

"Let's have none of that," he says. "My name is Sylvan, and that is what you will call me. Look up."

I do, and I find his hand extended to me.

"Sylvan Spencer."

I slide my hand into his. It's a broad hand and a firm grip—one he holds for longer than I expect.

"What do you wish to be called?"

"I . . . am B-Twenty-one."

"Ah, but here you will no longer be a number. What do you *wish* to be called?"

My blood pounds in my ears, and I cannot answer him. I cannot give him a name because I have one already, and anything else feels like a lie. Here, I am not Pria Nastasiya, *Beloved Rebirth*, and his demand for my preference feels false in this walled palace in the center of his oppressive empire. Like a mockery of the freedom I actually possess. I open and close my mouth, faltering under his gaze, trying to keep my hand from trembling in his grasp.

"If you will not choose a name," he says, leaning close, putting his lips by my ear, "then I will simply call you *mine*."

30

He releases my hand by sliding our fingers apart, as if I am his possession. Up close his skin looks unnaturally smooth, and his eyes are dark, almost black—except that glinting in his right eye, ringing his black pupil, are lines of copper that seem out of place.

Movement over his shoulder catches my attention, diverting my shock, and then a woman with brown hair swirling about her shoulders strokes her hand down his arm.

"Sylvan," she says. "I've made my decision."

"I expected no less." He doesn't look at the woman, but continues to study my face.

"You were right about him," she says. And then she gestures and Wallace joins her. He holds a tall, thin glass full of amber liquid that bubbles against the sides. "He's absolute perfection. And just *look* at his eyes."

The Autocrat at last turns from me at her prompting. "What about his eyes, my dear?"

The woman shivers and bites her bottom lip. "There's something there, don't you agree? He's wild—and wildly intelligent. Like an animal that's been trapped. One would almost think he has been free."

Against my will, I catch my breath. But Wallace gives no response other than to sip from his glass. The Autocrat narrows his eyes. "What a thing to say, Ashra."

Ashra, whoever she is—the Autocrat's wife, perhaps?—tosses her thick hair and says, "Can you imagine what he will be like when he is off the decipio? I must have him. We must have him. Do not lose."

A sneer of humor lifts the Autocrat's lips.

An attendant walks by, wearing a white suit like Richmond's and Elsa's and carrying a tray of drinks. The Autocrat takes one and hands it to me. "Drink," he says.

So I do. It's heady and sweet and the bubbles fill my nostrils. Whatever it is, it's alcoholic, but much more pleasant than what I consumed with Celine all those weeks ago. Around the rotunda, the Gentri float about in gowns and suits such as the Breeders wear—only with shirts under their jackets—talking in low tones barely audible above the music. But around the four of us—the Autocrat, Ashra, myself, and Wallace—no one else stands, as if people are too frightened to come near.

The Autocrat watches me drink until I empty the glass, and then he takes it from me and hands it to a passing attendant. Ashra does the same for Wallace. I try to stay cognizant, but my vision goes fuzzy around the edges, and I wobble on my feet.

"How are you feeling?" the Autocrat asks me.

"I am fine," I say, although it is a lie.

"Do you understand what is happening to you?"

"I believe I am a little drunk," I say.

Something sharpens in Sylvan Spencer's eye, and Wallace tilts his head my direction—clear warning in his expression. But I can't think what I've said wrong.

The Autocrat trails cool fingers down my neck—fiddles with the ruby on my shoulder. "I meant, do you understand what is happening to you here at Gentrification?"

I wish my mind was clearer. I wish I hadn't drank that whole glass of amber alcohol. I wonder how much of this is the decipio's fault, as well. I close my eyes and take a deep breath in through my nose. "I understand you need us to diversify your bloodline—the bloodline of the elite. I understand we are being raised to Gentri status for that purpose."

The Autocrat smiles. He takes my shoulders and drags his hands down my arms as though inspecting them for defects. "You were once merely part of the system. Here, you can be a princess."

The use of Celine's nickname for me shocks me out of my drunken stupor, and I raise my chin. Implications of what *diversifying the bloodlines* might mean strike me, hard. What his possessiveness might mean. In the UWO, no one belongs to themselves. Not even—or perhaps most especially not—the

Gentri.

Before I can say anything foolish, a chime sounds.

What were we supposed to do at the chime?

All around the room, Breeders separate from the crowd. As they go, members of the Gentri touch arms and shoulders, trail fingers through hair, caress waists.

Wallace steps purposefully around me and I remember myself, coming more fully out of the alcohol haze. The daises—we're to go to the crystal daises around the edge of the room.

I give the Autocrat what I hope is an apologetic smile—I hope it doesn't look like the sickened grimace that wants to claw out of me instead—and I walk to the nearest dais. The floor beneath my bare feet has become sticky with humidity or sweat, and when I step onto the dais, I struggle to find steady purchase with my slick feet on the cool surface.

Bright lights blink on around the perimeter, illuminating each platform. I cringe and resist the urge to raise my arm and shield my face. A buzz of excited talking has arisen amongst the Gentri, who arrange themselves in clusters before the daises. The Autocrat and Ashra come to stand before Wallace and me.

The music has stopped, and a strange air of anticipation hangs in the room. I don't know where to look, so I study Richmond and Elsa to keep my eyes off Sylvan Spencer's unnerving stare.

Richmond and Elsa part the crowd with two attendants trailing behind them, heading for two daises on the far side of the room—Elsa goes to the woman and Richmond to the man. They make a few quick movements, and when they step aside, the Breeders are left stark naked in the lights, their bodies gleaming and on full display. The Gentri hovering nearby make sounds of approval and gather even nearer to inspect the Breeders from all sides. Elsa and Richmond hand off the discarded clothing to their attendants and move on to the next.

I let out a hard breath as a wash of cold runs through me, and I quickly avert my eyes. If not for the decipio, I think I would faint straight away. Or run screaming—I'm not sure which. I should have guessed it would be something like this when I saw the daises, the pedestals on which to display us.

If I'm honest with myself, this is far from the worst thing the UWO has ever done to me. They have dehumanized me in more ways than I can possibly count. But we should have known

Gentrification would be something like this. They would not elevate us without objectifying us. No status in this world comes without a price.

Would I still have consented, had I known? Would Wallace? *He probably did know—or, at least, guessed.* I cut a glance sideways at him.

Richmond reaches Wallace a moment before Elsa reaches me, and I angle my face away from him. I can't look at him, at my friend. I won't add to his shame.

When Elsa's cold fingers undo the clasp at my shoulder, I close my eyes. The dress slides to my ankles and pools at my feet.

"Step out," she says, as if it's the most natural thing in the world to undress in front of a room of strangers.

I no longer feel guilty for making B-Twenty-one swap clothes with me in the X-1—for causing her momentary embarrassment. I lift one foot, kick the silk gown forward, lift the other.

She has no idea what I spared her.

I refuse to meet Sylvan Spencer's eyes, although I feel him watching me. His possessiveness keeps the other Gentri away, although they fawn over the other Breeders with loud comments and laughter. Like Wallace, I fix my gaze to a spot on the far wall—on a bronze star that seems to be as old as the building itself—and I wait. I wait for the nightmare to end.

31

My knees lock up and my eyes go fuzzy from staring at the same spot before Elsa's voice rings out amongst the Gentri, shaking me out of my self-imposed malaise.

"I'm afraid it is time for our guests to go, but as you know, the after party continues! Drinks and fireworks will begin on the green at midnight."

"When will the lab workups be available?" says a woman in a long orange dress. I try to focus on her, but when I turn to look, my eyes flit past the two exposed Breeders she stands between, and I blink away the image.

"Noon tomorrow, I should think," Richmond says. "We must take them to be tested now."

Elsa bows with an exaggerated flourish in my direction, but of course, she's bowing to the Autocrat. "Your Illustriousness?"

Sylvan waves a hand in a bored fashion. "To the green."

The Gentri shuffle out of the rotunda, and as the large room empties, several of the Breeders let out audible sighs—and even a few whimpers.

The sounds seem to amuse the Autocrat, who folds his arms and smiles. Then he catches my eye at last and says, "Until tomorrow."

Elsa remains in her stiff bow until he exits with Ashra, and then she straightens. "Do not leave your daises," she says. "Arms in. Stand straight."

I don't have much time to puzzle over her instructions, for Richmond taps something on his vid, and then my platform jerks to life and sinks into the floor.

It deposits me into a tiny room with just enough space for a cot.

I step off the crystal platform, which rises back into the ceiling once I do, and then I turn a circle. On the cot is a neatly folded set of white pants and a tunic. I stare stupidly at them, my heart beating in my chest. I should cry. I should *scream.* Damn this numbness! They strip everything from us, literally, and take away our very instincts to fight back.

But all I can push from my depths is a single throaty sob.

I snatch the clothes and put them on over skin pimpled against the cool air. Skin that should never have been exposed.

Then I curl on my side on the cot and tuck my knees to my chest. My wrist aches. Soon it will throb. Good. I close my eyes. I need the reminder that Holly implanted B-Twenty-one's chip into my wrist and that it has not always been there. I need the reminder that I am me and I am free.

I don't get more than a minute of rest before the door to my room opens. It has no visible knob but slides into the wall with a quiet *shish.* A med tech enters with a large tray, which she sets on the bed by my curled feet.

"Sit, please," she says.

I do, and she takes both my arms. On my right wrist, she affixes a plastic and metal cuff. It tingles against my skin, lighting up with data that I watch flash along its surface. Long ago—or what feels like long ago—I wondered at how these worked, amazed that such a small thing could read so much about us from so minimal contact. Such noninvasive methods the UWO had for taking care of us! Such marvels of technology!

But then Pax got me out, and I learned about microchips, and now I know the cuffs read what the UWO implants in us from our infancy.

A bitter taste creeps over my tongue.

The med tech swipes a cold, damp tissue over the crook of my other arm, and I flinch and look over.

"What are you doing?"

"Drawing blood," she says. She hooks another, larger cuff around my elbow so I can't bend my arm, and then she attaches a transparent tube to an opening on the cuff. "Try not to move if you don't want it to hurt worse."

"Worse?" But a moment later, a green light flickers on the cuff and a stinging pain stabs my inner arm. Blood, thick enough to look almost purple, fills the tube and travels along it to some hidden place beneath the cot.

The med tech merely raises her eyebrows and takes up a vid-screen.

I measure my breaths and try not to watch my blood flowing, thankful for Holly's diligence and Wallace's planning.

"What will you do with my blood?" I ask, hoping I sound merely curious.

"There are tests to be run—tests that require more than our usual methods."

"What for?"

The med tech looks up, her expression mildly incredulous. "The Gentri want to make certain they are getting their money's worth. Bidding starts tomorrow."

The green light goes off and the flow of blood stops. The med tech removes both cuffs. She informs me that the panel near the foot of my bed is another door that opens at a touch to a bathroom, should I need it. But she recommends I get some sleep, as it will be an early morning.

I sit and wait at least twenty minutes after she leaves, counting my breaths and feeling the weight of my hair down my back. Then I stand and press my palm to the door through which she entered. If I can get out into the hallway . . . find a computer console, perhaps . . . hack into it with the code and see if there's anything there of use to us . . . I can always feign being lost—confused—if anyone catches me.

But the exterior door won't budge, and I know it's for the best. It's too soon. And here, where they're keeping us, is too exposed. There will be no secrets kept on the computers here. At least, not outside the ones they keep from everyone living the conformity the Gentri have deemed necessary for them, while *they* exist here in their walled luxury—their costly decadence.

I have to get out of here. I have to. But I don't know if I'm strong enough to survive this.

32

I sleep surprisingly well—so well that when Elsa arrives the next morning with another technician in tow, she drags me from a deep slumber.

I push myself up, and something makes my head jerk to the side. Confused, I squint through a curtain of brown waves to find I've trapped my own hair beneath my hand.

Elsa laughs and rights my shoulders, setting me up like I'm a child. "You are not the only one who has done that this morning," she says. I am directed to use the bathroom and allowed to eat a sparse breakfast that feels and tastes like a Commune ration. By the time I finish, both Elsa and the nameless tech are twitching with impatience.

Elsa removes the tunic and pants I slept in so I am once again naked. Will the humiliation never cease? My hair feels soft and heavy against my bare back. I squirm with the urge to pull it over my front.

"Sit still please," Elsa says, and then she nods to the technician, who sets to work on me.

My face is washed and dried and fresh make-up applied—that's what they call it: *make-up*. Then the technician stands behind me with a curious machine that moves over my hair in sections, heating and steaming it, while Elsa considers a rack of clothing.

She settles on a single red garment—a suit of sorts—so tight it takes both of them to help me into it. Once both my legs are inside the rubbery material, it zips diagonally from one hip to the opposite shoulder in such a way that my breasts are pushed up to nearly spill out, and I can hardly breathe. It has no sleeves or straps, but Elsa chooses a heavy gold necklace to hang around my neck.

I touch it and look down. It's a coiled snake, the head pointing into the crease between my breasts, the curved tail nearly meeting the head. The eyes gleam, and Elsa says, "Diamonds." She guides me to look in the mirror.

My face is unearthly—someone I've never seen. They've darkened my eyes with black lines and . . . soot? . . . to make them appear mysterious, the brown iridescent within, the whites glowing. My lips are red like the garment I wear. My cheeks seem strangely hollow and my cheekbones sharp, higher than normal. And my hair . . . It's as straight as grass, parted down the middle, and hanging so far past my waist now it reaches the tips of my fingers.

I look like the snake they've hung around my neck.

"I don't understand . . . why . . ."

"The Gentri like to see"—Elsa cants her head and brushes a strand of hair from my temple—"possibilities. Tradition states the Mall Parade should present a unique look from the Gallery Party."

"So an informed decision can be made," I say. I know my voice sounds dull. I can't stop myself, now that I understand how Gentrification really works.

"That's right."

"Yet you put me in red again."

Elsa bites her bottom lip and gestures for me to put on a pair of gold shoes that are little more than platforms with ties over my feet and around my ankles. "It's his favorite color," she says. "Let's not pretend we don't know how your story is going to end."

Elsa leads me out of my little room and into an open space that mimics the rotunda above us. Several Breeders are already gathered there, Wallace among them. He is in flowing white pants and a shirt buttoned only to his naval. His hair is parted and dry instead of coiffed and curled and oiled like last night. He meets my eye and looks away. Bored. Carefully bored. He plays well at being on the decipio for one long immune to it.

Other female Breeders are dressed in pants or body suits like mine. All our clothes are skin-tight, designed to show our forms as surely as if we were naked again. All meant to put us on display.

"Are we ready, then?" Richmond walks amongst us and looks around with a critical eye.

"That is everyone. Follow me!" Elsa waves a hand and hurries ahead of the crowd to an open door beneath a stone arch.

The Breeders whisper amongst themselves as we follow. Today, everyone seems a bit more emboldened by the passage of a night, and perhaps the dulling of the shock after the first Gentrification event.

"Do you think this will be *it*?" someone says at my elbow. "Or will there be more to go through before we are chosen?"

I look at her—a girl a year or two younger than I am, I'd guess, with nearly black hair pulled into a loose braid and enormous brown eyes in an open and friendly face. They've dressed her in a shimmering mauve top that criss-crosses her chest in pale strips and leaves no curve to the imagination. Her pants are white, and her shoes mere slippers that look far more comfortable than the platforms I'm struggling to stay upright in.

"I'm B-Seventeen, by the way," she says.

I start, nearly turning my ankle as I stumble.

"Is something wrong?" She offers her hand and waits as I take a deep breath and right myself.

She's from a different Breeding house—another province. Of course she could have the same number I was once assigned.

Still, I can't help eyeing her with suspicion as we pass together into the hallway beyond the stone arch. "Sorry," I say. "It's just these shoes . . ."

She tilts her head and looks. "How they expect us to operate in clothes like these after what our lives were like before"—she blinks and flares her nostrils—"let alone be *naked*." Then she gives me a horrified, wide-eyed stare and says, "That is, I mean, they did tell us, in the prep. I don't mean to sound ungrateful. This is, of course, the highest honor—the best way I can serve the UWO. I-I recognize that my body doesn't belong to me, so I'm not saying it bothered me, but I—"

"Seventeen, you have a friend in me. I will not tell anyone about your misgivings." I place a hand on her arm and smile.

But she looks at my hand in alarm and shakes it off. With quickened steps, she moves beyond me and disappears into the crowd.

I take a deep, measured breath. She mentioned *prep*. So the Breeders chosen for Gentrification were prepped? That means only Wallace and me were truly taken aback by what happened at the Gallery Party. Although I'm not sure anything can ever fully prepare a person to be naked and on display for the pleasure of others.

A sudden brightness catches me off guard, and I raise my arms against it. Two attendants at the end of the hall have opened a grand door.

We're going outside.

The air is brisk, and none of us is dressed for it. But our comfort is not what the Gentri have in mind.

"Walk, walk, walk," Elsa says, hurrying ahead of us down a set of stairs so broad a crowd of people could march up it unimpaired. At the bottom of the stairs is a broad pond of sorts, with what looks like a fountain in the middle. At the top of the fountain sits a golden statue of a man holding a hammer and a woman holding a globe. It's at least twenty feet tall. We skirt around the fountain, and I can't help but be thankful for the brisk pace Elsa sets because it keeps my blood flowing in the cold air.

Beyond the pond and the fountain stretches a green lawn too uniform to be natural and too green for the time of year. It stretches to the horizon, bounded by what looks like a gravel walking path, and on either side sit rows and rows of buildings the likes of which I have never seen. They seem to be miniatures of the Autocrat's palace—white marble with pillars and domes and gardens and reflecting ponds and statues and gates wrought with patterns of flowers and ivy and stars and globes. Diaphanous draperies float from open windows and garden trellises, and the odd child clings to a closed gate and watches us with curious expressions.

It would all seem beautiful, pleasant even, if it were not for the wall that encloses it all and the presence of the Enforcers. Beneath every tree, and at every watchtower, faceless Enforcers stand grasping their Air-5s and watching. Even here, with all their exceptionalism, the freedom they play at is just a game.

"To the path," Elsa says. "We will parade once around. Speak only when spoken to."

The path shimmers under the morning light. Granite? I take several steps and let the others pass me, pausing to look closer.

Gold. Actual gold dust is scattered into the gravel of the path around the green. Gold dust like that which settles to the bottom of the mountain streams in Colorado Province. Gold dust like the gold in Pax's eyes.

A ripple of feeling goes through me, and I breathe deep. Have I been given decipio since I arrived? The Gentri do not take it.

"Walk with me."

It is not a question, and it comes from a man not used to being contradicted. I did not hear him approach, but now that he's here, I can't avoid him.

Nor should I, for Sylvan Spencer is surely the man to whom I should try to get closest, if secrets are what I need.

I look up and smile and say, "Of course."

The Autocrat's eyes narrow slightly as if I'm a puzzle he is interested in solving. He draws his fingers through my long hair and then settles his hand on the small of my back. With a firm push, he propels me forward.

33

I let him push me only until I get my footing secure as I wobble along in the platform shoes. Then I increase my pace until we are walking abreast and his hand only lingers, sending unpleasant chills down my already tingling spine. A cool wind rushes up the Mall, as they call it, blowing my hair back. He watches me until it settles again around my shoulders. His eyes travel to the snake's eyes, lingering above my breasts, and then back to my face.

"A snake. Interesting choice."

"Why's that?" I touch the necklace, self-conscious.

He blinks and those copper lines glint in his right eye. He blinks again, and the coppery lines narrow over his pupil. "Provocative. One might even say intentional."

"I don't understand."

"I wouldn't expect you to." He turns his face to the wind. "I imagine this is all a bit overwhelming."

"Only a bit," I say.

"You don't seem surprised by the children." He gestures at a boy, perhaps age four, who peers at us through a gate.

"Should I be? We are here to breed for you, after all." I can't keep the bite out of my tone.

He raises a perfectly sculpted eyebrow.

"That is . . . breed in the traditional sense." My mind races, hoping I'm not about to make a mistake. "They told us, in preparation for this, that there would be families. Children."

"Did they, now." He says it as a statement, not a question.

I swallow and own it. "They did."

A smile, small and almost imperceptible, creases just the corners of his lips.

We pass a group of three Enforcers on the path, and they straighten and salute the Autocrat. I can't help holding my breath, watching them, wondering if Pax has found a way in. If he has, will he be able to let me know?

But then I look around at the massive wall—seventy feet tall at least with guard turrets every twenty yards—and I have no idea how Pax will manage. Or how Wallace and I will manage to get out. It's a wall that serves two purposes: to keep people out, but also to keep those inside, in.

"You're wondering about the wall, aren't you?" Sylvan says. "It was constructed after the first wave of the Great Incursion as a means of . . . deterrent."

"I thought a peace was formed?" I say, playing dumb. Teasing him for information. "Why would you need a wall when we made peace with the Unfamiliars?"

"A ruler who doesn't look to the future—who doesn't consider all possible outcomes of a conflict—isn't a wise ruler. Wouldn't you agree?"

I incline my head. He's speaking of his ancestor, but he says the words as though he means them about himself.

"The wall has proven useful in preserving our way of life here."

"You mean the Gentri here in Washington."

"I mean everywhere."

I raise an eyebrow.

"Behind this wall, the Gentri live unmolested by the general populace—free to exercise the privileges of their superiority without inciting the jealousy of the citizens of Washington." He waves a hand vaguely at the horizon. "Or of the people of the UWO at large. And because of this wall, the populace remains unaware that the Gentri exists, which I'm sure you agree is for the best."

"If they knew, there would be riots. Uprisings, even," I say.

"Just so. Amongst the . . . uninhibited factions, that is." He shoots me a side-look and we stop before a towering statue nestled within a grotto of sorts. "Above all else, there must be uniformity to avoid envy, rage, dissension. Sameness is a pillar of life in the UWO. Absolute equality."

An attendant approaches carrying a tray of tiny plates of delicate food, the likes of which I've never seen, and tall glasses of shimmering amber liquid. Sylvan accepts a drink and a plate and indicates I should do likewise. We stand in the sunshine on the glittering golden path beside the statue and eat—something the attendant tells me is called *caviar* and *foie gras*. The flavors and textures are strange, and I sip the alcohol, taking care not to drink too fast and lose my head as I did last night. I consider the statue. The main part of it is gold—a golden man with a hammer striking a pile of marble rubble. The rubble is made of what looks like bits and pieces of a different statue—parts of an arm here, half a face there, a hand resting on a knee. On the other side of the golden man stands a silver woman, planting a flag of the UWO.

I don't ask. The meaning is clear.

We finish our food and hand the plates back to the white-clad attendant, but I cling to the glass, unwilling to down it. The Autocrat steers me on.

"The wall," he says, as though we hadn't taken an interlude, "concludes at either end at the capitol building."

I look over my shoulder. We've come quite far from his palace now; it's little more than a white smudge at the end of the lawn. "Which building is the capitol?" I ask, to confirm Luther's details.

"It connects to my palace, facing outward toward the city. On the city side, it looks much like any of the UWO buildings you have always known. This side, the grand side, is my palace. The wall connects at either side of the building." He folds his hands behind his back and gazes at his home. "The main egress is there, for those of us who get to pass through. Aside from the watchtowers, of course. But those are quite impenetrable to all but those with the highest access codes, I assure you."

He turns on his heel and continues in the direction we've been walking, leaving me to stare after him with a sick feeling in my stomach. Why has he told me these things? Is it customary to tell a Breeder how to escape her cage? Or is he simply letting me know how trapped I really am?

An Enforcer strides along the lawn beside me, almost nonchalant, and I turn my head to study him. But he carries on without a hint of recognition—without a twitch or nod or whisper of acknowledgement.

I catch a glimpse of Ashra and Wallace walking along the path behind us. She hangs on his arm and talks and talks, her voice carrying to me on the breeze, even though I can't make out her words.

"Twenty-one," Sylvan says in a commanding tone. He waits for me, ten feet up the path.

I sip my drink and join him.

"She is your wife," I say, when I come alongside him again. "Ashra."

"My second wife, yes. I am surprised you know the term."

"I learned it in . . . prep." I hope this is an acceptable answer. I sip my drink again. "Why your second?"

"My first became too old for my tastes, and I tired of her."

"Is she still here?" I have yet to see anyone as old as even Luther amongst the Gentri—although I'm certain that is in part due to the serums they have access to. Sylvan Spencer must be older than Luther, as he's ruled for so many years.

"She could still make herself useful, but those females who age out of the Gentri—whose husbands desire a new wife—they cannot be allowed to leave this place. There are secrets here. So I had her sterilized and put to work within these walls."

We carry on, our footsteps crunching over the gold-infused gravel.

"Do you wish to know who she is?" he says. "You do, don't you." He touches my cheek with his knuckles, an intimate brush that sends a shiver of revulsion through me. "It's your curiosity that drew me to you. You have already met her."

I meet his eyes then, and realization sweeps over me. "Elsa," I say. "Elsa was your first wife."

"And your exceeding intelligence." He breathes the words and steps so close our faces are mere inches apart. The copper lines in his right eye glint and flash. "I am going to enjoy every moment with you."

34

"Not until after the bidding war," Ashra says. "You know the rules." She steps between us with a flounce of her dark hair. "Although I can hardly blame you. She *is* exceptional."

"The rules hardly apply to me," Sylvan says with a snarl.

"But you must put on appearances."

He grasps Ashra's wrist so fast and so tight I don't see him reach for her, but suddenly she cries out and pales, straining against him as he twists.

"*I* must do nothing."

"Of course not, Your Illustriousness," she says in a trembling voice. "Never. I would never say such a thing except in jest." She struggles to perform a bow.

Sylvan releases her. He smooths his hair, and then he takes my jaw in a tight grip and jerks my face to his. He slams his mouth to mine and pushes his tongue between my lips, forcing them apart. I try not to gag as he sweeps my mouth. My drink falls from my hand, the glass shattering on the path.

But then it's over, and he releases me with a smirk and a twist of my face that makes me stagger back.

It was a kiss, but it wasn't. The mechanics of it were there, but he used it like a weapon against me, and now I want nothing more than to vomit onto the pristine grass beside the golden path at my feet.

Sylvan walks on, toward a statue that dominates the horizon. With a cursory look at me, Ashra follows, leaving Wallace and me to trail them—both seemingly secure that we will. Once their backs are turned, I wipe my mouth on my arm, shaking.

Wallace steps to my side and taps his fingers at my wrist. I look up into his eyes to find them brimming with rage. Deep rage.

Then he breathes deliberately and blinks a few times, and the mask falls back into place. He steps quickly to outpace me, and catches up with Ashra.

I wonder what would happen if I just walked away—went a different direction. Cut across the Mall lawn, perhaps, to join one of the other Gentri groups milling about with Gentrified Breeders in tow. Something tells me Sylvan Spencer would let me try his leash for a short time, but that I would pay for it, somehow, later.

So I follow, too. But slowly, only catching up to them at the base of the tallest statue that looms at the small crook of the path loop. Another path branches off and carries on beyond, down past a long rectangular pool, but here we pause at the base of a rise of earth on which stands the statue.

It's Sylvan. Or someone who looks nearly identical. But it must be hundreds of feet tall—impossible in its construction—and gilded with solid gold.

Sylvan regards his own likeness before turning to me. "Five hundred and fifty-six feet tall," he says, as if that's supposed to mean something to me.

"It's . . . *you*." I can't keep the awe out of my tone; I've never seen anything like it.

He gives a self-satisfied sniff. "Me, my father, my father's father. It took a hundred years to complete, so I guess you could say it is me—yes."

He takes my elbow and steers me away, up the far side of the Mall now.

We pass several other groups, each person bowing low and murmuring, "Your Illustriousness." Sylvan doesn't acknowledge any of them, but strokes my arm with idle caresses that make the passersby give me curious stares. When we return to the reflecting pool outside his palace, my feet and ankles hurt from the platform shoes, and I want nothing more than to sit and rest, but Elsa and Richmond are waiting.

Elsa takes my arm and chivies me onto a circular gold platform. I wonder if this one, too, sinks into the ground. She fusses about my hair, smoothing it down and shifting it behind my shoulders. She adjusts the snake necklace at my throat. Wallace stands on a platform beside me while Richmond prepares him in similar fashion. As the rest of the Breeders arrive with the assorted Gentri, attendants circulate and hand out vid-screens. One offers a vid to the Autocrat, but he declines with a wave of his hand.

Once all the Breeders are in place, I stiffen, preparing myself to be laid bare again before these people, but Elsa and Richmond make no move. The Gentri walk amongst us with their vids, looking between us and them—checking stats, I realize. The results of our blood work. Determining how much we are worth.

The evaluation must be timed, because Richmond calls for an end after a while and attendants re-circulate to collect the vid-screens. Then a very tall man with an austere bearing and wearing head-to-toe black steps to a platform that places him directly in front of the reflecting pool. He has a resonant voice that carries over the crowd.

"We will begin with B-Fourteen of Massachusetts Province. Male. The bidding will start at twenty million Order Credits."

I've never seen anything like the squabbling, the shouting, and the near-fist fights that break out at this, but after several minutes of chaos, B-Fourteen of Massachusetts Province goes for one hundred and fifty million Order Credits to a Gentri woman wearing a bright green dress who almost faints with happiness after she wins him.

B-Three, female, of Massachusetts Province goes for only one hundred million Order Credits.

I feel sick again—nearly as sick as I felt when the Autocrat kissed me.

Most of the Gentri peel off after acquiring their Breeders, but some stay to watch the rest of the bidding.

When it is my turn, the man in black starts the bidding at fifty million Order Credits. Silence falls over those remaining, and Sylvan raises his chin. With that gesture, I become his.

I step off the platform and look to him for further instructions, but he folds his arms, and we wait. Wallace is next. Sylvan acquires him with the same raised chin. Ashra smirks.

Sylvan takes my elbow and steers me away from the remaining Gentri and Breeders. I want to be strong and fearless, but I can't help the swoop that goes through my stomach. Even with the decipio in my system—I think without it, this would be the most terrifying moment of my life. As he marches me back toward his palace—toward the looming pillars and the dome that scrapes the sky, taking care always to keep me one step faster than I can comfortably walk in my ridiculous shoes—I know I'm stepping into an unknown far more dangerous than the one Pax led me into when we left Sanctuary. Then, I held Pax's hand—he didn't drag me by the elbow.

Pax. *Pax, are you here?* My eyes skim along the line of the building, along the encircling wall, along the green of the lawn.

The palace swallows us up and the door closes behind us with a resounding boom.

35

The resonance of the shutting door and sudden darkness of the interior shake me out of my depressive thoughts. I have a job to do.

Turns, I need to count turns. Memorize corridors, doorways, artwork, terminals—anything that can help me, and Wallace, get out of here.

Eventually. Somehow.

Sylvan leads us deep into the palace, through several chambers that open one directly into the next. The colors are bright and stunning, the artwork lavish depictions of UWO events, and the carpets thick beneath our feet. Enforcers stand in pairs at every doorway until we reach a set of tall golden doors, alone at the end of a corridor. Ashra peels off to the left with Wallace. I watch them go through a smaller, dark wooden door, and then I return my attention to the Autocrat.

Sylvan Spencer places his eye up to a glowing green panel—the eye with the coppery lines in it. The panel gives a soft ding and then the doors unlatch. He pushes them open.

Beyond lies an antechamber of sorts. Round wooden tables with feet shaped liked animal claws. Potted plants with trailing vines. Windows covered in red draperies of a fabric that looks heavy enough to smother me. Floor-to-ceiling artwork displaying the greatness of the UWO. After I've taken several steps into the room, Sylvan shuts the door behind us.

"Hungry?" he says.

I shake my head.

"Hm." He walks a slow circle around me, and then proceeds to the largest round table in the center of the room, on which sits a silver platter piled high with all manner of food: fruit, cheeses, nuts, cuts of cold meats.

He picks a grape and places it in his mouth, staring at me still. Then he picks something up from beside the tray—something that he conceals in his hand.

"Am I what you imagined I would be?" he says.

I think fast. Capricious, totalitarian, self-absorbed, cruel—yes, he's exactly how I imagined he would be. How *Pria* imagined he would be. But B-Twenty-one?

"I never imagined you at all," I say, a little breathlessly, for he's come close again. I square my shoulders. " 'Imagination is a building-block of creativity, which is a temptation to the spirit of individuality. And there can be no individuality in a functioning society.' "

His lips quirk. "Who said that?"

"You did."

"*Me*?" He laughs. "Surely not me."

"If not you, then your father. It was a maxim I memorized in the Agoge."

His smile broadens. "Ah yes. Your time in the Agoge was of great interest to me. It was no small part of why I chose you."

I try not to frown. Who *was* B-Twenty-one?

"How do you feel about your time in the Agoge?"

"I . . . don't feel. Anything." Is this a test?

Sylvan brushes a hand down my neck, curls his fingers around it, and pulls me closer. "You're such a pretty liar," he says.

I stiffen, thinking he's about to accost me with a kiss again, but instead he swipes his other hand up, and something sharp stings me on the exposed side of my neck.

I gasp and try to double over, but he holds me upright. "Some prefer to let the decipio wear off gradually, but I"—he pulls the syringe out of my neck, slowly—"prefer a more direct approach."

It's like when I was shot with adrenaline after being on the brink of death for so many hours in Denver Commune, except this time it's all my suppressed feelings that come rushing back to me instead of sheer energy. Terror and rage and loss slam into me in equal parts, and a primal scream rips out of me as tears rush to my eyes. I ball my fists to lash out at him, at this monster in a man's form who has assaulted me, and humiliated me, and *purchased* me, and who stands now in a position to do whatever he wishes with me. A man in a palace who lives according to his whims while others aren't allowed even the barest hint of personal preference—on threat of death.

Who does he think he is?

Sylvan grabs my raised wrists, his eyes flashing with pleasure. And I remember exactly who he is. He's the Autocrat of North America, and I need his secrets. Thousands of people's lives hang on what I can or cannot get from my time here. I need to use him as surely as he wants to use me.

"*There* you are," he says. The copper lines in his eye narrow and gleam.

A vid—of some sort. He has a vid installed on a lens over his eye. I am suddenly thankful for every measure we've ever taken to erase me from the system, every step we've gone through to make me into someone else.

I take several deep breaths in and out of my nose. I wish they were as cleansing as I need them to be. I release the tension from my arms one fist at a time, and he lets go of my wrists.

"You must be cold," he says. "There is a change of clothes in the next room for you." He gestures to a tall door with a golden handle shaped like an eagle's beak.

With a jerky tilt of my head, I go to the door and open it. He doesn't follow me, and I look back once, wondering if he'll stop me if I close it behind me. But he's made no move toward me so far, so I hurry into the room and close the door.

No lock. It figures. I look around the space. There is a bed large enough for four people, a wooden cabinet against the far wall, two windows on either side of the bed, a padded bench at the end of the bed, two end tables beneath the windows, an opening into what is clearly a bathroom, and a padded armchair in the corner. No exit other than the one I just came through. No way out unless I climb out a window, and I suspect that will not be an easy escape.

But of course I go and check. The drop is at least thirty feet, maybe more, to a gravel drive. Too far to jump without breaking bones, or worse. And a red glimmer along the edges of the window seals tells me there is some sort of alarm system. These windows are not meant to be opened.

I back away and return to the bed where a folded stack of

clothing waits for me. Underclothes, soft grey slacks, and a thick black shirt.

With a nervous glance at the door, I peel myself out of the ridiculous red jumpsuit. I dress in the slacks and the black shirt, which wraps me in warmth like one of Celine's hugs. Tears prick my eyes at the thought of her, but I push those thoughts away. She's okay—she has to be okay. There's no other option.

I find thick socks and supple black boots in the cabinet. The grey slacks are fitted tight enough to slide into the tops of the boots, which I lace tight around my ankles.

I straighten with a sigh and look at myself in a mirror on the wall. For the first time since arriving here, I feel a little bit like myself. Aside from the make-up and the long hair, which is so heavy my scalp and temples ache.

I have to face Sylvan Spencer again. I close my eyes and picture the antechamber, not recalling any computer consoles. But there wouldn't be, where he entertains guests. Perhaps in his personal chamber. A sick knot twists in my stomach.

No. I'm not ready for that.

A knock sounds. He must have grown impatient waiting for me.

I try to look confident as I open the door, even managing a smile.

He looks me up and down, and for a moment, I feel more exposed than I have yet felt. But I am off the decipio now—in a way, all my experiences will be new.

"Exquisite," he says. He leans close and presses his lips to my neck where my pulse beats rapidly. "And how do you feel now?" he whispers against my skin.

"Afraid," I say, answering honestly. "Alive."

He chuckles. "Come with me."

He takes my hand and leads me out of the antechamber. We walk in silence down the long corridor and I busy myself counting doorways as my hand slowly goes numb within his tight grasp.

"Why are you here?" the Autocrat says.

"For Gentrification," I say. "To diversify the genetic lines of the Gentri."

"Ah." He stops and swings me to face him. "But why are *you* here?"

My blood runs cold. He can't know. He can't possibly know. "Because . . . because I was chosen. Amongst all my sisters, I was chosen."

"And why do you think that is?"

A small release of pressure in my chest causes me to let out a breath. "Because you wanted me here."

"Just so." He taps my nose. "I grow weary of Ashra. I intended her to find a Breeder who pleased her as more than just a diversion. I am to be finished with her—soon. With Gentrification, with you, I am looking for my next wife."

I feel myself go pale as the blood drains from my face.

"I will have a new Empress if you prove yourself capable."

"Capable of what?"

He pushes me until I turn toward a pair of double doors. "Capable of partnering with me in my vision."

36

The doors open and we step into a hallway wreathed in darkness that lights only when the doors shut behind us. The light here is pale green, like sunlight through new leaves in the springtime. Like the light that used to filter in through the Looking Glass at Sanctuary. A white staircase and metal railing lead downward, sterile like a medical wing, but Sylvan turns us instead to the broad doors of what must be an elevator.

"Where are we going?" I ask. My voice bounces hollowly off the walls, giving the impression the stairs descend to a great depth. The change from the ornate colors and design of the palace to the spartan interior of this stairwell is jarring enough to make me shiver.

"We are going to see the Operation."

The elevator doors open, and we step inside. It gets colder the farther we descend, colder than it was outside, and I realize Sylvan's desire to have me change might have been more practical than kind.

When the doors open, it's to nothing of note. Everything is white: the walls, the floor, the ceiling—which glows to illuminate our way. We're at the end of a short hallway. To one side is the barest crack of a door, which must be where the stairs let out. Sylvan smiles, seeming to enjoy my wide-eyed discomfort, and then he leads me on, to the end of the hallway where another door materializes as soon as we're close enough to see the cracks.

When Sylvan and I stop in front of it, a panel brightens to life on the wall beside the door, lightly glowing with green. He places his eye to it as before, and then the door pops open and a buzzing sound fills my ears.

Voices, hundreds of them. Possibly thousands. My curiosity compels me forward, ahead of the Autocrat. The space before us is as long and as broad as the Mall above, and perhaps that is where we are—beneath the Capital Mall. It's as bright as day and lined with balconies and endless, endless doorways leading off into corridors both dark and bright. Technicians of all sorts bustle along catwalks, vids in hand, clearly in the midst of tasks.

But it is the ground floor—the floor at least a hundred feet beneath us—that draws my attention most of all. I stumble to the railing and gape down at the ranks of men situated there.

"Who . . ." I lick my lips—start again. "Who are they?"

Sylvan comes up beside me. From his pocket he takes a slate-grey metallic square, which he unlatches. He turns me to face him and tilts my chin up. I'm too dumbfounded, too caught in shock, to resist. He holds my right eyelid open and places something cold and wet onto my eye, something that hurts and blurs my vision. I wrinkle my nose and pull against him, but he says, "Close your eye until it adjusts."

So I do, because I want to understand. And after a minute or so, while the voices fill my ears and the cold air lifts the hairs on the back of my neck, the lens on my eye pinches and twitches and settles into place.

I open my eye slowly, almost certain my right eye will have become blind, but instead my vision has turned strangely off-kilter—almost like when I drank alcohol with Celine, and last night at the Gallery Party. I blink hard to clear it, but the vision in my right eye remains *different*.

"Blink hard three times to activate it," Sylvan says. "Three times to deactivate."

I do as he says, desperate for any change—any change that might make it just go back to normal, but it doesn't go back to normal. Instead lines of light appear, fanning out over my vision and outlining everything around me. "Now you are like me," Sylvan says. "Now you are perfect."

He takes my elbow and steers me back to the edge. Disoriented, I make my way by feel more than by sight.

"Look down," he says. "Focus. Widen your eyes and the vid-lens will intuit your demand."

Dizzy, I press my free hand to my temple and focus on the men below, who shocked me just moments ago. I wanted to see them closer. Now I . . . I widen my eyes, and the outlining light catches them and draws them near, near, near until I can see every detail of their faces. I cry out and close my eyes.

"Too close," Sylvan says. He draws a hand down the nape of my neck. "Release the desire. Relax your gaze."

With a shudder, I open my eyes again and follow his instructions. The men slip backwards until I have them where I want them, and then I hold them there. I grit my teeth and hold on, looking from one to the next.

"Who are they?" I ask again, with effort. I am no longer cold. Sweat slides down my face and neck.

"I call them the Freemasons. My first successful batch of Enforcer Clones. With them, I will cement my dominion over this world."

37

They are all the same, which is what first caught my attention, even at a distance. Attractive, like all UWO citizens—tall, broad, and strong, but young. Most as young as I am. Perhaps younger. And familiar . . . familiar in a way I can't quite put my finger on. Familiar as though I've met one of them before. But when would I have had the opportunity to do so? It nags at me, clawing at my memory like a word I know but can't draw to the surface. Perhaps—probably—it is a sense of familiarity born of the fact all UWO citizens are bred to look the same, and these Freemasons are clearly cloned to look like UWO stock.

But why *this* model? This person, whoever he was. Did he give his permission, the man whose genetic material they cloned? Or was he an unwitting participant in the march of the UWO's goals, in the march of scientific, evolutionary progress?

Sylvan is watching me—watching me with a critical stare that burns through my skin. Judging my reaction.

Clones. These are clones. I am not supposed to know human cloning exists.

"Clones?" I gasp the word, hoping my response is not too delayed—hoping it reads as shock and awe. Hoping it reads as the very real horror I feel.

Pax said he was unique. He said he was the only one.

There are thousands here. The main floor is filled with them. *The Freemasons*. "But they're human. *Human* clones."

"Clones of humans, yes," Sylvan says. "But not human themselves. No individuality, no will of their own, no true feelings, no souls. Just look at them. This batch—it's a perfect replica of humanity, but nothing more."

Hearing Sylvan Spencer speak words so close to what I've thought about Pax—spoken to his face . . . My stomach lurches and I grip the railing. My cruelty toward Pax has been astonishing. On par, apparently, with the Autocrat of the Unified World Order.

I rake my eyes over the masses of clones. Men who came into the world just like Pax. I watch them; I *see* them. The way they gather into friend groups, the way eyes light with amusement at jokes while others look away in disgust or disinterest, the way one smiles with only his eyes and another an open-mouthed grin. The way they make small distinctions in their dress and how they style their hair—even though they all have been issued the same tunics and haircuts. The same, and different.

I blink hard three times, shutting off my vid-lens, willing my sight back to normal. When I open my eyes, the slight off-kilter-ness remains, but the lights and lines are gone. I straighten and look at Sylvan Spencer. "They are spectacular. I had no idea—none."

His face splits into a diabolical grin. "You can hardly be blamed. This is top secret. It's been in development only this last decade."

"Ten years?" I look over the railing again, at the young men. "But they're . . ." I can't go on. Piecing together everything, it's . . .

"Growth hormones, stimulation." He runs a hand through my long hair—hair they gave me last night. "If we can grow bodies from cells to embryos, do you really think we couldn't accelerate the process?"

"And what will you do with them?" My heart races. I wish I had a means of recording this conversation, but the implant in my hip is worthless for that sort of thing.

"Release them to replace the human race, of course." He says it so nonchalantly, as if he's not discussing mass genocide. "Finish a job started over two hundred years ago."

I take a slow breath in and hold it. From the mouth of the Autocrat of North America: admission of the culpability of the Unified World Order in the Great Devastations. But I need more; I need proof I can take with me.

I measure my response with as much delicacy as I can muster as he turns to walk us along the uppermost level of the Operation compound to the nearest corner.

"But why?" I say. It's not difficult to insert a quivering horror into my voice.

"Humans are too"—he waves a hand—"unpredictable. If left to their own devices, they would rise again to nearly destroy the planet. Humanity had its chance, and they failed. Only some are fit to survive, and those some have already been chosen. It's time for a new wave of evolution to ensure the survival of the chosen few."

"But what about you and me? We're human, too, aren't we?"

We come to a set of stairs in the corner, which we descend, turning along the length of the massive space. I only stumble a little going down the stairs. The longer the lens is in my eye, the more I adjust to it.

"We are a higher form of human," the Autocrat says. "And soon, we will be the only true humans on the planet."

"Won't the Gentri die out if you do this?"

"Now that I have perfected cloning, why should I not live forever?" He gives a deep-throated laugh, but the darkness in his eyes tells me he's far from kidding. "Why should *we* not? Do you realize what I have accomplished? The perfection of the human genome! The Controlled Repopulation Program was always just an experiment to see if humanity could exist and flourish under controlled circumstances, but those circumstances failed us again and again. Flaws perpetuated like sand in the gears, viruses in the Tree of Life. But with the research I've completed here, the progress I've made, there no longer will be any need for *breeding*. No need for traditional humanity at all. The clones can be not only produced in a lab, but *made* to comply, unlike humans, who must be coerced."

"Made to comply?" It is only with great effort that I get the question past my lips without clear fear and revulsion showing on my face.

"Do you require a demonstration?"

"No, I—"

He places a hand on my arm and turns me back to the railing. With several quick blinks and a focus that speaks of the use of his own vid-lens, he tilts his head toward a corner of the room below.

On cue, a swath of Freemasons twenty-strong freezes mid-activity, crying out and dropping to hands and knees. Some of them fall to the floor and curl into the fetal position in clear agony.

Sylvan's nostrils flare as he stares at them, entranced.

"Stop," I whisper.

He takes a breath and lets them go. With a glance sideways at me, he says, "And also . . ." and waves a lazy hand toward the ground floor.

One of the Freemasons drops his sandwich, turns to his neighbor, and snaps his neck.

I skitter away from the railing. The noise of talking is loud enough in the space that I can't possibly have heard the bones breaking, but I imagine it nonetheless, and the imagining of it rings through my head. "I've seen enough—I understand," I say, pressing my hands to my stomach.

He smiles and drags a finger down my cheek. "There's no need to feel sensitive about it—to feel anything at all. They're not human. You see? *They* don't feel anything. They are empty inside. I created them—they belong to me."

"I see."

Pax, saying my name and pressing his lips to mine. Pax, taking my hand to comfort me in the dark. Pax, shielding me from harm again and again.

Forcing a bland smile to my face is one of the hardest things I've ever done, but somehow I manage it. "They are not human."

My words seem to excite him. His eyes light up and he moves closer to rub his nose along my hairline, breathing deep like he's smelling me. I grit my teeth and clench my fists so I don't shove him off.

"No more need for fragile infants or children," he says. "When we require more laborers, we will simply *make them.*"

"But . . ." My mind races back to every conversation I ever had with Holly about human cloning. She couldn't have been so mistaken about everything, could she? "But they still need to be born, don't they?"

"Of course they do." Sylvan sobers. He steps back and smooths his hair. "They do need wombs, at first. Have you guessed it—how we have made so many?" His gaze travels up and down me.

"Breeders," I say. "You used the Controlled Repopulation Program." It is no guess. Holly told me weeks ago, but for him I must pretend.

"That's my clever girl," he says, tapping my bottom lip. "For years, there have been thousands of clones birthed to Breeders—birthed and brought here." He pushes off from the railing. "Would you like to see the source?"

At my confused look, Sylvan takes my elbow and steers me with a hand to the small of my back. "We tried and failed for so long to find a suitable source for our batch of Enforcer clones, but none of them ever turned out quite right. Then one of our bio-science techs surmised we were working with genetic material that had been too *designed*, too manipulated. He remembered we had a Hunter in stasis and thought it best to start over from there—with a pure genetic base from before the Program. If we start with a pure base, we can then modify the genes to our liking."

"What's a Hunter?"

We step off the walkway and into a narrow, bright hallway before Sylvan answers. "Hunters were the first . . . Enforcers, I suppose you could call them. There was only ever a small corps of them, during the Great Incursion." We step through another doorway that slides open at Sylvan's command, and then we are within a room so cold I can see my breath.

Lining the walls are tanks large enough to hold full-grown people—about twenty of them, each one opaque. Sylvan goes to the nearest one and places a hand on it. It lights up from within to show a young man floating in frosty liquid. He is naked, but most of his body is distorted by the frost on the glass. I recoil, nonetheless, and not just because of his state of undress.

He's clearly dead and has been for some time. His skin is blue and his eyes closed and sunken. Clean in the center of his skull is a hole big enough for me to pass my thumb through. Tattooed on his chest beneath another hole—a hole through his shoulder—is a black number 1.

Despite these horrors, the likeness is unmistakable. His face is the face shared by all the men in the room beyond these walls, his jaw and nose and arms and hair. He is the first Freemason.

"He is"—I lick my lips—"How did he . . . I mean . . . Did the UWO kill him?" The bullet hole in his forehead stares at me like a third eye. It doesn't look like it came from an energy rifle.

"He is part of the history that built this world," Sylvan says. "He matters only in his contribution to making us great." He waves a hand, and the glass around the young man, the first Freemason, goes dark again.

With a shiver, I look around at the other tanks. More *sources*. More humans whose genetic material was taken to be cloned? Is this the only room like this, or are there many more? Somewhere in here, is there a man who looks just like Pax, floating in frozen stasis?

The thought unnerves me more than I care to examine. If I saw him, I don't think I would be able to contain myself. I duck my head.

"This way," Sylvan says, extending his arm. "If you are to be my Empress, you must see it all."

Must I?

This is everything I want, and he's giving it right to me—handing it over as if he knows what I seek. Why should he? I don't understand. Even as his *Empress*, there would be time to learn such things. I can't help feeling like this is a test, or worse, a trap. And here, far beneath the earth, there is no one to rescue me.

We pass through windowed rooms of lab techs, hard at work over equipment, and naked babies and children caught in green plastic chambers—hooked to tubes and wires, fast asleep. "The growth chambers," Sylvan calls them. Girls and boys, all strangely familiar, yet not. In another room, young Freemasons exercise, lifting immense amounts of weight. "The growth stimulations give them unnatural strength," Sylvan says. "An unexpected side-effect of the cloning process." In another room, five pregnant women recline on white couches. "Breeders chosen to incubate clones." Sylvan takes a deep, shuddering breath and smiles.

"Because . . . because clones are sterile, right?" I say through lips gone numb. "Animal clones are sterile. Human ones are, as well, aren't they."

"Sterile? Oh yes. Quite sterile. None of my clones can *breed.* We are using the wombs of these females to incubate embryos created in a lab. When the fetuses are fully to term, they will be removed and these female Breeders examined for further usefulness to the Operation. But we certainly cannot remove the reproductive blocks from the clones. Can you imagine what might happen?" He chuckles, inviting me to do the same. "They would reproduce like rabbits. They have the urges of animals—absolutely wild things, if I were to let them go." His humor vanishes and he stares hard at me.

My stomach twists into a sick knot, but I offer him what I hope is a benign smile, and we move on.

Beyond the cloning chambers, we step out into another cavernous space—a space as large as the one we first entered into. But here the smell is overwhelmingly toxic. It's a smell I know from fearful days in the wilderness, and from my nightmares. I gag and cover my mouth.

Below us stretches a Golem workshop. Enameled skeletons wait their turn on a slow-moving conveyor belt. One by one, they are fitted with a hydraulic system of piping—the "blood" of the beasts—and then they pass into an enormous machine that pulls them upright and begins adhering flesh to the bones. Completed Golems step out of the machine and arrange themselves in lines along the far wall. Waiting for what, I'm not sure. Probably instructions via the uplinks in their skulls.

They *are* just machines. I've known it for a long time now, but to see them in production . . . I sway and touch my head. *They are just machines*. The monsters of my childhood have been reduced to gears and plastic and bolts, and the men are truly beasts.

Sylvan is intent upon me. The Golems, above almost all else he's shown me today, should be a shock. No one in the UWO knows that the Unfamiliars—the Golems—are not actually aliens, let alone that they are, and have always been, manufactured *by* the UWO. I should scream or cry or rage.

But instead I do the only thing that comes naturally to me after all the shock I've sustained. I give in to the horror clawing at the back of my mind and pass out cold.

38

I wake with a jolt, clawing at silk. Heart racing, I bolt upright and take stock of my surroundings. A dark room, a soft mattress, the same clothes I wore to see the Operation. How long I've been out, I can't possibly tell, but it seems I've been returned to my room in the Autocrat's personal quarters and laid down on the bed.

And I'm alone—Sylvan Spencer is nowhere in sight.

I slide down from the high mattress, starting when my bare feet touch the floor. He left me clothed, but removed my boots and socks. The intimacy of the action unnerves me, but also gives me pause. *Why?*

So many *whys* race through my mind, threatening to crowd out the information I've gathered and the feelings weighing me down. After weeks of numbness, the emotions are now a blanket around my shoulders—both comforting and heavy. I curl my toes against the cold wooden floor and follow the motion with my eyes. Beneath me live swarms, thousands, of clones. *Freemasons*, built from the genetic material of one frozen boy.

They can be "made to comply . . . They are empty inside."

But they weren't—they aren't. It is as clear as day to me that those boys, those men, are individuals, no matter how similar they appear to one another. And I only saw them for a short while. The Autocrat may believe he has them all under his control, but Pax exists, and Pax belongs to no man other than himself.

And Pax is not empty inside.

He lives, he makes choices, he dreams. How many times have I seen him tormented by a nightmare about being *Fifteen* that he then tries to hide from me? He longs—for freedom, for me, even when he holds himself back. *He loves.* I can see it in his eyes, I always have.

It bowls me over, as it did earlier today. But alone, I don't have to hide it. I gasp and let the tears slip out, down the bridge of my nose, welcome after so long.

He is not empty. The UWO may have given him flesh, but they did not create who he is, on the inside. Pax is as human as I am.

And I can let myself love him.

I'm overcome with the need to see him. To tell him. To tell him I love him, and that I'm so sorry for the way I've acted—if it's not too late. But the only way I can fix this is if I can get out of here. And to do that, I need to first find what I need. What the rebels need.

I straighten, wobble, and press the heel of my hand to my right eye. It aches, especially now that I'm crying. I try not to rub it too hard, certain I'll just irritate the vid-lens, and I don't want to cause permanent damage to my eye. I sniff and blink hard several times, and the vid springs to life, lighting up my room in lines of light and words and numbers. With a huff, I stumble back against the bed and try to make sense of what I'm seeing.

It's too much—too much information everywhere, but the most is concentrated around the windows where the lines on the vid glow bright red and the words "perimeter alarm: active" run along beneath the window panes, shifting to stay in place every time I move. I close my eyes and take a deep breath. A headache is already forming between my brows.

When I open my eyes again, I notice four white dots in the corners of my vision, blinking softly, almost like an invitation. I raise my hand into my line of sight and splay out my fingers, as I've seen people do on vid-screens, and the images push out and expand so that I am looking at them at least ten feet in front of me instead of against my face. It is so much less discombobulating that I actually release a light laugh of relief. And then I start to experiment.

With hand motions, I can swipe things on and off the "screen"—in and out of my line of sight. With movements of my eye and focusing or unfocusing, I can draw elements in or push them farther away. I can highlight and click through to follow links, and I can give commands and pull up files, and I can—

I sit down hard on the bench at the foot of the bed. This thing in my eye, it is not a computer in and of itself—it is just a sophisticated vid-screen, and possibly the most sophisticated interface the UWO has ever developed. But a vid-screen interacts with either the UWO net or a computer, and if I can do all these things with it, then it must be connected to some computer, here, in the palace. Or it must have the capability to connect to a computer.

I leap back up, heart racing. Is it possible—is it *possible*—Sylvan Spencer put inside my head the agency of his own destruction?

How do I find it? Where do I look?

I blink once, hard, which I've discovered brings me to a sort of main screen. And in the upper corner is a blinking access bar. If I enter the code Wallace gave me, and this vid is connected to the Autocrat's personal computer, it should allow me access, shouldn't it? I raise my fingers and make a tapping motion, drawing up a keyboard. Shaking, I tap in the hacking code.

Immediately, my vision fills with files. "Unified World Order Record Files."

"On the Implementation of the Controlled Repopulation Program."

"On the Establishment of the Operation."

"On the Implementation of the Great Incursion."

"Annals of the Great Devastations"

Files on files on files, tabs overlapping in too many layers to count.

Sweat runs down my temple, and I cast a quick glance at the door, the screen of the vid-lens shifting with my nervous look. I bite my lip and type in the second code—the one that will download it all—all the files to the implant in my leg.

How long will it take? Will I know when it's complete? Will it signal me? I can't remember. Wallace told me the hack shouldn't set off any alarms in the UWO system, but does he know that, really? So much has been different from what we thought. Behind these walls lie true secrets.

As I wait for a signal that might never come, the *whys* creep in again. The Autocrat has given me everything I need. Information, access, time alone. He even told me how I could escape through the wall—that the main egress to the capital city is through his palace. The files on the screen blink as I turn a slow circle and look at the door that leads to the antechamber. Either he is foolishly trusting of me, or he desires for me to know these things. *But, why?*

I sit on the bed to wait, but I'm bursting with nervous energy—it's tingling down my arms and along my fingers. So I stand and pace, and go to my boots where they rest in the corner, finding my socks folded neatly on the inside. With trembling fingers, I put them on and then pace some more, back and forth across the room.

I can't risk staying here for too long, but to leave too early could mean missing something I need. And how will I know the way out, when it's time to leave? For all I know, Sylvan Spencer could be right outside the door.

To distract myself, I swipe through the files on the screen. There are mounds of data, and none of it is encrypted.

None of it is encrypted.

I blink hard twice at a file titled "The War in North Africa," which takes me to sub-files titled things like, "The Sub-Saharan Front," and "The First Implementation of the Famine," and "Pandemic Trials Amongst Indigenous Tribes."

I select one, but what comes up is just a list of numbers and letters beside more files: UWORF 675.1, UWORF 675.2, UWORF 675.3 . . .

Laughter, outside my door. I swipe at the screen, diminishing all the files, and blink hard three times. My vision returns to normal, but it takes me several seconds to reorient myself.

There it is again. Female laughter, loud and shrill.

I inhale, hold it, let it out. Either I stay here until Sylvan Spencer returns, or I take a chance and walk through that door. Hopefully all the files I need have downloaded to the implant in my leg.

Hopefully, far away in Asylum, Luther will get the notification that information has come through.

Hopefully I'll be able to get out of here, and Wallace with me. I square my shoulders and wrench open the heavy wooden door.

39

The laughing woman is Ashra. She stands with her head thrown back, a wild and mad grin on her face, and a bunch of grapes in her hands. Beneath her, on a divan, Wallace reclines—if it can be called *reclining* when he looks about as tense as a string on one of Moon's bows. Ashra, who is wearing a long silver dress that flows over her body like liquid metal, is feeding the grapes to Wallace one at a time. She forces another one into his mouth as I watch, and then she tilts her chin and casts a smile over her shoulder at me.

"You came out," she says. "I was wondering if I could lure you out."

"What are you doing here?" I say. "Isn't this the Autocrat's apartment?"

She straightens and drops the grapes into Wallace's lap. "It's my palace, too. Look at you." She walks to me, appearing almost to glide in her silver dress. She plucks at the sleeve of my shirt. "Quaint. Of course, he would want you comfortable, for what lies beneath."

I shiver and glance at Wallace. "The Operation," I say. I cut Wallace another meaningful look. Hold it. "He showed me everything. I . . . *got* it all."

Wallace sits upright and watches us closely. For as much as Ashra disparaged my attire, she's dressed Wallace similarly: grey fitted slacks, black leather boots, a heavy sweater.

Ashra looks between us, and her mouth twitches into a calculating smile.

I return my attention to her. "Where is he—the Autocrat, I mean?" I keep my voice calm.

"He got called away," Ashra says. "A meeting with the other Autocrats."

"Th-they're here?" I back up a step. "The Oligarch is here, in Washington?"

She laughs. "Don't be ridiculous. It's a remote meeting. They have much to discuss, and I can't help but agree with them," she goes on as if we should understand what she's talking about.

"With who?" I say. "The other Autocrats?"

She sighs. "Yes. It *is* risky, having you here. In fact, I think you should leave. *Now*." She raises an arm as if to strike me, but Wallace springs between us and grabs her around the neck. She struggles against his chokehold, but in moments, she goes still. He lowers her to the floor.

I press both hands to my racing chest. "What was *that*? Is she alive? You didn't kill her, did you?"

"She's alive," Wallace says. He straightens from his crouch and passes a hand over his brow. "Risky having you here . . . You. *You*. What did she mean?"

I gape and shake my head.

He rounds on me. "You got it. How did you get it?"

"In my eye." I pull down the bottom lid of my right eye. "See? He—the Autocrat—he forced this vid-lens onto me. And he showed me things that they're doing beneath the palace. He called it the *Operation*. When I got back here, I realized I could maybe use the lens to hack the system, so I did, and I think it worked."

"Did you put in the code, like I showed you?"

"Yes."

"*Both* codes?"

"Yes. The first one brought up files. Thousands of files. The second didn't look like it did anything, but you said—"

Wallace grasps both my arms and cracks a wide smile. "It did. If you put in both codes, it worked."

"How can you be sure?"

"Because I designed the program." He drops my arms and scans the room. "Can you pull up that vid—search for a way out of here?"

He doesn't seem surprised at the technology, not surprised at all that I have a piece of tech fused to my eye that can connect to the UWO net, or any computer within range. I blink three times and pull up the home screen—it's becoming familiar—splay my fingers to send it out, away from my face.

Every line in the room is limned with green or red. Red for an alarm system of some sort, as the display tells me. Cameras blaze at me like angry red eyes from corners and light fixtures, and I can't think why Enforcers haven't descended upon us yet. Beyond the central table, along the far wall, are several doors. Only one is green.

"That one, I think." I point. "The others are alarmed."

"Very good." Ashra's voice, hoarse with strangulation, sounds from the floor. "He said you were smart."

Wallace starts toward her, but she raises a firm hand to stay him. "Not again. My head can't take it."

"We're leaving," he says. "I can't let you stop us."

"I have no intention of stopping you." She laughs, but her laughter devolves into a coughing fit. "I want you to go."

"Why?" I say. In the halo of my vid-lens, she seems to glow, the light gleaming off her pooling silver dress. "Why are you helping us? We're no one—just a couple of Breeders."

She laughs again and shimmies herself into an upright seated position. Smoothing her dress in her lap, she says, "He would make you Empress in my place. Empress, while I am relegated to . . ." She lifts her lip into a cold sneer at Wallace. "A play thing." With a grimace, she gets to her knees, and then to her feet. "The cameras are not transmitting—I saw to that. Go now, through that door."

"You're letting us *go*?"

"Isn't that obvious?"

I give Wallace an incredulous look, one that he returns with grim calculation.

"I don't understand," I say.

"What's to understand? Sylvan would have you usurp my place—I'm not ready to go. Now pay attention! Through that door, you'll find a corridor to Sylvan's private quarters. Follow the corridor to the end. There is a false wall that opens if commanded with the vid in your eye. Look up into the corner. You won't be able to see the scanner, but it's there. Beyond the door is another corridor. This one takes you to double doors leading to Sylvan's office in the capitol building. Avoid his office and take a right instead at the hallway beside it. Follow it to a large window at the end of the hall. It's three floors up, but there are easy handholds, and there are no Enforcers on duty in the alcove outside the window—not this time of day."

"You're suggesting we climb out a window?"

"Three floors up," Wallace says.

"What about alarms? The windows here are alarmed."

"You can disarm the window," Ashra says. "With your vid-lens."

"You know about—about the lens he gave me?"

A bitter smirk twists her lips. She strokes the side of her face. "He took mine away. It was a twelve-hour surgery to have it removed. He gave it to you instead."

"Time to go," Wallace says, coming close and bending to whisper in my ear. "I don't like where this is going, I *don't* trust her, and the Autocrat could be back any moment. Let's worry about the window when we get there. If we have to break it—we break it."

I nod, mesmerized by Ashra as she sways and folds in on herself.

Wallace extends his hand, I take it, and we run.

I think Ashra will stop us, or say something else, or ask—as Holly did those months ago—to come with us. But she remains looking inward, and then raises her eyes to mine just as Wallace and I reach the door. Wallace opens it and ducks through first, checking the corridor for Enforcers. Before he tugs me through, Ashra smiles, and it seems a wicked sort of smile.

40

Neither of us asks the other to repeat the instructions. They were simple enough, and the corridor beyond the door is deserted. Our feet make no noise in the thick tread of the carpet, and when we reach the false wall, I look into both corners, seeking the scanner Ashra said I wouldn't see.

A soft click, and the wall swings out.

Wallace pushes on it, sticks his head out, and then gestures me forward. The hallway beyond is a stark contrast to the opulent chambers we've just left behind. Staid white walls and floors tiled and gleaming. No adornments other than the natural grain in the tiles. At the far end of the hall, a set of double doors waits.

Wallace and I exchange glances and then look over our shoulders. The hall stretches back to a gentle curve out of sight. Anyone could appear at any moment. The only way forward is to follow Ashra's instructions.

I can't shake the sense of being *herded.* Something doesn't feel right. None of this does. And from the look on Wallace's face, I can tell he's feeling it, too. Still, we go on. What choice do we have?

I take two steps to every one of Wallace's long strides. The Autocrat's office doors loom closer. He's meeting with the other members of the Oligarch. Does that mean he's in his office right now?

Shouldn't there be Enforcers outside his office, guarding it?

But there's no one—just us.

And the cameras. I trail my gaze along the crease where the wall meets the ceiling, my vid-lens showing me where they are. Ashra said the cameras in the Autocrat's personal quarters weren't transmitting, but she didn't say anything about the ones here, in the capitol building.

I quicken my pace.

We take a right at the double doors. The window isn't far—visible outside it are clouds and sunset-streaked sky.

Wallace gets to it first, and he leans on the sill and looks out and all around. "We're outside the wall," he says. "Only just, but we are. There's a spot of land here, this side of the moat."

I crowd in beside him so I can see. About five feet to our right, the concrete surface of the wall looms. And just beneath the window, the top of—

"A tree," I say. "There's a tree growing right here. If we can get beneath it, we won't be visible from any other windows."

"Or that guard tower." Wallace points up. "It will be all in the timing."

I bite my lip and look back down the deserted hallway. Our voices are too loud, this place too empty. "I don't like this."

"I don't like it, either, but we can analyze it later—after we're out."

I nod. Stepping back a pace, I focus the vid on the window. It glows red at the edges. "It's alarmed. What am I looking for? How do I deactivate it?"

"I could override it if I could see it," he says. "Try selecting the alarm function—there should be a way to click on it."

I use my finger to select the script running beneath the window, which brings up a screen full of numbers and letters. "Now what?"

"Scroll to the bottom of the page," he says.

I look all the way down, and the script moves with me.

"You should find a blinking cursor, or something—someplace you can enter data."

A sound echoes far down the hallway behind us. Voices drawing near. I jump and look over my shoulder, and the vid-screen blinks and changes, showing instead the lines up and down the hallway behind us. "No! No, no, no," I whisper, trying to reorient myself.

"Dammit," Wallace says. "There's no time."

My hands shake. I focus on the window again, draw back up the alarm and the data sequence.

The voices are getting closer.

Wallace kicks the window. Nothing happens. He kicks it again, and the glass groans. A third time, and spider-web lines appear.

I stand and blink hard three times to shut off my vid-lens as Wallace kicks the window a fourth time and glass explodes outward.

A siren wails through the capitol building and the light flashes a pulsing red. Wallace kicks jagged shards of glass out of our way and then shouts, "Come on!" He grabs my hand and pulls me through the window with him.

We're three floors up. We should be climbing carefully down, not jumping into nothing. We're going to break every bone in our bodies.

At least I got the files. They should have transmitted to Asylum by now.

At least Luther has what he needs.

At least Pax and Celine and everyone else will have a fighting chance.

At least—

We hit the branches of the tree with enough force to knock the wind from my chest. A limb slams into my stomach and I bounce backward into a tangle of smaller branches. My hair catches and tears as I continue to fall. Somewhere in my periphery, sounds of crashing and rustling indicate Wallace's downward progress.

Instinctively, I grab at anything I can until my scrabbling fingers catch and hold on a branch that doesn't break, and my legs wrap around another, and my hair—so much hair—is everywhere, holding my head at an unnatural angle. Everything hurts.

The alarm blares. Voices shout from above. Wallace lets out a groan and climbs around to my side. He touches my knee. "Climb, Pria."

I wrench my head, not so much disentangling my hair as tearing it from the tree. A cry of pain escapes my lips, but adrenaline pushes me forward, down, down the tree. Limb to limb and finally to the trunk. Wallace slides down ahead of me, jumping the last five feet. I practically fall on top of him.

Getting to shaky feet, he and I look out toward the city—toward Washington. Behind us is the wall, before us, the lapping waters of the moat, and beyond that a maze of buildings awash in the glow of the setting sun.

The moat. Our tree, the grass we came down on—it's on a triangular wedge of land between the archway where the water diverts under the capitol building front steps and where the building meets the wall. The only way to get off it is to scale the archway without falling in the water. Possible, but tricky. And I can't swim.

I cast a despairing look at Wallace. "They'll come for us, right?" I say, wiping a trickle of what I think is sweat from my eyebrow, but when I look at my hand, it's red with blood. "Elan and Holly and Pax. They're tracking us."

"They'll be able to find us," Wallace says. "If they're out there."

"Citizens, get down on the ground," a voice comes through a loudspeaker behind us, from up in the tower on the wall. "Get down on the ground, or we will shoot."

"Stay close to the wall," says Wallace. He pushes me against it, where their guns can't reach us, and we crouch together.

"We will shoot," the voice says again.

But no shots come, because they can't get the angle.

I can hardly breathe. Every breath sends stabbing pain through my chest bruised by the fall down the tree. Every moment I expect the bite of an energy gun.

A whoosh of air and a blaze of light. Three X-1s drop out of the sky and hover before us, churning up the water in the moat and training their guns on us.

The X-1s open their hatches and Enforcers spill out of two of them. From the X-1 in the middle, two Enforcers emerge, running, and before I can scream, I'm caught. One grabs me and I'm all flailing knees and elbows as the other roughly pulls and shoves at Wallace. The yawning hatch of their metal craft swallows us. It's over.

I'm thrown roughly to the floor, and the X-1 shudders and takes off.

41

Wallace is huffing and scrambling to get to his feet against the wall of the X-1. "It won't take them long to figure out you're not taking us back into the palace compound," he says. "You'd better punch it. Do you have a plan beyond *flying fast*?"

"I'm working on it, okay?"

It's Elan's voice, irritated, coming from the cockpit.

I bolt off the floor, my heart leaping, and immediately crumple back down as my body reminds me I leapt out a window not ten minutes ago. Sucking in a painful breath through my teeth, I grab my ribs and groan.

"Yeah, me too," Wallace says, rubbing at his shoulder as he goes to join Elan in the cockpit.

"Are you okay?" Holly hurries out of the shadows, her face pinched. "Did you get it? Of course you got it—you wouldn't have run if you didn't get it. You got it, right?"

I slide backward and bump into a solid body—a man who catches and steadies me. Pax. Of course it's Pax.

He pulls off his helmet and casts it aside. His expression is twisted, agonized. "When I saw you with Wallace, I-I didn't recognize you. I thought—it wasn't you. I thought he had to leave you behind, that he brought someone else." He raises a shaking hand to my long hair and runs his gloved fingers through it. "I almost went mad with rage. I would have broken that wall down one brick at a time to get you back, even if it meant . . ."

"If it meant what?"

He grimaces, a familiar anguished flash I haven't seen in a while. "Nothing. I'm sorry."

I drop my head to his forehead, weary and in pain. And so tired of holding back.

A crash rocks the X-1, and Pax and I fall into each other in a tumble of limbs.

"They're onto us!" Elan shouts. "Hold on."

Hold on to what? Pax slides into the row of seats behind him, and I slide with him, clutching his legs and ducking my head. Holly stumbles across the floor toward us and collapses onto one of the seats. She grips it with white-knuckled intensity. "Microchips," she says with a gasp. "I don't know how—like this—but I'll need to get them out of you. As long as they're in you, they'll be able to find you!"

The X-1 rocks again with another blast, and Elan drops us like a stone. Pax and I go airborne and then slam back to the floor.

"Maybe not," I say through gritted teeth. Wrenching myself upright, I sit next to Holly and buckle myself in. Pax buckles in beside me, and none too soon, as the craft lurches sideways and we all jerk against our restraints.

I pull up my vid-lens and focus on my wrist, connecting to the microchip within. Suddenly, before me, all of B-Twenty-one's data flashes by. "Come on, come on, come on," I mutter, scrolling through it. There has to be a settings screen, something that tells me it's transmitting.

"What are you doing?" Holly says. "What is she doing?"

"She's reading the microchip," Pax says in a low voice. "There's something in her eye. Some sort of vid."

"A vid-screen? They put a vid-screen *in your eye*?" Holly takes a shuddering breath. "They wouldn't have. That was experimental."

"They did."

Ah, there it is. In a pull-down menu, a "signal transmitting—active" message. The option to "deactivate" blinks just beneath it, and I blink twice at it, hard. It turns to benign yellow. "Microchip: OFFLINE" runs in a line across all the data.

"I did it." I lean my head against the side of the ship. "It's offline."

I wait until the craft is level and then unbuckle and hurry to the cockpit to deactivate Wallace's microchip.

Elan sits dressed in an Enforcer uniform, flying the X-1 with white-knuckled intensity, and Wallace is in the copilot seat. "Give me your arm," I say.

He glances at me once, and then complies.

The rear of the craft shudders and Elan mutters a curse. I connect with Wallace's microchip and find the menu easily this time. In just moments, he's offline.

"Okay, we're disconnected from the UWO net—does that help?"

"It would if we could shake our pursuit," Elan says. "At least they haven't picked us up on their tractors—"

A blast on our right strikes so hard, we spin in the air. I hit the ceiling and shout in pain, and then slam onto the control panel in between Wallace and Elan. Flashing lights and warning buzzers go off, and Elan says, "I'm going to have to put her down!" and then the nose of the X-1 points to earth.

Another blast hits us from above, and flames lick through the ceiling, filling the belly of the aircraft with smoke. Coughing, eyes streaming, I tumble off the controls and lay in a heap on the floor.

Someone is calling my name.

Elan and Wallace land the X-1 with a mighty crunch that jars every bone in my body. Leaves and bits of wood and forest bracken rain down on me through the widening hole in the roof.

Hands, many hands, lift me and carry me from the wreckage into a wood soft with evening light. Behind us, a bonfire—then an explosion that throws us to the ground.

And then, silence.

REFUGE

42

"Stay down! Nobody move! Let them comb the wreckage from above. The fire will hide our heat signatures."

Elan's words wash over me, and I shake my head, trying to clear it. I must have gotten stunned in the crash—perhaps even a mild concussion. Burning oil mixed with wood smoke chokes my nose and eyes. Above us, the sky is filled with the hum of circling X-1s.

"We'll need to go before they send in Golems, or ground troops."

Golems. Ground troops. *Freemasons.*

Hunters?

I groan and press my hands to my head. "How far are we from Washington?"

"Not far enough," Elan says. "Just southwest of the city."

"And now we don't have a way to get home," Wallace says.

"Sarah will take care of us, if we can just get to Refuge."

Beside me, Pax lets out a heavy breath that I somehow hear through the crackling fire and whispered words of our companions. He's poised in a crouch, half-shielding me, ready to spring into action.

"What is it?" I say.

His eye twitches. "Nothing."

"Liar."

He catches my gaze and holds it. Through the soot and blood smeared on his skin, his blue eyes are more striking than ever. He draws his mouth into a tight line, refusing to say anything more. The minutes tick by, and one by one the X-1s turn and zoom back toward the city.

"They've gone." Holly pushes up onto her elbow. "We can go now."

With a groan deep in my throat, I struggle into an upright position. Pax takes my arm and pulls, steadies me.

Behind us, Holly is all business. "What do we have for supplies? Did anything survive the crash? We'll need water."

"I grabbed a pack on my way out," Elan says.

"What about medical supplies?"

"In the pack."

Pax continues to hold my gaze. He takes his gloves off and casts them aside. With shaking hands, he grasps my face and searches, gritting his teeth against some invisible struggle. "Tell me the truth—are you hurt?" His voice cracks. I know he's asking about more than the crash.

I cover his hand with mine. Now is not the time to tell him what happened to me in Washington, but I will—when I can. "I'm okay," I say. "And it worked. It worked." I smile, but Pax doesn't.

Wallace drops to a squat beside us and hands Pax a knife, handle-out. "Cut her hair, will you?"

I furrow my brow. Pax releases my face and takes the knife.

"There's no way you'll make it through the woods to Refuge like that. I've lost count of how many times you've already almost lost your scalp." Wallace gets to his feet. "Hurry. We need to go."

Pax stares down at the knife, and then up at me.

It's a foolish thing, to want to keep this hair. Hair I didn't have until just twenty-four hours ago. Hair the UWO gave me to appeal to a horrible megalomaniac of a man. But yet—I've never been allowed to have long hair before.

And it's mine.

I shiver as Pax gathers my hair into a bunch at the base of my scalp.

"Wait," I say when I feel the cool knife press my neck. "Wait, please."

There are tears gathering in my eyes. What's wrong with me?

Pax sits back and considers me. Then he touches my cheeks, brushing my tears away.

"It's stupid," I say. "A stupid thing to cry about."

"It's not." He smooths the hair back from my face and tucks it behind my ears. Squints at my right eye—at the copper lines I'm sure he can see—but makes no comment about the vid-lens. "Do you want to do it?" he says. He extends the knife to me.

"I don't think I can. You do it. I-I'm ready now."

I close my eyes this time, and when Pax cuts my hair, a great weight leaves my head. "Is that okay?" he says.

I open my eyes to find him looking at me uncertainly. My hair falls to just below my shoulders—he didn't cut it to my scalp. I finger the ends of it and smile. "Thank you."

"Really, you two?" Wallace says, coming back around. "You can make eyes at each other later. Let's *go*."

There's another explosion in the aircraft, and we all cringe, throwing our arms up to shield our faces. But before the smoke has time to clear, Elan motions us forward, and Pax hauls me to my feet.

We plunge into the woods.

I'm immediately thankful the Autocrat dressed me in pants and boots, and not another ridiculous gown or pantsuit. In the gathering dark, tree limbs reach out to grab me, groping from the shadows without warning to strike my face and tangle in my hair and trip my feet. After the flight through the palace and the leap out the window and the crash of the X-1, I'm not even sure how I'm still going, but somehow I push on until the dark is full and we reach a pebbly bank at the edge of a swift stream, and Elan calls a halt.

I collapse to the ground, and I'm more than a little pleased to see Wallace do the same, although with somewhat more dignity. "We need . . . to rest," he says. "I do. Pria does. We can't go on like this all night."

"I know," Elan says. "I'm sorry. I just want to get us within range." He stands with arms akimbo and looks upward, as if checking the stars for some hidden sign.

"Within rage of what?" I struggle upright and hang my head between my knees.

"Refuge's sensors. Once they know we're out here, they'll come and pick us up. We crashed about forty-five miles southwest of Washington. Five miles to go—more or less—before we breach their sensor range."

"And what makes you think they'll pick us up?" Pax asks.

"They will." Elan goes to the stream, bends down, and cups his hands into it. "Trust me, they will." He splashes the water over the back of his neck.

Even though it's a cold night, I pull myself to the edge of the water and do the same. Exertion and pain have me sweating down my temples and back, and my mouth is dry with thirst.

As if reading my mind, Pax kneels and offers me a canteen of water. It's light green, like his Enforcer uniform, and there isn't much left in it.

My stomach gives a mighty growl as I drink deep from the canteen. I haven't eaten since the walk around the Mall earlier this morning. It's hard to believe so much has happened in one day.

"Can you manage just a little further?" Elan asks.

I wipe my mouth on my arm and hand the canteen back to Pax. "I can if Wallace can," I say with a look at him.

He raises an eyebrow and gets heavily to his feet.

"I'm sure you both have concussions," Holly says darkly. "Possibly some broken ribs. We should all be resting after that crash. But I suppose, as long as nobody passes out or starts coughing blood, we can press on."

It's harder to get to my feet this time than it was at the crash site. Lethargy is setting in, and when I stand, I sway.

"Whoa," Holly says, taking my arm. "Are you sure you can make it? Elan—"

"I can do it. I can walk. Just . . . slowly." I hug my hurting ribs and take a couple of stumbling steps, not even sure which direction I'm going.

"This way," Elan says, pointing. The only light is the moon glinting off the stream. I don't know how he knows which way we should go.

We splash across the shallow water, and the shock of wetness on my feet jerks me a little out of my reverie. Enough to see that it's no longer Holly holding my arm, but Pax. He shoots me a worried glance and pulls my arm around his waist, holding me steady against him. I loll my head on his shoulder, let my eyes drift to slits, and focus on putting one foot in front of the other.

43

Someone is driving nails into my chest one at a time. It's Sylvan Spencer, and he's smiling. *"You're mine. Mine, mine, mine."* I'm naked in front of the Gentri, and they're laughing. He kisses me, shoving his tongue deep inside my throat—

I cry out, waking, kicking against my captor, immediately regretful as the pain in my chest sharpens. It may not be nails, but it's almost as acute.

"It's okay. Pria, it's okay—you're safe." The bounds—no, arms—around me loosen, and my world tilts as I slide feet-first to the ground.

Pax.

Above us, an owl hoots.

"You passed out. Holly said you were all right, just overcome with exhaustion. That if I could carry you, we could keep on."

"Yes. It's fine." I press my ribs and double over, wincing. "Just give me a moment and I'll be ready to walk again."

A limb cracks nearby, and we all freeze, but it's just a deer—a liquid-eyed doe. She wanders past, freezing for a moment to stare at us.

Elan lowers his gun slowly. "Are you good, Pria?"

"Yes."

We press on, uphill now, and I still have no idea how Elan can tell where to lead us. I stay two steps ahead of Pax. I'm sure he's watching out for me.

We crest a ridge and a rotten odor fills my nostrils. "Elan—"

"I smell it."

"Something died here," Holly says.

"I don't think that's it," I say.

The ground beside me shifts, leaves and sticks falling away as a Golem rises in the murky darkness, its form unfolding from the ground like a waking beast.

"*Run*!" Elan shouts.

We scatter as the massive, mechanical monster looms upward in the gloom and swings wide long arms as if to catch one of us. I throw myself down behind a boulder, breathing in hard breaths that jab me with excruciating pain, and peer around. I'm alone, but Pax is ten feet away with his back pressed to a tree and his face turned to me. He gestures with both hands in a *stay down* motion and then un-holsters an Air-5 from his hip.

Behind me, Holly screams.

Pax bursts out of hiding, shooting as he runs. The Golem roars and Pax's shots are joined by more—Elan's? Holly screams again, a cry of agonizing pain.

Then bright lights blaze out of the sky—air ships?—and two quick thundering booms shake the forest. Bits of stinking flesh rain down on me and a scream catches in my throat.

What is happening?

The Golem gives a great creak as it collapses, and then there's an eerie silence, awash in the glow of the lights from above. Holly gives a gasping sob, and I scramble out of my hiding place, heedless of whether the ships are friend or foe.

Pax, Wallace, and Elan are gathered over Holly, working frantically. Blood is everywhere. At first I think it must be the blood from the Golem that is splattered on us all, but the pallor of Holly's skin tells me otherwise.

"Tie it—tie it off," Holly says through fumbling lips. "In the pack . . . bandages."

Pax holds his hands to her shoulder, but blood spurts out between his fingers. Elan yanks the pack open. Wallace exchanges a quick, sharp look with me.

Something lands in the brush behind us with a sharp metallic clang. I jump and press soiled hands to my mouth. The decimated Golem lies in a heap. Dangling beside it is the end of a rope ladder, its metal bottom rung knocking against the enameled bones, laid bare by targeted blasts.

People are descending. People in camouflage jumpsuits. I squint up, but their forms are hazy against the starburst of light. They jostle me aside—push past Elan and Wallace and Pax. Holly—they gather up Holly, who has gone limp.

My thoughts are coming in short, quick bursts, and I can't seem to make my brain process things in an orderly fashion. A woman takes my arm—urges me to the ladder, up the ladder. I don't resist. I don't think these people are UWO—if they are, they wouldn't have destroyed the Golem, right?

I climb up and up into the ship, which is long and thin and reflective like polished silver, and when I pull myself into the hold, a man greets me with a smile and a helping hand. "Quickly now," he says, "before any of the other sleepers wake up."

"Sleepers?" I hear Elan say in a strained voice.

"Golems like the one you stumbled into just now—powered down and programmed to respond to movement. The UWO has this entire range mined with them, almost all the way to our territory."

Elan gives a weary groan. "Sleepers. Never seen anything like that in Colorado Province."

"Colorado Province? You're a long way from home. What the hell are you doing all the way out here?"

"It's a bit of a story."

"We like stories—we're used to them." The man extends his hand. "I'm Juan, by the way."

"Elan."

The man looks at me next. He has an open, friendly face, tan skin, and jet-black hair. "Pria," I say, before he can ask. "Is our friend going to be okay?"

Juan looks over his shoulder. "Looks like they have her stabilized. We'll do what we can."

He doesn't make an empty promise. I appreciate his honesty, relaxing into it, even as my chest constricts further with worry for Holly.

"What's your name?" Juan asks Pax, who sits beside me, studying his hands. Hands coated in Holly's blood.

"It's Pax."

Juan tugs a rag from a pocket on his camo jumpsuit and hands it to Pax. "Nice to meet you. Don't see many of your type wandering these woods, not so close to Washington. Records would tell us not in over a hundred years."

Pax's type. I know Juan means someone who carries recessive traits, and not that Pax is a clone, but I can't help rolling the words around in my mind and watching Pax through slitted eyes.

Pax doesn't answer but accepts the rag and wipes futilely at his hands. His jaw is tight and sweat glistens on his brow.

Beneath us, the floor of the aircraft hums with movement, with flight. I can only assume they're taking us to safety—to Refuge.

44

Pax has a headache. His cheek is twitching, and he's measuring his breathing. It has been so long since I've seen him like this—and he was so clearly better when we *weren't* together—that now I can't help but notice the sheen of sweat on his upper lip, the unrelenting furrow between his brow, the way he's clenching his teeth.

But why now?

I rub the bridge of my nose, trying to loosen my own tension, and close my eyes. *I* have a headache. Of course Pax has a headache after what we've just been through. It doesn't necessarily *mean* anything.

After a short while, the aircraft descends and then lands with a soft *fwump*—a puff of air smoother than any landing I've ever experienced before. I crack open my eyes and look around, but all the strangers in the dim interior seem to be waiting for something. And then, after a few minutes, bright lights come up and several anxious-faced men and women squeeze past us with Holly on a narrow stretcher between them. "Make way, please," says one of them. "Tell Sarah we're taking her straight to surgery."

"No need—I'm right here."

Elan and Wallace get to their feet, Wallace wincing and holding his ribs in a way that tells me he's in much the same pain as I am.

"Sarah," Elan says, a smile in his voice.

"Elan. It's always good to see a familiar face. I never do know if I'll see anyone again, once they leave here."

The woman named Sarah is little more than a silhouette at the bottom of the ramp, backlit by lights far brighter than those at Asylum. Curious, I get to my feet as well and peer out at her. She's short, and a little plump, with a shock of greying hair pulled back into a knot at her neck.

"Well, come on down, I'm sure you're tired and hungry. You don't have anything to fear from us." Her eyes go to Pax as she says this.

I creep down the ramp. Something about Sarah draws me to her—something familiar, even though we've never met. When I reach her, she puts her hands in her pockets and stares back at me. Her eyes . . . one is blue and the other green.

She quirks her lips and then turns to Elan. "How's everybody at Asylum?"

"Luther is the same as always. Brant"—Elan hesitates—"he left, Sarah. Not long ago. Took about fifty followers and walked off into the mountains."

Sarah sighs. "He always did just want to hide."

"Is that not what you're doing here?" I say. And then I blush, because it sounds like an accusation.

"Not remotely." She smiles. "My name is Sarah Cohen, dear girl, and this is Refuge. My number two is Juan. You'll have met."

Juan smiles from the bottom of the ramp.

"Luther and Brant Cohen are my brothers. Luther married Juan's sister, Katarina, and together with Brant they left this place many years ago to seek a different path of resistance."

She turns and motions for us to follow. Although she's much shorter than either of her brothers, the family resemblance is obvious. She has Brant's cheekbones, Luther's rigid jaw and chin and at least one of his green eyes. Her hair is like theirs, although sprinkled with more grey. And in the soft curve of her cheeks, I see a little bit of James, Luther's son.

An unexpected wave of emotion rises up, choking me. I cough and look down, nearly tripping on feet that are too uncertain from the hours of exhaustion. Family. Genetic traits passed along from one member to another—like Celine and her brothers. It's such a rare and precious thing.

Sarah stops me with a hand on my arm. "Just a little further and we'll get you settled in. I promise not to ply you with too many questions tonight. Food, rest, care. Questions later."

"We should not stay long." The comment comes from Pax, and we all turn to face him. "We should return to Asylum as quickly as possible." He darts his eyes around the space, which is long and low and tiled in white. If I didn't know this was a rebel base, I would almost take it for a UWO structure. It is too sterile, too clean for a rugged outpost. Perhaps that's what has Pax concerned.

Because he is concerned. He's massaging the back of his neck where his clone implant is, almost as though he can't help himself, and his eyes hold a strange fear. Pax is usually able to hide what he's feeling better than this, so I frown at him and touch his arm.

"What about Holly?" I say. "We can't leave until she can travel."

He flares his nostrils and tightens his lips.

"I'll get you some medication," Sarah says, concern thick in her voice. "For the pain."

"I'm not in any pain," Pax says.

She looks him up and down with a quick, sharp glance. "Are you not?" she asks. "Hmmm." She turns, slowly, and leads the way again with Juan at her shoulder.

We follow, and I hang back to walk beside Pax, wincing with every step, every painful breath. My concerns seem small compared to his, though, whatever they are.

"Is your headache still bothering you?" I ask in a low voice.

"No," he says.

I sigh and turn to peer at him. But it's hard to feel hurt by his short tone when I'm so worried about him. "But it was on the ship flying in—I could tell."

He darts a look at me out of the corner of his eyes. "Well, it's gone now," he says, his voice sharp.

Elan looks over his shoulder, eyes narrowed.

Pax sighs. "Pria, please," he whispers. "Just leave me alone."

We leave the bright hangar through an automatic door into a narrow tunnel just as bright. The sensation of being underground is strong, pressing on me as heavily as Pax's censure. The tunnel allows only two people to walk abreast, which isn't very comfortable, so I fall behind him, leaving him alone as he asked.

45

The narrow tunnel off the hangar opens up into a main hub and much wider tunnels, and circular openings in the ceiling give the impression of skylights that might let in sunlight, if it was daytime outside. Furniture in muted greys and blues and greens—furniture that looks as though it was actually crafted for the space—is scattered around the hub, but no one occupies it at the moment. Sarah shows us into a tunnel that branches off to private rooms and promises to be back soon with food and medicine and an update on Holly.

Elan and Wallace and Pax each disappear into their own rooms, so I choose one and do likewise, finding a tiny space with a bed large enough for only me, a white armchair, and a bedside table. I sink onto the bed, which is neatly made with white blankets and sheets and a fluffy white pillow. On the table beside it, there is a vase with a yellow flower. Tears spring to my eyes, and I roll over sideways and curl into a ball.

I'm immediately regretful as my ribs protest, and then I remember how dirty I am, and I still have my boots on, too, but the bed is so comfortable that I push the regret aside and allow myself to sink into the comfort.

I'm about to doze off when a shadow falls over me and I look up to see Pax standing in the doorway. I left the door open. Pax has showered and changed out of the dirty Enforcer uniform and into clothes he must have found in his room. A white t-shirt and grey, loose cotton pants.

"I'm sorry," he says. He leans on the doorframe and grimaces, shaking his head. "I'm sorry I snapped at you earlier, in the hangar.

I shouldn't have talked to you like that."

I sit with great effort, biting my lip to hold in a groan. "What are you hiding?"

"Nothing," he says in an almost desperate tone. "Please believe me."

Minutes pass and he makes no move to leave or to say anything else. So I do. "You looked like you were in so much pain, flying here."

"I was, but then . . . it went away. It's gone now."

I shouldn't press. He doesn't like me to press. He asked me not to, but . . . "Do you think it has something to do with being a clone?"

He sighs and dips his head so his hair falls into his eyes. "Pria. I-I shouldn't be in here with you. I should go. I only came in to apologize—and to make sure you were okay."

"Don't go, please. Come in and close the door."

He gives me a cautious look but does as I say, stepping further into the room.

"Are you being controlled?" I ask, hoping to take him off-guard—hoping for an honest answer.

"No," he says. He folds his arms and looks at me with a measured calm that belies the discomfort I know he must be feeling.

"In the capital," I say, then take a deep breath. "There were other clones, Pax. A lot of others. Thousands of them."

He touches his chest as his calm wavers. A fearful light comes into his eyes.

"No, not like you. They were"—I close my eyes and waggle my fingers in the air—"like UWO citizens. Like they could have come out of the Program. The Autocrat called them the Freemasons. And he showed me the source—the first Freemason. He was just a boy, like . . . a young man who had died or been killed, I don't know when. It must have been long ago, because they said they had to use a *pure* genetic source, from before the Program. And they did *use* him. They used his genetic material to build others just like him. But, Pax, they *weren't.*" I launch myself off the bed, hissing through my nose as my head and chest throb. But I don't care about the pain. "I was wrong. I was wrong about you. The things I said . . . *I was wrong.*"

I reach for Pax, but he catches both my wrists and holds me

back. "What do you mean?"

I curl my hands into fists. "When the Autocrat showed me the Freemason clones, all he saw was a mass of automatons walking around in human flesh. He said they were empty inside. But that's not what I saw at all—they were individuals. They were *people*." I push against Pax's grasp, trying to move nearer, but he is unyielding. "Don't you understand? You're a person. You're just as human as I am—as anyone."

Pax's grip relaxes just enough for me to twist my wrists so I can slide my hands into his. "I'm sorry," I say, and I'm crying now, tears streaming unchecked down my cheeks. "*I'm* sorry. You are a person. And you are exactly who I've always known you to be from the very first day I trusted you enough to take your hand and leap. I shouldn't ever have said otherwise. I was cruel." I tilt my head and study him, the creases around his eyes, the whisper of freckles across his brow, his nose, his cheeks. "Please, please forgive me."

The lines smooth in his face, erasing all signs of stress. He tightens his fingers around mine and searches my eyes as though looking for a lie. "I forgive you," he says. "But you *weren't* wrong. I am . . . exactly what you said. I'm just a clone. I'm not like you, and there's nothing that can change that."

I stomp my foot. "Just because your genetic material was copied from someone else's doesn't mean *you* are the same person he was. The UWO doesn't get to tell you who you are on the inside—that comes from someplace else."

Pax's expression twists. "Where does that come from?" He takes a step closer so our toes are almost touching and his breath is warm on my face.

"I don't know. Maybe that's why they can't create it in a lab." I take his hand and raise it, slowly, to press his palm against my chest—over my beating heart.

"Pria—" He shakes his head and tries to pull away.

"No." I hold his hand tighter. Then I lay my hand on his chest, over his heart, our arms intertwined in the narrow space between us. Firm and reassuring and rapid beneath my palm, his heart beats, and beats, and beats.

"The same," I say. I close my eyes to feel him better. "We are the same."

We stand like this, and I hope my words are breaking through to him, because I'm breaking inside without him.

When I open my eyes, it's to find him staring at me with a furrowed brow and pursed lips. His hand goes to my shoulder, slides down my arm. "It's a nice thought," he says. "But nothing has changed."

"*Nothing?*" I can't keep the note of despair out of my voice.

"What I want to do, what I can do, what I *should* do . . . Those things rarely align." He rubs a lock of my hair between his fingers and then releases it with a sigh. "Most of the time."

"What does that mean?"

"It means I want to make sure you are safe and well, and as long as I can do that, I will. And to do that, I should"—he dips his head—"I should . . ."

My throat tightens and all my exhaustion rushes back to me as I watch him retreat into himself. I should be sleeping now, resting off injuries physical and psychological, but instead I'm playing mind-games with Pax. I sniff as more tears slide down my cheeks.

"I'm tired," I say. "And I want you to kiss me."

His mouth falls open, and he leans away.

"Don't tell me you can't! And please don't tell me you shouldn't. Just kiss me. Even if it's the last time you ever do."

Pax takes my face in both hands, stilling my tumbling words. I hiccup and bite my lip, staring up at him.

"Even if it's the last time?" he says.

I nod. A betrayal of my inner self.

He draws me to him slowly, and when his lips touch mine, he folds me up in his arms. I cling to him, fighting through the agony of deep bruises and cracked ribs. It's the first time we've kissed without the madness of desperation or the curious hesitation of unexpected firsts, and it feels like the first time I took his hand—full of endings and beginnings and a trust I cannot fully explain.

He's slow to pull away, reluctant. For a long moment we stand face-to-face, breathing the same air.

"Pax, I think I—that is, I know I-I-I'm in love with you," I say before I can change my mind. Before I am too afraid.

Pax straightens and gives me a deep, sad look—a look bordering on fear. Then he swallows hard, turns away, and leaves.

46

The feeling he leaves me with is something akin to lethargy. But that must be what deep grief feels like. Pax loves me—I know he must, but he will not say it or even give himself over to fully feeling it.

I sink onto the bed and wrap up in the blanket. It's not cold in the room—in fact, the temperature throughout Refuge seems perfectly regulated for comfort—but I'm cold inside. Covering my face to block out the light, I give in to the sadness.

When I wake, it's with the awareness that I fell asleep crying and I've slept for hours. Every joint, every bone and muscle aches in new and unique ways, and my eyes are swollen nearly shut. I blink hard several times and am rewarded by my vid-lens springing to life. I lie still, gritting my teeth and holding in all the groans of pain I want to release, until a jolt of panic rips through me.

My vid-lens—which is connected to the UWO net. Can they track me? *Are* they tracking me? I disconnected our microchips, but not this. And we've been here so long already.

I throw off the cover and try to leap out of bed, but my muscles cramp and instead I just sort of roll and fall. I cry out as my knees and arms hit the floor and the vid tilts crazily around the room.

"Pria?" Elan's voice, on the other side of the door. "Are you okay? I'm coming in."

The door cracks open to Elan's concerned face. "Did you fall?"

"My eye! The lens in my eye—they will track us! What if they're almost here already?" I gesture madly and take Elan's outstretched arm to let him pull me to my feet.

"You don't need to worry about that," Sarah says from over

Elan's shoulder. "Although I do recommend you disable the connectivity function so you will have peace of mind when you leave here."

"What . . . why?" Holding onto Elan's shoulder, I stumble into the main seating area outside my room. "What are you talking about?"

"We scramble all transmissions in and out of Refuge," Sarah says. "It's a sophisticated system that allows us to receive our distress code and communicate with our own, but the UWO cannot penetrate it."

"Not—not at all? Not even with this?" I point at my eye.

"No implant, microchip, uplink, or transmitter of any sort can connect to the UWO net or any ship or person or vehicle or any creation or agent of the UWO while within the radius of our scramblers. It keeps even the Golems away because they can't function inside our dead zone." Sarah comes to me and peers at my eye. "Although I've never seen a vid-lens before, I assure you we would know if our systems had failed."

I find the connectivity function on the home screen and deactivate it before I shut off the lens and follow Sarah to a couch. Pax stands beside it, poised with his hands clenched in fists. His face is pale with . . . shock? I watch him as I sit, but he seems caught in his own thoughts, trapped somewhere. And even if he did look at me, I'm not sure what I would communicate to him after last night. After I told him I loved him and he shut me out. Again.

I take a shuddering breath and look around. Everyone except Holly is present, along with someone who looks like a nurse. He wears a long white apron and is checking Wallace's eyes with a bright light. "If you have this technology, why not share it with the other rebel Nests?" I say to Sarah, desperate to learn more. Desperate for a distraction.

"I would—I have." Sarah spreads her arms. "But it takes infrastructure. What we have here is the product of two hundred years. Out there—where my brothers chose to go—you are always on the run. It's a different sort of life filled with different risks, and many dangers." Her eyes cloud over and she drops her chin.

"Katarina was happy with him," Elan says. "They were happy."

"Until she died." Sarah raises bright eyes. "But never mind the past. Let's talk of the present. Pria, you must want a shower, and we should examine you for fractures when you are through. The shower is through there." She points to a darkened doorway. A quick glance around tells me everyone else has already used it. I am the only one with the stink of battle still on me. "Towels and clean clothes are in a closet inside that room."

"Thank you, I . . ." I get shakily to my feet, gritting my teeth. "That does sound good."

The bathroom is bright and white like most of the spaces here, but with colorful accents to distinguish it from the bright, white spaces of UWO buildings. Flowers in bowls and vases, decorative rocks, cakes of soap that smell of herbs. I find a towel and underthings, light grey cotton pants like the ones Pax had on last night, and a white shirt.

The water is blessedly hot and presses into my shoulders almost painfully. I stay in for as long as I can stand the mixture of pain and pleasure, and then I get out and wipe the condensation off the mirror. My hair drips in wavy strands around a face smeared with running make-up. I frown. Why didn't it come off in the shower? It takes me several more minutes of scrubbing my face with a wet towel and the bar of herbed soap beside the sink before I'm finally clean and looking like myself. More or less. I'm not sure how long it will take me to get used to having hair.

I've never really had to dry my hair before, so I scrub it down as best I can with another towel, and then I dump all the wet towels and my pile of dirty clothes into a basket that seems placed there for the purpose. Taking up my boots and a clean pair of socks, I finally leave the bathroom.

There is a spread of food laid out on a small table, and my stomach growls in response to the smell of cooked meat—venison, perhaps?—and potatoes and vegetables. I go directly to it, but the male nurse intercepts me. "We should check you over first," he says, not unkindly. "It will only take a few minutes."

And so we go back to my room, and I am poked and prodded, and he determines I have two fractured ribs. Then he leaves and another nurse replaces him, a woman who instructs me to remove my shirt so she can wrap a tight bandage around my chest. "It will help with the pain while your ribs heal," she says. And then finally I'm allowed to eat.

Even though I'm practically faint with hunger, by the time I sit down with a plate piled high and start to dig in, I find I can't eat much without feeling nauseous. So I pick around the root vegetables and listen as Wallace and Elan fill Sarah in on the particulars of our Gentrification plan. Pax sits across from me in a pale blue chair, ostensibly listening, but by the way he keeps glancing at me, I can tell he's more aware of my presence than the conversation going on beside us.

"I cannot believe you got in and out like that"—Sarah snaps her fingers—"with everything you need, so easy." She shifts to look at me. "With so little cost."

And there it is. I swallow a bite of venison, the meat suddenly bitter in my mouth. "It frightens me," I say.

"What do you mean, Pria?" Elan leans forward. "It went off without a hitch."

"*Too* easily. And he didn't even . . ." I bite my lip and look down, trying to conjure up the words Celine used when she told me about sex. "The Autocrat. Sylvan Spencer. He wanted me. He *purchased* me. Gentrification wasn't an elevation, it was a—a—just another way for us to *breed* for them." My face flames red. "But he barely touched me, even though he had every opportunity. That is, he kissed me, but he didn't—" I shiver. "And he could have, but he didn't. Do you understand what I'm saying?" I cover my face.

Sarah places her hand on my shoulder. "You don't need to explain further. We understand."

I drop my hands into my lap. "It was as though he was more concerned with grooming me to be his Empress." I hesitate, unsure about how to explain what I mean. "I mean *me*. Not B-Twenty-one. I-I think he knew . . . me." I press my fist to my chest.

"That's impossible," Elan says.

"I know it is, but . . ." I round on him, on Wallace. "*Is it?*"

Wallace quirks his lips and doesn't answer.

"First of all," Elan says, "*how* would he have known you? And if he did, *why* would he have given you complete access to the information you were after?" He runs his hands through his hair until it sticks up wildly. "That doesn't compute. It must have been just a weird sense you got. Obviously it was an extremely unusual situation—"

"If he knew who you were," Sarah says, thoughtful, "the only reason he would give you any information is if he wanted you to have it." Her eyes are far-off and searching, her brow furrowed. "If that were the case, he must be very confident indeed that the UWO can come to no harm despite your having those files. And if he truly desires you, then . . ."

"Then what?" says Elan.

She sighs and twists her hands in her lap. "Then he must be supremely confident he can recover you for himself."

Across from me, Pax breaks a breadstick in half. "That will never happen."

Sarah gives her head a slow shake. "I have a bad feeling about this plan of yours. Sylvan Spencer has found his new Empress, and he does not give up easily."

"I can protect Pria from him. I will," Pax says.

"But what about the rest of the free people in the world?" Sarah asks. "If Spencer was willing to release compromising files to Pria, there is a chance the whole thing could have been a set-up. What if he's using her to get close to Luther?"

"We would know by now," Elan says. "Pria has been with Asylum for months."

Sarah purses her lips.

"It's too late, besides," Wallace says. "The files from the capital transmitted to Asylum the moment Pria hacked the system. It's done."

"The plan must go on," Pax says. "It's the only chance we have to bring down the UWO."

Sarah gives a frustrated huff. "Is it, though?" She leans forward. "Do you know how many people live here? How many have been rescued and are living and having children and growing and spreading? There are thousands and thousands of us, while the UWO Program breeds itself out of existence. We will outlast them, in the end. Sometimes simply to preserve life is the truest resistance."

Pax leans forward to meet her. "They will come for you eventually. Even here."

"They won't. They never have. They don't even know we exist."

"They will. And you won't be ready. That is why I—*we* must end them. Now."

Sarah searches Pax's face. "Why did Luther send you on this mission?" she asks, her voice low. "*You* . . . looking like that."

"I have a special skillset."

"But you're no topsider."

"In a manner of speaking, I am."

"But where did you come from? There are many like you in hiding, in a place like this, who have been born in hiding and will live in hiding their entire lives. But there haven't been people like *you* wandering the wilds for well over a hundred years."

Pax studies Sarah's expression with equal intensity, and something unspoken passes between them. "I will tell you," he says, "if you want to know."

Sarah stands and gestures for Pax to follow her. "I will speak with Pax alone."

47

I manage to eat a little more while Pax and Sarah are gone. The nurses give me some pain pills which take the edge off the worst of my aches and the jabbing pain that threatens with each breath, but nothing can take the edge off my distraction and concern for Holly, or my curiosity over Pax and Sarah's private conversation. Why did she want to speak with him *alone*? Wallace and Elan both know his story—the story he always tells about his upbringing and childhood, at least. That which he feels free to tell the world about who he is, since he cannot say *what* he is. But Sarah, as a rebel leader, must have her reasons for desiring private interrogations, same as Luther.

They are gone for a very long time.

Wallace talks to Elan in a low voice about our experience within the palace grounds, and I try to shut out his murmured words. I don't want to think about Sylvan Spencer or Ashra or any of the rest of it right now.

"Pria." Elan touches my shoulder, and I jump. "You haven't moved. Do you need anything?"

"No."

Behind Elan, Wallace gives me a pointed look. Only Wallace knows what Gentrification was like, and it's strange to think that he and I share this experience that had so many elements that should have been private. Our bodies on display before others, on *sale* . . .

"No," I say again. "I am fine, and I don't want to talk about it."

I am not, and I do, but not with Elan or Wallace. And not here, not yet.

"All right," Sarah says as she and Pax re-enter the room. "Your friend, Holly."

We all straighten. The gravity on Sarah's face makes my stomach drop.

"We've done what we can for her, but I'm afraid her arm could not be saved."

"She lost . . . her arm?" I say, trying to comprehend what that means—what that will mean for her future.

She nods. "I had hoped you'd all stay until we could fit her with a proper prosthetic, but now it's clear you should move on as soon as possible." She looks at Pax.

"Is she awake? Does she know?" Elan says.

"We'll wake her this afternoon."

Elan nods, his brow furrowed.

"Elan, Wallace," Sarah says. "Juan will be here soon to take you to see the science department. I had some thought you might be interested in the work we're doing here. He'll take you to Holly after that. Pax, Pria, come with me, please. I'd like you to see something before you go."

Pax seems different as we walk, less inhibited than usual. He looks around with interest as we reach the central hub. The skylights let in rays of sunlight and people gather in communal groups, talking. Young children play, and nobody stares at us or seems afraid. Sarah smiles and greets a few people as we pass, and then we turn into a wider and taller tunnel and ascend a set of stairs. Pax looks back at me—his mouth twitches as if he is tempted to smile.

"Sorry about the walk," Sarah says. "Refuge is a bit of a maze, and it was constructed section by section, at need. This is only a small part of it. We'll come to the tram soon."

A turn into a rectangular room with benches reveals an open space and a yawning tunnel to either side. "Stay back from the edge," Sarah says. "It will be here soon."

A whoosh of air and rush of shaking metal precedes the arrival of a sleek white vehicle along a track that runs through the tunnel. It glides to a halt, and then a door opens on the side facing us. A dark-skinned family with four children gets off, laughing. Sarah holds back to let them pass, and then she leads us aboard. "It's a short ride."

"Where are we going?" I stumble sideways into Pax as the tram starts to move again. He steadies me with a hand to my hip and then—when I think he will remove it—leaves it there, resting it lightly as though he's never had any discomfort in my presence. As though he and I, together, is the most natural posture he can take.

I raise startled eyes to him, but he's watching Sarah.

"We're going to my home." She tips up her chin and smiles slightly. "It's . . . a special place, even here, amidst all that's been built."

The tram glides along, making two more stops. Pax does not move from my side or lift his hand until its third stop when the doors open to a blank wall. Sarah presses her hand to the wall, and it chirps and opens inward. "After you," she says.

I step off the tram first, followed by Pax. The space beyond feels . . . old. The walls are still white, but there is a dinginess to them that betrays age.

We're at the end of a hall in what is clearly a home. Doors line the walls, and each door has a knob on it—an old-fashioned knob unlike the other automated doors we've seen at Refuge. The floor is a spongy material, grey, and a little springy. I walk further in, hesitant to invade Sarah's space, but curious. There is a claustrophobic feel to this hallway, these doors, this spongy flooring and these walls, that I haven't yet felt here at Refuge. Near the end of the hall, the space opens on either side to larger rooms, one of them carpeted. Beyond that, it narrows again to dead-end in a single, closed door. In front of the door there is a metal ladder that disappears into the ceiling.

"*This* is Refuge," Sarah says, coming up beside me. "Long ago, this was all there was. It all started here."

I frown—look at Pax.

"Come on in and I'll show you."

Sarah moves on ahead of us. The wider, carpeted space turns out to be a sitting room, across from which is a kitchen. She waves a hand toward the couch built along the wall in the sitting area and says, "Sit, please. I'll be right in."

Pax and I take slow steps into the space and turn a circle, synced with each other. The paint on the walls is scratched and peeling and the couch is fraying, although there are spots of obvious repair. An old vid-screen—so old it isn't even transparent—hangs fixed on one wall.

I catch Pax's eye, confused as to why Sarah brought us here. Confused about his relaxed manner. Just . . . confused.

"*Sit*," she says again. She edges between us, carrying a leather-bound book with yellowing pages. "I have something to show you."

Pax and I sit on either side of her as she opens the book in her lap. It is not, as I thought, a book of printed text, but a book filled with faded, handwritten pages.

"A journal," Sarah says. "The journal of Daniel and Emma Cohen, who founded this place."

"Cohen," Pax says.

"My ancestors, yes, and Luther's." She spreads a hand over the pages. "My family. They were just children. They must have been so afraid, but they built something here that has endured—that has allowed life to go on when the UWO would see it snuffed out. They outlined in here their vision for making this place a refuge for all, even when they didn't understand what was happening. For two hundred years, we've carried on their vision."

I trail my eyes down the page she has open.

> *"We welcomed two new refugees today named Jung and Grace Lee. Peter brought them to us. (Peter is still alive!) Jung was an electrical engineer, before, and Grace a pediatric surgeon. Daniel jokes I must have started praying again, because with the vision we have for the new addition off the south end and Harper's complications with the twins, these two are an answer to prayer. All I know is, I'm thankful they're here."*

I flip through the pages closer to the front of the book to find another entry in a different handwriting.

> *"Emma is pregnant. She says she's not afraid, but I can admit I am terrified. Found a bunch of medical journals in a storage cache behind a false wall in the pantry last week along with enough medical supplies to last us five lifetimes—if it was just us. Obviously we're going to take in as many people as we can, so we'll see how long it lasts. It's all labeled in French and Arabic and Swahili and whatnot, though. I'm guessing Dad stockpiled what he could illegally before the Incursion—not that it surprises me. Emma found translation software in the security room, so I guess it's time to get busy figuring out what all this stuff is. And how to birth a baby. Maybe I can find some anti-anxiety medicine while I'm at it."*

I page almost to the beginning of the journal and find a short entry in the same hand.

> *"I finished maintenance on the perimeter alarm so I can take Emma*

back outside for target practice. We are still far too exposed, though. I will have to come up with a better system of defense. If the Unfamiliars ever discover the bunker, I am afraid not even the hatch will keep them out."

The hatch. I look over at the ladder. "So in the beginning, this was the only place of refuge they had? Just this *one* bunker? And it was just the two of them living here alone?"

"There were a couple of others, although the details of what happened are unclear," Sarah says. "They never tell the full story, in the journal. But it seems as though Daniel's father, Travis, was the one who actually built this place. They also mention a friend, Crispin."

I stand and look around, picturing two young people living here all alone, figuring out how to survive, how to raise a child, how to prepare a place of refuge for others as the UWO rose to power. Did they even know it *was* the UWO causing the apocalypse they were living?

I walk to the ladder. "Can we go outside?" I say, looking up. "Does the hatch work?"

"Is it safe?" Pax stands as well.

"You can go outside." Sarah closes the journal and takes it to the kitchen counter. "We can. We are in the heart of Refuge. I thought you might like to."

Sarah climbs first with me at her heels and Pax behind me. At the top, she types in a code, and then a round metal door swings open and a shaft of sunlight strikes us, along with a burst of cool air. Shivering, I pull myself out and look around.

The hatch stands in the center of a clearing. At our feet lie some stones that might once have been the foundation of a small building, and to one side are a few standing bricks that could have been . . .

"A fireplace," Sarah says, staring at it as though she can still see it standing and functional. "This was once a cabin. We believe there were a couple outbuildings, at least." She points, drawing invisible shapes with her finger. "We've found remnants of a garden, as well. This spot—on this hill, they lived and breathed and survived while the Incursion killed millions—billions—of people."

"And over there?" Pax asks, pointing to a patch of land where some stones have been set up in a regular pattern. Beyond that patch, down the mountain, a blue lake glimmers.

"The graveyard." Sarah jerks her chin for us to follow.

I wrap my arms around my chest against the cold, but I'm not complaining. To be outside, in daylight, in the open forest—not behind the wall of the Autocrat's Gentrified palace grounds, but shrouded only in the veil of the natural world. I take several deep, cleansing breaths just for the glory of it.

We round the stones in the graveyard, our feet crunching over dead leaves and dying grass. Pax's eyes flit over the markers, and he squats beside one to look closer.

"We don't use this spot anymore," Sarah says. "We have a bigger plot on the other side of the lake now. But this was the first. This is where they're buried—Daniel and Emma, their children, their friends. The very first refugees who lived and died here."

Daniel and Emma. They share a grave with one stone marker over it and a short engraving, still visible, the letters irregular as though chiseled by hand. "Survival is Resistance," I read aloud. I bite my lip against a sudden impulse to cry and move to the next stone. "Travis Johnson." No inscription. And the next. "Crispin Freemason: He was a friend."

My mouth drops open. "Pax . . ." His name comes out a gasp, the barest of whispers.

But he hears me, and he's at my side in a moment. "What is it?"

I point to the stone with a shaking finger. "Freemason. Crispin *Freemason*." I look around at the bright sky, the blue lake, the reaching trees. What seemed peaceful a moment before now feels ominous. "This grave is empty."

48

Sarah approaches, her brow furrowed. "We know that grave is empty—we've always known."

Pax and I stare at Crispin Freemason's grave.

"I-I saw his body beneath the Autocrat's palace. I saw what happened to him." I grab my head and spin in a circle. "He's the source."

"The source of what?"

I look up into her eyes. "Human clones. Thousands of them, fully grown."

Sarah takes in a deep breath, holds it, lets it out slowly. And then she nods, and her eyes go to Pax. "We've suspected as much for a long time."

"They're called Freemasons," I say. "Freemason clones." A look of wide-eyed understanding comes over Sarah.

She glances at the grave marker. "We never knew why . . . We thought he must have died someplace else, where they couldn't recover his body. There are many empty graves here." She waves a hand over the graveyard and then wanders to a nearby stump and sits down, hard. "But you're saying the UWO used his body to create these Freemasons. Freemason clones. You saw them?"

"I did. The Autocrat said they can be controlled—compelled to do whatever he wants them to do." I close my eyes against the memory of the Autocrat forcing one clone to break another's neck. "He intends to unleash them to replace humanity, leaving the Gentri as the only true humans left in North America. I'm assuming the other two Autocrats have similar plans."

"That's a fair assumption."

A bird chirps and flies overhead with a noisy flapping of wings. I follow it with my eyes, squinting up into the sun. It feels strange to be discussing the destruction of humanity in such a tranquil place.

Sarah folds her hands. "He wants to take the work of the Great Devastations one step further," she says, her gaze distant. "The first Autocrat, Pritchard Spencer—along with the other members of the Oligarch—executed the Great Famine, Pandemic, and Incursion. But that's not enough anymore. Or maybe it's never been enough. They've never successfully uprooted everyone they intended to kill—everyone they deemed harmful to the planet and to the propagation of a pure human race. Now that they have a means of generating a workforce they believe they can keep compliant to them, they want to kill everyone left in the Communes—everyone who was originally deemed fit to live in their new world."

"But how do the clones help them get rid of the rest of—" I almost say *us*, but it's not true. I'm not one of these rebels in this regard. I was a Breeder, until I left. I was taken in by the rebels, declared a criminal by the UWO, but I cannot empathize with them in every way. Not in *this* way. So I swallow and look at my feet and say, "How do the clones help them get rid of the rest of you? Those they think are genetically unfit to survive."

"I would ask you the same," Sarah says.

"Me? How should I know?"

"The Autocrat showed you his Operation—did he say anything of his plans for wiping us out? I should think he has some plan—they have tried, and failed, for two hundred years to annihilate us. What did he tell you?"

I scour my memory, but I can think of nothing other than what I already told her—just that he wants to replace humanity with the clones, not how he intends to do it. "Nothing," I say. "He told me no plan."

Sarah exchanges a barely perceptible glance with Pax. "Perhaps there will be something in the files. If there is, I'm sure Luther and Wallace will find it."

"Will you come to the meeting Luther will call?" I ask. "He wants you to come."

"I will not."

"But—"

Pax places a hand on my shoulder, and Sarah says, "It is

imperative that I *do not.* Refuge must remain hidden."

"So you're just going to let all the rest of the rebels fight the UWO without you!"

"Trust me that this is the best way."

She's clearly hedging, and Pax . . . Pax isn't challenging her. In fact, he seems supportive of her position, holding me back.

"What is going on here?" I say, stepping away from Pax's hand. "What do the two of you know that you're not telling me?"

Sarah stands and paces. "There is another thing we must consider, should we win this fight against the UWO."

"*We* win. But you're not going to fight!"

Sarah goes on as if I haven't interrupted. She looks to Pax. "The uplink through which the UWO compels the clones is also what keeps them alive."

Pax says, "Yes."

"If, therefore, the UWO is destroyed, then their net will be shut down and the uplinks will have nothing to connect to."

"That's right." Pax's voice has a strange resignation to it.

I watch their exchange—the absolute certainty with which Sarah defers to Pax for his opinion on this—and my heart skips a beat. "You told her," I say. "You told her what you are. You didn't tell her the story you told me when we first met—you told her the truth."

"I did," Pax says, speaking softly. "She knows I am a clone."

The blood drains from my face. "You begged me never to tell any—"

"Pax's secret is safe with me," Sarah says. "His worth as valid as anyone else's here, under my protection. And that is why we must have this discussion. If we destroy the UWO, thousands of clones just like Pax will die. Maybe more. Who knows how many they have around the globe. They'll die for no other reason than that the UWO created them." She looks at Pax. "If we win, *you'll* die."

"No. No." I step toward her, shaking my head. "Not Pax. He was disconnected from the uplink as a baby. Pax is special. He's . . ." I look at him, and my heart constricts. "He's unique. He's been disconnected almost his entire life, and he hasn't died yet. Maybe the Freemasons will be the same. Maybe they won't have to die if we win."

Pax has gone very still, and Sarah draws her brow together. After a pause that stretches too long, I say, "You didn't tell her that part?"

A strange silence falls over the clearing in the wake of my question—a silence filled with things not said. And with the weight of . . .

Secrets.

I close my eyes and press my hands to my temple. "You didn't tell her that." He looks down, avoids my eyes. "Because it's not . . . it's not true."

My thoughts tumble over each other as things fall into place. "You've never told Luther, or Wallace, or Elan about being a clone. You never even told me—I had to figure it out on my own. But you told her, and you barely know her." I lower my hands and open my eyes. I don't ask why, because it is suddenly obvious. Here, in this place, in this dead zone where he doesn't struggle with headaches.

Where the signal to his brain can't get through.

"You're not disconnected. You've never been disconnected," I say.

Pax is still on the UWO net.

49

Pax raises his eyes to mine. "Clones *cannot* live without the uplink to the UWO net."

"But you're not receiving the transmission now, and you're standing here—alive."

"As with the animal clones," Pax says, "there is a period of delay before"—he waves a hand, as if seeking the right word—"expiration. The implant holds a residual amount of data in case of power outages or accidental disconnect. But the residual data is limited. It's a failsafe, just in case."

"Just in case?" I whisper, although I know what he's going to say.

"Just in case they need to execute a batch of us. Just in case any decide to go rogue."

So he's known he's not the only one. Telling me he was the only one was just another lie. I scrunch up my face. "But . . . you . . . Aren't *you* rogue? Why haven't they executed you yet? Aren't they tracking you through that thing?" Hysteria is rising in my chest, and I hug myself, as if I can physically hold it in.

Pax takes a couple of steps toward me, arms outstretched. "I am complicated."

"Please just tell me the truth. For once—*tell me the truth.*"

"The truth is complicated."

"Then un-complicate it."

Pax runs his hands through his hair. "The truth is I didn't tell you I was still connected to the UWO net because I thought you would tell Luther. And if you told Luther, that would have been the end—the end of me, the end of you, the end of everything. So I held it back to protect myself, yes, but to protect much more than just that. And I know I ask this of you over and over again, but I am asking you once more to *trust me.* I haven't done anything—*anything*—to earn it, but I need it. Your trust, for the world."

Behind Pax, Sarah's attention is riveted on us, as if my response means as much to her as it does to Pax.

"But she knows," I say. I wait. They both stay quiet. I look at the ground, to the bent blades of dying grass and the fallen leaves. Inside my chest, there is a wail of rage wanting to tear free, but stronger than that, the knowledge that I cannot abandon Pax. Not even now.

"You have my trust. You have my love. And I know it probably feels as though you did, but you never had to earn either."

He lets out a shuddering breath and takes another step toward me, but I hold up a hand. "I don't want to be lied to anymore." A sob catches in my throat, and I choke on it. I blink back the tears until I can speak again. The wind carries my hair across my face. I gather it to one side and say, "But I trust you. You have never done anything but help me, and if you say you can't tell me any more, then . . . okay. Okay, Pax."

Sarah's shoulders visibly relax, and she turns from us, walking several paces away to stare into the tree line bordering the clearing.

Pax comes closer, and I let him. "I told Sarah because I had to, to protect her," he says. "If I didn't, everyone in this place would be in grave danger."

"But you can't tell me about that either, can you." It's not a question. I look up into his eyes and sniff, wiping my nose on my sleeve.

He shakes his head, slowly, holding my gaze. Takes another step closer. "I told her because I *could* tell her, because of what this place is—what they've done here." He tips his face to the sky, letting the sunlight—coming in angled shafts through the trees—play across his cheeks, turning his lashes nearly transparent.

And then he smiles. Not some half-smile or twitch of the cheek, but a real smile that transforms his face—that transforms him into a different person. That shows his crooked tooth and wrinkles in his skin I've never seen before.

I release my hair to let it fly in the wind and just *watch* him. Here, he is free, and he knows it. And it has nothing to do with me or anyone else.

But he cannot stay here because he's already living off residual data. To stay would mean death. He has to leave.

I touch his jaw and draw him down to look at me. He doesn't seem afraid, not now, at least. His smile wavers and falls as he rakes his eyes over my face—my tear-stained cheeks.

"I'm sorry," he says. "I—"

"Don't apologize." With light fingers, I trace the line of his jaw to his ear, and then behind his ear to his hairline. It takes only a moment of pressing to find the implant, a hard ridge beneath the skin. I shift closer and circle it with the pad of my finger. Pax twitches once, but stands still, watching me.

"This is a silent place for you," I say.

"The first true one I've ever known."

I cant my head.

"The signal is sometimes weaker in very high altitudes, or very far from signal towers. And sometimes there are pockets where it can be hardly felt. Dead zones."

I widen my eyes. "The Golems. They can't operate well—"

"At high altitudes. Yes." He pulls a grim face.

"But you are not a Golem. You are not a machine. You have a heart, a brain, a soul."

"I am not a Golem," he says in a low voice, echoing me. "And when I first saw what those things were, I . . . It helped me to realize what I was capable of, as a *free person*." He swallows, and tears gather in his eyes. He blinks them away. "But the operative signal is the same. Only with me, it's woven deep into my brain."

"And it was never detected at Asylum because . . . because of . . ." I look down at my leg—my thigh where Holly placed an untraceable implant, made from material salvaged from the upgraded Golem uplink.

"Exactly," Pax says. "It's not an upgrade, like you all thought. The UWO has produced that casing for ages." He reaches back and takes my hand. Lowering it from his neck, he holds it—just holds it.

"You didn't say anything."

"How could I have?"

I want to know why the UWO hasn't found him and killed him after all this time. To know how he stays out of their watch, despite still being connected, but he can't, or won't, tell me. And the day is getting on. We have to go. Back to Luther and Bishop and all the rest. Back to Asylum. Back to the rebellion. Back, to start a war that might take all our lives.

What I wouldn't give just to stay here, with Pax, in these woods—in this silent place—forever.

"Pax . . . What does it feel like when it's *not* silent?"

"I cannot describe it." He squeezes my hand tighter, swiveling his head to look at Sarah for just a moment.

Then he returns his gaze to me and says, "I thought it would be best if I never said this, but here, where it's silent, I know I can. And I don't know if I will get another opportunity to say it—freely—ever again." He tucks a strand of my hair behind my ear and tilts his head with a sad smile. "I love you, Pria. I've loved you since before I even knew what word to put to how I felt."

All the air rushes out of me and my knees weaken.

"And I didn't know that real love was even possible for someone like me. But it is. And—and I want you to know that I love you even when it's not silent. I love you when it seems like I'm indifferent. Loving you has changed the course of my life." He looks down, crestfallen. "And it will change the course of my death."

I'm reeling. The joy that rushed through me at his words slams into a wall of devastation. *It will change the course of my death.* Because if we defeat the UWO, he will die.

Because he needs the uplink to the UWO net to survive.

My legs give out and Pax catches me as I fall. "No," I say, grasping at him. Together, we sink to the earth. "There has to be another way. Some other way. We can't—we can't destroy the UWO if it means your death."

"The files have already been sent to Luther. He will call the Nest leaders together." He says the words against my temple, his breath warm as it stirs my hair.

"Then we stop him! Sarah said it, too. If we win, it's more than just your life at stake—it's the lives of all the Freemason clones." I cast a desperate look over at Sarah where she hangs back, watching us. "Maybe we can . . . we can defeat the UWO without disrupting their network. We don't really *know* how Luther and the other leaders will end up doing it—what they will decide."

"The Golems are on the network," Pax says. "If we want any chance of fighting against them, I am certain we will have to destroy the signal."

"But you'll *die*!"

"I will. I have always been willing to—for you, for even a gasp of freedom."

"Unless we hijack the network," Sarah says. She's moved closer, but her expression is distant. "Instead of destroying it outright, we take control of it. We could save the Freemasons *and* you, if we could manage such a thing."

"If that were possible, why hasn't anyone done it yet?" Pax asks.

"Because it's not widely known the Golems are machines. Because we did not know about human clones. Because what use would hijacking the UWO network be if we are not unified? Because"—she tilts her head at Pax—"you make all the difference."

He goes still as if holding his breath. I struggle to my feet and face her. "You think you can figure out a way to take control of the UWO network?"

"I will not make any promises, but we can try. How else do we keep Pax alive when the UWO falls?" She rounds on him. "Come back," she says. "Come back, when it is all done. Let me help you. We'll work on hijacking the signal while Luther and the rest work on open revolution, and I will pray that by the time you need it, we will have control of the network. I know you can't stay now, but *return* when this mission is through. Return and let us make sure you are on a network signal controlled by us and that you are well. Choose to live. Your survival is important."

There's a note of challenge in Sarah's tone, and Pax still hasn't risen from the ground.

I bite my knuckles. "Pax," I whisper. "If they do this, you could live."

"Of course," he finally says. "Of course, I'll come back . . . when we're through."

Sarah nods, but her jaw quivers like she's about to cry. As she turns away to hide her emotion, I haul on Pax's arm, dragging him to his feet. I want to ask him why he hesitated—*why* he wasn't elated by Sarah's plan. But still I get the idea there is much between him and Sarah that was not spoken to me. Much that complicates matters like his life and death.

So I can only stand in his embrace and cry, and there is nothing I'd rather be doing. It feels as though we've fallen into each other, becoming one person in a way both of us have wanted to for so long. When we move, we'll have to face the reality of leaving this place, of leaving Refuge and re-entering a world hostile to us both.

After some time, Pax sniffs and inhales, his chest expanding against mine. With a heavy heart, I release my hold on his neck and, as I turn, he brushes my hair from my temple and presses a kiss to my brow.

"Pria, when we leave here, things have to go back to the way they were before. We can't—I can't be with you, like this."

I shake my head, confusion and sadness and elation all at war inside me. "Why?" I whisper.

He pulls me to his chest in a fierce embrace. "Someday soon everything will be clear, and then you'll know why. I hope you will still love me then. But in the meantime, in the silence and out, I will always love you."

50

Pax slides his hand into mine and we follow Holly to the hatch.

"Holly should be awake by now, and Elan and Wallace will have had their tour. I gave orders for a ship to be prepared, as well—I'd say it's ready. After you." Sarah gestures us down the hatch, forlorn and alien in the middle of the forest clearing.

Climbing back into the bowels of the earth feels as though we are exchanging the real world for a sort of shadow land. But I would take this shadow land any day over the one beneath the Autocrat's palace.

At the end of the single hallway Sarah calls the tram, and we ride to a part of Refuge we haven't yet seen. Pax is quiet and thoughtful, withdrawn back into himself, even as he holds tight to my hand.

We disembark on a broad and bright platform bustling with people in white aprons carrying vid-screens. Sarah leads us swiftly down a wide hallway, holding to the right to let a pair of nurses pass with a pregnant woman in a wheeled chair.

I hear Holly's voice before I see her. She sounds cheerful, almost too cheerful, so that when we round an open door into her room, her wide smile is not a surprise to me.

She's pale and her face is filled with strain, but her hair is neat and combed and she's sitting up. A loose white tunic covers her chest, but it can't hide that her right arm is no longer there. Her shoulder is bound tight with a thick bandage, and from the crook of her other arm runs a thin plastic tube connected to a bag of liquid.

Elan wears a careful smile, but Wallace stands at the foot of Holly's bed with his forehead knit over sad eyes. The tension in the air is palpable.

Holly flits her eyes over me and Pax, landing on our clasped hands. "Finally," she says, looking relieved, and a little surprised.

"Your ship is almost ready for you," Sarah says. "Juan would not have you travel so soon, but we think it is for the best for everyone—"

"I'm fine, really," Holly says. "This will heal and I will be fine. I can still do my work." Her eyes unfocus a little. "Some of it. I can at least advise. Teach. It will be fine." She blinks back tears. "I'm sure I'll still be of use."

"You don't have to be of use," Elan says. "You can—you should—rest when we get back. Take some time with Trent."

She looks at him with fear in her eyes. "Do you think this will frighten him? He won't know what to think. *I* don't know what to think." Holly lolls her head to look at me. "I'm . . . I'm so afraid I'll be useless now. The UWO would have just killed me."

"You're not useless," Elan says. "Don't say that."

"Holly." I release Pax's hand and kneel beside her bed. "You, your life, has value no matter what your body looks like or what it can do."

Holly mouths silently and relaxes her head against the pillow.

"She is on heavy pain medication," Sarah whispers. "She may be saying things she usually holds deep inside. Older beliefs and tendencies are coming to the surface."

I rise. "Can we really move her, like this?"

"We have to," Pax says. But he covers his face and rubs his eyes. "We have to go back, and we have to go now."

Juan comes in to prep Holly for departure. Several nurses wheel her out in a chair, and we're given detailed instructions about administering pain medication and watching for infection and how to change the bandages. Before we leave for the hangar, Pax touches Juan's shoulder and steers him over to me.

"Can you do anything about the vid-lens in her eye?" he asks. "Can it be removed?"

Juan peers deep into my eye for a long moment and then says, "Sit."

I perch on the edge of Holly's bed. He takes up a vid-screen and holds it over my face. On my side, I can't tell what he's doing, but his expression is grim. After a couple of minutes, he says, "The surgery to remove the vid is not *beyond* my capabilities, but it would take hours. And it's not without risks—she could go blind in that eye."

I recoil. "Ashra—the Autocrat's wife—she said he took it from her to give to me."

Pax tilts his head as alarm flashes through his eyes.

"She said the procedure took twelve hours. When he gave it to me, he said that now I was perfect, like him." I wrinkle my nose.

"Hmmm." Juan deactivates his vid and sets it aside. "If perfection means mutilation of the eyeball through integration of a foreign object, then, yes. He has made you *perfect*." He taps his lips. "Does it bother you?"

"It ached at first, and I had some vertigo, but that went away after only a few hours."

Juan stands. "I think it is a problem we will solve when you return to Refuge. But for now, it's time for you to get on a ship."

When we return. I will hold onto that hope.

"Follow me. I'll take you to your friends."

Juan leads the way, and Pax and I follow. When we leave here, this connection between us will be over. For whatever reason, out of the silence of this place, he cannot be with me.

But for now, I reach for him, and he takes my hand.

51

"Enjoy the ride." Sarah rubs a hand fondly along the underbelly of a sleek silver ship that is longer and thinner than an X-1. Two Refuge pilots are already waiting in the cockpit.

One of Sarah's people comes around with new, heavier, shirts and camouflage jackets and pants. We separate to different sides of the ship to change. I hand the soft cotton clothes back to Sarah, but she waves me off. "Keep them. Take them back to Asylum. You probably have precious little to call your own there."

Pax returns from the far side of the ship, tugging his new black shirt down over his torso. I catch a glimpse of the vivid, raised scar from where the S-hook pierced him in the crash months ago. That's how long I've known I love him. Since that crash. The scar is a visual reminder of what I almost lost and how my heart has been changed forever.

We zip into the camouflage jackets, and Wallace takes a long look around the hangar. "I am coming back, after," he says. "There is real work I can help with here."

"You will be welcome. You *all* will be welcome." Sarah gives Pax a long stare.

"Thank you," Holly says in a hoarse voice. "For saving my life."

Sarah takes her hand. "Of course."

We board in turns after Holly, who is helped onboard by a pair of nurses. Then the nurses leave and the door begins to shut, enclosing us in an interior that feels dim after the bright hangar. The others find seats and strap in, but Pax takes my arm as the ship hums to life and pulls me to him.

I gasp in a breath. "We said it was the last time—"

"I know." He takes my chin. "I lied."

I throw my arms around his neck and kiss him. He squeezes me so tight I can hardly breathe and my cracked ribs cry out in protest, but in moments we will leave the range of Refuge and it will be the end and—

The ship tilts and accelerates and we stumble, breaking apart. Pax winds his fingers into my hair and pulls my face to his. In the barest of whispers, he says, "Whatever happens, never tell anyone you know what I am. Do you understand?"

I nod.

He kisses me again, a quick stolen moment before he gasps and buckles, his face going pale.

I flutter my hands over his shoulders, seeking purchase—a way to keep him upright.

"It's okay. It's fine. I'm fine," he says. But he's not. He's not fine.

"Unless you intend to stand there making love the whole trip, you two should really strap in," Wallace says in a droll tone.

Pax catches my hand and holds on tight, but he's trembling. We find seats near each other and buckle our straps. Pax lets out a heavy breath, and when I glance over at him, it's to see a tear sliding down one cheek.

I catch my lip between my teeth and look away. It's over.

INITIATIVE

52

I want to sleep, but I can't. Pax can't either. He bounces his knee and drums his fingers. Holly rests on a stretcher laid across several seats, but she is awake, too, staring at the ceiling of the aircraft. Only Wallace sits with bowed head and closed eyes. For a man so rarely still, the posture looks unnatural.

Elan is in the cockpit. Everything is eerily silent, and I don't remember how long this flight is supposed to last. Maybe it will be faster than our flight to Washington, now that we're in a Refuge aircraft and not an X-1.

I slip into a sort of lethargic trance—easy to do in this strange, bright, white ship. Now that we are at altitude, it's difficult to tell we are flying. It's so smooth.

Eventually, Holly dozes off. Pax closes his eyes, but beneath his lids, his eyes move. I don't think he's dreaming—*thinking* is more like it. His jaw is rough with beard growth and every freckle stands out against his pale skin. I wonder if his freckles would match the person whose DNA he shares—if even their freckles would mirror down to the last one. The thought is enough to make my chest hurt, and I shift to stare at the curved wall instead.

What if there are a thousand Paxes just like there are a thousand Freemasons?

He would tell me; he would warn me.

Wouldn't he?

Every now and then, the aircraft makes a slight adjustment that reminds me we're airborne.

Elan returns with something clutched in his hand. "Medicine time for Holly." He gently shakes her awake. "We'll be there soon," he says. "How's your shoulder?"

She cracks open her eyes and looks blearily up at him. "Hurts," she says. "How far?"

"Not far. Half hour."

She nods and sits and takes the pills he offers.

The ship tilts downward as Holly pops the pills in her mouth. She slides on her stretcher with a gasp of pain, and Wallace wakes with a jolt. I widen my eyes at Elan.

"I'll be right back," he says.

Wallace unbuckles and follows him, and I go to sit with Holly. Sweat glistens on her face. "Are we still going down?" she asks. "It feels like we're descending."

"We are," Elan says, joining us again. "A heat signature appeared on their scanners. It's a man, and he's running. We're not close enough to any of the Communes for it to be a Commune citizen."

"We shouldn't stop," Pax says. "We should keep going."

"He might need our help, Pax," Elan says. "It's the right thing to do."

"What if it's a trap?" Holly says in a thin voice. "Is there any way the UWO could be tracking us?"

I meet Pax's eyes. Would he know? *Does* he know?

The ship touches down before I have a chance to make up my mind what I think.

The two Refuge pilots emerge from the cockpit, shouldering large black energy rifles. "Stay here," says the woman, her long, dark ponytail spiraling down her back.

"Like hell," Wallace says. He and Elan open a locker near the front, revealing more guns. No Air-5s, but they all look like energy rifles to me. "You three stay here," Wallace says with a pointed look at Pax, Holly, and me. "We'll be right back."

The lowered ramp lets in a blast of cold air, and I shiver and ball my fists. But then the ramp closes, leaving us in the white interior.

Holly sits up, wincing. "One person, alone, in the middle of nowhere?"

Pax pulls his mouth to the side and walks to the curved wall. He places a hand on it and then steps back in surprise as a four-foot square of the wall fades to a transparent sheen.

A window.

I hurry beside him and look out.

Wallace and Elan are shadowing the two pilots from Refuge as they stalk toward a line of trees. Despite their mission to help this person, they stay low and ready with weapons raised.

A man bursts from the tree line. He stumbles, holding his stomach, doubled over, dragging one foot. Our people pause and raise their weapons higher—I think they might be shouting something at him. And the man looks up.

"Pax, is that . . ."

"Brant," he says.

We rush to the door and Pax slams the release button.

"Brant?" Holly looks around in alarm.

"He's injured. We have to help him."

"You'll need me." Holly makes to stand.

"Wait here! We'll bring him to you." And then I take off running after Pax.

But Elan holds up a hand to stop us as Wallace and the other pilots hold their ground.

"Something's wrong," says the pilot with the ponytail.

"He's injured—Why are we just standing here?"

Wallace catches my arm. "He's not. *Look* at him."

Brant continues his halting half-run toward us. His mouth is flecked with foam and his skin is blotched with dark bruises and red streaks.

Wallace is right—he's not injured.

"He's sick."

53

"Gone. All . . . gone." Brant sways like a falling tree and collapses to his knees.

I creep toward him, but Pax steps ahead of all of us and says, "Stay back," in a sharp voice.

"It's . . . all," Brant says, his voice hoarse. "It's coming." He grabs Pax's arm. "Can't—stop it."

"What's coming?" I say.

Brant's eyes are rolling wildly. "Families. They—using families." He dissolves into a coughing fit that brings up flecks of blood.

I cringe, wanting to pull Pax away from him, but I stay back like he told me to.

"*What's* coming?" I say again.

"Pa—" Brant looks at Pax as he coughs again, and again, and tears stream from his eyes. He groans and vomits a mixture of bile and blood. It splatters over Pax's chest and neck, splashes onto the side of his face before he can look away.

"Pax!" I scream.

Brant shudders and falls limply to the ground.

"Don't touch him!" Holly shouts from far behind us.

"Too late," says a voice that's not one of ours. But I recognize it.

I spin around.

"*Moon?*"

She stands at the edge of the tree line, holding a bow and arrow and staring at Pax with grim eyes. "It's too late now—you are infected. You should never have touched him."

Pax stands slowly, letting Brant slip fully to the ground.

I look from Moon to him, covered in blood and bile, and back to

Moon again. A cold feeling settles into my gut. "Infected with what?" My voice sounds foreign to my own ears. "Moon, do you know?"

She steps toward us, out of the trees, and opens her mouth to answer. "It is th—"

But then the trees come alive with the force of—something—rushing toward us. I gasp and stumble back, but Pax flings himself in front of me. Like a wind, two Golems pass us by, roaring and shaking the earth. A third appears behind Moon a moment before lifting her in a fluid motion that sends her bow flying.

"No!" I scream as it throws her and continues stomping through the grass.

I have no weapon—nothing with which I can fight. So I run. I run toward Moon's body, lying crumpled on the ground. Pax runs with me, but he does not touch me, and I know we are thinking the same thing with each beat of our feet on the earth.

Infected, infected, infected.

Moon lies at an odd angle, her head bent to one side, and when I touch her forehead, she twitches. A pulse beats weakly in her neck.

"Moon," I say. "What is it? Tell us what it is."

"Burn it," she says. "Burn . . . the bo—dy."

I clutch her shoulder. "The body? *Brant's* body?"

A tiny smile tilts just the corners of her mouth as her breath leaves her.

Behind us, the world is in turmoil. Golems roaring, energy rifles blasting, earth crashing, people screaming. Wallace, Elan, the pilots—fighting for their lives.

The Golems aren't after Pax and me. It's a mercy or an oversight—but I know which. These machines cannot show mercy.

I stand separated from Pax by at least six feet, but he backs away further still. "Don't come near me," he says. "Just stay back." He looks at his hands as if seeing them for the first time.

A Golem turns toward us, roars. Torn flesh hangs from bones exposed by multiple shots to its body. I cringe back just as its head explodes from some shot behind it, showering the vicinity.

Two people lie on the ground near the Refuge ship. Who, I can't tell. Dead or alive, I can't tell. Blood is everywhere.

Pax grits his teeth, gives me a long look, and then runs toward the fight. He slides beneath a reaching Golem and comes up with an energy rifle.

Pax is fighting. He's infected with some terrible disease, and he's fighting, and I'm just standing here, paralyzed with uncertainty.

Because my brain can't make any sense of these Golems who ran past us without touching us. But it's not the first time Golems have ignored me when Pax was nearby—when Pax was with me. Ignored me, or attacked without leveling a killing blow.

I grab the sides of my head, weave my hands into the unfamiliar hair and curl it into bunches. *Am I going crazy?*

My feet betray me, carry me toward the fray—right into the midst of it. Two Golems still stand, still fight. The other lies in pieces, although some of those pieces twitch and move like half-crushed spiders. In almost a trance, I step behind the Golem Pax and Elan are fighting.

"Pria, are you crazy? *What are you doing?*" Elan shouts. "Move! I can't get off a shot with you standing there!"

But Pax lowers his weapon with eyes wide and comprehending. He shakes his head once, as if to tell me, "Don't do it."

"Do you want to *die*? *Pria*!" Elan is desperate now.

No. I don't want to die. I just want to know.

The Golem turns, as if sensing me. It lowers on its haunches. For a heartbeat, we are face to face, the creature and I. The stench is almost overpowering, but there is nothing behind its eyes. It roars—a mechanical sound. A sound without breath to stir my hair.

You don't scare me. My heart feels like it will beat out of my chest.

I brace a foot back and raise myself higher. "So kill me already."

It roars again.

"But you're not going to, are you?"

I release a huff of a laugh and lift my lip in a sneer. With a twist of my heel, I turn my back on it.

The Golem grabs me by my neck and yanks me into the air.

54

I can't breathe—the pain sears into my chest and down my spine.

I can't breathe. Stars explode in my eyes.

I can't—

I fall through space and land in a heap. Something heavy and noxious falls on my legs. The Golem. I hack and cough as air returns to my lungs, but my chest is on fire. Ribs already cracked scream at me and my vision streams with tears as Elan swims into view, hovering over me, dragging me from beneath the fallen Golem.

"Are you alright?" He slaps my cheek, bringing me back to full awareness. "What were you thinking?"

"I was . . ." I loll my head and cough, cough again, try not to burst into sobs. Massaging my throat, I squint at him. "I thought it wouldn't kill me."

"*Why* would you think that?"

"I don't know." It's hard to remember why, now.

I hug myself and look around. It's all over and my friends stand in postures of defeat. Hands on hips, heads hanging, shoulders slouched. At the ship, Holly makes her slow way down the ramp.

"Can you stand?" Elan offers me his hand.

Nodding, I take it and let him pull me to my feet.

Pax stands apart from the rest of us, and he is somehow calm. He holds the gun he took from the fallen Refuge pilot in a lowered grip, making no move to come closer.

"Stay there," Holly says. She gives him a wide berth. "I need . . . I need . . . a medical kit."

"There has to be one on the ship," Wallace says. "I'll get it."

"They're dead—there's nothing you can do to help them," Elan says, looking at the fallen pilots. "And we shouldn't linger."

"It's not for them." She passes her hand over her eyes. "Did Moon suffer?"

"No," I say. "I-I don't think so. It all happened so fast." Moon, dying. I raise my eyes to Holly. "She said to burn the body. She must have meant Brant. Why would we do that?"

"It would be the only way to ensure it doesn't spread—his infection. It must be viral, but I'll know for certain once I test it."

"But you can't touch him. You said so yourself. Pax is already—" I cover my mouth as tears choke me.

"I won't. That's what the kit is for."

Wallace returns, jogging, and hands her a white case. "Everything you need should be in there. Would you like assistance?"

"No. Everyone not already exposed should stay back. I'll do this alone."

"I'm already exposed," Pax says. "Let me help."

She looks him up and down. "Very well."

I don't know if I'm imagining it, but as Pax walks after Holly, he seems *altered* to me. He stumbles slightly and winces as though the sun hurts his eyes. But then they are gone and all I can do is speculate.

"What do you think it is?" Elan says in a low voice.

"I can guess, but I don't want to." Wallace sighs and moves to one of the fallen pilots. "What are we going to do about them?"

"We have no time to bury them here. Let's take them on board—Luther will see they get a proper burial at Asylum. Moon, too."

As Luther and Elan set about moving our dead companions to the hold of the ship, I shield my eyes and look out to where Holly is bending over Brant's dead body. She removes something from it and places it carefully in a container Pax holds. I wish I could see more clearly what they're doing. And then I remember my vid-lens. With three blinks, I activate it and focus hard on them, zooming in.

Holly wears a plastic glove and a face mask. She's taking blood from Brant's arm . . . the blood is going into a vial, which she hands to Pax. She stands and removes the glove with some effort, tosses it onto Brant's body. She gestures at Pax, and he seals the container and sets it aside. Then he takes off his jacket and sets it on top of Brant, and then his shirt. His boots and socks. And . . .

his pants.

I blink and pull back, letting the lens zoom to normal, and then deactivate it entirely.

Moments later, a plume of smoke rises from where they are standing. The plume becomes a billow that fans out over orange and red and gold flames. Ahead of it, Holly walks back to us with Pax in her wake, barefoot and nearly naked.

"That's done," she says once she's in earshot, her voice still muffled behind the face mask she wears. "But we will have to quarantine Pax until we can be certain."

Pax looks sadly vulnerable, standing in his underpants, holding a medical container filled with samples from Brant's body. On his neck and face there are still traces of Brant's blood. But he isn't stumbling anymore, and he doesn't look so pale.

"How will we quarantine him?" I say.

"There are . . ." Holly grimaces and cradles her shoulder. "There are biohazard suits at Asylum. Until we get there, he stays in the back of the ship, and no one goes near him. Pax, it would be wise for you to put on a face mask, too," she adds, raising her eyebrows.

"Everyone on board. Let's go," Elan says from the hatch door.

My feet thump hollowly against the bottom of the ship as I move to sit as near the front as I can. Of all the things I thought would drive us apart, I never thought it would be this.

55

Elan has radioed ahead to Asylum, and when we land in the familiar hangar, the door opens to nurses waiting with a bio-suit for Pax. Doc is there, too, with a wheelchair for Holly, and they are all hustled away before I can pause to think about where they will take Pax and what they will do with him.

Only Elan and Wallace and me are left, until we hear steps on the ramp and Luther appears. He raises his hands to the frame above his head and appraises us with tired, but approving, eyes. "You did it."

"Not without loss," Elan says.

"No." Luther looks at the bodies of the dead pilots laid out neatly on the floor in the rear of the ship—at Moon's body. "No, not without loss." His voice cracks. Then he crumbles, his face twisting into a mask of grief. He stumbles backward and falls to his rear, slumping over his knees and burying his face in his forearms.

I gape, horrified, but Elan hurtles the nearest seat and rushes to him, lays his hand on Luther's shoulder. "There was nothing we could have done for Brant. He died quickly, but he wasn't alone in the end."

"His body?"

Elan clenches his jaw. "We burned it. I'm sorry. We had no choice."

"You could have brought him here—to be buried."

"We couldn't. He was infected with . . . something. A virus. Moon was adamant we burn him."

Luther groans. "My brother."

"I'm sorry. I'm so sorry, Luther," Elan says.

Luther looks up, and there are tears streaking his face. "What about the rest of them? Carlisle and Ameera and Jin and Simu and—"

Elan looks over his shoulder at me. Those names—they must be some of the fifty others who left Asylum with Brant.

"He—he said *all gone*," I say. "I don't know if that means . . ." I lick my lips and start over. "He was alone. He might have just *left* the others. There's no reason to assume they are all dead."

Luther takes a shuddering breath.

"There's still a chance," I say. "Maybe Brant was coming to warn us about something. He did say that *it* was coming. That they would use . . . our families . . ." I rub at my forehead, trying to make sense of Brant's last words.

Elan's eyes dart back and forth as if he's thinking.

"I'm going to get to work on the files," Wallace says, his voice carefully calm. "Luther, when you're ready?"

Luther doesn't answer. He sits with shoulders shaking.

"I'll watch him," Elan says. "Go on."

"Come on, Pria," Wallace says. He takes long, quick strides, and I follow in his wake to his workshop. He goes straight to his bank of computers and calls to life a vid-screen. "Let's decrypt those files you stole from the capital. "

But all I can think about is Brant. And Pax. "You think it's the Pandemic, don't you?"

He pauses in the middle of typing in a code. "I do. We don't need Holly's blood samples to confirm what we already know."

I grope my way to a bench and sit down hard. "But that's—it's extinct. The UWO eradicated it in the years after the Great Incursion. Two hundred years ago." Then I laugh and slap a hand over the sound, because the lie—all the years of indoctrination—slips so easily out of my mouth.

Wallace raises an eyebrow and looks slantwise at me.

I rub my hands over my face. "Gaia Earth, what will we do?" I mumble.

"The best thing we can do, right now, in this moment, is work on the UWO files." The lights of his vid-screens play out across his face. "Dammit! Where are those files? I don't see any encryptions." His eyes flit over his screen. He taps another to turn it on.

"This all makes sense, doesn't it," I say in a dull voice.

He doesn't ask me what I mean. Wallace came out of the UWO,

same as me. He knows.

"A plague is much more efficient than hunting us down with Freemasons. No, *they're* just to replace the Commune citizens in essential working-class tasks—once everyone is dead. A plague can go where people can't, and where Golems could never find us. People can run away from bombs—can rebuild and start over, but a plague can kill us all in great swaths. A plague is the ultimate efficient killer."

"All you need are carriers," Wallace says under his breath.

"Like family members," I say.

"Like family members." He gives me a long stare, and I think of my family here. I think of Celine, and Henri, the only family I've ever known. Wallace sees it on my face.

"They are out there, somewhere, Pria. We don't know where. You can't do anything to help them yet. All we can do right now is get into these files and bring the rebel leaders together. Start the uprising against the UWO before they wipe us out."

The files. The proof of how the UWO orchestrated all the Great Devastations. I close my eyes. "You're searching for encrypted files, but they're not."

He jerks his head to face me. "What?"

"They're not encrypted." I march to one of his screens and search what he has pulled up. "UWO Record Files, that's what you're looking for. There were thousands of them."

"Why the hell wouldn't they have encrypted the information?"

"I took it from Sylvan Spencer's personal computer. Maybe he felt there was no need?"

Wallace blinks and stares long at his vids. "You're right," he says. "You're right, they're just . . . here. Nothing to crack into or decrypt. All I need to do is run a search for the relevant information to show the other leaders." He cuts his eyes at me.

"I know. It's too easy."

"Yes," he says, with pursed lips and wary eyes. "Way too easy."

56

I find Holly and Elan in a lab in the infirmary, hunched over a scope. Holly looks up when I enter. Her face is pale, and I don't know if it's because of her injury or because of what she's looking at. Maybe it's both.

"What is it?" I say.

She hesitates, biting her lip. "It's the Pandemic," she says, and I deflate. "But it's much worse than that." She pushes back from the scope. "It's a mutated strain. The Pandemic virus worked fast, but it could only be spread through body fluids. This one . . . it's virulent. It might spread through the skin. Contact could be all it takes." She looks at her scope again, with fearful eyes.

"Mortality rate?" I ask.

"Nobody who contracted the first Pandemic survived—not a single recorded case." Holly closes her eyes. "I don't know why this one would be any different."

Coldness washes through me. I sway.

"Pax didn't touch anyone when he came in, did he?" Elan asks.

Holly shakes her head. "No. We were very careful."

I make my way to a chair and sit. "But we don't know for *certain* he's infected. Let's wait and see if he shows any symptoms before condemning him to death."

"Oh, Pria," Holly says, and tears brim in her eyes. She gestures at her scope, at the transparent slide with a smear of red on it. "This is Pax's blood sample."

Elan says something I don't hear because of the rushing and roaring that fills my ears, and then Holly says, "I'll know more once I run Brant's tissue sample about—"

I catapult off my chair and vomit into the trash can beside the desk.

This isn't right. The UWO can't have gotten him, after everything.

I wipe my mouth on the back of my hand and turn blurry eyes on Elan. "You have to find Celine and Henri and bring them home."

Elan is so pale he looks as though there is no blood left in his face. He backs out of the room and then takes off running.

"Pria, I'm so sorry," Holly says, but I ignore her.

I wander out of the infirmary to the wing adjacent. Pax's room isn't difficult to find, with two security guards posted outside. They eye me warily as I approach.

"I just need some time to talk with him."

"You cannot open the door," one of the guards says.

"I understand. Please, can you give us some privacy?"

The guards exchange a look and then move further down the hall, out of hearing range, but not out of sight.

I stand and stare at the door for a long time before I knock. "Pax? It's me," I say through the wood.

Nothing.

"Are you there?" I can't keep the alarm out of my voice.

"I'm here." A heavy thump, and then a dragging sound against the door. He's sitting against it, on the other side.

I turn against it and do the same, sliding to the cold stone floor. I rest my head back and close my eyes, pretending we are in the same room talking. "You have the Pandemic virus."

"I know."

Of course he does. "They say you won't survive."

Silence.

"And I cannot see you or touch you or—" My voice catches.

"It's going to be okay," Pax says. Calm. How does he sound so calm?

"I don't think it is." I dig the heel of my hand into my eye. "I can't do this without you."

"You don't need me," Pax says. "You don't have any idea how strong you are."

"That's not true. Without you, I would be dead ten times over. I would have been killed in Sanctuary before I even knew my whole life was a lie. You set me free. You *chose* me."

"We chose each other."

I drop my head into my hands. "We've come so far. I don't want you to die."

"I don't want to die either."

We're both silent for a long time with the weight of things unsaid—of things we can't say. With a shaking hand, I wipe away a tear that is tracking toward my chin.

Finally, Pax says, "Pria," and his voice sounds heavy with hesitation. "If I die here, I want you to look in the box in my apartment. The one that used to be under your bed. But only if I die. Do you promise me?"

"The box?" I frown. "Do you mean the one that has pages of letters in it from the girl who lived there before we moved in? That's the only box I know of."

"That's the one. Promise me."

"Okay, I promise." And then I hunker over my knees and rest my forehead on my crossed arms.

57

I wake to a hand on my shoulder, shaking me.

"Huh—what?" Befuddled, I sit, wincing. At some point in the night, I keeled over sideways on the floor beside Pax's door. The hard floor has been digging into my shoulder, and every bump, bruise, and cracked rib is punishing me for it.

"It's been twelve hours," Holly whispers. "When was the last time you talked to him?"

"I . . . don't know. When I left you?" I scramble up and knock on the door. "Pax? Are you awake? Are you okay?"

"I'm here. I'm fine," he says.

I let out a relieved laugh and sag against the door.

"Pax, it's me, Holly. What symptoms are you displaying?"

There's a brief moment of silence before he says, "None."

Holly frowns, a crease appearing between her brows. "Okay," she says. "Still asymptomatic."

It's all I can do to keep from hugging the door.

Holly wrestles a face mask on one-handed—she's already wearing a glove. "Move away, Pria," she says.

I edge back.

"Pax, I'm coming in for another blood draw. Roll up your sleeve to your elbow, please, and stand back from the door. Put this on." She slides a second face mask under the door.

The guards unlock his room. The door squeaks on rusty hinges as one of them opens it wide, and Holly disappears inside. She reemerges a couple of minutes later carrying a vial containing dark red blood. She nods at the guards, and the door closes again.

I raise my eyebrows.

"He seems . . . fine. Healthy even."

I let out a hard breath.

Holly shakes her head and gives me a pained look. "Pria, he *has* the virus. We've already confirmed that. We just don't yet know how long it takes for this strain to display. I'll keep running tests, and maybe he can"—her voice breaks and she lowers her chin to compose herself—"he can help us understand this thing, before the end."

"Before the end," I say. "You mean before he dies. Why don't you just say what you mean?"

But I know why she doesn't. Doublespeak and euphemisms are hard-baked into the vernacular of the UWO, as if by putting a different name to things they change what they really are. Holly was raised on that as much as I was, but I'm tired of it.

But that's not Holly's fault, and I shouldn't take my grief and frustration out on her.

"Yes, before he dies," she says. "I'm so sorry, Pria."

I nod, my throat closing around the apology I want to speak.

"Would you like to come with me to run this sample?" she asks.

I shake my head. "I'll stay here." Talking feels like choking. My neck hurts, too—a reminder of the Golem attack. I touch my bruises and turn back to Pax's closed door.

Holly leaves, her quick steps carrying her down the corridor.

I push my hands into the small of my back and stretch, working out the cricks. My hair feels heavier and greasy, and I wish I had something to tie it back with. Arms akimbo, I pace in front of Pax's door, trying to untangle my thoughts—trying to ignore the guards who have retreated to a respectful distance.

I stop pacing and rest my forehead against the wood. He's still infected. It's *festering*, waiting to manifest. We don't know how long it's going to take for him to die.

"Pria?"

But it isn't Pax who says my name. I lift my head and look, bleary-eyed. "Celine?"

"Pria!"

My friend—my best friend. My chest constricts and tears spring to my eyes, and I cover my mouth as she sprints toward me. I rush to meet her and we collide in a tangle of limbs.

"You're back! You're alive! They didn't get you." I laugh through my tears. She smells of dirt and sweat and wears the same clothes she left in and her hair has grown a little so I can't see her head tattoos. But she's here, and she is wonderfully familiar.

"I'm okay. We're back." Celine sniffs and pulls away to appraise me. She grabs my shoulders. "*You're* alive! You survived the capital! I didn't—I didn't—I honestly didn't think . . ." She drops her head to my shoulder and sobs.

I pat her on the back until she says, "Oh stop it. You're still terrible at that." With both hands, she wipes her streaming eyes. "What's going on? I just saw Holly in the Hall—Pax is in quarantine?"

"Didn't Elan tell you?"

"No, I haven't even seen him yet! Do you know where he is?"

"He's looking for you—he left yesterday, to warn you about the Pandemic and bring you home!"

Celine shakes her head, eyes wide. "Pandemic? Like, the eradicated-two-hundred-years-ago Pandemic?"

I nod. "They've brought it back."

"*Celine*!"

She swings around, and Elan is running toward her from the end of the hallway. Letting out a small choking sound, she leaps into his arms and wraps her legs around his waist. They murmur together for a few moments before he sets her down and says, "They radioed me—let me know you and Henri came back. I got here as soon as I could."

"Okay, now I'm sure at least one of you can tell me *what is going on*." Celine looks between us. "How did Pax get infected?"

"By Brant," Elan says. "We came upon him on our way back from Washington. He was infected. And he's dead now. Did you or Henri come into contact with anyone on your trip?"

"Oh my—" Celine covers her mouth with her hands. "No—I told the same to Holly. No one, not since we left Asylum."

Elan sags against her and his eyes close. "That's good. Good news," he says.

"I have more good news!" Holly says, rounding the corridor. She's rushing back, her eyes wide. "I can't explain it, but Pax isn't sick. At *all*. No trace of the virus is left in his blood. I ran the sample from yesterday again just to be sure, and I-I ran the sample from today *three times* just now." She's gaping, stunned. "Yesterday, he was infected. Today, he's not. Pria—he's well."

I stagger against the wall. Pax is not dying. Celine and Henri are back. I sink down to my knees, overcome with emotion.

"It should be impossible," Holly says.

"Are there records of any people surviving the Pandemic virus from two hundred years ago?" Celine asks.

Holly shakes her head. "In our med-tech training, they told us it was eradicated by quarantining everyone who was sick—and everyone who had been exposed or who they feared had been exposed—until they died. There was no cure, no immunity ever developed. Eventually it just ran out of people to kill. The Great Incursion started while the Pandemic was still ravaging the world, wiping out even more potential hosts. A virus can't live without a host. We were *told* one of the greatest achievements of the UWO was stopping the spread of the Pandemic. That if they hadn't taken control, it would have wiped out all humanity."

"But the Pandemic virus was *never* out of their control," Elan says. "It was always a dog on a leash. They pulled it back once. But now they intend to let it off its leash for good." He takes Celine by the shoulder and hugs her tight.

"But what about Pax?" I say.

"I can't explain it," Holly says. "I really can't. He fought it off . . . somehow. *Overnight.*"

I shudder and say, "Then *let him out.*"

"Right—of course." Holly gestures for the guards.

"He fought it off," Elan says. "That means there's hope for others."

Holly casts him a dark look. "It's the Pandemic. No one fights it off."

"But he *did,*" I say.

The guards open the door, eyeing Pax warily as he comes out. He removes his face mask and crumples it in his hands. "So I'm *not* dying?"

"Not even a little," Holly says. "You just became the first person in the history of the world to survive the Pandemic."

58

Pax clears his throat and skirts his eyes to me where I'm tearfully hugging my chest. He flexes his hands and blinks, stretching his mouth tight as though he wants to say something, but can't.

I give him a watery smile. "You"—I sniff—"I'm just so glad—"

But then a furry mass attacks me, licking my hands and bumping my legs so hard it nearly bowls me over.

"Down, Arrow!" says a familiar voice, and Henri comes striding to meet us. "Sorry about that, Pria." He helps me gain my balance with a firm hand to my elbow, and once I'm settled, he brushes my hair from my face and gives me a serious look up and down. "You made it back in one piece—in spite of everything. Are you okay?" His eyes flit to my hair, my neck, back to my face.

My shoulders sag with the weight of the question—what people like Henri don't know about the toll it takes to try and answer it honestly. So I just nod and shrug.

Henri breaks into a careful smile. "At least it's over now. And I will admit you are a sight for sore eyes. I missed you."

"I . . . missed you, too," I say honestly.

His smile broadens, and then he takes my chin and plants a solid kiss on my temple, the gesture familiar and promising of things to come.

I freeze and gape as Henri pulls away and lets out a satisfied sigh. He slings an arm around my shoulders and says, "You don't have to talk about any of it until you're ready, Pria. I'll be ready to listen when you are."

"O-okay." Dragging my gaze to Pax, I find him standing with a tight jaw and rigid spine, looking at Henri with cold uncertainty.

"Pax!" Henri extends a hand. "You made it through, and you brought her back. Well done, man."

Pax shakes Henri's hand and gives his chin a sharp jerk that I think is supposed to be a nod.

Holly gives Pax a critical stare and then turns to lead us all down the hall. "Despite Pax's recovery, we cannot discount the danger this poses—to everyone here, and to everyone everywhere."

I stare slantwise at Pax until he looks at me. Does he see what I can't say? That I'm near to fainting with happiness he's still alive. That I didn't know Henri would greet me like that.

Pax's face is a stoic mask, but in his eyes is a depth of jumbled emotions. I wonder if he's thinking the same thing I am—that he survived because he's a clone.

A gasp inadvertently escapes me, and Pax brushes my fingers with his, as if to comfort me. But just as he makes contact, a grimace of pain crosses his brow. He shoves his hands into his pockets and looks ahead.

We enter the cave used as the dining hall, and Celine says she's starving.

"I'll get you something," Elan says. He kisses her—a lingering kiss—and then heads to the counter where Orson's crew is just setting out breakfast.

"No coffee," she calls after him.

He turns and gives her a questioning frown.

"Not today." With a weak smile, she says to me, "I don't know what I want more, this breakfast, or a shower."

The last shower I had was a hot one at Refuge. I let out a longing sigh and cross my arms.

"What is it, princess?" Celine pokes my ribs.

I dance away. "Just thinking."

"About?"

I wish I could tell her—about everything. The burdens of all my secrets feel too heavy for me to continue to bear. But I must. "Refuge," I say. "We stayed there for a night. It was nice. I had no idea a place like that existed."

Celine raises a slim shoulder. "I've never been."

"But Elan has—been there before, I mean."

"Yeah." Celine fingers her lips as her gaze turns distant. "He took the news to Sarah and Juan after Katarina died. Didn't seem like something that should be delivered via pigeon."

"I suppose not."

Celine's gaze returns to present and she taps me on the nose. "Are you really okay? Did those elite bastards hurt you?"

Tears that are always too close to the surface well in my eyes again. I look at my feet and bite my lip.

Celine strokes her hand down my hair to my shoulder, and then she pulls me tight to her side. "You don't ever have to go back. You're home now. You can rest. "

She's wrong, but she doesn't know it. If rest was an option, I could have stayed at Refuge with Pax. But Pax isn't done, so I'm not done. I raise my eyes to him. He's watching me, of course, his gaze filled with sadness.

"What about your mission?" I say to Celine.

"We found him." Celine's voice turns strangled. "He's alive. He's being kept in a compound of some sort. Like a factory. Everything Henri heard was true. We actually *saw* him, Pria, working the grounds behind this big wall. But the wall is hardly guarded. Henri said there should have been a lot of Golems around, but there weren't more than a few. Maybe it's so remote they don't bother with much consistent security. That's why we came straight back—because a rescue is possible, and we need a crew to rescue him. All of them."

"How many?"

"A couple hundred prisoners, maybe. People of all ages. People like us."

People like us. I catch Pax's eye. Celine and Henri's father. *Family.* Being kept as prisoners by the UWO . . . who can now *make* their own clones, who they can compel to obey. What do they need human prisoners for?

"Celine, what if . . ." I look to Holly for help, to Pax. But Pax is preoccupied, massaging the back of his neck.

I grit my teeth. "What if those prisoners are carriers of the Pandemic?"

Celine goes pale, eyes wide. "Oh . . . come on," she says. "Don't say that."

"I have to say it." I clasp my hands. "Celine, *think* about it."

"I don't want to think about it!" Her face contorts. "I want my father back!"

"Pax." I turn, seeking his help, but Pax has keeled sideways, paler than I've ever seen him. "*Pax.*" I hurry to his side as he doubles over a table.

"Don't—*don't*—rescue them." He grabs the back of his neck and falls to his knees. "Pria . . . is . . . right." Then he vomits and collapses in a heap and clatter of fallen chairs.

59

I leap at him. "Pax!"

Elan cuts a look at Holly. "Are you *sure* he's okay?"

"His blood is clean," Holly says, but even she backs away.

"He's not sick with the virus—it's his head," I say. "Give him some space." But he doesn't need space or air. Pax has passed out cold. I roll him onto his back, shoving away the chairs he became entangled in when he fell. His pulse beats strong in his neck, but he's dead weight under my hands. "Help me, please."

"All right, come on." Henri kneels beside me. He raises Pax's shoulders and lets out a surprised breath. "Heavy guy. Where are we taking him?"

"Take him home." And suddenly Luther has joined us, disheveled with deep circles beneath his eyes.

Elan takes Pax's ankles and between him and Henri, they lift Pax.

"Why does this sort of thing keep happening to him?" Celine says, sticking close to my side as we all follow Luther. "I know you know why."

"I don't," I say. It's a half-truth.

She grasps my arm. "Is he dying? Can you tell me that, at least?"

"I don't know." I take a shuddering breath. "I don't know, and it's killing me."

Celine takes my arm and rests her head on my shoulder. "He *knows things*. Somehow," she says in a low, haunted voice.

I scrunch up my face and pinch the bridge of my nose. Pax just knocked himself out cold to tell Celine not to rescue her own father. He said I was right—about the possibility these mysterious prisoners could be carries of the Pandemic virus?

I skirt my eyes to Celine, on edge. "If you believe that . . . that he knows things, then we should listen to Pax."

Celine's expression darkens and she lifts her head from my shoulder.

We catch up to the others at the end of our corridor. Luther unlocks Pax's apartment, opens the door, and flips the light on. With gritted teeth and straining muscles, Henri and Elan heft Pax through the door and sling him—a little unceremoniously—onto his bed.

"I'll stay with him," I say.

"Good," Luther says. "The rest of you come debrief with me." Luther tilts his head and the others follow him out.

Henri lingers a moment and gives me a lopsided smile. "I'm sure he'll be all right," he says. "He seems to have a way of pulling through difficult situations."

"Yes. He does." I look at Pax's face, peaceful in unconsciousness.

"Well, I, uh . . . I guess I'll see you later. " Henri rubs the top of his head, no longer bald after the weeks of travel in the wilderness. He casts an uneasy look at Pax and leaves.

I close the door and lean my back against it, throwing the lock. With slow steps, I move to sit on the edge of Pax's bed.

Hands shaking, I unlace and remove his boots. As I set them neatly beside his bed, I see the corner of a box underneath. The box that used to live under my bed. The one he said to look in if he died—*only* if he died.

I swallow hard and look at his sleeping form. My fingers tingle with curiosity as I fidget with the corner of the box.

Before I can change my mind, I drag it out and look inside. Nothing seems out of place since the last time I looked in it. Stacks of papers with lines of handwriting on them. Personal notes and drawings. I dip my hand along one edge, feeling down deep, feathering the pages as I go.

Then I feel it—a space of air between pages, as if something has been shoved there for safekeeping. I prod the space and find the cool edge of something metal. I pull it out and hold it up with trembling fingers, disbelieving my own eyes.

My memory drive.

60

My memory drive. Pax took it. Not Charlie. *Pax.* And he planted pieces of some other smashed object beneath my bed so I wouldn't go looking for it. His deception was deliberate and manipulative.

Questions flood my mind, but they are immediately driven away by clarity.

Of course Pax took it. He didn't want me to have it. He told me to throw it away. He said I shouldn't read it.

Pax groans and shifts, muttering in his sleep.

I jump and palm the drive, but he settles again.

So what am I going to do now? It's mine. He stole it . . . *He stole from me.*

But how many times has he asked me—begged me—to trust him?

It's my whole life.

But he didn't destroy it. He kept it here, safe and hidden. He must intend to show it to me someday. To give it back.

With a deep breath, and hoping I won't regret it, I replace the drive between the papers, and then I slide the box back beneath the bed.

I stand and brush off my knees. With arms akimbo, I stare down at him. His eyes move beneath his freckled lids. He's waking up, dreaming now.

"Fifteen," he mutters. "I'm . . . fifteen."

"I know. You're fifteen, Pax." I sit and lay my hand on his forehead, hoping to pacify him. "But what does that mean?" Because it was not an Enforcer number; of that, I am now certain.

He wouldn't dream about a persona he adopted to fool the UWO. Dreams, nightmares, run deeper than that.

He jerks awake, pupils dilated, and grabs my wrist in a grip so tight it hurts. I sit still, letting him focus on me—letting him get his bearings. And when he does, he relaxes with a deep exhalation and releases my wrist. Covering his face in both hands, he rolls to his side, putting his back to me.

"I . . . can't . . ."

"I know," I say.

He sits up, dangling his legs off the other side of the bed.

We sit back-to-back for a long time.

"There are some things that nearly kill you to say, and . . . do," I finally say, speaking to the far wall. "Don't answer. Just stay quiet if I'm correct."

Silence.

My pulse increases. "Your headaches are because of the uplink to the UWO net, I'm sure of it. But you said they aren't controlling you, and I-I'm choosing to believe you. Nothing about you—about us, together—would make sense if they were controlling you."

Pax remains silent.

I take a deep breath and cover my face, thinking. "If they knew where you were, we would all be dead, so you must be hiding from them somehow. I don't understand how these things can exist at the same time—your connection to the UWO net and our ongoing safety." I turn to look at the back of his head, at the red-gold hair mussed from sleep. "Are you hiding yourself? Is that the effort you're putting in *constantly*? Is that why you're always in pain?"

Silence.

But then he says, "In a manner of speaking." His voice sounds so choked with emotion, I hurry around the bed to him.

He sits with his head dangling between slumped shoulders, tears streaking down his face. I fall on my knees before him and take his face in my hands. It might cause him more pain, but I can't bear to see him like this—alone, without comfort. "What can I do? Tell me what I can do."

He swallows hard and shakes his head—a feeble shake. "I'm coming apart, Pria. I don't know if I'll make it. I don't even know—" He gives a cry of pain and grabs the sides of his head, his hands over mine. Then his eyes roll back and he slumps over sideways onto his pillow.

"Pax!" I shake him, but he's out again. With a desperate sob, I crawl up on the bed beside him and curl along the length of his body, holding him tight.

61

Hours later, tensions in Luther's office are high.

"Henri, Celine, even you two must admit that now that the Pandemic has resurfaced, it changes everything." Luther runs his hands through his hair, eyes roving the surface of his table, seeming lost.

Celine's fists are clenched. "Luther—we can't just leave them to rot."

Luther rounds his table with weary steps and slumps into his seat. "We must at least consider they are being used as carriers for the virus, and that rescuing them would endanger everyone here."

"Why? Why would we assume they're carriers?" Henri says.

Luther lifts one arm in my direction, the other he extends toward Pax.

"Because," I say with a quick glance at Pax, "Brant told us, as he was dying, that *it* was coming. That they would use *our families*."

I look again at Pax, feeling torn between the certainty he displayed earlier that we should not rescue them and the longing my friends feel to reunite with their father. Pax sits now with his jaw clamped tight and his skin pale, like he's trying not to vomit. Which is probably the case. After his second fainting episode, he slept for hours. My ears warm, remembering how I fell asleep curled around him—how we woke up tangled together, both of us relaxed in each other's presence in a way we had only felt during our brief respite in Refuge. But of course, as soon as he was awake and aware, we retreated to different sides of the room.

I clear my throat and finger my collarbone. "There's no way to know if Brant meant the Pandemic, but . . ."

"But you don't know." Celine hugs herself. She turns into Elan's arms.

"They weren't sick, though," Henri says. "I mean, they were prisoners—thin, a little malnourished maybe, but I think I could tell if they were dying of the plague. We surveilled the compound for three days, and nobody dropped dead."

"Maybe they haven't been infected yet," Holly says.

Celine looks up with dark eyes. "Maybe we should rescue them before they are."

Pax makes a pained sound in his throat and bends over his knees, lacing his hands behind his neck.

"But we can't be sure they'll be clean of implants," Bishop says. "We must also consider that."

Henri mutters a curse and Celine gives a whimpering sound of disbelief. "So we're like Brant now? Hide out here and take care of our own?"

"Except Brant is dead," Luther says, "and probably everyone who went with him."

Celine shuts her mouth tight.

"I'm with Luther," Charlie says, and it's the first words she's spoken. "We don't know enough about the situation."

Luther nods. "My first priority has always been the people *here,* under my care. My second priority is taking out the UWO."

"If these prisoners are to be carriers of the Pandemic, the best way we can help them will be to destroy the UWO," Charlie says. "And we must do it before word gets out that there is a new Pandemic."

"Why?" I ask.

"Panic," says Luther. "Everyone will panic and flee. Do as Brant and his followers did. And look where that got them. We must meet *now.*" He pounds his fist into his palm. "Now that we have the evidence we need, it's time to call a general assembly."

"The Nest leaders will come to one now," Wallace says. "Everyone will come. Pria got everything. Files on the production of the 'Unfamiliars' for the purpose of the Great Incursion. Files on setting up the Controlled Repopulation Program to purge humanity of *undesirables* before establishing a higher human race. Files on how the Oligarch consolidated power in the years before the Great Devastations even began—about how they flooded what they called *Third World Nations* with strands of the Pandemic virus to test it, how they incited the Great Famine and the wars that followed it . . ." He gives a disbelieving laugh. "We have them in their own words. They are not agents of order, helping humanity to survive in some sort of new world utopia. They are masters of destruction."

"Well, yeah," says Celine. "We already knew that."

"Wrong." Luther stands. "We already *guessed* that. Now we know, and so will everyone else." Some color has come back to his face. "They will not kill us with a second Pandemic. They will not replace us with clones. We will unite and fight, and we will survive."

Pax lifts his head, and there is a resignation in his expression that frightens me a little. "When?" he says in a hoarse voice. "When will you call the assembly?"

"Right away. Bishop can draft an encrypted message and send it to all the heads now. We'll send proof that we have the files and request the assembly on the last of this month."

"I'll send the pigeons," Bishop says.

But my stomach feels queasy. All I want—all I've wanted since Pax showed me the truth—is to fight the UWO. To bring down this sick, horrible world they've created. But in Luther's eyes is a crazed gleam I haven't seen before, and I want to feel that fire, too. But none of them have really seen the might of the UWO as I have.

My misgivings are starting to come together. To take shape. From the flawless ease of the mission, to calling together the Nest leaders and convincing them to rise up and fight. What if an attack is exactly what the UWO wants? What if they only want to draw us out? I skirt my eyes to Pax—thinking about what Sarah Cohen said about why she stays hidden. *There are other ways to resist.*

Pax tightens his lips and closes his eyes.

Charlie raises her chin at me, drawing my attention. "I hear old Sylvan Spencer chose you *special* from the Gentrification pool. Pity you didn't kill the bastard before you left."

"It's a pity she had to go at all," Henri says, his voice deepening to a near growl.

Charlie huffs and looks away.

I tilt my head at her. "Is that why you *really* wanted me to go?"

She draws back. "What do you mean?"

"To Gentrification. Were you hoping I'd kill the Autocrat?"

"Please. You don't exactly strike me as the murdering type."

Something feels off, and I can't quite place it. I wander to stand beside Pax, who shifts in his seat. "I'm nervous about this plan for the general assembly."

Luther looks at me, eyes sharp. "Tell me more."

"Well," I say, rubbing my forehead, "our first plan—to get the files from Sanctuary—failed, badly, because somehow they knew we were coming. Then Charlie arrived, and told us about Gentrification, and we suddenly had a way to the capital itself, where we could get the actual files."

Charlie's staring at me with her bright blue eyes like I've gone mad. "So *what?* I knew the previous plan had failed. I had intel of my own, and I shared it. That's what we do, between rebel Nests."

"You brought Dougal here, and he tried to kill Luther."

"I *knew* he was a UWO agent. I brought him here for Luther to deal with!"

"But how did you know about Gentrification in the first place?"

Charlie rounds on Luther. "What is this? An interrogation?"

"Where are you going with this, Pria?" Luther asks.

"Something feels *off*," I say, "and it has since the mission. Charlie said it herself—Sylvan Spencer chose me special, and I wasn't even there as me. But, Luther, *he knew me.* I thought so at the time, and I wasn't imagining it. That man knew me and chose me and marked me"—I point to the vid-lens in my eye—"as his future Empress." I turn a circle, taking in the room. "He has no intention of letting a band of rebels destroy everything he's built. He's far too smart for that."

"So what would you have us do?" Luther shouts, surprising me. He swings his arms wide. "Nothing? Keep running until they find and kill us all? Hide and build an underground society like Sarah? What good is passive resistance in a world like this?"

"Living is never passive," I fire back. "Surviving is never passive."

"If we don't fight, we are done."

"But what if we're playing right into their hands? They built this world—do we really think they aren't paying attention? They control *everything* in it." The room is getting smaller, the walls pressing in. I grab the sides of my head. Spin.

And then Pax is there, catching me around my waist and holding me steady. "Not everything," he whispers into my ear.

I touch his chin as his grip on my waist lessens, and he steps back.

Pax turns to Luther and says, "We will fight them. Because if not now, when?"

Luther nods. "And for that, we need the agreement of the general assembly of the Nest leaders. All of them."

62

"We'll host the general assembly here," Luther says, looking around. "We have the space, and I've worked for years to build the infrastructure for it. We are in a central location. It's ideal."

"But if war is decided upon, we will need to strike at the capital," I say. "Wouldn't Refuge be a better location?"

Pax grows very still, as if he's listening to something I can't hear, or holding his breath.

I look back and forth between him and Luther, uncertain.

"Refuge is too far for the Nest leaders on the West coast," Charlie says. "They won't go so far for just a meeting."

"And Sarah will never have it," Luther adds in a quiet voice. "She has never agreed with me on this. It will have to be here."

Imperceptible to everyone but me, Pax lets out a soft breath.

Luther's eyes gleam with pleasure. "We are finally on our way to *true* freedom."

"Or annihilation," Celine mutters. She takes Elan's hand. "Are we done here?"

"For now."

She gives a sharp nod and leads Elan from the office.

After a moment of hesitation, I move to follow. Nothing seems clear anymore. Nothing simple or easy—if anything ever was.

Celine is holding tight to Elan's arm, in close conversation with him. She looks back at me, catches my eye, then returns to the whispered conversation with her husband. Henri follows close on my heels, Pax beside him. It's impossible to ignore the two men walking in step behind me, tension crackling. The silence between them is deafening.

We come out into the main area of Asylum, and Celine and Elan stop to face each other.

"Now," Celine says. "It has to be now."

"I don't want you to go—not like this." Elan grabs Celine's shoulders. "Doesn't my opinion mean anything?"

"Of course it does! I love you. But if we don't go now, we may not get a chance." Celine looks around at the few people milling in the space.

Amongst the few, I spot the two Breeders we liberated from the UWO on the way to Gentrification—the two whose identities Wallace and I took. I frown in their direction, distracted, but Celine goes on, drawing me back.

"We wouldn't need a lot—ten or fifteen people, maybe, judging by what we saw. They clearly don't expect any sort of attack there, and we'll have the element of surprise. Since you crashed my X-1 we can take the Refuge ship." She gives Elan a dark look.

"You're going to rescue them," I say, keeping my voice low, mindful of listening ears. My stomach drops. "Celine, you can't."

"I have to."

I cast a devastated look at Pax. "But . . . the Pandemic!"

"Pria, *none of the prisoners were sick*." She shakes her head. "I don't expect you to understand this. You don't have a—" She sucks her breath in and stops.

But I know what she was about to say. "A father."

She shrugs a slim shoulder and avoids my eyes.

I step closer. "A mother. Any family at all."

Celine raises her eyes to mine. "If we wait, and the UWO really does intend to use them as carriers, maybe we can rescue them *before*—"

"Please . . . don't," Pax says in a hoarse voice. Then he coughs and stumbles back—sits down hard in a nearby chair. He hangs his head between his knees.

"What is *wrong* with him?" Henri says.

"I don't know." I rub my forehead. "But you should *listen to him*."

"Pria, I can't. I just can't." Celine is crying now. "He's my father. I have to go."

"No," Elan says. "I will. Me and Henri. We'll recruit the right people and we'll go. You stay here. I'm begging you."

Celine looks back and forth between me and her husband and her brother. "But I saw the compound. I know what it's like and what it will take to get those people out."

"Henri saw it too." Elan looks to him. "You aren't the only one who can do this. And I need you—I need you to stay here."

"Fine. I'll stay. But you had better come back!" She dashes tears from her eyes and frowns at Elan.

Elan catches her around her waist and kisses her, hard. "I will return, I promise. For both of you."

I wrinkle my forehead. Both of who?

"Stay with Pria while I'm gone. Most of your stuff is still there, anyhow."

Celine gives a feeble nod.

He takes off running toward the hangar. Celine turns to Henri and raises a finger, but he says, "I know, I know. I'll watch out for him." He kisses her on the forehead, then he turns to me.

With an uneasy glance at Pax, he says, "Pria . . . I understand now."

I open my mouth, wanting to explain. Wanting *this* not to be the moment to have this conversation.

"It's okay," he says. "I get it. I should have seen it a long time ago, but I didn't want to. You said there was nothing between you, but with you and Pax, it was always like you were"—he struggles to find the right words—"doing this dance, you know? And you just couldn't figure out who was supposed to lead. I thought I could cut in, but I can't. Because this music isn't playing for me."

"Henri," I say in a small voice. "I wish I could have loved you the way you wanted me to, but I will always love you as a friend."

He grimaces. "I know you mean well, but that's not really what a guy wants to hear when he's finally figured out he can't be with the woman he loves."

"Will we be okay?"

"Sure we will. Someday." He lets out a breath that is somewhere between a sigh and a groan. "If we all survive this." Then he whistles long and loud. "I thought we'd have longer to rest before heading out again, but . . ." He shrugs. "I guess we'll rest when we're dead."

"Don't say that." I touch his arm. "Please."

He shrugs me off as Arrow comes pelting toward him from some far-off corner of Asylum.

"Sure, Pria. Sis—I guess I've got some recruiting to do."

He straightens his shoulders and heads off after Elan.

"No," Pax says in a feeble sort of way. Then he coughs again—and spits out blood.

"Gaia Earth," Celine says. "Pria . . ." She raises horrified eyes to me. "Are we—am I *doing this to him*? Somehow?"

I shiver against the cold that washes through me, and I don't know how to answer her, because *I don't know*. "Can you, um, help him up? Sometimes it gets worse when I try to help."

She gives me a perplexed grimace. "When you—"

"I know. I can't explain it."

Celine shakes her head and goes to him.

"I . . . failed," Pax says, muttering the words to himself. Then he focuses on Celine, and on me, and he steadies a bit. He waves her off. "I'm fine now. I just need to rest."

"You don't look fine." Celine peers at him. "Your eyes."

She's right. Pax's eyes are bloodshot, like he's been screaming, and his face is pale and sweaty. He darts a look at me, pleading.

"He'll be okay," I say, even though I have no idea if it's true. Even though it's the biggest question in my head right now. "Go rest, Pax."

Pax struggles to his feet. "I'm going to my room. I'm . . ." He looks around, lost. "I'm going home."

I watch him stumble away, helpless.

"Tell me what's really going on, Pria."

"*I can't*."

"Is the secret worth him dying? Is the secret *that* he's dying? Because that boy is clearly dying."

I burst into tears and slump into a chair. "I can't help him. I don't know if anyone can."

Celine sighs and sits beside me. She rubs a bracing hand between my shoulder blades. "I didn't mean to say that you don't have any family. That was cruel. You do have family. You have me." She offers me a watery smile.

I return her gaze. "You're my sister," I say.

She nods. "Pria, are any of us going to survive this?"

It doesn't seem as though she's looking for an answer, but I say, "If you saw what I saw in the capital . . ." I dig my hands into my scalp.

She takes a strand of my hair and tugs gently on it. "How did they *do* this?"

"It must come from the same sort of biotech they use to make the scar-erasing serum," I say. "You should have seen it before Pax cut it."

"*Pax* cut it?"

"He had to. We never could have gotten to Refuge otherwise—it was catching on everything."

"Elan told me about the crash." Celine shudders and hugs her middle. "And the clones."

I take a deep breath and wipe my tears and say, "Do you ever wish you could leave here and go to Refuge? Live with Sarah?"

"I didn't before. It seemed like . . . the coward's way, you know? But now I do, sort of." She leans her head on my shoulder. "Pria, I'm afraid."

We sit like that for a long moment as people move around us in the large, open space. The two former Breeders get up and leave, passing us on their way out. I glance at them and the female one catches my eye. She holds my gaze a second longer than is comfortable, but then she hurries after her companion and the moment passes.

63

Celine and I make our way home—to my apartment now, I guess—and when we turn into our corridor, I see a form slumped at the end of the hall.

"Is that—" Celine says.

"Pax!" I leap into a run. I should never have let him walk home on his own. I skid to my knees beside him. "Pax—Pax, wake up." I lift his head, and a trickle of blood runs from the corner of his lips. "Please don't be dead, please!"

He groans, letting out a heavy breath. "I'm . . . fine."

"*No, you're not.*" I punch him on the shoulder, immediately regretting it.

"Ow."

"Celine, get Holly."

"No." He grabs my hand. "Celine, don't." He finally cracks open his eyes.

"She can help you," I say. "It's time to *let her* help you. She won't judge you, I know she won't."

I feel Celine's eyes burning a hole in the back of my head.

Pax lowers his lashes as if he's too tired to hold his eyes open. "I'm not worried about judgment. If we tell her—if we tell *anyone*—it will only get worse."

Behind us, Celine mutters something in French. Then she comes forward and squats beside Pax. "All right, you. Pria said I need to help you up—that she shouldn't do it for some reason. So let me help you, already."

I stand back and watch my diminutive friend haul Pax to his feet. "Our apartment or his?" Celine says.

"Mine," Pax says at the same time I say, "Ours."

I cant my head. "How can I keep an eye on you over there?"

"You don't need to keep an eye on me."

I stomp my foot.

"He's *really* heavy," Celine says.

"Fine." I hold out my hand for his key. He digs it out of his pocket and hands it over. "But I'm not leaving until I know you're not going to keel over dead."

Celine helps Pax to his bed. I plant myself at his table and fold my arms.

"I'm going to eat lunch and then have a nap," Celine says. "You two"—she shakes her head—"try to work this out. Whatever this is."

After Celine closes the door, we descend into silence.

"You have blood on your face," I say once it becomes clear Pax isn't going to fall immediately asleep. "You're coughing up blood now?"

He touches his chin. "It will pass."

I roll my eyes to the ceiling, trying not to scream. "How would you feel if it was me and our situations were reversed?"

In a soft voice, he says, "I would be losing my mind."

I nod, my face contorting. "I am. I'm losing my mind, Pax."

He hauls himself off his bed and moves to the table. Pulling out the seat opposite me, he sits down heavily. "I'm so sorry. I never intended for you to love me."

"So you've said."

"But I . . ."

"What?"

"I'm glad that you do. It's selfish, but I am. If you didn't, I think I would be dead already." He drops his face into his hands.

A knock, loud and confident, sounds on his door. We both turn to look.

I go to open it, and find Charlie on the other side.

I back up a pace, surprised. What can she want with Pax?

But she says, "I knew I'd find you here. Can we talk? Alone."

"Me?" I touch my chest.

"Yes, you." Charlie crosses her arms and gives me an appraising look. "I think your lover will survive a few minutes without you."

I step into the corridor with Charlie, closing the door behind me.

She looks at me with piercing blue eyes. "I wanted to tell you I'm sorry."

"Oh?" This is so unexpected, it's all I can get out.

"Yes, I . . ." Charlie massages her wrists. "The last time we were alone, I said some things I shouldn't have. I made accusations. Nyck would have been ashamed of me. He didn't like it when I drank—and especially not when I . . . hurt myself." She flits a glance at me—lowers her eyes again. "So I'm sorry for what I said and what I did. It's a version of me I don't like very much, and I'm working on it." She takes a deep breath that raises her shoulders. "And now that Nyck's gone, I have to figure out how to work on it by myself. I'm also sorry I tried to take your memory drive. I wasn't thinking clearly. Nyck wouldn't have wanted that either—he would have wanted you to know who you are."

I nod, but I don't really understand. I don't think Nyck knew me well enough to care much about that.

"I said it before, but I'll say it again and . . . and I actually mean it this time. I do hope you learned what you needed to off that drive."

I shake my head. "I never looked at it. You were right that I shouldn't have taken it from the Commune. It was stolen from me." I brace myself for her explosion of anger, for accusations.

Her nostrils flare and her eyes widen, but she raises her chin and says, "Did you tell Luther?"

"No, I . . ." How to answer—how to explain that I thought it had been destroyed, but know now that it wasn't. "I didn't," I say.

"And yet, you survived Gentrification, so whoever took it didn't reveal your identity to the UWO."

"No. No, they didn't." I sound guilty. Over her shoulder, Pax's closed door seems to hum with the secrets it's hiding.

But Sylvan Spencer knew me, somehow. My mind goes to the box under Pax's bed, and I try to twitch the thought away.

Charlie watches me for a long moment. "Your drive is here somewhere, and somebody took it for a reason, girlie. You suspect the UWO of manipulating us—that's clear enough. Our mission. Our uprising. I sure hope you're wrong."

"Do you think . . . you don't think the answer is on my memory drive, do you?"

She shrugs. "I guess you won't know that unless you find it."

64

I enter my apartment and slam the door. Celine looks up. She's pushing a stack of clothes off her old bed, making space to sleep, probably. "Things go that well with Pax?"

"Not Pax. It's . . . something Charlie said in the hall just now."

Pax says to trust him. He believes he's doing the right thing. That he's doing everything he can. That he is trustworthy.

But what if he's wrong?

I groan and flop onto our couch.

"She got into your head that bad?"

I peer at my friend. "Celine, Pax took my memory drive. I found it in his apartment."

"He what? Why would he do that? I thought you found pieces of it—destroyed."

"I did. Or, I thought I did. He must have planted them." I sit forward. "He was upset when he found out Helene gave it to me. He told me to throw it away and not look at it. I guess he was serious enough to break in here and steal it."

"So go and get it!"

"I can't just . . ." I gesture broadly. "I mean."

"Why not?" Celine sits on her bed and bends to remove her boots. "Have you at least confronted him about it?"

I purse my lips.

"Of course you haven't." Celine yawns. "Listen. It seems to me there is a lot that you don't say to each other that maybe you should."

I hold back from pointing out that Celine didn't tell Elan how she felt for a long, long time. Even I could see how much went unspoken between the two of them, and I hardly knew a thing about love or relationships then.

"I need to sleep," Celine says. "Will you turn the light down?"

"Of course." I heave myself up, feeling as though I weigh twice as much as usual.

As I turn off the main light, Celine says, "Just talk to him, Pria. I have a feeling nothing good can come of it staying hidden."

"But he asked me to trust him."

She gives a sleepy shrug. "Doesn't mean he's always right." She rolls over and is almost immediately asleep.

Then I'm in the hall and staring at Pax's door, at war with myself. I've just determined to go inside when Bishop appears at my elbow. "Pria, will you come with me? Luther wished for me to record your observations so we have them ready to present to the assembly."

"Oh . . . of course." I cast a backward glance at Pax's door.

When we reach Bishop's archives, I shuffle inside and am immediately awash in the familiar smells of old books, parchment, wood, and musty fabric. But instead of feeling comforted, I feel suffocated—suffocated inside this mountain.

"What's wrong?" Bishop says. "You seem unsettled."

I turn a circle around a stack of boxes filled with as-yet-unsorted finds, and then I ask, "How do you really feel about Luther's plans?"

"They are . . . the best we can do, given the circumstances."

"The circumstances."

He adjusts his glasses. "We are too scattered and divided. We have been for decades—since this all began. That was part of the UWO's strategy. If they couldn't kill everyone who was different, and everyone who opposed them, they could at least keep them separated enough they would never be a threat. Hope they died off on their own. But that never happened. We've just grown in numbers." Bishop is puttering around, collecting a recording cube and a vid-screen. "So now, apparently, they are going back to old tricks."

"They're going to use a virus."

Bishop touches the side of his nose. "They've tried and tried to infiltrate us, with no luck. They've tried to bomb us, and we always rise again. But a virus, a resurgence of the Pandemic"—he stills—"that just might work."

"But Luther thinks there might be enough rebels now to challenge the UWO."

"It's not without great risk, of course. And it requires us all to come together. It is where he and Sarah most diverge. She always said if we banded together, the UWO would destroy us. Luther said if we stayed divided, we would all be swept away."

"Sarah didn't try to make us stay at Refuge," I say. "She told us to hurry back here. That's why we came back so soon. It was a risk, with Holly being so badly injured. And Sarah intends to try and hijack the UWO network I-I believe." Pax had said nothing of Sarah's plans to anyone since we got back, and now I wonder if it was supposed to be a secret.

"Sarah said that?" Bishop blinks at me. "But she isn't coming to the assembly, is she?"

"No . . . no. She said she wasn't."

"Peculiar." He fiddles with the recording cube, turning it over and over in his hands. "Did anything unusual happen at Refuge?"

I frown, unsure what Bishop might consider unusual. "She met with Pax, alone. After, she said we should leave right away." *After Pax told her he was a clone.* I divert my gaze, fearful Bishop might see what I'm hiding.

"Pax. It always seems to come back to him, doesn't it?"

"It does," I whisper.

"Luther might be interested to know about Sarah's meeting with Pax, and her plan to hijack the UWO net. He'd sure like to know his sister approves of his plan, for once, but he may be confused as to why she still will not come."

"I don't want him to be suspicious of Pax," I blurt out. "Not after how long it took him to trust him."

"Are you suspicious of him?" Bishop raises his brows.

"No! He's not . . . I mean, he's with us. He's for us, Bishop."

"I've no doubt about that. He loves you very much."

I swallow hard and look down. "He has something of mine—something that might help me to understand who I am. He's hiding it."

"So ask him for it."

"It's not that simple."

Bishop sets his hand on my shoulder. "Of course it is. It's just a question between two people who love each other."

I groan and cover my face.

"But for now, I have been tasked with recording your observations of the capital. You need tell me only the facts—I don't wish to pry into anything that will make you too uncomfortable."

Me—naked, in front of Wallace and the Autocrat, and the rest of the gallery of Breeders. Naked in front of all the Gentri. Sylvan Spencer shoving his tongue down my throat. My face flames hot with discomfort and the weight of memories I've tried to keep hidden. "I can tell you all about his *Operation*," I say, banishing the thoughts. "I will begin with—with the Freemasons."

65

Hours later, I leave Bishop's archives feeling as though my brain has been scooped out and left behind. I gave him all the details I could recall, down to the personal features of the Freemason clones and how it felt to have the vid-lens slowly meld itself to my eye. I'm hungry and tired and I don't know what time it is, but I have a vague feeling it's after dinnertime.

There is still some food in the dining cave—a stale loaf of bread and a simmering pot of stew. I pick up some to go.

"Pria!"

I turn at Luther's angry voice.

"Did you tell them to go? Was it Pax?"

Them—Henri and Elan. "We told them *not* to go," I say. "Pax tried to stop them."

Luther halts before me, hands on hips. "They took twelve of my best fighters with them. *Twelve.* That leaves us vulnerable and puts everyone at risk." He swears under his breath and massages his chin, studying me. "What are we going to do?"

Does he want an answer? I search his face. I don't know what he's going through, what he's feeling after the loss of his brother. The stress he's under. "I guess we wait until they get back and hope for the best. What else can we do?"

Luther huffs a humorless laugh. "Ever since you got here—you and Pax—I have felt like all my plans are being controlled by someone else. When you arrived, Pax said he'd brought you to us because he'd heard from Mack that we wanted a Breeder. And it was the truth—we did, although I can't for the life of me imagine why *Mackenzie*, who never went by Mack, would reveal something like that to a stranger like Pax. So Pax, he just . . . found you, and brought you, to us. How does one *do* that? I have gone over and over it in my head, Pria. It's just too damn convenient. Nothing about the UWO is ever easy or convenient." Luther steeples his fingers near my face. "But every time I've questioned Pax, or you, I can detect no deception. So either you're telling the truth, you're both expert liars, or you're lying and you don't even know it."

"What does all that have to do with Henri and Elan disobeying your commands?" I can't keep the affront out of my voice.

"I don't know. Nothing, probably. Something, maybe?" Luther coughs a humorless laugh. "I feel in my bones it's all connected, but I just can't see how."

I set down my food, my hands shaking. "We're not liars. We've done nothing but help you—and at great cost to ourselves, I might add."

Luther spreads his arms. "I know!" He wanders a few steps from me and then says again, "I know."

I wait until Luther has disappeared down the tunnel back to his office. All the while, words Etienne spoke to me months ago waver to the surface of my memory. *"You could be spies and not even realize it."*

With quivering fingers, I reach to the back of my neck. There's nothing there—nothing I can feel. I'm no clone. But does that mean I'm not something else?

I leave my food behind; I'm not hungry anymore.

When I get to Pax's apartment, I open the door without knocking.

He's gone. Momentary panic grips me as I take in his empty bed. But I'm not here for him.

I drag the box out from under his bed and root down through the papers to the memory drive. I don't need to ask his permission or ask why he took it. It's mine—I'm taking it back. And this time, I can view it all on my own.

Just like I did with the microchip in my arm.

I take it to the table and sit. With a deep breath, I pull up the vid in my eye and search for the drive on the table in front of me.

It's there. I connect to it and am directed to a series of files that flash across my vision in white and red. "Primary Viability." "Secondary Viability." "Tertiary Viability." "Agoge Training, Year 1." I select that one.

There are mountains of documents—more than I could ever get through—and videos, too. I click on one labeled only by a date, curious what they found to be worthy of recording.

There are many little girls, all lined up, all wearing identical knee-length green tunics and all with dark, bobbed hair. I can't pick myself out amongst them; we are all so similar. We look to be about age four. We're outside in some sort of open field, but surrounded by a high and curving wall. It's the Agoge arena—I remember that, but I have no memory of this scene, or of the severe woman who walks back and forth in front of us, inspecting us.

We're barefoot.

One little girl reaches for a blade of grass.

The woman slaps her hand with a long white stick she carries. The video has no sound, but the girl recoils with an open-mouthed exclamation.

The woman walks and the children stand.

After a minute or two, the girl reaches again, dancing a little.

"Don't," I whisper.

The woman whips around and strikes her again, this time across the shoulders. The girl falls to her knees, crying.

The woman stands and watches until the girl regains her feet and steps back in line. The other little girls don't even whisper to each other. The woman turns to look straight into the camera and then continues her slow walk up and down the line. Once or twice, another child wiggles in place, but no one other than the grass-picking girl really moves. I know it's coming, but it still grabs my chest when the little girl breaks the line again—to dart forward, pick up a rock, and throw it at the woman.

Instead of slapping the girl, this time the woman grabs her by the arm and drags her off camera. She doesn't cower as the woman takes her, nor does she fight—she maintains a stiff back and a raised chin until she disappears from sight.

The little girl was me. But I have no memory of this.

I swipe the video off the screen, sniffing, unsurprised to find tears sliding down my face.

I scroll aimlessly through the files, skipping ahead by years. I open another video file from when I was ten. I remember this one—it was a physical examination, and I was in a cold room, stripped naked, and standing with my arms outstretched looking straight ahead at a blank wall.

As a child, I didn't know what the purpose was. I thought some instruments were taking my measurements. I had no idea the wall was a one-sided window, that people were watching me. Filming me. Taking notes on me.

The notes appear along the side of the video of my scrawny, prepubescent body. Height, weight, age, measurements of my waist, legs, ankles, thighs, hips, shoulders, arms, neck, head. And then the annotations: "Hips too thin." "Tracking too tall." "Nose too prominent." "Troublesome curl to hair." "Eyes not optimum distance apart."

At the end of all the notes, a "Preliminary Recommendation:" *Field Laborer.*

I sit back and close my eyes, stomach churning. But . . . How did I end up in the Breeding Program if they thought I was so *flawed* at age ten?

I scroll ahead farther. Notes on my marks at things like memorizing the maxims of the Autocrat—I shiver, thinking of Sylvan Spencer's hands on me—and more videos. Me, exercising with my peers. Me alone in my room. At lessons.

Notes in the video margins repeat the same things: "A propensity for curiosity." "Asks an unacceptable number of questions." "Memorizes the maxims but does not apply them." "Difficult to discipline." "Could prove resistant to decipio—will require testing for higher dosage."

That one gives me pause. Is there something here? Some clue? I search on.

My eyes are growing blurry, and I still haven't figured out why they made me a Breeder if I didn't fit the physical or mental ideal. Then, I find a note on a file marked to my thirteenth year, just weeks before I was sent to Sanctuary: "Psych evaluation suggests candidacy for the Denver Initiative."

I sit up straighter and focus on that phrase. The Denver Initiative. I blink twice at it, hoping for a link to carry me to an explanation, but nothing happens. I tap on it with my finger—nothing.

"The Denver Initiative?" I minimize the file on the screen and pull up a search bar. "Denver Initiative," I type in.

Error message.

I frown. Not a "file not found," but an *error*. Like there's a block built into the drive on that phrase. I try each word separately, but without success.

The door creaks open and Pax steps in. He looks between me and the drive on the table, and his eyelids flutter slightly as he narrows his focus on my eye.

"Please tell me you didn't—you aren't . . ." His nostrils flare and he tightens his jaw.

"What's the Denver Initiative?"

He closes the door softly behind him and then comes toward me, arms outstretched like he's approaching a wild animal.

I close out my vid-lens and stand to watch him warily.

"I wish I could explain."

"That seems to be a common excuse, with you."

"It's not an excuse." I expect him to reach for the drive on the table, but instead he takes my shoulders and gives me a deep and earnest look. "It *is* an explanation."

I frown. "*What?*"

"It's the only one I can give you, in the noise."

I glance down at his hands on my shoulders, brow furrowed. "Shouldn't you be launching yourself to the opposite side of the room about now?"

Pax's face falls. "Forgive me," he says. Then he drags me to him and kisses me, kisses me with a strange tension that makes me tighten against him instead of melt into him. He's not in pain, but something is wrong.

He lifts me up and walks me back against his counter, digging his hands into my back as if he's afraid I'm going to fade into smoke if he lets go.

When he sets me on his counter, we pull apart and I look at him with bleary eyes. "Pria," he says, his voice raspy, "someday soon, you'll understand everything. I promise."

Something stings my thigh. "In the silence and out," Pax says. "Remember." He holds my neck and steadies me, his face buried in my shoulder as I slide into oblivion.

66

I rise to the surface of consciousness little by little, dipping in and out in such a way that I know it's a process of days rather than hours. Whatever Pax dosed me with, it was powerful.

"In the silence and out."

He loves me. He loves me, he loves me . . . he loves me . . .

"Remember."

The knowledge circles around in the darkness. Somehow, he thinks he did it for my own good.

When I finally fully wake, it's to find the nurse, Mona Lisa, blinking over me with a smile. She pats my head and shuffles off. To get Doc or Holly, I suppose. I can't bring myself to care. I groan and shift my shoulders, my back. Everything aches.

Groping along my body, I find the line of an IV taped to my inner arm.

"Pria." Holly enters my sight. "Finally. I was beginning to wonder if you would ever wake up."

"What?" My voice sounds like it hasn't been used in days. I close my eyes to block out the bright lights.

"Pax brought you straight here after it happened. I've never seen him so worried."

"After . . . what happened?" I open my eyes. Surely he didn't tell her he injected me with something.

"He said your vid-lens malfunctioned, or that's what it looked like. That you were together, and one moment you were fine, but the next you weren't. That you grabbed your eye and screamed, and then you passed out. You've been in a coma ever since." Holly gives me a keen look, as if inviting me to challenge the story.

I shift higher on the raised bed, arms shaking. He lied. *Of course he lied.* I say nothing.

"I've run every test I can with my limited resources here. There doesn't seem to be any damage to your eye, that I can tell. How's your vision?"

"Fine," I say. "Normal."

Holly raises a small bright light to it. I flinch, but let her check me.

"Pax has hardly left your side. Predictably," she says.

"Where is he now?" I ask, trying to keep the tremor out of my voice.

"Working with Wallace on the files, but he asked me to send word if you woke up. Do you want me to have someone get him?"

"No, that's okay. I'll go to him."

"Not yet, you won't. You just came out of a coma. I'll need you here for at least another day. Two or three, most likely."

I level a resolute gaze on her. "Holly, I need to leave the infirmary. Now."

"Why? What do you have to do?" She checks my IV bag. "You're not part of the general assembly, and you can't help with the quarantine center, in your state. You can rest now—you should rest now."

"The general assembly . . . Holly, have the leaders started to arrive?"

"They're all here. The assembly is tomorrow."

"Tomorrow! But that would mean . . ." I press my hands to my eyes. "Have I been out for *two weeks*?"

"Just shy, yes."

I lower my hands, flushing. "Why am I not invited to the assembly? I was the one *in* Washington. I put my life on the line. I saw the Autocrat's *Operation*. Luther should know my testimony is the most valuable one he has. It doesn't make any sense to exclude me."

Holly bites her lip and avoids my gaze. "Right. Maybe I spoke out of turn. Maybe he only meant because you've been here, in the infirmary." She shrugs.

But I know she's lying. I remember what Luther said to me the last time we talked. *"Either you're telling the truth, you're both expert liars, or you're lying and you don't even know it."*

My hand wanders to my thigh—to where Pax injected me with

something. My neck and face flush red with fear, with rage, with . . . uncertainty.

"Celine has been by to visit you almost as often as Pax. I'm sure one or the other of them will be back soon." Holly's voice sounds unnaturally high-pitched. Too cheerful. "Just rest, Pria. You've done enough. Doesn't it feel good to know you're finished?"

Am I?

"I guess."

As soon as Holly leaves, I sit up—my head swims only a little—and I carefully remove the IV from my arm. On unsteady feet, I tiptoe to the curtained doorway and look out.

A few people mill about the infirmary corridor, but no one I recognize, so I move out into the flow and try to act normal. Once I can see the exit, I increase my pace to a jog until I burst free and head for the hangar. If Pax is with Wallace, then that's where I'm going.

People I pass give me perplexed looks, and it's not until I'm almost to the hangar that I remember I'm wearing one of the short and flapping infirmary gowns. But I don't want to go all the way back to my apartment now, so I pull the ties tight and keep going.

Until I come to the hangar, where I stop short.

A wide space has been cleared of all vehicles and a fence has been set up. Around the exterior of the fence, enclosing a buffer of about five feet, a white chalk line has been drawn on the floor. Inside the fence is a *large* group of people. Probably two hundred or more.

"Pria?" I see a familiar form unfolding himself from the floor.

"Henri?" I take a few hesitant steps toward him. "What is this?"

He casts a disgruntled look at the fence and gives it a rattle. "Quarantine. This is Luther's compromise."

They're back with the prisoners already, because it's been two weeks. I press cold fingers to my forehead.

"Celine told me you were sick."

"You could say that." I turn a dark look on Wallace's door, then back to Henri. "Are *you* sick?"

Henri drapes his arm on the fence above his head. "Nah. Holly tested us, and everyone here is clean. But Luther said we have to wait in quarantine, just in case. After the general assembly, everyone can go free." Henri looks over his shoulder. "There are people here from *everywhere.* If the UWO *did* intend to use them as carriers of the virus, they could have let them loose to return to their families and wiped out every rebel Nest in North America." He lets out a hard breath. "If that was their plan, it's a good thing we rescued them when we did, before it was too late."

Then he steps back a pace and holds out his hand toward a dark-skinned man with greying hair. "Pria, this is my dad, Antoine."

Some of my fog clears as I look from Henri to Antoine. He's older but not old. His back is stooped, as if from hard labor. His eyes are crinkled at the edges—and kind.

"I'm so glad you're here. It's very nice to meet you," I say. I suddenly feel like I should be wearing something nicer than a medical gown.

"And you, young lady," Antoine says. "My children have told me so much about you. The Breeder. The very special Breeder."

His words ring in my ears, circling around with my memories.

The very special Breeder. *"You're different than the others."* Some of the first words Pax ever spoke to me.

That little girl, barely more than a toddler, slapped for stepping out of line.

That child, noted for being physically *un*remarkable amongst her peers.

That young teen, whose psych evaluation made her a candidate for the *Denver Initiative.*

And a cloned man willing to put her in a coma rather than tell her what it means. One who chose her and told her she was special and brought her here to destroy the UWO.

Without me, Antoine Rousseau wouldn't be standing there, reunited with his son. *I* set off a series of events that led to this.

Or did I?

"I'm sorry, I need to go," I whisper. And I run to Wallace's workshop.

67

When Wallace lets me in, I breeze past him and walk a circuit of his workshop. "Where is he?"

"Pax? He left over an hour ago—said something about needing to check on a pigeon."

"A pigeon."

"That's what he said."

I open and close my mouth, and as I turn to leave it strikes me that Wallace has been going through all the UWO Record Files. "Wallace, have you come across anything labeled the *Denver Initiative*?"

"Not that I recall."

"Do you think you can check for me?"

"Is this really important right now?"

"I think it might be, yes. I think it might be very important." Maybe. Maybe the Denver Initiative is just some top-secret breeding program. But maybe it's much more.

"Anything else?" Wallace raises an eyebrow. "I'd really like to get back to work. The general assembly is tomorrow and Luther has me digging up every last detail we can use to make sure everyone votes in favor of going to war."

"No, that's all. Thank you."

He nods curtly and turns back to his vids. "Come back later and I'll let you know if I've found anything."

I leave again, in search of Pax. If he's seeing about a pigeon, he's probably in Lovey and Moon's old apartment.

I hurry into the bowels of Asylum, threading my way through the tunnels, creeping, conscientious that Holly could be looking for me. My shoulders prickle with the sensation of being watched, being followed, but I shake it off. Of course I would feel that way, since I fled from the infirmary. As I pass a narrow tunnel that branches off from the dining hall, the sound of sobbing arrests me.

Sobbing—a woman, loud and wrenching. The tunnel is dark and looks like it narrows to nothingness. I slow and peer inside. I don't think this tunnel is used for anything; it's just a natural fissure in the rock. But the crying woman has wedged herself deep within.

I can't just walk on by, even as I prickle with impatience to find Pax.

With hesitant steps, I make my way within the fissure. "Hello?" I say. "Who is it? Can I help you?"

The woman sniffles. "Thank you. I-I don't want to be alone." Her voice sounds familiar, echoing in the narrow space off the rock walls.

I edge closer to her. She's little more than a huddled mass near the end of the fissure.

"I don't feel like I belong here. I've tried, but everyone judges me."

She raises her face and I can just make out her features. It's the Breeder—B-Twenty-one. I hunker down beside her, my knees knocking into the wall on the far side of us. "I know how you feel," I say. "It was difficult coming here for me, too. And not everyone wanted me to be here."

"So what made you stay?"

"Well . . ." I scratch the side of my face. "I had Pax. He's my friend who brought me here. And I believed in what these people were doing."

"What are they doing?"

"They're trying to . . ." I'm suddenly uncertain how much I should say. They'll have been debriefed, surely, but I don't know with what information. I cock my head to the side and say, "They're trying to make sure everyone gets to live and live free."

"Even people who don't deserve it?"

"I don't think there's anyone who doesn't deserve to live, but I understand that might be hard for you to—"

"Even criminals?" She's risen onto her heels. Her eyes are burning, intense . . . and dry. No tear-stained cheeks.

"That depends on what you mean by criminals," I say, hands tingling.

"I mean people who break the law. The law that is established by the governing powers. That's how it works, isn't it?"

She strikes before I have time to counter, slamming my head into the rock. Stars burst across my vision.

I kick her in the shin with the heel of my foot, and I wish I weren't barefoot. She's farther into the fissure and has nowhere to go. Following through on my momentum, I knee her in the stomach and jab for her throat. But it hardly fazes her. She's strong—unnaturally so. She grabs my hand and twists until I cry out, pushing me back to the wall. I try another kick, for her groin this time, but she twists and slams her hip into mine. With a deft maneuver, she flips me face-first to the rock, my arm pinned behind me.

"Stop messing around," says a man's voice. "Someone is going to notice."

Breathing hard, I dart my eyes to the opening where a tall silhouette takes up the lighted entrance.

"She fought back."

"So? You're at least twice as strong as she is. Dose her already." He steps into the tunnel and folds his arms. "We were always going to have to carry her out of here."

His face . . . I can't get any words out with my cheek and mouth pressed tight to the rock wall—just a whimper of disbelief that I didn't realize it before now. The Freemason clones looked so familiar, and now I know why. He's a few years older than the ones I saw, and his hair is still shaved nearly to the scalp. But the male Breeder—B-Four—is unmistakably a Freemason.

Which means he's not a Breeder—was never a Breeder at all. And neither is this woman into whose trap I readily walked.

Which means the UWO planted him on that X-1. Both of them. *Both of them are clones.* Because they knew we were coming. They knew our plan. Planted them . . . to get them here?

I try to scream, but the sound won't come. And then the darkness takes me.

68

"You pulled her out too early. Pulled *us* out. I had everything under control." Pax's voice. *Pax?*

A scoff—female. "After all your delaying, I'm surprised we were able to bring it together at all. You're lucky Mother has such a soft spot for you. Did you at least manage to kill the med tech before you left?"

"No. There were too many people around. And I've said it since the beginning—the med tech's inconsequential. Killing her would only raise an alarm."

An exasperated sigh. "The Freemason should have done it."

A grunt of assent from . . . the Freemason?

"No matter—they'll all be dead soon. And it's a good thing, or we'd all be facing retirement."

I cry out and rip my eyes open. A light blue ceiling and blasting cold air. A sterile bed I've woken up in before. My arms are shackled to it, and my legs.

The female Breeder . . . no, *clone* . . . Twenty-one . . . She bends over me. "She's awake," she says unnecessarily.

The Freemason, the one who posed as B-Four, smirks in the corner.

"Well, aren't you going to say something?" says Twenty-one, looking across my body. She's not talking to me. "This is your moment—the moment of your unveiling."

Pax leans over my bed, his expression dispassionate. "I suppose I must, since this is the end," he says. "We're back where we began."

"Wha—" I look between Pax and Twenty-one and Four, standing in relaxed confidence in the corner. It can't be true. Pax must be playing them. This can't be real. He can't be with them. "No," I say.

"Like all successful journeys," says a familiar voice. "You should end up back where you started, don't you think?" Mother comes into the room and Pax and Twenty-one step away. She places her hand on my forehead.

I gape, following Pax with my eyes, tears sliding down into my hair. But he gives me nothing—no wink or twitch or nod or hint of a smile to tell me he has a plan. It's as if he has been replaced with someone else.

Replaced with someone else.

He can't be my Pax. I stare him down, searching for any sign. There are thousands of Freemasons—how many others who look just like Pax does the UWO have? This isn't Pax. *It isn't.*

"You're not—" I say. "You're not him."

Pax gives me a cold look. "I am. There are no others like me, I told you that before."

"But—"

"I met you first here, in this room. I convinced you to flee with me. We found the rebels led by Luther, Bishop, Celine, Henri . . ."

As our friends' names roll off his tongue, my heart seizes and I clench my teeth to keep them from chattering.

He raises his shirt. My ears are ringing and I don't know when he stopped talking. On his abdomen is an unmistakable scar—a scar from a terrible crash and an S-hook that pierced his side. "I assure you," he says in a low voice, "I am your Pax."

My sob rips out of me, my face twisting as my eyes well with fresh tears.

"Oh . . ." Mother frowns, wrinkle lines appearing between her perfect brows. "Pax, I do believe you've hurt her feelings. How long do you think it will take her to hate you, after the performance you turned in?"

Twenty-one snorts a laugh.

"I did everything you told me to," he says, lowering his shirt.

"That you did, my boy. My *good* boy. How useful you've been." Mother glides to him and smooths a hand down his shoulder. "We'll have to come up with a reward for you. We know you find this form pleasing," she says, waving a hand toward me. She taps her lips. "Since you cannot have this one, perhaps we can arrange for a copy to be made. Surely Sylvan wouldn't mind that."

"Whatever the Autocrat desires."

A strangled cry of protest bursts out of me. Pax doesn't even blink in my direction.

"Oh, now, don't cry, Seventeen. Your tears are wasted on him." Mother turns back to me with a bemused smile. "Clones cannot *feel.* They can only act and react. And do as they are told. You fell in love with little more than an animal with his urges, his . . . perceived needs." She shudders dramatically. "You should be *thanking* us for keeping him on a leash, for your sake."

I clench my teeth against a rising need to vomit.

"Sylvan would have pitched quite the fit if anyone else had *really* touched you." Her eyes turn cold, appraising. Then she takes a cleansing breath and says, "Speaking of which, he should be arriving any minute. Freemason, go and wait by the gate for his arrival. You two get her up." Mother gestures for Pax and Twenty-one to assist me.

They unshackle my wrists and ankles and each takes an arm. Pax's grip is tight and unyielding. Cruel. Each of them is stronger than I am—I don't stand a chance.

I stumble along between them as they strong-arm me out of the room and through the med-wing. My clothes . . . they've dressed me in some ridiculous gown, long and diaphanous and flowing and cut low between my breasts to the base of my ribcage. And red. *His favorite color.* Dizziness and horror overwhelm me and I trip so Pax and Twenty-one have to drag me.

"Pax," I say, choking on tears. "Pax, please."

He is unmoved.

"She still thinks it was all real. Even after what you said, Mother. Humans are such emotionally stupid creatures." Twenty-one pinches my cheek.

Before I can stop myself, I'm sobbing—great, heaving sobs that prevent my feet from moving and obstruct my vision. Pax and Twenty-one lift me from the ground by my arms, until we are before the Looking Glass space, in the gathering room.

Sanctuary is empty, quiet, a tomb. I look around in terrified, jittering glances until Mother comes and faces me. With a critical gaze, she slaps me. Once, twice, three times. I gasp and lean back, taking several bracing breaths.

"Stop that," she says. "Stop that right now. You are ruining your looks for him. He will not be pleased. Stand up straight, shoulders back, and stop sniveling this instant."

Mother's slaps, for all their cruelty, have an immediate effect on me. Something about them snaps me out of my fog of grief and into the present with a clarity I haven't felt since I woke up.

Or maybe it's that whatever drug they gave me is wearing off and the pain is giving me the push I need.

"Liar." I straighten, but not because she told me to. "You're a liar."

Mother laughs through her nose. "I should think that would be obvious."

I sniff. My nose is dripping and I can't wipe it because Pax and Twenty-one are still holding my arms, but I don't care. I step back until I'm no longer straining against them. "You can't create a copy of me because I'm too *designed.* You need a pure genetic base—someone from before the Program. You have no intention of rewarding Pax at all."

Mother smirks. "I see you paid attention during your tour of the Operation. I told Sylvan he shouldn't show you too much, but he *insisted* we give you everything so there would be no doubt your pesky rebel leaders would meet together in one space. *I* said to show you the clones was a risk we shouldn't take." She lifts her lip. "Especially since you already knew about Pax."

Pax's grip on my arm falters just a tad—almost a twitch . . . of surprise?

"But Sylvan didn't believe me. He said he wanted to *test* you. That no human could love a clone once they saw what clones *really* are. He thought Pax would have alerted us if you knew, because of the danger it posed to our mission. "

Mother walks close to us, so close I can see the lines of lighter brown in her dark eyes. Then she turns to Pax and places a caressing hand on his face. "It's all right, Pax. I understand why you tried to hide it from us. You didn't want to be pulled out of the mission. But you needn't have worried. She was *just* stupid enough to trust you still, so you could continue to operate within that rebel rat's nest." She clicks her tongue. "I guess that's what love does to people—it makes them stupid." She pats Pax's cheek. "I forgive you for what you . . . *tried* to hide."

"Thank you, Mother."

She paces away from us, hands behind her back. I glance at Pax, willing him to look at me, but his profile is rigid—eyes staring straight ahead. The color is high in his cheeks. Does it mean anything? *Did anything we went through mean anything at all?*

"*Where* is he?" Mother says, almost to herself. "I wish to be done with this."

Sylvan Spencer is coming for me. He will make me his Empress, just as he said he would. He'll defeat the rebels. And I will never know why I was chosen. Why Pax was sent to me.

Panic overwhelms me. I can't go down without a fight.

"What is the Denver Initiative?" I say, blurting the words.

Mother stops her pacing and a predatory smile comes over her face. "Where did you learn that phrase?"

I stare at her in silent rebellion.

"*He* didn't tell you. We would have known." She tilts her head and then says, "Ah, yes. Your memory drive. That you got from your little attempt to erase your identity. How amusing."

She knows. Everything. Pax has been a direct line of intel the whole time.

She rolls her eyes, flicking at the air with her fingertips. "Honestly, the lengths you rebels go through to give yourselves the illusion of anonymity. As if we would ever lose track of you for one second. *You*."

But they did.

At Refuge, in the dead-zone, they lost track of us. Their signals couldn't get to Pax there. There, he was invisible. We were invisible. At least, I think we were.

Mother sighs. "Nevertheless, you weren't meant to see that file." She throws a dark look at Pax and then shifts her gaze back to me. "But to know that phrase . . . Did you learn how to read?"

I clamp my mouth shut and Pax's grip on my arm twitches again.

Mother squints at me. "Fascinating."

Twenty-one says in a caustic tone to Pax, "You're just lucky your mission was almost wrapped by the time she saw it, before she could go blabbing to everyone about the Denver Initiative." Then she looks at me, taking in my wide tear-filled eyes. She smiles. "Look how confused she is. Pathetic thing."

There's a deep chuckle coming from the doorway, and I turn my head to see the Autocrat stepping into the room with the Freemason at his heels.

"The Denver Initiative," the Autocrat says, "is the two of you. So lovely to see my two agents standing side by side, mission complete, finally with no more need of secrecy between you." He waves his hand in a flourish over Pax. Over me. Then he removes a pair of light-grey gloves and sets them on a divan—the one that used to be my favorite place to sit and watch the world through the Looking Glass, now newly constructed after Pax blew it up several months ago. "The Denver Initiative was established to be the final solution to our rebel problem, and I would say it has done a magnificent job, wouldn't you?"

It's a good thing Pax and Twenty-one are holding my arms, because I can't stop my legs from giving out. And when I rake my eyes up to his face, Pax is finally looking back at me, his expression dark with disdain.

69

"Oh, release her, already," Sylvan says. He unbuttons his jacket—grey, like his gloves—and sits on the divan. He pats the seat next to him as if inviting me to a friendly chat. "What harm can she do, now?"

They drag me over; they don't even bother to carry me. Then Twenty-one lets me go and Pax lifts me and sets me on the divan. I turn my face to his—searching, searching.

"In the silence and out."

"Forgive me."

"Oh, look. She still loves you. She *still* hasn't grasped the depth of your betrayal." Sylvan grabs my chin. "You will. And you will love me instead, because I am his creator and he is just a created *thing*." He settles me to his side, under the crook of his arm, and forces me to look out the Looking Glass. It's snowing now. The purity of the scene belies the abhorrence of everything going on within this place. "Do you want to know when I first chose you?"

Yes, desperately. But I can't answer; his hand is holding my jaw shut.

"I watched you, and others like you, your whole life. The ones we could break, we broke. But others . . . endured." He caresses my cheek. "I was always watching for the ones who didn't conform. Some said we should set you aside for hard labor, but I said no, not with all our *problems*. You see, for years and years—since the advent of the Unified World Order—there have been people like you who flourish outside our world. Who just . . . won't . . . *die*." He pinches my cheek so hard I gasp and lean away, but he grabs the back of my head and leans in. "Deviants," he whispers. "You found that you quite fit in with them, didn't you."

I grit my teeth and stare out at the falling snow.

"*Didn't you?*"

I flinch. "Yes," I gasp as he releases my jaw.

He takes a deep, steadying breath. "But *how* to deal with them? My forefathers stopped short with the Devastations. They were too cowardly to carry them through to completion—too afraid of going too far. As if such a limit exists!" He laughs. "After, we kept hunting the rebels with our Unfamiliars and our Hunters, but the machines have always been flawed, unable to operate in certain places. So we dissolved the Hunter program—merged it with Enforcement, and the Unfamiliars became agents of containment, little more. We still used them to hunt out rebel activity, but we were aware their limitations would prevent them from effecting the wholesale eradication of the rebel problem following the Great Incursion. And then"—he raises an epiphanous hand—"our salvation came from another division, entirely. The science of human cloning."

I cut my eyes to Pax.

"Him, yes, but not *him*." Sylvan sits back, releasing my face. "*His* model was the first truly successful model. But there was much trial and error before *he* was achieved. The Personal Automated Xeno-Sapien."

"The . . . PAX," I say.

A smile plays along Sylvan's lips. "Do you not wish to know why he looks the way he looks?" He seems to be getting perverse pleasure out of this. "Why we wouldn't craft our first to look like those of us who have been perfected? Why we chose a defiled base as our first model?"

I don't need him to tell me why. "Because it wasn't about you," I say. I take a shuddering breath and refuse to look at him, or Pax, or anyone. I stare straight out the window. "It was about them—the rebels."

"Very good. We thought if we had one that looked like *them*, we could send him in as a refugee, gain sympathy, gain their trust. They always were about welcoming freaks." He sneers, but then softens as he studies Pax. "Although I will admit I chose a base model with red hair because I am rather partial." He bites his lip, but then shakes himself and blinks. "*That* was the original goal of the Denver Initiative. Creating a 'refugee.' In fact, our first cloning labs were here, beneath this very house. Our first incubators were amongst the Breeders of Sanctuary."

I swallow hard and close my eyes. Breeders who are conspicuously missing from this quiet, vacant place. Have they killed them all?

"But then," Sylvan says, raising a finger, "we captured—"

"Mack." I cover my face. "You captured a man named Mack. Six years ago."

"She's figuring us out now, Sylvan," Mother says. She sits on my other side and strokes my hair back from my temples, tucking it behind my ears. "Go on, Seventeen. What do you think *Mack* told us?"

I level a poisonous glare on her. "I think you tortured him until he broke. I think his real name was Mackenzie and to clue in his friends that he had been compromised, he gave you a different version of his name. I think Mack told you all about Luther and his ability to tell if someone is lying, and I think Mack told you the rebel Nest he came from didn't *want* another refugee—they wanted a Breeder, but he wouldn't tell you why. So you couldn't just send in a clone after all. You needed a Breeder, too. Even if you didn't know what for."

Mother bites her lip as clear pleasure crosses her face. She raises her eyes to the Autocrat. "Such a clever girl. Not as stupid as I feared."

"Six years ago," Sylvan says, "we didn't have any who could pass for Breeders manufactured yet, and none that could be ready any time soon. Our efforts to reproduce what we had achieved with the PAX model were in full swing using other genetic bases, such as the Freemason, but the march of science does take time. We feared also that sending in a clone to play the part of a Breeder would set off suspicion, for it is impossible to manufacture a clone to truly act, feel, and behave as a human does in *all* ways. Clones can only imitate humanity, and those who take their imitations as true agency *want* to be deceived."

He means me. He means that I wanted to be deceived by Pax.

I clamp my teeth hard against his manipulative words and dart a look at Twenty-one.

Sylvan waves a dismissive hand. "She is brand new—she'd never have been accepted by the rebels like you were. Even Pax barely managed to earn Luther's trust all these months. All the trials we concocted for him to 'prove' himself!" He shakes his head with a sneer. "The mission nearly failed and failed and failed again. If not for you, Seventeen, it all would have been for nothing. We had to send in a true human, guileless"—he lifts my hair, smells it, whispers the words against my cheek—"innocent."

I shudder and lean away. "So once you had intel from Mack, you needed someone like me."

Sylvan tugs on the lock of my hair he has captured in his hand. "We admitted a whole *pool* of girls just like you to the Breeding Program here at Sanctuary. Girls who were too curious, too creative, too sympathetic to things that were *other*, too . . . strong-willed. All the qualities that would make them naturally rebel, if we removed them from the decipio and introduced the right stimuli. We studied you—all of you—watched you go through your first carries, and slowly eliminated the ones who assimilated too readily into the Program. But *you* never did. You retained those qualities I saw in you as a child. So I chose you for the Denver Initiative because you intrigued me. *I* chose you, Pria. You, who I've watched your whole life. You are so different. And I knew, when it was through, I would have you for my very own."

I shiver as he places a kiss on my neck—shiver as I realize some of the first words Pax ever spoke to me were parroted from this vile man who has stalked me from my birth. Who believes I belong to him.

Sylvan sighs against my skin. "I've been so patient—sharing you. The Initiative came first, of course. And once you were chosen, we had to prep your PAX clone. Compatibility was key, and that was not something we were willing to leave to chance."

Sylvan stands and walks to Pax—draws him over to me. "He had to be just right, or you wouldn't have taken to him, and the extraction would never have worked. Because despite your propensity to rebel, for a Breeder any man is a great shock, let alone such a flawed one. So *this* version of the PAX we crafted just for you." He draws his hand down Pax's face, not unlike he's done several times to mine. "And he has performed spectacularly, just as I designed him to—to play on your sympathies, to play to your empathy, to *make you care*. I wove a tale into his mind of sad origins and abandonment and wandering—set deep into his implanted psyche so it was more than a lie; it became part of who he was. Luther could never detect it as falsehood, even as Pax himself knew it to be false. Pax"—he gives him a disdainful look—"is nothing but an empty shell of my creation. *I* know you better than anyone alive. Everything you have ever loved about him, I put there."

Deny it! I want to scream at Pax—to jump up and rail and pound on him and kick and scream until I can't anymore. But he just stands there, calm and composed with a bored indifference to that monster's hand on his shoulder. "I don't believe you," I say hoarsely. "I don't. I won't."

But I do.

Sylvan tilts his head toward Pax. "What was the first question you ever asked her?"

Pax takes a deep breath. Is he steadying himself? "I asked her what her name was."

"*That* was an important question. It was to establish a connection between the two of you. You see?" he says to me.

"It was my idea," Mother says.

"That's right, it was. But *I* was the one who knew her name. I knew it. Tell me, Pax, did she actually tell you her name?"

Pax meets my eyes, looks away. "No."

"But she thought she did, didn't she?"

"Yes."

"Who told you her name?"

"You did."

Sylvan's face hardens. "And who punished you for using her name when she hadn't actually shared it with you yet?"

A barely perceptible shiver runs over Pax's face. "You did."

"You could have ruined everything before we had even begun. But you see, Pria"—Sylvan returns his attention to me—"the mind believes what it wants to believe. You always wanted Pax to be real, and so you filled in the gaps in logic, the spaces that didn't make sense. And in doing so, you proved to me that I had chosen the perfect person."

I am crying in earnest again. I simply cannot help it—to have my stupidity, my gullibility and vulnerability, my desire to be deceived, so laid bare . . . "The perfect person," I repeat, feebly.

"Yes indeed. The perfect person to kill them all."

70

"So it was all . . . all of it . . . *all of it* was manufactured to manipulate me." I dash my hand across my face. "To manipulate me into bringing him to—to a rebel Nest."

The Autocrat twitches his lips into a smile, Mother watches me with poisonous precision, and Pax—Pax offers a somber nod.

I flinch. "The sti-stimuli . . ." I skirt my eyes beyond Pax to the Looking Glass. Remember a splash of red blood—a girl sacrificed to a hungry mountain lion. Me, the only one of all my sisters to break down in horror. And before that, a pregnancy, terminated. A spiraling depression I couldn't escape. Doors left open when no one was around but Pax, who never should have been in a place like Sanctuary in the first place. Pax, a man sent to lure me into following him—who fed me stories and stories and stories that I just *believed.*

Because how could they have been lies?

So convenient that he had survived in Sanctuary for so long. That he knew the way out of Sanctuary. That he had a cache of supplies in the woods and clothes in just my size. That he knew how to remove my microchip—that he knew *about* microchips. That he had safe places for us to go to again and again and again. Every interaction we had after leaving Sanctuary—each one flashes before my eyes—was crafted to do one simple thing: get me to trust Pax. Trust him as my protector, my provider, my friend. To make me believe I could not survive in the outside world alone. Make me believe his story and let him lead me into the mountains.

"Even the Unfamiliar attacks," I say, slipping back into the vernacular of the UWO. "You sent them . . . to frighten me, to attack me so he would *save* me . . ."

"Of course," says Sylvan.

"Well," Mother says, "we had a miscommunication that one time . . ."

Sylvan shifts and sucks on his teeth.

I look up, and I know exactly what she's talking about. "On the mountain—when you almost killed us."

"It was Pax's fault," Sylvan says with a testy snap. "Communication was sometimes unreliable, and when he didn't send any message hinting at *why* you were leaving the rebel compound that day, we thought you were making a run for it. We thought it would be best to . . . drive you back."

"I was just . . . learning to hunt," I say. "That's all. And you almost killed me." My eyes close and I replay the attack on the mountainside—the Golems tearing through our ships. Pax shielding me with his body. Pax yelling *stop*, as if he were talking to someone else.

"It was not our intention to kill you, but I will admit it was a close thing. And, as it turns out, the better for it. You went scampering back to the rebels *terrified* of our power." Sylvan turns and stares out the window. "Every Unfamiliar attack was an orchestration. Anything to keep you together—reinforce your trust in him and your desire to help those deviants."

A flush of fearful rage races through me. "What have you done to them? Did you—did you *bomb* Asylum?" I gather my strength and leap to my feet.

"Bomb them?" He chuckles. "No." Sylvan faces me. "Why would we go through all this just to bomb one Nest? Or two? We have bombed many rebel Nests. Though satisfying, it is a foolish strategy that does not, in the long-term, work. Our problem has always been the scattered nature of the rebels. What we needed was a means to gather people from all the Nests into one place."

"For the Pandemic virus," I say, going cold. "That's your plan. That's the endgame."

"It is not a game," says Mother, sharply. "Do you consider the survival of the dominant species of humanity a *game*? It's the mission of the Denver Initiative. It is Pax's prime directive and compulsion, and he cannot act against it. The only way to destroy the rebels is from within, and Pax is programmed to do just that. Gain the trust of the Breeder and, through her, gain access to the rebel Nest controlled by Luther. Infiltrate the highest ranks of the rebel Nest and determine what they wanted with you. Report any significant intelligence relating to the eradication of the rebels in North America. Manipulate and aid the rebel leaders into a gathering of forces against the UWO. And then"—she smiles—"we would be finally able to deliver the killing blow."

My heart skips a beat. Not because I'm terrified for Asylum, though I am, but because Mother is missing something.

Our mission to Sanctuary was for files to use as fuel for joining all the rebel Nests. In a sense, our mission was exactly the same as the UWO's mission—to gather all the rebels together. But our mission *failed*, because Mother didn't release the files. She gave us nonsense. Why would she do that, if she wanted all the rebel leaders to gather, same as we did?

Because she didn't know what we wanted the files *for*. She didn't have that piece of intel when we went back to Sanctuary.

Because Pax didn't give it to her. He resisted the compulsion to obey.

My heart is beating wildly. *They didn't know.* They should have known, because Pax should have told them. Getting the files from Sanctuary months ago would have meant the UWO's goal—a meeting between Nest leaders—would have happened much sooner. That was exactly what Mother and the Autocrat wanted—what Pax was *programmed* to do. So they say.

I twist my sweaty fingers until I can't feel them and I stare at Pax, willing him to break. Willing him *not* to break. Willing my hope not to be in vain.

"Someday soon it will all be clear, and then you'll know. I hope you will still love me then."

"Why don't you just take her and leave, already?" Twenty-one says. "If you tell her everything, we will be here all night."

I catch my breath, waiting for Sylvan to explode at the casual address, but he merely smiles and says, "I want her to understand. With understanding comes acceptance, and I prefer an Empress who accepts her position over one who must be kept a prisoner."

I swallow hard, sure he'd take just as much pleasure from keeping me a prisoner.

Mother sighs. "Pax found out what Luther wanted with my files *after* our little charade here when you hacked my system and I let you escape. If I'd known ahead of time, we could have played all this out much sooner."

My heart thunders in my chest and I hardly dare to breathe. Pax didn't find out *after*; he knew before we left.

Mother goes on. "We had already compelled him to take you back to Asylum and keep you close to Luther, so we needed a new way to get you the files Luther wanted, without making it obvious it was coming from UWO sources. So Sylvan called for Gentrification."

"It was long overdue, anyway," Sylvan says, grinning. "I fed the intel about Gentrification to a Nest allied with Luther's—one a little less scrupulous than his. I assured it would make its way to you."

"The intel came through Charlie," I say. "But you sent that man—Dougal—one of your own. And you compelled Pax to kill him." I press my hands to my stomach.

"Luther *still* didn't fully trust Pax—he needed a push," Sylvan says.

I grab my head and think through everything that happened, from Charlie arriving with Nyck Ridley and Dougal, through Denver Commune to erase my identity, through getting my memory drive from Helene.

Helene.

"The woman who helped us in the Commune—"

"Is quite dead." Sylvan yawns.

I huff and return to the divan, sitting down hard.

Pax, in the Commune, to guide us—*me*—back out. Pax's strange and intimate knowledge of the layout of Denver Commune. Pax, never objecting to the plan to Gentrify me.

All Pax ever had to do was put on an Enforcer uniform, and none of us questioned too deeply how easily he moved among the UWO. Save for Luther. And Charlie. The rest of us didn't question it because Pax gave us what we needed, and what we wanted.

And after everything, they got what *they* wanted: all the rebel Nest leaders together, to infect with the Pandemic so they would take the virus back to their Nests and their families where it would spread across the continent and kill every last human.

But Pax didn't always *do* as they compelled him, and—

I cough out a laugh. Slap my hand over my mouth and laugh again.

"What?" Mother says sharply.

"We rescued those prisoners you intended to infect. *They aren't sick*. And Pax—" *told us not to rescue them. A warning—he knew what Mother and Sylvan intended.* I swallow the words. I start again. "My friends rescued them. And they're all back in quarantine in Asylum and *none of them* are sick." Mother and Sylvan exchange a caged, pleased look.

"Please," Sylvan says, his voice preternaturally calm. "You are merely telling us of our own success. Of course you rescued them—you were supposed to rescue them. That was the point of the entire Initiative. They may appear not to be sick, but I assure you"—Sylvan leans close to me—"they are quite infected. Your rebellion—every rebellion in North America—is finished."

"It's not," I say, denial beating against my ribcage.

"It is." Sylvan's voice turns cold and clipped. He turns his attention on Pax, and his demeanor sharpens. "Despite the *efforts* of my creation to sabotage me right at the end."

Pax's face drains of all color, and he stiffens.

"I knew you told those rebel rats not to rescue those people nearly the moment it happened," Sylvan says. "It is why you are no longer of any use to me." He tilts his head and Pax's composure breaks.

With a garbled cry, Pax falls to his knees, coughing blood onto the white floor.

71

Sylvan ignores Pax's strangled coughs. He talks louder, to me again. "Using the other two *just* as decoy Breeders would have been such a waste of resources. I had them watching him, of course. He thought I didn't know he was hiding things from me—that the punishments were mere electrical impulses sent automatically through the implant whenever he tried to disobey his primary objective—but I knew. I always knew he was *testing* his limits." He widens his eyes and Pax arches his back and groans.

"*Stop it!*" I try to fling myself over Pax, but Mother catches me and holds me back.

"Ever since he started *rutting*, he's been difficult to control. You have no idea the monitoring it's taken," Mother says.

"Come now—I've held tight to his leash." Sylvan's eyes are maniacal as he presses closer to Pax, bearing him to the ground. Pax spits more blood as he writhes. "Except when we've *needed* him to draw her close."

Mother makes a *tsk*ing sound.

"Haven't you ever dealt with a wild animal before? It's exhilarating." Sylvan smooths Pax's hair from his sweat-streaked forehead.

"I have, and I know how dangerous it can be. I told you we should have put him on the decipio."

I whimper and struggle against Mother, who shoves me into Twenty-one's arms. "Deal with her."

The Freemason steps out of whatever corner he's been lurking in. He watches Pax with a fascinated tilt to his head.

Sylvan bares his teeth at Mother. "And I told *you* she never would have trusted him on the decipio. Besides, clones don't need decipio to control their feelings. Because they aren't true feelings! They're the instincts of an animal. And like an animal, he was obedient while I held him close, but the longer he was out of his cage, the more he became feral. And now that he's served his purpose, like an animal, it's time to put him down."

"He's not an animal," I say, my voice hoarse and weak. "*He's not an animal.*"

Twenty-one laughs. "Shut up."

Pax groans and shudders and rolls onto his back. Sylvan is toying with him. He's going to end it soon. He's going to end Pax.

But I see it clearly. In his agony, I *see* it. No matter what Pax's *primary objective* was, he chose again and again and again to betray it—for me. Maybe he didn't even realize it at first. Maybe he surprised even himself, because he'd believed what they said of him. But then he started to change, to see *himself* as human, and his feelings for me deepened, and his choices transmitted through his implant as rebellions against his primary objective. He chose to live, and that was resistance. And in time, those betrayals began to hurt him, to cost him. He was supposed to make me trust him, and they did their job too well, because I fell in love with him.

But they never believed he was capable of loving me in return.

And that is where they've fatally underestimated him.

And me.

"I trust you, Pax," I say, just loud enough for him to hear. "In the silence and out. You are not what they made you, on the inside."

Twenty-one digs cruel fingers into my arm. "We are *exactly* what they made us. You don't know anything about it."

"You're not," I say, looking into her dark eyes. "You want to blame Sylvan for what you're doing to me, but you can't. You're just a horrible person who *enjoys* hurting people."

She parts her lips as if to protest, but the truth of it strikes deep in her gaze, and her grip on my arms falters.

Sylvan Spencer raises his lip into a snarl, animalistic. "And you're just a Breeder bitch who won't let go of the toy I threw in her kennel. I—"

But his voice cuts off with a gargle as Pax's bloody hand grasps him around the throat.

Pax grits his teeth, holding the Autocrat steady. "I—have had—

enough—of *you* in my head."

Sylvan's face turns purple as he claws at Pax's hand.

"Sylvan!" Mother rushes at him, but Pax knocks her away with his other hand and she goes sprawling on the floor. He stands, legs shaking but arm steady, until he holds Sylvan Spencer by his neck, high above his head.

"Enough," Pax says.

"Stop!" Twenty-one redoubles her grip and shakes me. "I'll snap her neck. You know I can do it."

Sylvan gurgles and kicks his feet.

I throw an elbow toward Twenty-one's face, which she readily dodges. She puts me in a headlock. "Let the Autocrat go."

"No," I gasp.

But Pax breaks. The rage in his eyes clears as the lines in his face fall into despair. He lowers Sylvan to the floor and then shoves him away, hard, so he falls backward over the divan. Pax takes two quaking steps toward me, arms outstretched. Blood dribbles from one of his ears.

"Let her go," he says.

And then the room behind him lights up with fire and light and sound. I have only a moment to see Pax glance over his shoulder before he tackles us to the floor and we go down in a tangle of limbs and splintering furniture and glass.

72

Airships are firing, on and on. And then they stop, and a cold bite of wind blows snow into the space. I am pinned under Pax's warm body.

Warm . . . and dripping blood.

With a gasp of panic, I wriggle out from under him—my ridiculous red dress catching and tearing—and roll him onto his back. "Pax, Pax, please be okay. " I grab his face, his neck, his cheeks.

Beside us, Twenty-one lies with gaping eyes and a hole in her chest the size of my fist.

Pax takes a deep, rattling breath—and another. Weeping, I press my forehead to his chest. He flutters his hand over my hair. "In the silence . . . and . . . out," he says.

I nod against him.

We love each other.

Someone makes a dash for the opening in the wall that used to be the Looking Glass. There's a shriek, followed by scuffling, and then sobbing.

"It's over." It's a woman's voice, but it's not Mother.

I look up, squinting through the dust and the blowing snow. "Sarah?" I say, but my voice is no more than a breath.

I turn bright eyes on Pax. He smiles, weakly, and gestures for me to help him up.

Footsteps crunch over broken glass—heavy footsteps laden with purpose.

"Pax? Pria?" Sarah says. "You alive in here? My apologies, we didn't mean to shoot *at* you."

"You're just in time." Pax leans heavily on me as we limp out of the shadows.

Beyond Sarah, uniformed rebels from Refuge are hauling a restrained Mother into an open vessel that has landed in the clearing outside the Looking Glass. She shrieks and writhes, twisting against her captors. "You're all going to die! You can't stop what we have begun. You'll never—" A Refuge soldier shoves her head-first into the hold of the vessel.

My heart chills as I watch the scene, but Pax just looks at Sarah. "The decipio?" he asks her.

She holsters her energy rifle as she steps over a section of blown-out wall. "There won't be any more decipio coming out of the capital ever again. Your coordinates for the production depot were spot on, and my people are dismantling the Commune plants as we speak." She grins and slaps Pax on the back.

He flinches but gives her a grim smile. "And the antidote?"

"In production. It will go into the water supply within the week."

Pax sits down heavily on a charred piece of the divan, sliding out from under my arm.

"Antidote," I say, "to the Pandemic." My mouth drops open as my eyes dart back to the vessel that holds Mother. "Sylvan said they didn't fail. He said the people at Asylum would all be dead soon. He said—"

Pax takes my hand and squeezes. "Sarah . . . has it covered. It's going to be okay. *They're* going to be okay."

"Luther knows to keep them in quarantine until the antidote is administered," Sarah says.

"So they really are sick!"

"They will be. They were infected with a pill designed to slow-release the virus into their systems. It wouldn't reveal in any blood tests on arrival to Asylum. None of them appeared sick—technically were sick—when Henri and Elan brought them back. But they would have been."

"How do you know all this?" I ask.

"When it came to the Pandemic," Pax says with effort. "I was . . . compelled to hide it from you. I didn't even know about it until Brant. He got away from them, somehow. When we found him, I was to stop him, to hide his illness. And I was supposed to ensure the rescue of the prisoners—to be timed to whenever Luther called the general assembly."

"So the leaders would contract the Pandemic," I say. "But instead you tried to prevent the rescue of the prisoners."

Pax nods. "Sylvan had the Pandemic engineered to be released when all the leaders met together. For so long, that was my primary objective—get the rebel Nest leaders together. If he could infect them with the Pandemic and send them home to their Nests, they would kill everyone. There wouldn't even be a revolution." Pax shifts and winces, takes a deep breath. "Once I understood, I tried to disobey the compulsion. I tried to tell Celine and Henri *not* to rescue the prisoners, but giving that warning was in direct contradiction to my primary directive, and it . . ."

"It almost killed you."

He raises pained eyes to me. "That's why I couldn't do more, say more, to prevent their rescue. And of course, I failed, because Celine and Henri were determined. The two clones must have overheard and told on me, as well, because for all his posturing, Sylvan Spencer could never read my mind, even if he could yank on my *leash* when he knew I was resisting." Pax's lip twists. "After Elan and Henri left, I did the only thing I could and sent a pigeon to Sarah. Because of how he punished me, I couldn't have told Luther. There was still so much I had to do to try and make sure you survived and Sarah succeeded with the rest of our plans, and I was barely holding on—"

I stop him with a kiss, pulling him close for just a moment. His eyes glaze and he tightens against me, straining all his muscles, but then he relaxes with a deep sigh.

Sarah gives an approving nod, her lips twitching into a smile. "Given the circumstances, it is amazing what you did, Pax. What we all managed to accomplish. By the time any of them start to show symptoms, the antidote will be ready for Holly to administer it to them. You really did it. You liberated North America without a war—without sacrificing the Freemasons. And you came out alive. You didn't expect that."

"*You* did it," he says. "I just . . ." He wobbles and nearly falls off the divan.

I catch him.

Without sacrificing the Freemasons. The UWO network. I cut a glance at Sarah as my heart skips a beat. "The network is still up. You hijacked the system! Pax is going to be okay!"

Sarah's face splits into a grin. "We di—"

There is a scuttle of movement and the Autocrat rises from the ashes behind us. With a sneer twisting his blood-streaked face, he thrusts his hand at Pax, and Pax goes rigid. His eyes roll back in his head and he falls to the floor.

Then Sarah is shouting, and a man is leaping through the shattered glass, energy rifle raised. The snowflakes are bright white against his dark skin, and sunlight glints off his single gold earring. *Etienne?* I think, just before he shoots at the Autocrat, twice, three times. Sylvan crumples, blood spewing from his open mouth as he throws back his head in a final, defiant laugh.

Pax lies face-down in the ashes, blood trickling from both ears, his neck twisted at an odd angle.

"Sarah!" I scream, my voice a shrill siren. "Sarah, he's dying! He's dying, help him!"

Rebels from Refuge rush in, surround us, and then carry him away. I follow in their wake, trying to keep a hand on Pax—to keep close to him as they strap him to a stretcher on board one of their shiny silver ships.

And then we are airborne.

73

The infirmary at Refuge is too neat and tidy after the chaos of the fight at Sanctuary, the blood, the disarray.

Juan is talking to me, his voice sad. Resigned. He sounds far away, or like my ears are stuffed with cotton. "Pria, did you hear me?" he asks. "I'm so sorry, but the implant was damaged beyond repair. We had to remove it. If we'd left it in, it would have poisoned his blood."

I nod. Lick my lips. "Can I see him now?"

Juan rubs his upper lip and shifts from one foot to the other, stalling. "He's still under the induced coma." His eyes are dark with concern. He thinks I don't understand, but I do. "Without the implant, Pax has no residual data stored on which to live, and no way to be reconnected to the network."

"He has a *brain*." I think I say it out loud. Maybe I whisper it.

"Yes, but . . ." He sighs. "This is a whole new area of science. We have never operated on human clones before, never studied how their implants interact with their brains. We don't know if—"

"Can I see him?" I raise my eyes. "That's all I need to know."

Juan stares at me a moment longer, and then he takes my hand in his. "Pria, I'm trying to tell you we don't know what he will be like when he wakes up. *If* he wakes up. He might live only a minute or two. Maybe an hour . . . a day? Or he might die the moment we bring him out of the coma. And if he does wake up, he might be different. He could have a whole new personality, or no personality at all. The implant chip at the back of his neck was wired throughout his brain, and—"

I stand. I'm still wearing the tattered red dress, but someone has given me a white medical jacket to wear over it, and black military boots for my feet. I walk slowly into the next room, where Pax is.

He lies on his back with his head covered in bandages so thick they're like a helmet. He's hooked up to a machine that is beeping at regular intervals.

"Clones cannot *live without the uplink to the UWO net,"* Pax told me in the graveyard above this place.

I sit in a chair facing him, studying his features and clenching my fists—trying to keep my breathing under control. Trying not to panic. How many more like him were there? How many more were created for the Denver Initiative just to be destroyed because they didn't fit . . . *me.*

The beeps of Pax's machine increase in frequency, and his eyes start to move beneath his lashes. I lean forward, anticipating. Dreading.

He opens his eyes groggily, one lid at a time, and then closes them again, as if the light hurts. I touch his cheek. He tries again and struggles to focus.

"It's me," I say.

"Pria?"

My heart feels like it will burst. I nod as tears sting my eyes. He knows me.

"Do you know who you are?"

Confusion crosses his face, knits his brow.

"What's your name?"

"I . . . don't know."

I bite my lip to hold in a whimper. "You're Pax," I say, brushing my knuckles down his cheek. "Pax. Do you remember that name?"

"I remember . . ." He squeezes his eyes shut. "I remember . . . I am a PAX-model clone. I am Fifteen. I am PAX-Fifteen."

I can't speak, so I lean over him, my lips a fluttering kiss on his forehead. He doesn't move. I think he may be asleep again. I want to burst into tears, but I don't want to trouble him. I don't want to make him as afraid as I am.

I push my chair back and lurch to my feet before stumbling out into the hall. There, I press my hands to my chest and try to keep from hyperventilating. Nurses skirt around me with sympathetic gazes until I hear a voice that breaks through my fog.

"Pria!"

I open my arms, and Celine barrels into them.

"He's going to die, Celine. And he's . . . different. It's like he's reprogramming, or something." I cling to my friend and sob onto her shoulder. "They took out his implant because it was killing him, but now he will die because he doesn't have it. He might not even be *him* anymore, but I can't stop loving him, and I don't know what to do. What do I do?"

Celine lets me cry until I can't anymore, and then she sets me back and takes my face in her hands. "That implant didn't make him love you—he loved you despite it. And that kind of love never goes away, no matter how deep it gets buried. So you march back in there and you *tell him* who he is. He saved us all—you both did. Now you get to save him. It doesn't matter how long he has left to live. His life is worth it."

I square my shoulders and take a bracing breath. "Thank you," I say. She squeezes my arm and then shoves me toward his room. Ducking back inside, I find him staring at the ceiling with glazed eyes.

"Hi," I say in a quavering voice.

He turns his head slowly toward me. "You look . . . afraid?"

I nod.

"Of what?"

"Of what will happen next. That you won't . . . remember . . ."

"I remember you," he says. "I could never forget you."

I draw up my chair so I am close to him. "But you don't remember everything."

"I have . . . blanks." He taps his forehead. "Why do I have blanks?"

"They took out your implant." I can't keep the despair from my voice. "The doctors here at Refuge did. They had no choice. The Autocrat tried to kill you. Do you remember?"

Pax's eyes lose focus with confusion, but then he says, "He was the noise in my head, always telling me what I had to do, what I could and could not do." He runs a weak hand down my cheek. "He wanted me to manipulate you, but he didn't want me to love you."

I stretch my lips tight and nod. "When he tried to kill you, it destroyed your implant. And now the implant is gone. And that means . . ." I can't say it. I grasp his hands and cry over them.

"It means I will die."

I nod against our clasped hands. "Sooner or later—there's no way to know. They don't even know how you're still alive. You could die now, in my arms. Or in an hour, or—" I choke on my words and give in to silent, shoulder-shaking sobs.

"But I'm finally free, and so are you."

I sniff and look up into his clear blue eyes. "I would happily be a slave to the Autocrat if I knew you would live a full life," I say fiercely.

But Pax shakes his head. "It was never about saving me. Better to die a free man than a slave to the Unified World Order. I knew I was working toward my death and your liberation from the moment I started loving you."

He sighs and lets his eyes drift closed.

"Pax!" I shake him.

"Mmm?" He peels his eyes open again.

I throw my arms over him, sobbing, and he grips my back a moment before his arm slackens.

"I am so tired," he says. "Can we rest a bit?"

I climb onto the bed beside him and curl my body around his, as close as I can get. I can hold him, but I can't hold on to him. He never belonged to me. The UWO may have designed and programmed him for me, but he is a free man. He will die a free man.

For now, though, we will sleep. And I will hope for the morning.

74

Celine wakes me with a soft hand on my shoulder. "Pria?"

I jolt upright with a gasp and swivel my head, eyes groping for Pax's face. It takes a moment for me to register that Pax's body beside mine is warm, and his heart is beating beneath my hand on his chest. I nearly collapse with relief.

"How long has it been?" I say.

"A few hours. Juan wants to check his vitals, but he didn't want to disturb you. I volunteered." She tilts her head toward the hallway. "Come on and take a break—let the medics work." I take her hand and climb down from the bed. With a last glance at Pax's sleeping form, I follow her into the hall. Juan and a couple of Refuge nurses pass into the room in our stead.

Celine stops me and squeezes my hand. "I need to tell you something. Before you find out some other way and give yourself a heart attack."

"Oh?" I rub the sleep out of my eyes and blink at her.

She takes a deep breath. "Etienne is here. He's been working for Sarah these last few weeks, and—"

"He killed the Autocrat," I say, the daze wearing off. The soldier who shot Sylvan Spencer. It *was* him. "I saw him. I remember."

Celine wraps an arm around my shoulders. "Etienne is trying to make things right—in his life . . . with you. He's too ashamed to come and see you, yet. But I thought you should know. He hopes you'll forgive him for what he did." She takes a deep breath. "I forgave him. I hope you aren't angry with me for that."

"Of course not. He's your brother."

Celine gives me a closed-lip smile. She takes my hand and leans her head on my shoulder. Silence stretches around us, and then she says, "Sarah has a brilliant team, you know."

I don't answer, because I can't bear to give voice to my hope—the hope Celine shares—that Sarah's team will find a way to save Pax.

"I mean, if they can make an antidote from Pax's immune blood . . ." Celine whistles long and low. "They can *literally* save the world."

Pax's immune blood. He was infected, and then he wasn't. "Clones are immune." I say. "I did wonder—when Pax survived."

"Pax figured that out, too. He risked sending a tiny blood sample to Sarah via pigeon and asked her if she thought they could manufacture an antidote and a vaccine from his blood. She set her people right to work on it, and . . . they did it. Now that Sarah has access to the Freemasons, she has an unlimited supply of blood to work with."

"The Autocrat didn't want his clones contracting the Pandemic," I say. "So when the virus ravaged the continent, he could send out his clones to take up the work that needed doing." I shake my head.

"Sarah is going to administer the vaccine to everyone, just to be safe. But we think we got ahead of the Pandemic before it got out."

"How many more prisoner compounds are there?"

"We don't know yet." Celine twists her lips. "Henri is going to go, with my dad, to look for them—to set prisoners free."

"But you're not going with them."

She gives her head a slow shake, her smile turning sly.

"Because you're pregnant."

"I *knew* you knew."

It feels good to laugh. I grab her shoulders and squeeze her as hard as I can. In the midst of my devastation, this is a great joy, worthy of my full celebration.

We pull apart and Celine wipes away happy tears. She says, "Is it stupid to say, after everything we've been through, that I am afraid? Of *this*?" She presses her hands to her stomach.

"It's not stupid at all. It is fearful, and . . . wonderful."

Celine's smile falters. "The UWO took your baby from you."

"Two babies, and even the memories of the pregnancies. I will never know what could have been."

"There's still time." Celine takes my hand and looks meaningfully at Pax's room.

I quirk my lips and look down, avoiding her gaze. Clones are engineered to be sterile. But I don't say it, because she means well.

Instead I squeeze her hand. "Is Luther upset he didn't get his war?"

She laughs. "Oh, Pria. I've never seen Luther so happy in my entire life. He'd be here now, but he's conferring with the Nest leaders and managing the quarantine and the antidote. The people in the Communes are waking up now, with the decipio shut down. Refuge hijacked the UWO net and they've been broadcasting nonstop that the Autocrat is dead. The Golems have been taken offline. UWO loyalists are outnumbered." She grins. "News is already spreading to the other Continents. The rest of the Oligarch will be running scared in no time."

I listen to Celine's report with mounting exhilaration. It just feels almost impossible.

But . . . Pax is still dying. He gave his life for this.

Juan and his team of nurses exit Pax's room. As they walk past, Juan inclines his head and says, "He's still with us. The wound is healing—that's the most I can say."

"Thank you."

I leave Celine and return to Pax's beside, for whatever time we have left.

75

Someone brings our things from Asylum to Refuge. Even Pax's motorcycle, salvaged from the woods beyond Denver Commune. Henri found it, perhaps? A peace offering. I once again have clothes that fit me and a sense of belonging—a sense of home.

I don't think I'll ever leave Refuge. Even after Pax dies.

It's been a week. A week, and I count every minute of every day, knowing each one could be our last. Juan reminds me at every turn that I should not hold on to too much hope, but how can I not hope as Pax's color returns, and his appetite, and his strength? His memories trickle back like birds alighting on a tree, and when I catch him frowning into the middle distance, I know not to bother him, but to let him sit and think and be.

I stay in his infirmary room as much as I can, because he wants me there, and because there is no other place I'd rather be. I am the only constant in his memory, he says. So I stay, we stay together, with our meager belongings from Asylum piled around us.

Celine and Bishop bring me out to eat lunch, and life begins to feel normal. But when I get back to Pax's room, I find his bed turned down with fresh sheets and the lights off. Our personal belongings are stacked along the wall as if ready for a move.

"He's not here," Holly says from behind me, unnecessarily.

I spin around, my heart thumping. "Where? Where did he go?"

She raises her hand. "He's *alive.* He's fine. In fact, they discharged him."

I give her a hard and frightened stare, but she tilts her head and says, "He'll be okay, Pria. Trust him." With a small smile, she tucks her vid-screen under her arm and then turns back for one more thing. "I know"—her voice catches—"I know he saved my life. He was supposed to kill me, and he didn't. I know what he did for me, and for Trent." She jerks her chin in a nod and hurries out, overcome.

I turn to head out the door in search of Pax, and run headlong into Sarah. She laughs, making sure I'm stable, her hands on my shoulders. Then her smile wavers. "I can see you're looking for Pax, but before you find him, I have to tell you—"

"Oh Gaia Earth, what?" I press my hand to my racing heart.

"We've completed a model of a new implant that could work for Pax—for any human clone, if something like this ever happens again. We could uplink him back onto the network."

I gasp, but Sarah sighs, chewing on her lip. "Installing our implant would have been all experimental, but it could have meant his survival."

"What do you mean, *could have* meant? *Would have* been?"

Sarah looks at the floor. "He said no, Pria."

My knees go weak and I slump against the wall. "But *why*?"

"You will have to ask him for yourself." She tilts her head to the hallway, indicating I should follow her.

So I do, even though my feet weigh me down with every step. I follow her to the tram that takes us to her apartment at the end of the line. The first Refuge. From there, I don't need her to tell me where to go.

I climb the old ladder until I reach the hatch, which is open to the cold air. A light dusting of snow covers the ground, and over by the graveyard sits Pax with his back to me on the bare tree stump. His head wrappings are gone, all that's left a single bandage that covers a long scar down his scalp to the base of his neck. His hair, shorn off a week ago, is beginning to grow back in tiny spikes of gold that catch the light when he tilts his head—the only indication he gives me that he knows I have arrived.

I make my way to him, and when I'm close enough, he says, "I remember everything about us now."

I touch his shoulder. "Tell me."

"I remember how you looked when you woke up and saw me for the first time. How I felt when I discovered you didn't know how to read. How it felt when I first held your hand. How you *saw me* and weren't disgusted. How amazed I was that you valued my life on that roadside when I almost went over the edge. How you valued me enough to put your own life in danger." He stares off into the sky, his face full of awe, and then he looks at me. "I started to fall in love with you for all those reasons and more."

He's turning something over and over in his hands—something that flashes in the light. He stands and faces me and places it around his neck. It's the S-Hook that pierced his side when we crashed in the Golem attack, now threaded to a leather strap. His wound . . . his scar . . . it's a defining mark that sets him apart from any others who look like him.

I step closer and slide my hand under his shirt, touching the scar. "I knew I loved you when you suffered this. I almost lost you, and I couldn't—I couldn't imagine life without you." I blink back tears. "I would have done anything to save you, and I still would."

Pax closes his eyes. "I remember what it felt like the first time we kissed, when all I wanted was to be close to you, and then the noise in my head"—he opens his eyes—"the compulsions started to drive me away."

I nod. I understand now.

"I had to save you, so I tried to stay away. But I had to save them, too, our friends. The compulsions were . . . *awful*." He lets out a hard breath. "When I got on the outside and saw—saw that what they'd told me about you and so much else was a lie, I saw that maybe in loving you, I would be strong enough to disobey them. But I found that if I disobeyed the compulsions too directly, they somehow always knew, and then they punished me."

"But he—they—couldn't read your mind," I say.

"No. . ." He frowns. "It was hard to act against them. But I could hide information from them, as long as I didn't think about it too directly. Sometimes I could convince myself there was a way that omitting intel was fulfilling the compulsions. I practiced keeping my mind blank, but I couldn't *not* pay attention or just leave Asylum, because I was the only one—the only one—who knew about the Denver Initiative who had *also* turned against them. I could play the role of loyal agent to the UWO and loyal rebel agent simultaneously—I had a chance of using their own Initiative to destroy them, if I could only figure out how."

"But it almost killed you."

He shrugs. "I expected it to—in the end. I hope you know I *wanted* to tell you everything. I wanted to tell Luther. To a degree, they expected me to—to act out, I guess, in small ways. But large rebellions, and regular ones, were noted and . . . punished. They could *tell* when I acted against the compulsions. I came to realize my independence could only ever mean my death, and your death, and then they would just start anew with a new clone, a new Breeder, a new rebel Nest—even if it took them years. If they were to be stopped, I had to maintain absolute secrecy.

"And then . . ." Pax tilts his face to the sun and smiles—actually smiles. "And then we came here—a place the UWO has no knowledge of. A silent place. But we couldn't stay for long."

"Because you were off the network."

He twists his lips. "I had enough residual data to last. But, no. We couldn't stay for long because they would have grown suspicious of my silence. There are dead zones where the signal is weak, but to go silent completely . . ." He shakes his head. "They would have come looking for me. They would have descended on the last place my implant transmitted from, just outside Refuge. My presence here put Sarah and her people in the gravest danger they have ever been in. That is why we could not stay."

"I see," I say, and I do. And it chills me to know how close we came to bringing destruction on Refuge.

"But realizing this was a truly silent place meant that I had finally found someone with whom I could share my secret, and someone who could help me in my subterfuge. I could work with Sarah—tell her everything, without the compulsions wrecking my head."

"But why couldn't you tell *me*?" It's a plaintive question, but I ask it anyway. I clench my hands into fists and hug my chest, feeling once more the heaviness of all his lies, all his secrecy.

He takes my face in his hands. "I wanted to. I wanted to so badly. When we left here, I didn't have to hide knowledge of Refuge from them, because it was a place that didn't exist to them. But you were part of the Initiative. If I'd told you, that would have been knowledge I would have had to carry away from this place—outside the dead-zone. Knowledge I would have had to keep hidden until the end, and I didn't trust my strength for that. I was already coming apart."

I nod, tearfully. And then he's embracing me, and we cling to each other, chests rising and falling in tandem.

"I was born to a clone surrogate in Sanctuary," Pax says, breathing the words into my hair. "I was PAX-Fifteen. I don't know the name of the Breeder who was my mother, but I know I came into being eight years ago. When I reached a twenty-year development level, they removed me and the other PAX models from the growth stimulation hormones and let us progress at natural rates. I called them my brothers. The UWO told us we were the same, but we were not—we were unique, each one of us. We were studied day and night, and Sylvan Spencer was there, sometimes in person, but always in my head, compelling me. And then one day, the compulsion come over me to—to kill them. To kill them all." His arms tighten around me. "And I did. And they sat there, staring at me while I snapped their necks. The last of them had tears in their eyes, because they knew why I did it, and I knew why they didn't stop me."

Pax pulls away and looks at me. Tears stream down his cheeks. "But now I think, what if I could have stopped myself?"

I open my mouth to protest, but Pax shakes his head. Takes my face in his hands again, kisses my forehead. "No. I know you came up here to convince me to accept the implant Sarah's people made for me, but I want you to know why I can't do it, Pria. I won't. I won't ever give another person that sort of control over me, no matter their good intentions. I may die today or tomorrow or the next day, but I will die with a free mind. I will never willingly allow another person to control my actions."

I grab his face. "But I don't want you to die."

Pax lifts me up by my waist and holds me tight. I pull his face to mine for a kiss, and he gives in. I kiss him until I'm breathless, and then I kiss him some more because he's right. He's right not to take the implant.

When we finally pull apart, I say, "I want to be your family, for whatever time we have left."

Pax traces my face, his breath warm in the cold air. And he smiles. "For whatever time we have left."

Sower

76

He rolls his shoulders and then returns to the work, the good work of turning over the soil and prepping our land for planting season. Sleeves pushed up to his elbows, sweat dripping from his brow and his beard, trousers coated in dirt that won't come out, no matter how many washes. I never tire of watching him work the homestead, and of watching how the homestead shapes him. The man and the good earth he's stewarding, bringing new life from the ground year after year.

A child runs past me, squealing happily. Celine waddles after her, and then pauses at the chicken fence where I'm leaning. She puts her hands into her back, stretching out her very pregnant belly. "If you stare at him, does it make him work faster?"

With a dry chuckle, I go back to tossing handfuls of feed to the chickens. "When is Elan coming home?"

"Tonight." Celine quirks her lips. "Holly says if he's gone too much longer, he'll miss the birth, so he'd *better* get back." She puts her hand on her stomach. "I told Zoe he'll be bringing Uncle Henri."

Zoe runs past again, in the opposite direction, curls flying. Celine sighs and moves to follow. "You've always stared at him like that." She twirls her finger as she walks away. "From the moment I met you. It's never changed."

I watch Celine go and then return my gaze to Pax. He's taking a break—leaning on the plow we built together using an old manual Bishop found—surveying the small plot of land we call our own in the dewy hills of Former Virginia, close enough to Refuge to be part of the community, far enough away for the peace Pax craves.

Bishop says the word for an unexplained supernatural phenomenon is *miracle*. If that's so, then every minute of the last three years has been just that—a miracle. A gift.

I finish tossing the chicken feed, aimless with it now. Pax catches me staring at him and smiles, raising his hand to wave. I wave back and find, as I often do, that tears are in my eyes.

And then the child in my womb kicks—or stretches or leaps. I cannot be sure which. It is far too early, and I have been too scared to hope. Too scared even to speak the hope aloud.

A mother. I will be a mother, and Pax will be a father. Against all reason and logic, somehow, it has happened.

I place both hands over my stomach, and Pax—far away in the field—tilts his head. He gestures to me, concerned. Perhaps he thinks I'm sick. He knows I've not been myself for weeks. I close my eyes and take a deep breath.

Miracle is just the word I need. It's just the word to tell him about the flutter of movement beneath my pressing hands. It's the only explanation I have.

And because none of our days are promised to us, I will wait no longer to tell him. I will not be afraid, because Pax is still here, and even if tomorrow he is not, I am strong enough to be a mother.

And now, I will carry part of him with me forever.

With trembling legs, I step out into the field, into the good earth we have sown. I go to meet Pax, my partner, my husband.

The End

BEFORE *THE BREEDER CYCLE*, THERE WERE THE GREAT DEVASTATIONS...

HUNTER

1

"The travel ban remains in effect indefinitely as death tolls continue to rise in Haiti and the Dominican Republic. All attempts to stop the Pandemic have been as ineffective amongst the island nations as they were in Africa. Rumors of cases in Mexico have already caused widespread panic and rioting at the wall—"

"Daniel, turn that off. It's too early for death and destruction."

Mom's heels clack on the linoleum, and I dim the kitchen vid to sleep mode. Pictures of mountains and idyllic pastoral scenes slide one after another across the now-silent screen. I swallow the last bite of my cereal and take my bowl to the sink.

"You have what you need for today?" Mom smiles at me, adjusting her earrings. They're out of fashion. Everything she wears is out of fashion, but she does the best she can. I try not to think about the college fund she's worked so many long hours to fill.

"Yeah. Yeah, I've got it." I finger the two paper tickets in my jeans pocket and clear the nervous lump in my throat.

"Do you have enough money for the flowers? I have a little extra cash."

"No, Mom. I've got it covered. They're not that expensive."

"Are you sure you don't want to get roses? They're so much nicer." She fumbles with her purse—a worn, faux-leather, shell-pink handbag with a thin shoulder strap. "I have some tip money in here from Sunday night. Burt came in, and you know he always over-tips me."

I roll my eyes and grab my keys off the counter. "Mom, I've told you a thousand times. She likes daisies. I'm getting her daisies. This is about her—not you."

Her hands still and her knuckles whiten, just a little. "Okay, sweetheart, okay." She touches my elbow. She wants a hug—she always wants a hug before school these days. I think she's realizing I'm going to be gone next year. "I just can't believe you're actually, finally, going to ask her out. And to the prom, no less."

"It's not a big deal." I catch her up in a quick side-arm embrace. When did she get so thin? I can feel her ribs through her sweater. "I'm going to be late if I don't go now."

"All right. Get going. Message the store later and let me know what she says."

"I will." The store. Because Mom got rid of her vid six months ago to help save money for my college fund. I grab my backpack and jog to my car, trying not to feel guilty. But when I turn back to look at my mom—her dark hair not yet graying despite the wrinkles creasing her face, clutching her Star of David necklace in one hand and her store smock in the other, smiling on the patio of our fifty-year-old baby blue prefab house—I know she wouldn't have done anything differently.

I hope Emma says yes, and not just for my sake.

My ancient sedan takes several tries to crank, and then I'm on my way. I have a half hour to get to Gia's Flowers and pick up the daisy bouquet I ordered on-vid yesterday and then camp out in Emma's usual parking spot at school before she gets there. Should be just enough time. I skipped my morning run so I wouldn't be late, but I'm still pushing it.

I leave my sedan running in the parking lot of Gia's so I don't have to wrestle with it when I go back out. Over the store counter, Gia's vid is playing the news of the plague that Mom made me turn off this morning. The story has dominated all news outlets for over a year.

"Lord God Almighty." Louisa, Gia's assistant, crosses herself and stares at footage of charity workers in HAZMAT suits clearing dead bodies in Haiti. "What if the rumors are true and it *has* reached Mexico? What's to stop it from coming here?"

"Nothing," Gia says, emerging from the back with my bouquet.

"Hi, Daniel, sweetie. Here you go." She puts a hand on her hip and stares at the vid-screen while I swipe my wrist-vid to pay. "First the famine, now this."

"God is judging us," Louisa whispers, crossing herself again.

Gia huffs and cuts her eyes my direction. "Is that all, sweetie? Need any chocolate to go with those? On the house today." She winks.

"Uh, no. No thanks." I cast another look at the heaps of dead bodies on the vid, clutch the bouquet tighter, and head outside. The bell on the door jangles, and then I'm back out in the fifty-degree weather. Despite the cool temperature, the sky rumbles in the distance with the promise of storms. I zip my jacket to my chin, squint at the clouds over the tree line, and yank open the heavy door of my car.

I don't want to think about the worldwide famine that killed so many people in the Third World nations three years ago. Or this strange plague people call the Pandemic that's been sweeping across the globe. Not today. Not right now. In America, we haven't had to worry much yet, and I don't plan on starting today. Today I want to think only about asking Emma to Prom.

The school parking lot is filling up when I arrive, but Emma's spot is still empty and I let out a relieved breath. I pull in near where Emma usually parks and kill my engine. Instead of getting out, I grip the wheel and go over what I'm going to say for the hundredth time.

It's just an invitation to Prom—not a wedding proposal. And it's senior year. It's my last shot. Now or never. I take a deep breath, hold it, let it out.

Emma Blackstone and I have been best friends for four years, ever since she blazed like a star into my quiet life in this sleepy town and befriended me when no one else would. Mom says Emma is the sort who has a soft spot for *wounded souls*. I guess that's me, even though I've never told Emma my whole story. On her first day at school she walked up to the group of bullies pushing me around and demanded they leave me alone, and . . . God. I've been in love with her ever since. Not that she knows, of course. But we're tight, Emma and I, even though she's a cheerleader now and has other friends, too. There isn't any reason she should say no. I shouldn't be so nervous.

A car door slams, making me jump, but it's not Emma. Just a

group of giggling girls. Juniors. I know all their names. At a school our size, everyone knows everyone else. I should be thankful for that, because I doubt someone like Emma would ever have been friends with someone like me at a bigger school in a bigger town.

I shake myself and check my wrist-vid. I've been sitting here for ten minutes already, and the parking lot is almost full. Emma will be here any second. In fact, she's usually here by now.

I get out of the car and sling my backpack over my shoulder. With shaking hands, I pick up the bouquet and dig the Prom tickets out of my pocket. Maybe it was stupid of me to buy the tickets without any assurance she'll say yes, and maybe she'll see it for what it is—an act of desperation. But at this point, I just don't care. I'm all in.

Thunder rumbles again and the sky darkens. Is it going to start raining before Emma gets here? Dammit. I really don't want to have to do this in the crowded hallway full of lockers where everyone can see, and judge, and laugh.

A sudden sharp wind almost pummels me over, and I stumble against my car, smashing the bouquet. Kids around the parking lot shriek, some of them startled, others laughing, and most run for cover as papers and debris tumble with the wind. I give a shout as the Prom tickets are ripped from my hand to join the swirling mess.

"*No*. No, no, no!"

Another gust, and I barely keep a grip on the flowers.

Teachers are running outside and gesturing students into the building. I fumble with my car door and toss the half-ruined bouquet onto the driver's seat. Then I slam the door and spin a circle. I have to find those tickets.

"*Daniel*. Inside, now!" Mrs. Roy, the vice principal, stands on the school steps, waving her arms.

"I lost my Prom tickets!"

"They keep a record of purchases in the office," she shouts back. "Get inside!"

I start toward her, but then there's Emma, running across the parking lot, her golden hair in disarray and her clear eyes—one blue, one green—bright with excitement.

"Can you believe this weather?" She grabs my arm and hangs on, turning her face to the sky. "I'm *so* glad I made it before the rain."

"Where's your car?"

"At home. It wouldn't start this morning. I had to walk."

"I could have picked you up."

She shrugs and releases my arm. "I didn't want to bother you."

Another gust of wind knocks us together, and we barely stay upright. The sky is now churning, and flashes of lightning shoot from cloud to cloud. There's a metallic groaning like a lamppost bending.

"Daniel Cohen and Emma Blackstone, *get in this school building this instant.*" Mrs. Roy is practically apoplectic.

I look around. We're the only two students left in the parking lot and the storm is getting more intense with every passing moment. Emma and I start jogging toward the open door of the school.

And then sirens go off. Emergency sirens. Eerie relics of the Cold War era. I only know this because they demonstrated them for a history class one time, but they've never actually been used for anything—not in my lifetime. Emma looks at me, eyes wide and perplexed, and I stop, staring off into the swirling clouds as though I can somehow find the source of the wailing siren. Mrs. Roy seems frozen in horror, her mouth agape and her limbs splayed out along the crash bar of the door.

"What's happening?" Emma shouts, grabbing my hand.

"I don't know."

The metallic groaning sounds again and the sky darkens even more.

A set of car headlights pulls into the parking lot. It's a brown jeep I'm well familiar with. One that probably cost as much as the mobile home the driver lives in with his grandmother.

Emma releases my hand as quickly as she'd grabbed it, and Crispin Freemason pulls alongside us. He sticks his head out his open window. "What's up with these sirens?"

"No idea." Emma tugs on the straps of her backpack. "Guys, we should get inside before it rains."

"Roy looks like she's going to have a heart attack," Crispin says.

"Can't say I blame her," I say, but Emma's comment niggles at me. *Before it rains.* Where's the rain? All this wind and thunder and lightning, but still not even a drop or hint of rain.

Another blast of wind—the strongest one yet—sweeps through the parking lot, and the door Mrs. Roy has been holding slams shut in her face, pushing her back inside. Emma screams as she falls backwards onto the ground, and I tumble on top of her. With a tremendous groan and crash, the scoreboard on the football field across from the school slams to the ground.

"*Holy* . . ." The rest of Crispin's shouted expletive is lost in the wind.

"Daniel." Emma's voice is urgent and scared in my ear as we scramble into a crouch. "Daniel, I've never been in a storm like this before. I've never even *seen* a storm like this. We have to get inside, we—"

"My car's closer," I say. "It's just right here. Come on. We'll sit it out, or . . . or drive to my house. It will be all right."

"What about Crispin's jeep?"

The tingle of static electricity warns me a second before it happens. "*Get down*." I pull on Emma's shoulders, but she's already hunkering down when the lightning strikes the line of cars parked behind Crispin's jeep. It strikes and strikes and strikes again until I can't see anything but hot white fuzz and all my hair is standing on end. Somewhere in the background, the sirens are still wailing and Crispin is shouting.

I blink, trying to get my eyesight back, and just as I do, the sky turns almost black above me. Something enormous drops onto my car with enough force to crush it. Something that moves with gangly limbs like a human—but not like a human—and strides from the roof of my car to the ground to stand over Emma and me.

Emma's scream is so piercing her voice goes silent, and I look up and up into the face that towers above us. Red, glowing eyes and greyish skin that sags off a vaguely humanoid skull—it has virtually no nose and a lipless hole for a mouth. The creature is of such obviously alien origins I can only gape.

Gape and swallow my own scream as I'm struck with the absolute certainty we are all about to die.

Available Now!

www.kbhoyle.com/books
Amazon.com

ACKNOWLEDGMENTS

After years of runarounds and publishing misadventures and mishaps that delayed the writing and publication of this book, I'm just so happy to finally get it out in the world that I'm going to keep these acknowledgements short and sweet.

To my family, always. My husband, Adam, and my four boys, Caleb, Joshua, William, and Edmund. To the very best editor I have ever known, Hayley German Fisher, who always makes my words 1,000% better. To the best beta reader I could ever ask for, Maggie Rapier. To the narrator of *The Gateway Chronicles* audiobooks, Dollcie Webb, for your unflagging encouragement. To the members of the CaPC Book Writing Group for your feedback, prayers, and listening ears. To my agent, Ben Grange, as we work toward bigger and better things. And thanks—last but not least—to you, my readers, for your patience in waiting for this final entry in the series. I hope it is everything you want it to be and more.

Don't miss *The Gateway Chronicles* A young adult fantasy series also by K. B. Hoyle

Darcy Pennington hates her life. She is an insufferably average teenager with no true friends, crushing social anxiety, and an indescribable sense of not fitting in anywhere. When her parents force her to attend Cedar Cove Family Camp the summer before her eighth-grade year, Darcy once again finds herself on the outside of an established social circle. But going to Cedar Cove is just the beginning, and when Darcy stumbles through a magical gateway into a new world called Alitheia, she must convince five other teenagers at the camp to not only befriend her but follow her on a journey beyond their world and their wildest dreams to save Alitheia from an ancient, shadowy foe. Gnomes, magic, prophecies, dangerous adventures, and desperate love await Darcy and her five companions, and for six years they must travel back and forth to fight a war invisible to everyone in their own world. But it's a war to save all they hold dear—a war that just might demand everything of Darcy Pennington.

Books 1-6 Available Now!

www.kbhoyle.com/books
Amazon.com
Audible.com
Barnes & Noble
Books A Million

ABOUT THE AUTHOR

K. B. Hoyle fell in love with fantasy literature when she walked through a wardrobe at age six, and she never looked back. She is the recipient of several international book awards and honors, including the Gold Award for Best Young Adult Series from Literary Classics for *The Gateway Chronicles*. She lives in Alabama with her husband and four sons, and she is never without a story on her lips. Visit her at www.kbhoyle.com to learn more about her multiple titles, to subscribe to her newsletter, and to learn how you can invite her to speak at your school, festival, or special event.

Contact K. B. Hoyle at author@kbhoyle.com

Made in the USA
Las Vegas, NV
01 October 2023